A
MEASURE
of
TRUST

Sarah Hale

ISBN 978-1-0980-1742-2 (paperback)
ISBN 978-1-0980-1743-9 (digital)

Christian Faith Publishing, Inc.
832 Park Avenue
Meadville, PA 16335
www.christianfaithpublishing.com

This is a work of fiction. Names and characters are derived from the author's imagination and are used fictitiously. All the real-life places and locales mentioned in the story are used fictitiously.

Printed in the United States of America

To every person who has supported me throughout this journey, you have given me encouragement and words of kindness along the way. I love each and every one of you.

*Trust in the Lord with all thine heart; and lean
not unto thine own understanding. In all thy ways
acknowledge him, and he shall direct thy paths.*

—Proverbs 3:5–6

CHAPTER 1

Charleston—April 11, 1896

Jackson Lorton opened the side door to the downstairs salon. He was in awe of the beauty before him. Abby, his wife, was meticulously pinning his daughter Annabeth's long blonde hair up. It was her wedding day, and the bride-to-be looked exquisite. He watched the scene with a measure of pride. He couldn't help but smile. These were his girls—his treasures.

"Patience, will you stop! I don't need any more face powder. That is the third dusting you've given me. I'll look like a ghost if you're not careful."

"This isn't more powder. It is a bit of rouge. You tend to be on the pale side. I'm trying to give you a glow."

"Girls, stop. You look lovely, Annabeth."

Abby Lorton cupped her daughter's chin. "All brides glow regardless of paint and powder. You'll be no different." Abby kissed her cheek tenderly.

Patience turned to notice her father watching. "She does look beautiful, doesn't she, Father?"

"She takes my breath away."

His oldest daughter smiled. Her father was the kindest man she knew. She hoped she and Jonathan would be as happy as her parents. "You two better get out there. We are just about to begin." When his wife and youngest daughter passed, Jackson gave them a quick kiss.

When they had gone, he turned to his eldest. "Are you ready for all this?"

"I think so." Annabeth gathered her bouquet.

Jackson smiled. "I mean all this." He made a motion with his hand, and she caught his meaning of marriage in general.

"Yes, Father, I am."

She noticed an emotion cross his face. "Do you have reservations about me marrying Jonathan?" She would never do anything she thought her father may not approve of. He was that big of an influence in her life.

"No, he is a good man." He paused and took her hand. "I want to be sure you are marrying for all the right reasons." He acted as if there was something more he wanted to say.

Annabeth squeezed his hand. "Say it. Whatever it is, I will listen."

"I want to be sure you are marrying for love and not because all your friends are marrying."

Annabeth closed her eyes and smiled. "I can assure you I am marrying for love."

The bride and her father descended the steps of Laurel. The plantation mansion had been Abby's childhood home. Abby, the only daughter of Franklin and Lorraine Sheridan, walked these same steps twenty-four years ago right into Jackson's arms. He prayed his daughter's marriage would be as fulfilling as his. When the pair reached the main hall, the musicians began to play. A mist covered Jackson's eyes. A flood of memories swept over his soul. He was giving his little girl to the man standing next to the preacher. It seemed like just yesterday he was holding his firstborn in his arms.

Jackson placed his daughter's hand in Jonathan Taylor's. He kissed her forehead and went to take his place by his wife. Abby rested her head on his shoulder, looking longingly at the couple prepared to take their vows. Reverend Scottsdale began the marriage ceremony. "Who gives this woman in holy matrimony?"

"Her mother and I," Jackson replied.

The reverend continued, "If anyone can show just cause why this couple cannot lawfully be joined together in matrimony, let them speak now or forever hold their peace."

The couple looked at each other. The reverend paused for a moment.

"I would like to say something," a soft voice from a few rows back shocked the crowd. The bride and groom turned. Lillian Eversole stood, wringing her hands.

"Jonathan"—her voice held thick emotion—"a year ago you asked me to marry you, and I said no. I made a mistake. Please don't do this." She let out a tiny sob.

"Well, you have some nerve," Patience blurted out, and Annabeth's arm stopped her sister from advancing toward the woman.

The crowd was shocked, and Jonathan just stood there, looking at Lillian. This was the first Annabeth knew of any attachment between the two. The look on Jonathan's face told a story she didn't want to read. It showed her all she needed to know. "We obviously need to discuss this matter," she whispered to the groom. "If our guest will excuse us," Annabeth's voice cracked ever so slightly. She took Jonathan's hand and led him into the adjoining room.

Abby and Jackson were at a loss as what to do. Jackson personally wanted to whip the Taylor boy. Abby had a constant stream of tears down her face. Patience stood glaring at Lillian Eversole. TJ, Annabeth's younger brother and best man, stood staring at the couple. The reverend was dumbfounded, and the guest sat silently.

"You don't want to marry me, do you?" It was hard to get out, but Annabeth pushed the words through the emotion. Jonathan just stood there with a look of shock. His face was pale.

He took her hands. "I... I do love you, Annabeth"—he wouldn't look her in the eye—"as much as I can."

What did that mean? She was afraid to ask. "So you were settling for me because she turned you down. Did you think our marriage would last, beginning on one big lie?"

"It's not like that." He dropped her hands and moved to stand in front of the window. "I moved on. I had to." His words were quiet. The man she loved had a face of torrent emotion.

"But you never stopped loving her." His head went down. "Why did you waste our time? Why did you feel the need to put me through this?"

He made his way toward her. She stepped away. "Just go, Jonathan," she said with more strength than she knew she had.

"Please, Annabeth." He put his hands on her arms, cupping her shoulders.

"Don't do this, Jonathan. Just go."

Jackson met Jonathan in the hallway. His anger was at an all-time high. Never had he been this willing to use his fist. "I... I don't know what to say," Jonathan mumbled as he met the man he truly admired. It was one of the reasons he asked Annabeth to marry him.

"You are the worst kind of man, Jonathan Taylor. I am glad my daughter will not be your wife." With that, Jackson hurried to his daughter.

This couldn't be happening, Annabeth thought. Her heart was shattered. She had known Jonathan Taylor for most of her life. They had been friends before—before what? Before the woman he genuinely loved had turned him down, and he would have to settle for second place. She shuddered. What a fool she was.

It didn't take long for her father to enter. He put his arms around her. "I'm fine. I—we just need to tell the guests."

He pulled her back and looked at her tear-stained face. "I will see to it." His tone was soft. "I'm sorry, honey."

"No, I want to address them." She grasped her father's hand and headed back to the stunned crowd.

Annabeth made her way to the front of the room. Everyone was slightly shocked to see her reappear. "I'm sure you understand there will not be a wedding taking place today." Her voice faltered a bit. The friends and family were sharing in her sorrow. The Taylors left looking for their son.

"Knowing the good people of Charleston as I do, I invite all of you to stay for the"—she paused—"I am not sure what to call it. *Reception* doesn't seem quite right." She tried to smile.

"Call it I-didn't-get-stuck-with-a-cad party." Patience could never hold her thoughts or her tongue. She received a stern look from her sister.

"Please stay and eat the delicious food that has been prepared. I insist."

Everyone was in disbelief as to how a jilted bride could be so calm. Most of them knew the character of Annabeth Lorton to be good but not this good.

Jackson and Abby escorted their daughter to the dining hall. There was a plethora of good food most of which the bride herself had made. The wedding cake she so painstakingly constructed mocked her from its grand display. It was more than she could take. Raising her glass of punch to what should have been well-wishers, she smiled. "If you don't mind, I need a hot bath and a good cry. I bid you good evening."

Abby and Patience followed her to her room. There, Annabeth broke down, crying endlessly as she attempted to remove her wedding gown. Her fingers trembled as she tried to unbutton her dress. Her mother went to help her.

"I could just pulverize that Jonathan Taylor," Patience said as she plopped on the bed. Her lavender chiffon dress was billowing around her.

This sort of thing would never happen to her, Annabeth thought. Her sister was beautiful and vivacious. Her long dark hair had soft curls as opposed to Annabeth's blonde hair that had to be crimped if she wanted any wave. Patience was the perfect height and weight and curved in all the right places. Annabeth was a bit chunky and certainly had an overabundance of an upper curve.

"This has nothing to do with you, you know," Patience said, taking in her sister's contemplative look.

"It has everything to do with me." Annabeth turned to her mother as if to ask for some sort of explanation.

"I think what Patience is trying to say is don't blame yourself."

"No, I am saying it has nothing to do with the way she looks. It is not because you are a lesser woman to some degree. It is merely a man not being brave enough to handle his feelings maturely. Father would never behave that way."

The other women just stared at the eighteen-year-old. How did little Patience get so wise?

*****

Jackson Lorton couldn't sleep. He had listened patiently to his wife's tears. He held her until she fell asleep. He couldn't get over the hurt his little girl must be experiencing. Annabeth was a quiet soul. She never let her feelings of disappointment show, although he knew she hurt as much as anyone. He rose quietly to not wake his wife and headed down the hall.

Jackson gently cracked the door to Annabeth's room. She was not in her bed. Knowing a moment of fear, he opened the door wider. Annabeth was kneeling in front of the window seal. Her head was bowed. "I know I must thank you, Heavenly Father"—Jackson heard his daughter praying; he stood numb—"for what happened today. I know in time I will see the why, but for right now, my heart is broken."

He heard a sob. His first inkling was to scoop her up in his arms, but he knew she needed her Heavenly Father much more than her earthly father. He continued to listen.

"I love Jonathan. I want the best for him. and only you know what that is. Please, Lord, give me the grace to forgive him and Lillian. I don't want to be bitter."

This was Jackson's undoing. He slid to the floor outside his daughter's room. With tears sliding down his face, he closed his eyes and leaned his head back on the wall. "Oh, Lord, she is so precious."

*****

The Lortons sat at the dining room table waiting for Annabeth to arrive. It was obvious no one had slept much. Annabeth entered the room and greeted her family, "Good morning."

The smile on her lips did not reach her red puffy eyes. "Good morning, dear." Abby rested her hand on her daughter's back as she sat next to her mother.

Jackson was careful to read his daughter's expression. It was better this happened now instead of later in the marriage, but he couldn't voice the sentiment. His daughter was not ready to hear it.

"I have never been more proud of you than I was last evening, Annabeth." Patience looked at her sister intently. "You were all class and grace. Let Lillian Eversole attempt to be the woman you are. Jonathan Taylor gets what he deserves."

Annabeth smiled at her sister. "Thank you, but let us remember that up until yesterday we didn't have an opinion on Lillian either way. This isn't her fault, and Jonathan couldn't help it either." All this was said with tears pooling in the corners of her eyes.

Jackson looked at Abby. They had done something right in the raising of their children. He thanked his Heavenly Father.

"Father, how about a lunch date today? The last thing I want to do is play the wounded victim. I have something I would like to discuss with you. Mother, can I meet you later for a little shopping? I need to see about returning some of the gifts."

Her parents sat stunned at their daughter's ability to bounce back, but had she? Patience knew the answer. Her sister was up to something.

Later that day, Annabeth laid out her plan to her father. "You want to go to West?"

"Yes, I want to visit Uncle Thad and Aunt Merry. Indefinitely."

"I understand you feel like you need to get away, but that is an awfully long way. I am going, to be honest. I don't like the word *indefinitely*."

"This town isn't for me, Daddy. I'm not Mother or Patience. They were born for this life. I'm clumsy and awkward." He started to speak, but she quickly continued, "I don't fit in. You know that as well as I do. Please, let me go. I need to go."

He had no answer for her. He knew she needed to go. "I'll send your uncle a telegram and ask him if he has room for you."

"He has room." She smiled knowingly. "I would like to surprise him and Aunt Merry. I will telegraph Tommy at the bank in Sheridan and make the arrangements."

"You have thought this out, haven't you?" Annabeth just smiled, but it still didn't go any farther than her lips.

*****

Annabeth stepped off the stage, the toe of her boot hitting the edge, causing her to misstep. Her satchel hit the ground, spewing her books everywhere. She righted herself before she was spewed to the ground. Lucky for her, no one seemed to notice. She gathered her belongings and put them back in their rightful place. She smoothed her pink traveling suit and tidied her hair. She couldn't go to the bank looking disheveled. She stood a little straighter and with her head held high entered the Sheridan bank.

"May I help you?" the older man at the counter asked from behind the teller's cage.

"I am here to see Mr. Thomas Sheridan.

"Do you have an appointment, miss?"

"No."

"You must have an appointment."

"I can see he is alone in the office. It will only take a minute of his time."

The man raised his eyebrows; at least, she thought he did. The hair over his eyes was barely there. "You must have an appointment." His tone was final.

"If you would just tell him Annabeth Lorton is here to see him, I am sure he would spare me a moment."

He frowned and turned toward Tommy's office. "He won't see you without an appointment."

Annabeth watched as Tommy's head shot up, and he moved from around his desk. "Annabeth, you weren't supposed to arrive until tomorrow." His arms enveloped her, and he kissed her cheek. "C-come into my office." He took her bag and offered his elbow.

He escorted her to his office. She sat in the chair, and he sat on the edge of the desk. "I-I had p-plans to meet the stage tomorrow. Y-y should have sent a telegram."

"I wanted to surprise you."

They talked for a few minutes. Annabeth had forgotten that Tommy stuttered. A few years ago, he had come to stay with them. Thomas Sheridan was doing a banking internship with her father. He had excellent control over his stuttering; but when he was excited, it was more pronounced. He had learned that if he held something in his hand, it helped his stuttering. You rarely saw him without a pen or a small smooth wooden object his brother Jonah had carved for the specific purpose.

"I want to take you to lunch." He hopped off the desk and pulled her chair back. "I am rather hungry," she confessed.

He opened the door, and she preceded him. The hem of her dress caught on the chair, and she faltered just a bit. Tommy steadied her. "I am so graceful." She chuckled and gave her skirt a little shake.

They strolled along the boardwalk, her hand in the crook of his arm; headed their way were two women. The ladies slowed their pace as they approached. Tommy nodded in greeting. "Miss Hannah, Miss Josie."

The women said hello and paused slightly. Tommy moved forward, going past the girls. "Those two acted as if they wanted to say more. Why didn't you stop? Are you that hungry?" Annabeth knew Josie Miller was the only girl in town Tommy Sheridan cared about. When he visited Charleston, he had mentioned her more than once to Annabeth. "I know what you're thinking, but Josie has made it very clear she does not want me to court her."

Annabeth turned to look at the women who had stopped to watch Tommy's procession. They quickly entered the Feed and Seed. They had been caught staring. "That did not look like the actions of a girl not interested." Tommy just shrugged his shoulders.

They entered the cafe and sat in front of the large pane window facing the boardwalk. "You haven't told your folks I am coming, have you?"

"Not one word. I haven't told anyone, but don't be surprised if Hawk 'senses' it and finds you."

They both laughed. Hawk was Tommy's brother. They weren't blood brothers, but both had been adopted.

Fifteen years ago, Annabeth's uncle Thad Sheridan married Merry Margret Quinn. The two opened their home to boys who had no other place to go. Through the years, several had passed through the doors of The Sheridan Home for Boys. A few stayed permanently and were adopted by the couple.

Tommy was the first. His parents perished in a fire, and the Sheridans took him in. Hawk followed. He was older than Tommy and Lakota Indian. Eventually, Hud, Franklin, Jonah, Gil, and David all became Sheridans. Annabeth had only met Tommy and Hawk, but she felt as if she knew the others by her aunt's frequent letters.

After lunch, Tommy escorted Annabeth back to the bank. They had business to discuss. "I have been making inquiries around town, Annabeth, and I believe I have some prospects for you." Tommy was opening the folder he pulled from the corner of his desk, pen in hand. Annabeth sat quietly waiting for him to continue, her heart beating out of her chest.

"First, I think I have found a place for you to open your business. Do you remember Dr. Lapp's wife, Lydia?"

"I can vaguely remember her, but I feel I know a lot about her from my conversations with you. The Lapps are very special friends of your family."

"They are. Since Dr. Lapp retired, he and Lydia have opened a dress shop in an old mercantile. They only use half the space, and I have approached them about renting out the other side. There would be some remodeling that would need to be done, but I think it would suit your needs. They are supposed to get back with me this week if they are interested.

"That sounds promising." Annabeth tried to curb her excitement.

"Now, about your living arrangements. We both know my parents will want you to live with them. So I already have a place for you to stay in town. A place I think both our parents will approve of. I doubt you remember Sheriff Dan Bullock."

Annabeth shook her head. She had little to no recollection. She was only five when her family visited; it was hard to remember people by name. Perhaps when she saw them, it would jog her memory.

"Dan married later in life. He married a widow a few years back. Gertrude Stanton was traveling through with her son to California. They stopped here for a few weeks, and Gertrude stayed. She and Dan married shortly after, and she turned Sheriff Bullock's large house into a boarding house."

Annabeth tried not to show it, but she was a little disappointed. She was in hopes of finding a place to open her business that she could also live in. Annabeth wasn't sure she had prepared as well as she thought. How was she going to pay for room and board and her supplies for the bakery she dreamed of opening? Tommy sensed her change in mood.

"Are you okay, Annabeth?"

"I'm not sure I can afford room and board and all I need for the bakery."

"Let me explain your living arrangements. I think it will be amicable for you and your bank account." His grin was huge. "When you are not at the bakery, you will work for the Bullocks—cleaning rooms, helping in the kitchen, and such—in exchange for a room. They know the boarder I am suggesting has another job. You will be able to spend as much time as you need at the bakery."

"Tommy, you have worked everything out perfectly!" She moved toward him and wrapped her arms around him. She gave him a huge hug and kiss on his cheek. All this was done amid the whole bank watching, including Josie Miller.

*****

The Lorton family was wealthy. When the Panic of 1893 led to the current Depression, life changed for the Lortons. Jackson Lorton was a smart and shrewd businessman. He anticipated the impending depression and prepared his bank and his personal finances. His household became primarily run by his family. Each one of them cleaned, cooked, and became ground keepers. The Lorton-Sheridan Lumber Mill only took a small hit.

The depression wasn't over, but things were looking up. Jackson and Abby guided their children on how to be self-sufficient. Annabeth was thankful for the lessons she learned. She felt it would benefit her here in South Dakota.

"Shall we head over to the boarding house so you can get settled in?"

"Yes, that would be lovely. I need to get my trunk from the stage office. I don't mind telling you my head is spinning. I couldn't have done any of this without your help, Tommy. I do appreciate it."

He pulled out her chair and escorted her to Dan's house.

Gertrude Stanton was a whirlwind of a woman. The moment she laid eyes on Annabeth, she removed the satchel from her hand and directed her trunk to be put in the living accommodations adjoining the house. "We have this room with a tiny kitchenette just off the side of the house. I think it will be perfect for you, Annabeth. It has its own entrance and exit, yet you are still close to the house. It's practically a tree house. It sits so close to that big oak. I was cleaning it just now, and the acorns hitting the roof nearly scared me to death."

The woman finally took a breath to lay a hand over her heart as if she could still feel the startling episode. Trudy, as Dan like to call her, was a very petite woman. She had nearly silver hair and soft blue eyes. Trudy was wiry and full of vim and vigor. She was the kind of person you instantly liked. "Tommy, you take her on out there. I will be along in a minute." Tommy proceeded toward Annabeth's new home.

The lodging was built up to butt against the house just below the second story. It was as if the room were on stilts. A plank-like walkway led to the cottage nestled beside the tree. "This is most unusual. It is a far cry from Laurel."

Annabeth followed Tommy in. "I had stayed here a couple of times when I worked too late, or the weather was bad. It actually is an interesting and peaceful place. I think you will enjoy it."

Tommy was taking in the homey touches Trudy had added. There were flowers on the table and delicate curtains pulled back to allow the spring sun in. "Now the fireplace is stocked with wood, and there is more just outside the door here."

Trudy had joined them. "It may be warm during the day, but these Dakota nights can be rather chilly."

"I doubt she will be staying here tonight, Trudy. Annabeth is my father's niece, and he doesn't know she is coming. I would be surprised if he and my mother let her out of their sight for a day, perhaps two."

"Well, of course. Now, don't you worry about a thing. Your trunk will be fine. It would be pretty stupid of a man to rob the sheriff's house."

"Annabeth, why don't you stay here and get some rest? I will pick you up on my way home. Today is Pa's birthday, and Ma always fixes a big meal. If I can bring you, I will win for best gift this year." His smile was such a sweet feature of Tommy Sheridan.

"I like the plan. After I rest a bit, I may sneak over and see Hawk."

"That won't be necessary." Dr. Hawk Sheridan stood at the door. Always quiet when he approached, he startled the unsuspecting group.

"Hawk!" Annabeth ran to him. "How did you know I was here?" she said as she put her arms around him. "I saw you and Tommy leave the cafe. I knew in an instant who you were." He turned to face Tommy "Ma never said anything about this. Do they know?"

Tommy shook his head. "Big surprise for tonight. This will be great!"

The three stood talking until Annabeth let out a suppressed yawn. "Somebody needs a nap," Hawk said as they all chuckled. "We will catch up tonight. How long are you staying?" he asked.

Annabeth looked at Tommy. "If everything works out, permanently."

Hawk embraced her. "I'll be praying it all works out. I don't know how you got Uncle Jackson and Aunt Abby to ever let you leave, but it sure is good to see you."

*****

Merry Sheridan had just taken the venison roast out of the oven. The meat needed to rest. She stirred the noodles cooking in a pot of broth. These were two of Thad's favorites. The Depression had taken its toll on the Sheridan Home for Boys, but the Lord always provided just what they needed. She was particularly feeling blessed today; her entire family would be present for the meal. Hawk and Hud had their own homes. Tommy's and Jonah's works kept them in town a lot. Franklin and Gil were in the throes of discovering girls. That left David, Merry, and Thad the constant three at the table every night.

"Merry, where do you want this?" A beautiful woman with leg braces and crutches came through the back door. Molly Gilbert had married Hud Sheridan eight years ago, and the girl had not stopped smiling. She and Avery, Hawk's wife, had been a bright spot in Merry's life. Not to mention the four grandchildren she now had.

Five-year-old Quinn followed his mother in and went straight to his grandma. "Where's Uncle Franklin?" the towheaded boy said as he gave Merry a hug around her legs. The boy was infatuated with his uncle Franklin. Franklin was Hud's biological brother, and Quinn had picked up on his pa's close relationship with this particular uncle.

"He is out in the barn with your grandpa." The boy barely stopped for the kiss Merry placed on the top of his head. He darted out the door. "Do you know how many times I had to stop him from coming over here? He is so excited about Hawk's boys coming tonight. You would think they never see each other. And if he asked once, he has asked a dozen times what kind of cake we are having. I finally told him it would be prairie dog cake for him." The two women laughed.

Hud and Molly lived a stone's throw away in a small house on Sheridan's property. Hud was the son who loved farming. He stayed close to help his pa. The two had been able to keep the farm afloat so far in the Depression. Again, another reason to be thankful, Merry said to herself. "I had Thad and Franklin put a makeshift table up outside. We will leave the food in here, and everyone can fill their plate and then head outside. I think it is warm enough."

"It is, and that is a great idea. The more there are of us, the more cramped we are at that table." She pointed to the large table in the dining area.

"I'm not complaining, mind you," Molly said, "and six months from now, there will be one more Sheridan." Merry's eyes were wide. She knew Molly and Hud had been trying to have another baby. Molly had miscarried last year, and it broke her heart. "I'm so happy for you."

She gave her daughter-in-law a kiss and a hug. "We are going to tell everyone tonight. Of course, Hawk already knows."

The Sheridan family began to file in. Franklin and Gil had arranged the table and chairs outside, and Thad was stealing a kiss or two from his wife. He once told her his sons may have sons, but he would forever be a newlywed, and so he was. His sons had learned well from their father. A show of public affection was on display when the Sheridans got together.

If it hadn't been for Piper's tears, you wouldn't have known the doctor and his family had arrived. Seven-year-old Hunter Sheridan and his six-year-old brother River had learned a thing or two from their father. One was the ability to move without being heard. They surprised their grandpa with a calculated attack, and the ruckus began. It wasn't long until David and Quinn joined in.

"What is the matter with Piper?" Merry moved to take her granddaughter out of Avery's arms. The little girl snuggled into her grandma's embrace. "She is just moody today. That is the only excuse I can give."

"She takes after her mother," Hawk said as he placed a rather long kiss on Avery's lips.

"Standing in a room full of Sheridans, I'm certain they know whose gene the moodiness comes from."

She didn't need to say any more. Hawk Sheridan was by far the moodiest of the group. Hawk just kissed her again. "Tommy's going to be a little late," Hawk told his mother. "And I believe he is bringing a girl."

This got everyone's attention.

"Yeah, who is she?" Jonah had entered in behind Hawk and Avery. "I lost thirty minutes of valuable time being subtly pumped by Hannah Miller and her sister Josie for information.

"Yes, I bet that really bothered you, seeing Hannah Miller," Franklin piped in, laughing and nudging Gil who stood beside him. Jonah just frowned.

"I take it she is someone new in town?" Merry inquired.

"I've never seen her," Jonah replied.

"You don't see anyone but Hannah." Another stern look came from Jonah toward Franklin.

"Should we wait?" Thad asked, surrounded by his grandsons.

"No, he said to go on, but he will be here."

When they were gathered around the table, Thad looked at his family. His emotions were high. God had blessed him. First, with love and a helpmate who held the same dreams. His oldest son, Dr. Hawk Sheridan, was a real miracle. The Lakota Indian came to them after his father had been gunned down in the streets of town nearly fifteen years ago. He married Avery Piper, who was originally from Austria. Had she returned to her homeland, she would have been very wealthy and hold a title. She and Hawk married the same day as Hud and Molly.

Hud and Franklin came to them about twelve years ago. Abandoned by their prostitute mother, the two lived a rough life until they found their way to the Sheridans. Hud, loving to farm, settled early in staying right where he was, doing just what he was doing. His wife, Molly, had been a friend of Hawk's during college in Baltimore. When her disabilities got in the way of a teaching job, Hawk brought her home, right into Hud's awaiting arms; and the rest was history.

Jonah just showed up one day. The boy was born missing a part of his left arm. He had run away from every orphanage until he hit the Sheridans' boys' home. The place felt like home. His gift of woodcarving landed him a job doing furniture repair for Mr. Tyler, the owner of the general store. He also had begun to build and design furniture for the store. He was in love with Hannah Miller, and he was pretty sure she was in love with him. There was just one problem: Owen Miller, Hannah's father, forbade her to see him. He was an orphan. There was no telling what kind of past he had. This was Mr. Miller's reasoning for not liking Jonah and Tommy.

Gil and David were the sons of a widow neighbor. Thad and Merry were present when David entered the world and Olive Gilliam left. Her dying words were a request for the Sheridans to take and raise her boys; they had done so with great zeal.

Fifty years of joy and sadness filled Thad Sheridan's heart. He had had good times and bad times. Looking at what sat before him, he wouldn't change one single thing. "Lach, would you say grace?" Lachlan Kennedy and his family had joined the group. Lachlan and Thad had grown up together in Charleston. He was the closest thing Thad had to a brother, and he had made his way West back in '83.

If only his sister Abby and her family lived closer, Thad would feel complete. Just as the prayer ended, something caught Thad's eye. "It can't be." Thad started to rise as he saw his son Tommy come from around the side of the house with a beautiful blonde on his arm. It only took a few strides for Thad to reach the girl. Her arms went around his neck, and he lifted her off the ground.

"Annabeth, it is so good to see you." He kissed her forehead and sat her down. Merry took her turn, hugging and kissing the girl.

"Are you by yourself?" Merry asked, not sure why the girl would be here. She knew a wedding was planned. Merry just couldn't remember the exact date.

"Yes, I—" She wasn't sure what to say. Her aunt and uncle knew something was amiss but knew this wasn't the time to address it.

"I know I am not blood family, but do I get a hug?" Lach made his way over.

"You will always be Uncle Lach whether you were born into the Sheridans or not. We won't give you up now." She leaped into the big man's arm. The rest of the onlookers just stood there. Everyone knew who Annabeth Lorton was; but why she was here, they had no clue.

"Let's get this celebration started. I am starving," Tommy said as he found a plate and headed to get some food Annabeth followed.

Soon the group had settled in with gentle conversation, mostly directed to the newest arrival. "How long are you staying, love?" Thad asked his niece.

"I'm not sure." This raised more than one eyebrow. "Can we talk about it later? I just can't think amid all this beauty. I didn't appreciate it when I was last here."

The group obliged her request, and the meal was finished in a leisurely fashion. After supper, Thad, Merry, Lach, and Jamie Kennedy sat on the front porch drinking coffee. Annabeth sat nestled between Thad and Merry on the swing. She had told them all earlier about her wedding mishap. They were very supportive and didn't ask too many questions.

"So let me discuss my reason, my plan for coming West." They all sat quietly. "I have been corresponding with Tommy, and I plan to open a bakery in town. I know we are in a Depression, and it seems crazy, but this is what I want to do. I prayed about it and had mother and father pray too. I talked Father into giving me my dowry to get started." The adults were quiet. She misunderstood their lack of comment. "Do you think it is a bad idea?" She looked at her uncle.

"No, I think it is a good idea. I was just thinking of where you would put it."

"Oh, well, Tommy has been working on that for me. He has asked the Lapps if they would be interested in renting the other half of their dress shop to me."

"Now that is clever. Women can buy their dress goods, then go to the bakery, and discuss the patterns, right, honey." Lach was saying to his wife, Jamie, knowing she and Molly could spend hours discussing dresses for his twin daughters. "And if they eat enough, they will have to go get more material." His smile was infectious, and Thad couldn't help but laugh.

"Can you be serious for two seconds?" Jamie gave her husband a stern look not containing a bit of a threat. "It is a good choice. Where will you live? You would be spending a lot of travel time if you stayed out here." Merry looked perplexed.

"Tommy has helped me with that also. I will be staying at Dan and Trudy's. When I am not at the bakery, I will be helping them in exchange for room and board."

"Sounds like you and Tommy have everything under control." Merry started the swing moving.

"I know it will take a lot of work. I don't even know if I have a ghost of a chance. I just know if I don't try, I will never forgive myself. What do you think, Uncle Thad?"

"I think we are a family built on faith, Annabeth. Give it to the Lord and see what happens. You know we will help you all we can." He smiled at her, and she laid her head on his shoulder.

"I will tell you this. I came out here and found exactly what I was looking for." Thad's eyes went to his wife's. "I've never been sorry." The other three people on the porch could testify to the same sentiment.

CHAPTER 2

August 1896

"Thank you, Mr. Tyler, for opening up the store a little early. I am almost out of flour, and I have a big order to fill tomorrow." Annabeth's bakery The Dowry was a big success. She was no dummy. Annabeth understood the new would soon wear off, and then she would know for sure if her bakery could stand on its own goods.

"Thank you, Miss Lorton. You keep me in cookies and pies. What more can a man ask for?" The old bachelor patted his ever-present belly. His hearty laugh was contagious. Annabeth had turned her head to smile at the generous man when she ran smack dab into a boulder. She landed on her backside covered in flour.

"Are you all right, miss?" the boulder spoke.

"Why don't you watch where you are going?" Annabeth asked rather harshly. More because half her flour now covered them both.

"Me? You shot out of there like your tail was on fire." Did he say that? He probably shouldn't have used that phrase, but it was out there now. He extended his hand, and the little miss slapped it out of the way.

"I don't require any more of your help, sir! Just look what you have done."

His dark-brown eyes had a fire in them. Shaking his head, he stepped over her and went his way. Several onlookers were appalled at his behavior, yet it didn't seem to bother him. Mr. Tyler came to her rescue and helped her up. "You go on and get cleaned up. I will send over some more flour in a little bit." She started to protest. "Now we will work something out later. You go on."

*****

Will Stanton entered the sheriff's office, brushing the flour off his dark shirt. That woman wasn't paying any attention coming out of the store. When he saw her, it was too late. Well, he offered to help her up. He only offers once. He frowned when the flour wouldn't completely come off his shirt.

"What can I do for you?" The sheriff came from the back room.

"I'm Will Stanton." The man offered his hand to Dan Bullock.

"Trudy's nephew. We weren't expecting you until tomorrow."

Dan shook the man's hand and motioned for him to sit down. "I had the opportunity to come a day early. I hope it doesn't cause a problem."

"Not at all, but I am not sure Trudy is ready."

There was a ruckus outside, and the sheriff stood. Two teenage boys were fighting in the alley. "I better get out there. Why don't you head over to The Dowry and get a cup of coffee? I'll take care of those two and then show you around town. Then we can head home. I think your aunt Trudy would be ready by then."

"The Dowry? What's The Dowry?" the stranger in town asked.

"The best little bakery in the West. You head on over. Ask for the apple cinnamon muffin. If they tell you they are out, tell them I said you can have mine. They save me one back each morning."

Will headed toward The Dowry. *What a stupid name for a bakery,* he thought, but who was he to have an opinion? If the food was good, and it must be because of the crowd of people exiting, the name mattered little. When he stepped in, the smell of coffee and cinnamon filled his head. He did love the smell of coffee, almost as much as he enjoyed the brew itself. He made his way over to a corner table and sat down. The establishment was small—just a few tables—but there looked to be room for expansion. It was clean—very clean—and appealing to the eye.

The woman behind the counter was staring at him. She looked to be middle age with dark-black hair streaked with gray. He didn't know why she was staring. When he smiled, she smiled right back. He nodded, and she nodded and then burst into laughter. Was she touched in the head? He sure hoped she wasn't the owner.

The waitress at the other table turned; and when she did, the toe of her shoe scuffed the floor, causing her to lose her balance. She regained her stance, facing him. It was the little miss from earlier. Her face dawned recognition, and a slight flush claimed her cheeks. "What can I get you?" she asked, staring directly into his eyes.

"Coffee and one of your apple cinnamon muffins."

She sat the coffee cup down and poured. "We are out of the muffins."

She was to the point. "They came highly recommended by Sheriff Bullock. He said I could have his."

"We are out of muffins," she stated flatly as if that was the end of it.

"Could I see the owner, please?" She turned to leave. "Leave the pot," he commanded.

"Leave the pot? I'm not leaving the pot. There are other customers." One other customer was currently in the building, drinking tea. "You have another one back there brewing."

He threw his eyes toward the second pot. "Leave the pot and get the owner."

She dropped the pot onto his table, sloshing his already-poured coffee.

"Something like that doesn't come in this place every day. He is a dream." The lady behind the counter continued to stare.

"Vivian, he was very rude. I don't care how dreamy you think he is." Both women were now facing the man in the corner. He was drinking the coffee looking out the window.

"A man like that, a man that masculine, is rare. Reminds me of my first husband. He was something."

Vivian Ascot had outlived three husbands and was on the lookout for number four. She was midfifties and had no children. Each husband left her with more and more money. She didn't have to work, but she chose to just to stay in the thick of things, she would say. "He wants Dan Bullock's muffin. He said the sheriff told him to tell us he could have it. When I told him we had no more muffins, he asked to see the owner."

"What did he say when you told him you were the owner?"

"I didn't tell him."

Vivian took the apple cinnamon muffin put back for Sheriff Bullock and put it in plain sight of the man at the corner table. She winked at the man and smiled again. "Vivian, why did you do that?" Annabeth asked in a whisper.

"Because that man likes games."

One of the customers stood at the counter ready to pay. After she took the man's money and gave him his change, she approached the dark-headed man, pouring himself another cup of coffee. The action irritated Annabeth. "You wanted to see the owner?"

"That's right." His eyes drifted to Vivian watching from behind the counter. She pushed the muffin a little more in his view. He stood to get the coveted muffin, but Annabeth stepped in front of him. He reached over the top of her and took the muffin. "Thank you, ma'am." He winked at Vivian and returned to his seat.

"You realize you gave that gentleman back too much change," he said with a mouthful of the prized muffin. "Better not let the boss know you made that kind of mistake. With your rudeness, that may cost you your job."

"My what?" Annabeth crossed her arms over her chest.

"Your job."

"That is not what I meant, and for your information, widows and widowers get a discount here at *my* bakery.

"Your bakery? That figures." Will plopped the final bite of muffin in his mouth and drained the rest of his coffee. He handed Annabeth the correct change and flipped a tip to Vivian. "Thanks, sweetheart," he said as he left the bakery.

"He is a smooth one." Vivian tucked the coin into her dress pocket. "And a looker. Annie did you see that smile? And those eyes could melt a girl plum into a puddle. He'll be a tough one to slow down unlike 'Old Reliable' Rawly Smith. Here he comes."

Rawly entered the bakery. He was the blacksmith; he came to town a few weeks after Annabeth. Since the first few weeks of his arrival, he had cautiously been trying to woo her. She was taking it slow, telling him she just wanted to be friends. She was not yet ready to fully trust any man. Rawly usually came to the boarding house on Tuesday nights for supper. "I'm going to be a little late tonight, but I will definitely be there." He was a nervous, shy kind of guy. He had blond hair and blue eyes with an average build. He had huge forearms because of his blacksmith work and was always nicely tan.

"That will be fine. We can wait for you." Annabeth barely looked at him.

He was sorely disappointed. "No, don't wait. Just know that I will show up sometime."

"Okay," Annabeth said as she put away supplies, not paying much attention to the man staring at her. Rawly left as dully as he entered.

"Well, that was like a drizzle compared to the thunderstorm that just left. Can't you feel it? It is like a ten-point buck walked through followed by a rabbit." Vivian was hanging the Closed sign on the door.

"Don't be unkind. Rawly is a nice man."

"Reliable Rawly won't get the job done. He doesn't have the fervor to sweep a girl off her feet. I see you're pretty sure-footed these days."

Annabeth stepped out the back door. She was not interested in being swept off her feet. She wanted her business to be a success. She needed to prove to herself she could make her bakery grow. "Hey, Ms. Lorton, you gonna have any do-overs today?" A boy came running from the schoolyard.

"I might. You come back at noon, and I will see what I have." The boy smiled and went back to the other children.

"What are do-overs?" The muffin man startled her. How long had he been standing there?

"When I bake, if I make a mistake or I don't think the product is as good as I want it to be, I do it over. I give my less-than-perfect ones to the schoolchildren." Why was she telling him all this? He moved to get her attention.

"After our first meeting, do you think I could have a do-over?" Those eyes held nothing but trouble, she thought as she looked deep into them.

"After this morning, I am surprised you think you need one." She returned to the bakery. His soft laughter made her angry. Who was he anyway?

At lunchtime, Annabeth handed out her do-overs to the children. They really weren't do-overs. They were cookies baked with love for all the kids. She knew there were some who had very little to eat or may have lost a parent. This was her way of helping the hungry and the fatherless just like the discount for the widows. She did her best to be Christ-like.

Once she was done, she headed back to Trudy's. She typically brought home leftovers from the bakery to supplement the evening meal. She placed her basket on the table and found Trudy. "What needs to be done?" she asked her friend.

"If you could take the linens off the clothesline and make up the third bedroom upstairs, it would be a big help. My nephew is coming to stay with us. He will be here tomorrow. It has been thirteen years since I last saw him"—Trudy stopped to think—"or maybe fourteen. No, it was thirteen."

Did it matter? Annabeth shoved the thought aside. "How old was he then?"

"Let me see." Trudy calculated in her head. "I would say he was around fifteen. He was almost full grown then. I can just about imagine what he looks like now."

"I brought some bread and leftover pie home. I put them on the counter. When I am done upstairs, I will start on supper preparations." Annabeth left to gather the linen.

"You earn way more than your room and board. We should be paying you."

"Nonsense!" she called over her shoulder.

Annabeth spent her time fixing up each room. When she came to the third one, she wanted to make it extra special for her friend's nephew. She took her time adjusting the mattress. She put the fresh linens on it and a lovely quilt. Now to make sure there were no lumps, she lay down. She rested in several spots, adjusting and readjusting the lumps of feathers until they were just right.

Will Stanton made his way through the back door of Bullocks Boarding House. He set his bag on the floor and took a seat at the table. Kicking his feet out, he waited for his aunt to come through the swinging kitchen door. Sure enough, she did, stopping just short of screaming. "William Stanton, you scared the living daylights out of me! When did you get into town? You weren't supposed to be here until tomorrow. How long are you staying? Are you hungry?" She wouldn't let him answer one question before she spewed another. He just smiled and waited.

"I got in early this morning. I'm not sure how long I am staying, and I'm always hungry if your cooking is as good as I remember." He stood, and she wrapped her arms around his waist. She reached up to kiss him on his cheek. "Point me to my room, and I will get this eyesore out of here." He picked up his worn satchel.

"Last door on the right. The room should be ready."

Finding the door to the third room slightly ajar, Will entered quietly. There she was, the little miss from earlier, curled up asleep in the middle of the bed. He leaned on the doorframe. Should he drop his luggage on the floor, startling her awake? He looked at her all peaceful. She probably could use the rest, and hadn't he teased her enough? He quietly put his baggage down and left.

He returned to a sandwich, coffee, and his aunt's many questions. "How are your mother and father? It has been several years since I have seen them. I know my sister-in-law's letters indicate all is well, but how are they truly?"

"They are doing well, and they send their love."

"And your sisters—are they well?"

"Everyone is fine, Aunt Gertrude, or should I call you Trudy?" He smiled, and she blushed.

"I have grown to love that name." She sighed just a bit, and he knew his aunt was happy with the sheriff.

"Dan seems like a good man. The town sure doesn't say anything negative about him."

"And why would they? He is good and decent." She seemed a little offended. His hand covered hers.

"That's what I am saying."

"I'm a little protective I guess." She smiled for her apology.

"I guess." He leaned back and patted his stomach and yawned.

"Why don't you go up and sneak in a nap?" Trudy cleared the dishes. "You must be tired from traveling."

"I might just do that, but I noticed how big your sofa is. I might just stretch out on it."

"As you wish. This time of day, the curtains will need to be drawn. You go on. I'll be right there."

Will pushed his way through the swinging door and pushed Annabeth, her arms filled with linens to the ground. She just sat there. Was he put on earth to be her thorn in the flesh? It sure seemed like it. "Go ahead and step over me," she said with a huff. So he did. He was on the first step when Trudy entered.

"Oh my, Annabeth, are you okay? What on earth happened?" She looked toward her nephew for answers.

"Don't worry about adjusting the curtains Aunt Gert—Trudy." He smiled. "I'll just head up to my room. Something tells me Goldilocks might think my bed is just right." He laughed all the way up the stairs.

"What? What did he mean by that?" Trudy was helping Annabeth up.

"I think it means he enjoys reading children's books."

That was Trudy's beloved nephew. How long was he going to be staying? All sorts of things were running through her head. If he was a buck like Vivian described, then Annabeth was a field mouse.

"Annabeth?" Trudy got her attention. "Are you all right, dear?"

"Yes, I am just so clumsy. I think I would trip over my own shadow."

"That was my nephew, Will. Did he introduce himself?"

"No, not officially."

"No matter, I will introduce you tonight at supper. He is currently our only tenant, so we can eat in the kitchen tonight." Trudy was headed back into the kitchen.

"Don't forget it is Tuesday."

"Oh yes, that's right, Rawly will be joining us."

"He did say he would be late tonight but not to wait on him. I don't think he would mind eating in the kitchen."

Will stretched out on the bed. He was exhausted. The trip from Atlanta had been a long and grueling one. He was ready for a holiday away from any big city. He had had his fill of the riotous towns battling the effects of the Depression. The railroad collapse, the bank failures and Coxey's Army's march on Washington in '94—he had been involved in them all. Thank goodness, he had not been involved in the Pullman strike that same year. That had turned out to be a disaster.

His mind raced. Sleep was nowhere in sight. He rose and began unpacking his things. He wasn't sure how long he was staying; his gut would tell him when to go. He pulled out the worn Bible his mother gave him several years ago and laid it on the bedside table. He removed his clothing and put them in the chest of drawers. When he did, his silver Pinkerton Detective Agency badge fell to the ground. The thud sounded extremely loud in the still room. He bent to pick it up. He needed to put it somewhere it couldn't be found. As far as his family knew, he traveled around doing odd jobs. He was a drifter, a drifter working for the agency. He wanted to continue to keep his employment concealed.

Will read his Bible for a good part of the afternoon. He never minded being alone. It suited him rather nicely. When he heard Dan's voice, he washed up and went downstairs. Annabeth was at the sink, peeling potatoes. Dan was sitting at the table, drinking a cup of coffee, telling Trudy about his day. His aunt was all ears as she stoked the fire in the stove.

Dan kicked out a kitchen chair and motioned for Will to sit. "I reckon you met Annabeth this morning at The Dowry." The sheriff poured his newfound nephew a cup of coffee. Trudy looked at Annabeth. *Is that what she meant by "not officially"?*

"Yes, and if it hadn't been for Mrs. Ascot, I wouldn't have gotten your muffin today. Miss—"

"Lorton," Annabeth supplied.

"Ms. Lorton didn't seem to think I was honest about it."

"Vivian Ascot would give any man a free muffin." This came from Trudy. Vivian had been Trudy's rival from the very beginning. There was still a little animosity there for Trudy. Vivian had moved on. All this was said without Annabeth's participation in the conversation. She was thinking about her bakery. She was always thinking about the bakery. How could she make it better? What new confections could she come up with? She wished she had her own kitchen instead of the small kitchenette to work in at night. She often went to the bakery well before five in the morning just to soak it all in.

Suddenly, a dish towel went swirling through the air, hitting her in the face. "This is exactly why you and I were covered in flour this morning. You don't pay attention. My aunt asked us to go into the living room where it was more comfortable."

Annabeth surveyed the empty room. She had missed the request. He held the kitchen door open for her. "So neither of us ends up on the floor," he said as she passed by him.

*****

The four had just sat down to eat when there was a knock at the door. Dan started to get up. "I'll get it. It is probably Rawly." Annabeth smiled as she patted Dan's shoulder. As expected, Rawly Smith stood at the door. He was handsome and kind and always thoughtful. Tonight he had a small bouquet of flowers.

"These are for you." No kidding, Will nearly said out loud as he heard the exchange from his seat in the kitchen.

"They are lovely," Annabeth took a deep breath, "and they smell wonderful. Thank you." Rawly followed her into the kitchen. He wasn't expecting to see another man at the table. "Rawly, this is Will Stanton, Trudy's nephew."

Will stood and leaned across the table with an outstretched hand. The blacksmith put his hand in Will's. "This is our blacksmith and close friend Rawly Smith." The two nodded and released hands. Were they close friends? Rawly wondered. He hoped they could be much more.

Will dominated the mealtime conversation. He asked Rawly dozens of questions about his blacksmith shop and the town. Rawly, in turn, asked Will a few questions; but his answers were vague. When everyone had eaten, Annabeth rose to clear the table. Will's hand stopped her. "You kids go on into the parlor. I'll help with the dishes."

There was more than one strange glance thrown his way. "Did I say something offensive?" he addressed the table. They all schooled their features.

"No, son, I guess we didn't expect it. You caught us off guard," Dan spoke for the group.

Annabeth and Rawly remained still. Will looked at Rawly. "Do you want *me* to take her into the parlor?"

Will started to move as if he would. Rawly grabbed Annabeth's hand and led her into the sitting room but not before her foot hit the chair, knocking it over. Before she could pick it up, Will had it back in its proper place, laughing wholeheartedly.

Will spent the next few days meandering around town. He visited every business, trying to get his bearings; he wanted to get a feel for the territory. Just about every business he went into in Sheridan, South Dakota, a person by the last name of Sheridan was employed there. Such a dominant family. He wondered if they were a good kind of dominant or bad. He knew where he could get the answer.

He headed over to The Dowry. Vivian Ascot loved to talk, especially to him. He had made it a point to stop in for a midmorning snack since his first day. The bell above the door jingled, causing Annabeth to look up and then back down. It was only Will Stanton. He made his way to the counter and leaned over.

"Have anything saved back for me?" He winked at Vivian.

"Not unless you are the sheriff," Annabeth answered.

"What's good today?" he voiced his question to Vivian. "Everything, but I think those cream-filled pastries are probably the best."

"I'll have two of those and coffee." Vivian retrieved the danishes and the coffee pot. When she went to the table, he pushed the chair opposite him out with the toe of his boot. "Have a seat. I would like to talk to you for a minute."

Vivian sat down, and he pushed the extra pastry her way. "What's on your mind, Will Stanton?"

Annabeth watched from her place in the kitchen. The bakery was empty, or she would have reprimanded Vivian for sitting with a customer.

Will Stanton was an odd fellow. He held no job and wasn't particularly looking for one. He had hair the color of a muddy river, dark eyes, a strong chin, and a very expressive face. He hadn't really said why he was here or how long he intended to stay. Will Stanton was kind of a mystery. What could he and Vivian have to talk about?

"Everywhere I go, Vivian, I run into Sheridans. I would like to know a little bit about this family the town is named after. I am assuming it is named after them. You'll never convince me it is coincidental."

Vivian nibbled on her pastry. "If you want to know about the Sheridans, honey," she said it loudly so Annabeth could hear, "you might want to talk to the owner. Her mamma is a Sheridan."

Will motioned with his finger for Annabeth to join them. She moved to the table standing next to Vivian. "What is it you wish to know about the Sheridans?"

He studied her for a moment. She was average looking. Not ugly but not striking. Her hair was a golden blonde and seemed to be thick, and she had blue eyes. Now that was what transformed her into something worth looking at, he thought. They were big, bright, and sincere. She couldn't lie if her life depended on it. That is what he saw in Annabeth Lorton.

"Just wondering if they are upstanding people or if they are a little on the domineering side." He noticed her bristle at his remark. "It does seem they are involved in almost every form of commerce in town." He gauged her reaction. Would she retaliate?

"I hardly feel I would be the best one to answer that as I think they are wonderful people. Perhaps instead of asking about them, you try to get to know them personally."

"How would I go about doing that? Where or with whom do you recommend I start?" He leaned back in the chair and crossed his legs at the ankle. He hoped he wasn't being too obvious, but he was here to do a job. There had been a ring of thefts along the southeastern coastal states. Money, jewels, and other small but pricey items had been stolen. A few of the items had been showing up in mining towns near Victor, Colorado.

A sheriff in Victor had alerted the detective agency of some suspicious goods being sold in his town. For the past five weeks, Will had been following lead after lead. His investigating had brought him to Sheridan. But why?

"You can meet them at church on Sunday if you are inclined to go." Annabeth brought him back to the conversation at hand.

"You don't think I am inclined to go?" he asked her, taking a long swallow of coffee, never removing his eyes from hers. She shrugged her shoulders. The bell alerted her of a customer, so she left Vivian to deal with Will.

*****

Sunday morning Will made his way to the pew with Trudy and Dan. He was inclined to go to church. When he was able, he never missed. Growing up, he made it his goal to know the scriptures. The purpose had served him well. It had kept him on the straight and narrow in the midst of the job he found himself in. He was getting a little tired of always being on the move. He promised himself this would be his last assignment. He decided when it ended he would pick the place in his travels he most enjoyed and make it his home. He was pretty sure it wouldn't be Sheridan, South Dakota.

It didn't take long for Will to determine who Thad Sheridan was. The man entered the church and drew the respect and well-wishes of everyone. Thad, Merry, and David sat on the pew with the Kennedy family. On the bench behind him were the doctor and his family. It surprised Will to find out the town physician was Lakota Indian. A doctor's office certainly could be a place someone could ship stolen goods to, and no one is the wiser.

An older couple sat with the doctor as well as a family with a woman with crutches and leg braces. The town's bank vice president sat behind the doctor. The bank is always under suspicion. There was a man with a missing left arm and two boys in their late teens sitting with the banker. The blacksmith and the baker entered.

Rawly Smith ushered Annabeth to her seat and then sat at a conservative distance from her. Not even close enough to slip his arm around the back of the pew, Will thought. Somebody needs to teach the man a thing or two about subtlety in courting. He watched the two for a moment. Annabeth sat with perfect posture. Her face never deviated from the pastor.

Rawly's face kept glancing toward Annabeth. A time or two he would survey the crowd. Rawly was looking for anyone looking at Annabeth. Will almost chuckled out loud. The man had no security in the affections of the little miss. Rawly caught Will looking, and Will grinned. Rawly needed something to spur him on, or he would be courting or trying to woo Annabeth for years. The Holy Spirit checked him. He should be paying attention to the sermon.

After church, Trudy introduced her nephew to Thad and Merry Sheridan. Merry immediately asked the Bullocks and their nephew to Sunday dinner. "The Lapps are coming over, but thank you for the offering." Trudy smiled.

"Would you mind if I go to the Sheridans?" Will asked his aunt. "Of course not. You go on. Who wants to be with us old people when you can spend the day with people closer to your age?"

"It's not that," Will said.

"No, he would like to get to know the people the town is named after. He wants to know if the Sheridans are good or—"

"That's enough, little miss." Will stopped Annabeth. Thad just stared at Will with a questioning look.

"I'm just curious about the family a town would change its name for. If there is something wrong with that, so be it." He was a bold one.

Thad was weighing the young man up. "Well, at least you're honest. Come to dinner, and you can ask us anything."

Will pushed his pony down the road following Rawly Smith's wagon. They were traveling at a fairly good clip. *Why doesn't he slow down?* Will mused. Rawly could enjoy this beautiful day with the little miss and take advantage of some stolen moments. Will shook his head. He didn't have to worry about the blacksmith being involved in any mischief. He wasn't even savvy enough to romance a woman.

When they reached the Sheridans, Will was surprised. The farmhouse was rather modest. It had obviously been built onto many times. There was a sign at the edge of the property that read Sheridan Boys' Home. He tied his horse to the back of Rawly's wagon.

Will watched as Rawly allowed Annabeth to exit the wagon on her own. He mentally rolled his eyes. Greenhorn. About that time, Annabeth slipped; and Will caught her around the waist just before she landed in the dirt. He still had her in his arms when Thad came out on the porch. The look on his face was that of a protective father. Will released her. "Are you all right, Miss Annabeth?"

She was smoothing the bodice of her jacket and adjusting her hat. "Yes, thank you, Mr. Stanton."

She tripped as she climbed the few steps to her awaiting uncle. Rawly followed her.

Will went to enter, but Thad put his hand on the man's chest, stopping him. "You come with me," Thad said as he stepped off the porch and headed toward the barn. Once inside, Thad spoke. "I don't know who you are, son, but you are a little too bold for my taste."

"With all due respect, sir, she was falling." Will wasn't going to be pushed around.

"I'm not talking about Annabeth. I am talking about your eagerness to find out something about my family. It is more than idle curiosity."

Uh-oh, Will thought. He may have run into someone who could be on to him.

"I never was good at social graces. I pretty much say what I am thinking. If I want to know something, I ask. All I seem to hear about is the Sheridans. I just wanted to meet them."

"Oh, you are going to meet them, but I am warning you. We pay close attention."

Thad left the building. Will stayed behind for just a minute. How come he felt like he had been to the woodshed? He needed to be very careful.

Could a table be fuller? Thad and Merry sat at each end. Quinn, Hunter, River, and David all sat at a little table in the kitchen. Dr. Sheridan and his wife sat with Hud and Molly Sheridan on one side. Tommy, Rawly, Annabeth, and Will sat on the other. Franklin and Gil had been invited to have dinner with a family in town who had eligible daughters. This was a regular Sunday event. Jonah had declined to come.

"Where's Jonah? Is he ill?" Molly asked Merry.

"He just said he couldn't come today."

"I b-bet he is m-meeting Hannah Miller somewhere. It is the only w-way he ever g-gets to see her," Tommy commented.

"Well, that won't get him anywhere with Mr. Miller, them sneaking around," Thad added.

"I don't know why they don't elope. They are both over eighteen," Avery said. "I know Hannah is crazy about him. She stops by the office sometimes just to ask about him."

"I guess there is something to be said for going about courtship the right way," Rawly added. *Well, you sure ain't giving a stellar example of how it is done,* Will said to himself.

"None of us in this room has had conventional courting." Merry looked at her husband with a little grin. What did she mean by that? Will's face must have shown his question.

"Merry and I were married less than a week after meeting one another," Thad supplied.

"Yes, and they haven't stopped courting," Tommy said with a smirk.

"What about you two?" Will looked at the doctor and his wife. "You mean, how did a beautiful Austrian noble get tied up with a Lakota Indian?" Hawk asked sarcastically.

The doctor's eyes were very penetrating and somewhat intimidating. Will felt like he might have hit a nerve with the doctor. Somehow the question didn't seem that important anymore.

"I didn't mean it the way you are taking it. Can we just settle on the fact you two look very blessed?" Will shut the conversation down. Avery knocked her husband's knee with her own. At times he still held on to a little bitterness in regard to their past.

In all this, Annabeth sat quietly. Will Stanton seemed to create havoc everywhere he went. He wanted to meet the Sheridans, but his actions were bringing out the defensive nature of each one. He will never see them the way they are if he doesn't shut up.

"Are you okay, Annabeth? You have barely touched your food." Merry drew her attention from Will.

"Oh, I am fine. I am not very hungry today. I hate that because I know the food is so wonderful, Aunt Merry."

"Maybe you are working too hard."

"She is," Will blurted out.

All eyes were on him. He stopped just as he put a fork full of potatoes in his mouth. What did he do now? He just told the truth.

The men spent the afternoon pitching horseshoes. Annabeth wondered if Will was able to keep his mouth shut or if he was causing chaos. She joined the women in the kitchen. They had all promised to give her recipes for her bakery. She was anxious to share with them some of her ideas for The Dowry.

Annabeth could have stayed at her aunt's all day. The home was warm, and inviting. Laurel was warm in its own right. Her parents tried to make it so. However, it was still a plantation home and was never as open as Thad and Merry's seemed to be. She was determined her home, if she ever had one, would be a place people wouldn't want to leave.

At dusk, everyone was packing up to leave. Leftovers were neatly packed away in the wagons. Merry always had treats for her boys and their family. The sudden approach of a lone rider surprised the group. Owen Miller stopped short of the front porch. "I just want you to know your Jonah has gone and done it. He has taken Hannah against my will and eloped." The man was a mixture of fury and defeat.

"I am sorry you are upset, Mr. Miller, but both Jonah and Hannah are of age." Thad's words did not seem to help the man.

"He is just the man I thought he was: not to be trusted."

"Now, hold on there, Miller. My son abided by your rules for more than a year. He tried every way he could to get your approval."

The man frowned. "He will never be welcomed in my house." The disgruntled man turned to leave.

"Mr. Miller, if you do that, you won't see your daughter either," Merry said.

The man stopped only long enough to face Tommy. "Don't you get any ideas, young man. I have set Josie straight on you. Don't even think of trying what your brother did." With that, the man left. The family went back inside for a few minutes.

"Did you know about this?" Hawk Sheridan asked his wife.

She grinned. "Maybe." They all liked Hannah and Josie Miller and were tickled to have Hannah in the family. It was going to be rough on the couple. Thad suggested they take time as a family to pray for them.

*****

Will brushed his horse, fed her some oats and headed to the back door. There, at Annabeth's door, stood Rawly saying good night. It was pitiful! A full moon, warm breeze and Rawly was just flapping his jaws. *Kiss her,* Will willed the man to do so. It never happened. Will went to his room, and Rawly left Annabeth on the doorstep.

From the window in his room, Will could see into Annabeth's tiny living room. She sat in a chair and removed her shoes. Reaching up, she unpinned her hair; and the locks came cascading around her. Was she crying? It sure looked like she was.

Sensing someone was watching, she went to the window. Finding Will looking at her, she stared back. He had seen her tears. How many times would she be humiliated by a man? The tears flowed a little faster, and she let him see them. If he could take it, so could she.

From the window, he blew her a kiss and closed the curtain. He turned off the light and sat in the chair; the scene haunted him. Rawly Smith was a fool if he didn't pick up his pace. Annabeth would make him a good wife. It was evident she loved him but was taking her cues from him. Will needed to stay out of it. He didn't have time to play Cupid.

Will's mouth was suddenly dry, so he made his way downstairs. He was startled by Dan Bullock sitting at the table. "Did you have a good time at the Sheridans?"

"Yes, there are some good cooks in that family." Will patted his stomach.

"Thad tell you any about his Texas Ranger days?"

Will was taken aback. Thad Sheridan had been a Texas Ranger. Now that was a surprise he wasn't expecting.

*****

Every day Annabeth worked harder than the day before. Yesterday a shipment of peaches had come from her hometown distributor. She took a huge chance. The risk of them being spoiled by the time they reached her was high. They arrived nearly perfect.

Early morning she arrived at the bakery, ready to create. She made a few peach pies and decadent peach tarts. She put some of the peaches up to dry to use in the winter. Her mind went to last night. Rawly had come to help her unload her shipment. He was a little difficult to understand. His actions caught her off guard. He kissed her not once but twice and rather passionately. Her stomach fluttered just as it had done when Jonathan had kissed her. Look where that got her: left at the altar. Would she ever understand the male species or be able to trust one again?

"My goodness, girl, how long have you been here?" Vivian waltzed in, hanging her hat on the peg by the door. "Those smell heavenly." She inhaled deeply. Her eyes closed. "I can't believe Rawly Smith hasn't dropped a ring on that finger of yours. I guess I shouldn't be surprised. I bet we will be having the same conversation this time next year."

Annabeth felt very emotional. The statement almost brought her to tears. "Be nice, Viv."

"Honestly, Annabeth, has he even laid his lips on you once? And I am not talking about a peck on the cheek. I'm talking about a real I-am-in-love-with-you kiss." Annabeth blushed.

Vivian didn't see her face, or she wouldn't have kept talking. "I don't know that he has that much spunk in him."

"Yes! Vivian, yes!" Annabeth's emotions got the best of her. "He has kissed me—passionately if you must know."

"Well, it's about time." The deep voice of Will Stanton went down Annabeth's spine like fingers on a chalkboard. Her back was to him, and she shut her eyes. How long had he been standing there, and why didn't they hear the bell alerting someone had entered? She took a deep breath.

"What can we do for you, Mr. Stanton?" Annabeth tried to stay professional, but Vivian was Vivian. "You're here awful early. We don't usually see you until close to nine. Your timing is impeccable. I guess we both were wrong about 'Old Reliable' Rawly. He sure fooled us."

Why couldn't Vivian leave it alone? It was clear she and Will had discussed her relationship with Rawly. Annabeth felt sick. Would she ever get out from under a cloud of constant embarrassment? Vivian thought she knew everything there was to know about romance because she had been married multiple times. Annabeth was seething. She stopped herself from being angry at her coworker. Vivian also knew all about losing not one but three husbands to death. She even knew the pain of not having children of her own.

Annabeth had a change of heart. When she turned, she placed a kiss on Vivian's cheek and then stretched to kiss Will's. "Thank you both for taking such an interest in my love life. Now, Will, what can we do for you?"

Will was momentarily shocked by the little miss's action. She had every right to be upset with the two of them. Not only had he eavesdropped, but he had also had multiple discussions with Vivian about the couple. She could have told him what for or kicked him out of the bakery, but she didn't. She laid those soft, warm lips right on his rough cheek.

"I came by to ask you to save back some of whatever that is I smell baking. I have asked your uncle to meet me here at ten along with Hud, Hawk, and Tommy." Annabeth tried to reason why he would invite that group for a midmorning snack. "And," he continued, "I want that corner table and lots of coffee."

"May I ask what type of meeting is going to be taking place in my bakery?" She started putting back four tarts.

"There will be five," he said as he watched her put the four tarts in the pie safe. She pointed to the tart in the back.

"Vivian already put one back for you."

"That's my girl." He smiled with a nod toward the woman wiping down the counter.

"You didn't answer my question," Annabeth said as Will left the bakery.

"And I don't plan to."

He headed toward Tyler's mercantile. Annabeth was a little nervous. He couldn't be discussing her relationship with Rawly with them. If he does, will he tell them what he heard just now? Her mother taught her to keep her emotions in check. Abigail Lorton would have never blurted out she had been kissed passionately. Annabeth put her hand to her forehead.

"You okay, honey?" Vivian rested a hand on Annabeth's shoulder.

"It's just a headache."

"You sure it's not a heartache?" Annabeth frowned at the comment. "What you need just walked out that door."

Annabeth let the comment slide. She wasn't going to let Vivian's words get her riled up; besides, they had customers to tend to.

At a quarter to ten, Will returned. He came around the counter and got a cup and the pot of coffee and headed to his table. He had a lot of nerve. Annabeth tried to ignore him. Vivian just encouraged him. Slowly the Sheridan men strolled in. Before long, four men, who worked constantly, found the time to sit with a stranger. What was going on?

Annabeth greeted her family with mugs of coffee and peach tarts. "Those look wonderful, honey. It's no wonder your bakery is doing so well." Thad had his arm around his niece's waist. "I'm proud of you, Annabeth."

She blushed, knowing he had to say that because he was her surrogate father here in the West.

After the pleasantries, Annabeth got the feeling they were waiting for her to leave. "If you need something, just give me a holler."

When she left, Thad turned to Will. "All right, son, why are we here?"

Will looked at the four gentlemen facing him. "I wanted to apologize for Sunday. I know I stepped on more than one set of toes. Maybe even a time or two." The four men sat quietly. Will continued, "I am a person who says what I am thinking. I know it may not be the right thing, but that's what I do. I meant no offense. I hope we can be friends while I am in Sheridan."

Thad sat up and leaned his elbows on the table. "I reckon we can forgive you." He stretched his hand across the table to shake Will's. "Your admission explains why you are still a bachelor."

Hawk took a drink. "No woman I know would put up with a man who said what he was thinking all the time."

"At least not one in the Sheridan household," Hud declared.

There was a roar of laughter that got Annabeth's attention. When she looked up, she saw five little boys, not men, at the corner table. They were laughing and nudging one another, grinning from ear to ear. "That is a good sound." Vivian came to stand beside her. "Find you a man with a good laugh and passionate kisses, and you'll find a gem. I don't know if I have ever heard Rawly laugh. Does he laugh, Annie?"

She didn't answer. She couldn't. She never heard Rawly laugh.

At noon Annabeth had to tell the men at the corner table it was closing time. Who knew men could kill nearly two hours just talking, laughing, and telling stories? The boys said their good-byes and exited The Dowry. "Vivian, I need to go to the post office. I will be right back." Vivian nodded, and Annabeth grabbed her shawl and left the bakery.

The gentlemen were still standing on the porch, talking. She maneuvered around them and down the steps, missing the last one. Hud caught her arm just in time, preventing her from hitting the ground. "Thank you, Hud."

She went a little farther. The group watched as Annabeth gracefully stepped in a small pile of horse dung, causing her to slip. Embarrassed that someone might be watching, she acted as if nothing happened; but the men on the porch saw the whole thing.

"Her center of balance is all messed up if she wasn't so top heavy." Will barely got the statement out when he felt all eyes on him. "I just meant—"

"We know what you meant." Hawk stopped him.

"You know, I—"

"We know the hole you're digging can't get much deeper you better move along," Hud added.

Will decided it was time for him to move along. He headed toward Tyler's with the sound of laughter behind him. He smiled to himself. He liked the Sheridans. He prayed they were as good and honest as they appeared.

*****

Will plowed into his investigation. He started with Tyler's Mercantile. Will had offered to help Mr. Tyler unload his goods. He knew with times being a little tough the man couldn't afford to pay him, so they set up a trading system. Will would help out in exchange for goods he might need. This was the perfect job to investigate the mercantile and watch the town.

He had been there for two weeks and turned up nothing. He knew Tyler needed the help, so he continued just in case. Will had also taken to helping Dan. There was no deputy in Sheridan. Dan would do evening and night checks randomly, but there was nothing consistent. Will offered to patrol since they weren't letting him pay for room and board. He would do night walks of the town. He would do it at different times as not to have a pattern.

One morning around three, he noticed a dim light at the back door of the bakery. There was a shadow of a person hunched over. He made his way to the corner of the building just in time for the light to go out. He ever so quietly advanced on the perpetrator. "Stand up real slow and put your hands where I can see them."

"I'd like to put them around your neck for scaring me so." Annabeth stood with her hands up.

"Miss Lorton, what are you doing out at this time of morning?"

"I could ask you the same thing. Don't just stand there. Help me find the key. I dropped it when my light went out."

The two ran their hands along the back stoop. "I'll never find it." She sighed. "This kind of thing always happens to me."

"Here it is." He felt for the keyhole and slipped the key in; opening the door, he let Annabeth in. She found the lamp and turned it up just until there was a soft glow. Will walked in behind her.

"Do you always come this early?" "Every once in a while I do, when I can't sleep, or I want to try a new recipe. I try to be quiet. I am not sure how soundproof these ceilings are. I don't want to disturb the Lapps."

"I didn't realize they lived above the store."

"When Dr. Lapp retired, he turned the practice and the house over to Hawk. They moved in here and opened the dress shop."

Will nodded, looking up at the ceiling.

"You can go now, and thank you for finding my key." Annabeth wanted to be alone.

Will didn't want to go. "Why did you call the bakery The Dowry?"

It was none of his business, but she didn't feel she could be *that* rude. She put her apron over her head and tied it around her waist. "I used the money my parents had put back as my dowry to open the store." She pulled a bowl off the shelf and went to a cabinet to get her dry ingredients.

"I am surprised your folks let you have it. It's customary to save it for the wedding."

"They did give it to me for my wedding."

"Oh." He looked at her, wanting more but was afraid to ask. A few scenarios played through his mind. Annabeth never talked much about herself, so he didn't know her history. He was about to find out more than he bargained for.

"In early spring of this year, I was to be married. Matter of fact, I got down the aisle, right up until the reverend asked if anyone had a reason the two of us shouldn't be married, and that was the end."

Will was stunned. "Do you mind me asking what happened?" She had opened this Pandora's box. She might as well give him all the gory details.

"A woman I barely knew, but he knew quite well, stood up and asked him not to marry me. He was in love with her and a year prior had asked for her hand, and she had turned him down. She changed her mind. Needless to say, he was still in love with her." The pain was evident in her voice. "I had known him all my life and never knew the two were—" She couldn't find the words. Her heart ached to rid itself of the enormous grief she carried. "What kind of man asks a woman he doesn't love to marry him?" This was said in a sorrowful whisper.

"A man like me."

Did she hear him correctly? He had positioned himself on the counter. His feet were dangling; and his head was down, his hands gripping the edge. When he looked up, his eyes locked with hers. For a few heartbeats, something passed between them. The villain was facing the victim.

"Christina and I met through mutual friends. We began courting. At first, everything seemed to be going well. We had a lot in common and could converse about most anything. Then I began to notice how manipulative she became. She pouted about most things and made me feel guilty about everything. I got it in my head that perhaps her actions were due in part to my lack of a proposal. If we married, things would go back the way they were in the beginning."

Annabeth just stood there looking intently at him with those big blue eyes on the brink of tears.

"Her mood did change for a while, but when we started the wedding preparations, she was back to her old ways. I began to notice how her mother treated her father. I saw a life of continually trying to please someone who was never going to be satisfied. The night before the wedding, I called it off."

"Our situations are quite different in some respect. Jonathan was willing to marry me without loving me. He was prepared to go through life married to someone he didn't love. Did you do the right thing, Will? Did you love Christina?" Her voice cracked.

"I loved her as much as I could."

A sob escaped Annabeth. "What does that mean? Please tell me what that means when a man tells you he loves you as much as he can."

Her pain and agony hung on to Will like a thick coat. "I don't know if I can explain it." He wanted to ease her suffering but not sure he could.

"There is part of a man that exists only to thrive and live for a certain something only the right woman can give him. I loved a lot of things about Christina and could have married her without that certain connection. Neither of us would have been happy. A man who willingly goes into marriage only loving as much as he can knows he'll never be happy. He will die emotionally and kill his wife's emotion as well. Please know that Jonathan loved your beauty. He loved your sweet temperament and the sound of your laughter. That's what he meant by loving you all he could. This has nothing to do with you." She was so overcome she could barely speak.

"That's what Patience told me the day it happened. She said it had nothing to do with me." She made eye contact with Will. She wanted to tell him how much his words had meant to her, but she was afraid of the onslaught of tears welling up in her soul.

"Who is this woman called Patience that showed such brilliance?" His smile was contagious.

"Only the best little sister in the world."

The sun was just starting to peek over the horizon. "I better get out of here." He hopped off the counter. "Look at it this way. Jonathan's loss will be another man's treasure." He headed out the back door. "I'll be back at my usual time. Make sure Vivian keeps something back for me."

*****

Will made his way to the bank. If Tyler's Mercantile wasn't involved in moving the stolen goods, perhaps someone in the bank was. He was pretty sure he could rule out Tommy Sheridan, but he still had to investigate everyone. He met with Tommy about opening an account. In doing so, he was able to ask a few questions about how the bank sustained itself during the panic and the following Depression.

The bank was across the street from the mercantile, so he could keep a close eye on who came in and out daily. He also turned his attention to other local businesses. No one escaped his eye; but still, he was getting nowhere. He contemplated letting Dan Bullock in on the investigation, but it didn't feel right—not yet.

CHAPTER 3

*T*had looked out over his wheat crop. It was beautiful. The Lord had blessed him again. "You ready to get started?" Hud stood beside him, putting on a pair of gloves.

"I was just admiring the Lord's handiwork." Thad put his hand on his son's shoulder. "Let's go harvest this crop." Franklin and Gil had joined the two men as they headed to the field.

They worked for several hours, putting the wheat into the thresher. A sudden pop stopped the process. When Hud turned to investigate, he saw Franklin running to his pa. Thad lay on the ground, blood oozing from his shirt. He struggled to get up. "Pa, lay down." Franklin was easing his pale father back down. Hud ran to the scene.

"Gil, take one of the horses and ride into town. Tell Hawk what happened and that we are on our way. Franklin go get the wagon and Ma." The boys did as they were told. "Pa, stay with me."

Thad looked pale and clammy. Hud was tearing his father's shirt to see where the blood was coming from. He had a wound where the shoulder met the chest. It was bleeding pretty good. The shoulder and upper arm were already swelling and changing colors.

Hud took off the bandanna he had tied around his neck and placed it on the wound. "I'm okay," Thad croaked out.

"Humor me and lie still." Hud looked at the thresher. One of the pulleys had snapped and hit Thad.

It did not take long for Merry and Franklin to arrive. "What happened?" She knelt by Thad; and tearing off the rest of his shirt, she looked at the injuries. Hud explained what happened, only lifting his hand from the wound when his mother asked.

"I'm fine Merry," Thad said as he closed his eyes.

"Let's get him in the wagon." Hud, Franklin, and Merry lifted him into the wagon. It must have been sheer willpower because Thad Sheridan was not a small man. Merry climbed in the back and held pressure on the wound, supporting his upper body with hers.

"Stop worrying, Merry. Hawk will take care of this."

"If you could see your own face right now, you wouldn't tell me not to worry. You are as white as a sheet, cool and clammy."

He reached up with his other hand and stroked the hair from her face. "My love."

Hud hit a rut in the road, and it shot pain throughout Thad's body. He clenched his teeth and then fainted.

Gil burst into the doctor's office. "Hawk!" he called out in sheer panic.

Hawk came out of the office, and Avery came from the kitchen. "What is it?"

"It's Pa. The thresher broke and hit him in the chest. He is bleeding real bad. They are on their way in the wagon."

Avery, who was a trained nurse, went directly into action. She began preparing a room with every possible piece of equipment.

"I'm going to head that way," Hawk said as he picked up his saddlebags. "Gil, go get Dr. Lapp. I may need his help."

"I will go tell Tommy." Josie Miller had been visiting Avery and had quietly stayed in the background. She turned to Avery. "I can take the children with me. I will get them to Molly. That way, you won't have to worry about them."

Avery reached out to take Josie's hand. "Thank you, Josie. That will be helpful. You boys, go get your overnight things to take to Molly's. Show Josie where Piper's things are." In a split second, Avery was suddenly alone. She anticipated every possible injury. She prayed for her father-in-law, and she prayed for her husband. Gil's report didn't sound good.

Hawk reached the wagon in record speed. Hud slowed just enough to let Hawk on and Franklin off. "He fainted," Merry said. Her face was streaked with tears.

"Move your hand. Let me see." Hawk gently moved his mother's hand. Thad's shoulder was mangled. The cut was deep, but the bleeding had slowed. There were several smaller cuts down his arm and bruising across his chest. Hawk put his fingers to Thad's neck; his pulse was steady.

Hud, Hawk, Gil, and Merry carried Thad into a room with a table donned with a clean sheet. Instruments were in a pan of liquid. Dr. Lapp and Avery stood ready to assist. Dr. Lapp nodded to his wife, and she turned to Merry. "We need to wait outside, dear." Merry did not want to leave her husband's side, but she knew she had to.

As the door shut, she heard her husband cry out in pain. She dropped to the floor in tears. Hud scooped her up and held her close. "Let's pray."

Josie Miller showed up in the lobby of the bank, asking to see Tommy. Mr. Smithers, being Mr. Smithers, asked if she had an appointment. "It is an emergency, sir."

"You must have an appointment," he said smugly.

Josie shoved past the man and entered Tommy's office. Tommy stood when Josie burst into the room. "J-Josie, w-what—"

She didn't let him finish. "Your pa has been in some sort of farming accident. He is at Hawk's. Dr. Lapp is there too. I am taking the children to Molly. Can I borrow the bank's buggy?"

"H-how b-b-bad is it?" Tommy's stuttering always made Josie hurt. She knew how hard he tried to control it. "I heard Hud say he was struck by something when the pulley on the thresher broke. He had passed out on the ride into town. It looked like he was bleeding from the upper chest area. Hud had quite a bit of blood on his hands and shirt. Your ma is with him."

Tommy swallowed hard. If Hud and Hawk were with his parents, he could see that his niece and nephews got to Molly and then come back. "I'll drive you out to Molly's." He loaded the kids in the bank-owned conveyance and headed out of town.

As they went past Miller's sawmill, Owen Miller saw his daughter with that Sheridan man. He stepped in front of the carriage. "I warned you, Tommy Sheridan."

Tommy's emotions were making it difficult to speak. "M-m-my p-p-p—" Oh, why did he have to stutter?

Mr. Miller had a look of disgust on his face. "Spit it out!" Mr. Miller raised his voice. Josie's hand clasped Tommy's.

Hunter emerged to stand up behind Tommy. "My grandpa has been hurt bad, and Uncle Tommy is taking us to Molly's, so stop yelling at him." Hunter then added a few more words in his father's Lakota language. None of the adults knew what he said or cared to know.

The young boy had obviously put the older man in his place. "I'm going to help Molly with the children," Josie informed her father.

His countenance lightened a little with the seven-year-old's reprimand. "Be back before dark."

He turned his back to return to work. "I will be back when I am no longer needed," Josie spoke. Her father turned to look at her.

"I'll have her back before dark." Tommy found that with Josie's hand in his, he could control his stuttering better. "I would appreciate it if you would find Jonah and tell him our pa is at Hawk's," he added.

The man frowned but nodded in confirmation that he would. Josie's hand remained in Tommy's for the duration of the ride.

Jonah saw Mr. Miller headed his way. Something was up, and it wasn't good. He stopped his work. "I'm here to tell you your father is at the doctor's house. He has been hurt, and that is all I know." Mr. Miller turned to leave.

"Thank you, Mr. Miller." Jonah was heading toward Hawk's.

"This doesn't mean you're welcome in my house. I'm just relaying a message."

Jonah's anger got the better of him. "I sure pray my pa isn't too badly hurt. Hannah needs a father." Jonah noticed just a slight change in the man's posture. He would never apologize for the statement. It was true. The few weeks he and Hannah had been married, not one time did Owen Miller contact his daughter or allow Evie Miller to see her own child. Josie covertly came several times. It kept Hannah from being lonely for her family.

Will noticed quite a bit of activity at the doctor's house. He recognized Franklin and Gil sitting on the stoop. Will told Mr. Tyler he was headed over to see if everything was okay. When he reached the boys, they told him what happened. They were replaying the accident, trying to determine what went wrong.

"It was an accident, fellas, plain and simple. Don't be tagging anything else on to it, and don't be asking yourself what your role was in it." Will's words brought the boys back to the present. "Best spend your thoughts in prayer."

He stepped foot into the doctor's office. Merry sat on the settee next to Hud, looking at the door that kept her from her husband. No one had been out to tell them anything. It had been over an hour. Jonah and Hannah were sitting on the other couch, her hand wrapped in his. Her head was on his shoulder.

"Has anyone told Annabeth?" Will said in a quiet tone.

Merry looked at her boys. "I don't think so. She would be here."

He didn't wait for a sure answer but headed toward The Dowry. The bakery had closed for the day. When he peered in the window to see if Annabeth was working in the back, he saw it was empty.

He headed to the boarding house. He found her and Trudy in the kitchen. "Will, what are you doing home this time of day?" Trudy noticed a strange look on his face.

"Annabeth, your uncle Thad has had a farming accident. He is over at Hawk's." Annabeth arrived as Hawk was exiting the room. Merry ran to her oldest son. "His left shoulder and upper arm are broken. We have that lined up and splinted. He had a pretty deep laceration that had to be cleaned out. It had a lot of dirt and debris. I am not sure about any internal injuries. There is some bruising on his chest that I need to keep an eye on. He will be here at least forty-eight hours before you can take him home. He is going to be out of commission for a while. He's not going to like that."

"Can I see him?" Merry was trying not to cry again.

"Let me and the boys move him to a more comfortable bed. Then you can see him all you want."

It took all the Sheridan men and Will Stanton to carefully move Thad from the surgery table to the bed in the next room. He moaned when they lifted him and when they laid him down.

Merry immediately went to the bedside. Thad was pale. She bent and kissed his forehead twice. Never had any of the Sheridan boys seen their parents kiss just once. It was always twice. It had always been that way. Thad's eyes fluttered open, and a small smile graced his lips. His right hand came up to stroke his wife's face. Then his eyes closed again.

Merry was not going to leave his side. The family gathered in Hawk's living room, their heads down and their emotions spent. Hawk nodded to his best friend. Hud led them in a beautiful prayer of thanksgiving and then spoke, "If I know my wife, she has a ton of food cooked. Why don't we all head home and talk about getting the harvest in? Pa is not going to be able to participate. I want to have a plan when he starts worrying." Hud motioned them all toward the door. He stopped in front of Hawk and gave the man a massive hug. There was a brotherly bond between the two that transcended any bloodline.

"Let us know what we need to do," he added. Hawk nodded.

Rawly Smith was waiting outside the doctor's house. "I saw all the horses and the wagons. When I saw you and Stanton go in, I knew one of your family members must be ill." He had clasped Annabeth's hand. "I finished the job I was working on and came right over. What can I do?"

Annabeth turned her head to look at the house behind her. She briefly got a peek at the uncle she loved so much. He looked very pale. "Take me out to my uncles." She leaned heavily on Rawly.

"You coming out, Will?" Franklin asked. "You know you're welcome."

"I am going to head over and talk to Mr. Tyler. I will tell Dan and Trudy what happened if that is okay." He looked to Hud.

"I would appreciate that. Maybe let Pastor Grey know as well."

"Sure, and count me in with those harvest plans. I'm going to help." Will hopped off the porch and headed toward the mercantile.

*****

Tommy was the only one of the older boys who hadn't returned to Hawk's. He felt Molly needed help with the children. There was a reason he was a banker and not a doctor or a farmer. He couldn't stand blood and people he loved suffering. He didn't mind to help with the farming, but he didn't particularly like it. His pa knew that from the beginning and helped him with his banking career by sending him to Charleston before the panic to do an internship with Jackson Lorton. It changed his world.

Josie had stood up to her father. When she clutched his hand and didn't let go the whole ride home, he knew her resistance to courtship was purely her father's influence. He felt things were changing. He shouldn't be thinking about the woman standing before him with light-brown hair snuggling his niece. He should be thinking about his pa, but Josie was making it difficult.

Piper wouldn't go to anyone but Josie. The little girl had fallen asleep in her arms. "Where can I lay her down?" she whispered to Tommy.

He took her into his parents' bedroom, and she placed the child in the center of the bed. The little girl had her thumb in her mouth and a sweet expression. Tommy stared for just moment; he felt the nearness of Josie. Her hand rested on his upper arm, and he turned to face her.

"I love you, Tommy Sheridan." Her other hand now rested on his chest. "And if you don't kiss me this instant, I think I may die."

His lips softly and slowly caressed hers. Her arms went gently around his neck. Something triggered in his mind; he knew now what his folks meant. Every time they would kiss in front of the boys, which was frequently, the boys would always complain. His pa would say, "One of these days, boys, you'll change your mind about kissing." That day had come.

Having the feeling they were being watched, Tommy broke the kiss but kept his arm around Josie. Piper was sitting up rubbing her eyes. "It's not like she hasn't seen kissing before. Hawk and Avery are master craftsmen," Tommy whispered, and Josie snickered.

Piper reached for Josie. "Lay down and go back to sleep, Piper. It's my turn," Tommy whispered. The girl flopped back down. Tommy picked up where he left off.

*****

Thad slept for twenty-four hours and had developed a fever. It prevented him from going home. Merry was worried, but Dr. Lapp and Hawk assured her that rest was the best thing for him. It had now been a week, and he was still at his son's. It was driving him crazy. Hud had sent word the harvest was coming along nicely and not to worry. The news did not do a bit of good. Thad thought about the harvest constantly.

Thad Sheridan was a hard man to keep down. Only God and perhaps Merry could stop him. He thought about that. Why had God slowed him down? There had to be a reason. He picked up the Bible by the bedside and began reading.

The door opened, and Will Stanton poked his head in. When he saw Thad was awake, he spoke, "Mind if I come in for a minute?"

Thad welcomed the visitor. He had sent Merry home to rest. She had been staying both day and night. He wanted her to spend time with David. She had been away from their youngest for too long.

"Come on in. How is the harvest going? Did you get the north field done?"

"You need to stop worrying about the harvest. Hud is a task-master. It's getting done. Matter of fact, he let the boys go early so they could go fishing. He and I just finished up for the day. I believe he and Molly have a date tonight."

Thad smiled. "I appreciate you stepping in and helping us out. I will pay you when I get back on my feet."

Will shook his head no. "I do need a favor."

"Sure, what can I do for you, in addition to paying you for your work?"

"Merry said you were hardheaded."

That got an even bigger smile from Thad.

"I need your help, and I need your confidentiality in a matter."

Thad read the seriousness on Will's face. "Unless it negatively affects my family, you will have it." Will let out a big sigh. "Just start from the beginning, son."

"I'm not here just visiting. I am here investigating this town." Thad never flinched or took his eyes off Will. "Stolen goods from the southeast are finding their way to the Western mining towns in Colorado—Victor, to be precise. I have followed all the leads, and they stop here."

"Goods are being smuggled here and then moving on? Victor is about four days' ride from here." You could see the wheels turning in Thad's mind. "Who are you working for?"

"The Pinkerton Agency."

Thad raised one eyebrow. "Dan knows what you are doing?"

Will's head went down. "I don't know Dan Bullock. I couldn't be sure the town sheriff wasn't involved. I know he is a good man now, and I will tell him eventually, but I have a method of investigating. I don't like people in my way."

Thad understood full well. "This would explain your eagerness to meet the Sheridans." "Where would you have started?" Will asked.

"The Sheridans." Thad conceded. "Why are you telling me all this?"

"I need your Texas Ranger skills to help crack the case. I figured while you are laid up, you could use your brain for something other than worrying about a harvest that is almost in."

Thad chuckled. "I know all the businessmen in town, but you have to start with the most obvious first: the mercantile, the mill, and the bank."

"That's why I am working for Tyler. I've opened an account at the bank, so I have reason to be in there frequently."

"There is a lot of activity at the mill. I'll keep my eye on it while I am here. I can see the back entrance from the window. I'll put some thought into it."

Annabeth knocked on the door. "Uncle Thad, are you awake?" she called softy.

"Come on in," he answered as Will stood to open the door.

"Oh, I'm sorry. Did I interrupt something?"

"No, honey, come on in. What do you have with you?" He could smell the treats from where he was sitting.

"I brought you some cookies. They are not Aunt Merry's cinnamon sugar cookies, but I thought you might like them. I can verify they are good. Hunter, River, and Hawk ate half of them before I could get to your room."

He motioned her to bring them to him. "They're just oatmeal raisin." He pulled out a large cookie.

"Just oatmeal raisin," he said as he took a huge bite. "This is pretty tasty. There is something in them that isn't usually in oatmeal raisin cookies. What is it?"

"It is a secret. I'm glad you like them."

"Hear that, Will? It is a secret ingredient. Help me figure this out." He handed the man a cookie.

Will took a long inhale and then bit into the morsel of good-ness. He knew instantly what made the cookie extraordinary. He laughed. "I know what it is. Come on, Annabeth. I will walk you home. Your secret is safe with me."

She looked perplexed. Had Will figured it out, or was he just being Will?

Thad disrupted her thoughts. "Annabeth, I appreciate you coming to see me every day and how you have helped Merry with the meals during the harvest, but you look worn out. Promise me you will get some rest. Take it easy this weekend. I can't have you wearing yourself out. My sister would have my head."

"I'm fine, and I can assure you tired or well-rested my mother would worry."

Will held the door for her, and the two left, Thad watching intently. Rawly Smith better get a move on. Thad finished his cookie.

"Orange."

"What?"

"Orange zest in the cookie."

"I don't know what you are talking about." Annabeth played dumb.

He smirked. "Yes, you do, and don't get cute with me." He grabbed her hand and looked at the tips. They were tainted with the remnants of orange peel. "You can't fool me."

Rawly happened upon the two, Will's hand still holding hers. She tried to pull it away, but he wouldn't let her. He figured he needed to help things along. Rawly's eyes went from the clasped hands to

Will's face. Will had a different look on his face, one she hadn't seen before. He took her hand and slapped it into Rawly's.

"Better hold on to that, or someone else will," he said as he made his way across the street to the post office.

There was a stack of mail for Trudy and a telegram for Annabeth. "Can you see Miss Lorton gets this, or do I need to send the boy?" Mr. Jacobs spoke with garbled speech. He had so much chewing tobacco in his mouth; no one could understand him. He was a rotund man with bushy black hair and a thick mustache. His heart was a heart of gold.

"I will see she gets it. I am headed that way now." Will took the telegram. He couldn't help but read it. Patience Lorton was getting married in the spring to Preston Middleton of North Charleston. "Well, Lottie da!" Will said aloud. Would this hurt the little miss, or would she be happy about it? He knew her face would tell all.

Annabeth had said good-bye to Rawly at the stage depot. Every other weekend he went to see his mother. He left on the last stage Friday and returned on the first stage Monday. Will watched the touching good-bye. There was nothing. No peck on the cheek, no hug, not even a kiss on the hand—just a smile. He reckoned that would do for some women. Christina expected them all; Annabeth should get them all. Perhaps he should pull Rawly aside and give him some pointers. About that time, he saw Annabeth nearly knock over a display outside the Feed and Seed. Someone needs to get her off the street before she hurts herself. Will trotted over and caught up with the little miss.

"Where is Old Reliable off to?"

"You spend too much time with Vivian."

"You have to admit it does fit him. Where is he going?"

"He is going to see his mother."

"Well, that explains a lot."

She frowned at him. "What are you talking about? What do you mean?"

"Never mind. I have something for you." He retrieved the telegram from his pocket and handed it to her.

"I knew it. I told her this would happen. She denied any attraction, but it was written all over him." She looked up at Will. "I assume you read it."

He shrugged his shoulders. "May I walk you home?" He presented his arm. She wouldn't take it. "Chicken." He nudged her. When they got in front of the sheriff's office, he stepped inside. "See you at supper."

*****

Dan Bullock was rarely caught off guard. When Will told him who he was and what he was doing in town, he couldn't believe it. "You're sure?" he asked.

"This is where the trail ends. The goods are shipped here, and then they disappear and resurface in Victor. Victor is a four-day trip from here." Will laid out all the evidence. He discussed his course of action and what he had done to try to find who and how the goods were getting to Sheridan. "I have Thad watching the mill from his sick bed. He is the only other person who knows my identity. I would like to keep it that way." Dan nodded.

There were three new boarders that evening at supper. Annabeth and Will were to eat in the kitchen. Dan and Trudy would eat with their guests. "Who are the new boarders?" Will asked as Trudy and Annabeth were fixing supper.

"A Mr. Jones and his two sisters. They are here from the east."

Something didn't settle well with Will. "How long are they staying?" he asked his aunt as she fluttered around the kitchen.

"A couple of days?"

"Have they paid you yet?"

"Well, no, not exactly."

"What are you thinking?" Annabeth asked.

"If it is what I think, the town could be in for some swindling. When did they get into town?"

"I don't know and stop being so suspicious. If anyone in this town warrants suspicion, it would be you. A drifter with no family, no job. What if the town looked at you that way? Honestly, Will."

Trudy frowned. "I saw the ladies go into Lydia's dress shop around noon." Annabeth reported.

On that, Will left. Will met Ezekiel Lapp as he was putting the Closed sign out on his wife's dress shop. "May I talk to you for a minute?"

"I don't think my wife has anything to fit you." Ezekiel let out a little chuckle as he opened the door.

"I don't know. I hear she can make just about anything."

The distinguished older man nodded. "What can we do for you?"

"Did a couple of new women come in here, maybe by the last name of Jones?"

Lydia came from around the counter. "Yes, around noon."

"Did they ask to take dresses back to the boarding house to show their brother with the promise of sending him back to pay?"

"Yes, but Zeke wouldn't let them." She frowned at her husband.

He turned toward Will. "I read the paper too, son. They are swindlers, and Trudy better get them out of her house."

When Will returned, the Joneses were leaving via the upstairs window. He waited for them. "Leaving so soon?" The group was startled. "Let's take a walk." He escorted the trio to the sheriff's office.

"I'll need to telegraph the marshal," Dan said as he put the perpetrators in jail. They were known for this form of robbery all over. Dresses, furnishings—whatever they could get to make a profit.

"I already did." Will smiled. Dan felt as if he was losing his town and losing his edge. "Did I overstep my boundaries?" That was the last thing Will wanted to do.

"No, thanks for your help."

Will was beat. He wanted to go to bed so he could make another late-night round of the town. He didn't even turn on the light. He just removed his boots and lay down. He hoped Thad might have caught some sort of activity at the mill. His investigation of the bank and the mercantile had been futile.

"Who are you?"

Though her words were soft, they caught him completely by surprise. He sprang from the bed. Annabeth sat in the chair in the corner. "What are you doing here? You shouldn't be in my room." He was trying to distract her from the conversation she wanted to have.

"I asked, who are you?"

"Come on, go," he said, grabbing her arm and heading to the door. No, wait, she can't go out the door. Dan and Trudy were downstairs in the living area. If his door opened, they would hear it. She pulled her arm free.

"You knew those boarders were criminals. You are either a criminal yourself or a lawman. Which is it?"

She was standing entirely too close to him in a dark room with moonlight peeking through the curtain. He noticed the open window. She had crawled through the window. His hand encircled her waist and brought her a little closer. "Which do you want it to be? I could be either for you, Annabeth." His words were said in the most bothersome way. He leaned in as if he were going to kiss her. He could feel her shaking. In an instant, she was out the window and traipsing down her boardwalk. She tripped going into her little house. She won't be sneaking into his room anymore. That is for sure.

*****

Thad Sheridan returned home on Sunday. As gently as possible, Merry drove him slowly toward their place. He was going to be limited for a few months. Hawk had set him up with some exercises to strengthen the muscles around the bone while keeping everything in line. Molly had made a huge celebration dinner, inviting all the family to welcome Thad home. The house had not been the same while he was gone.

The Kennedys, Lapps, and Bullocks were invited to share in the celebration. The house was wall to wall with people, which pleased Thad. He wanted to thank everyone for all their help. The harvest wasn't entirely in, but it would be shortly. Will had been a part of it; and for that, he was invited.

"I'll just sit here next to you, Annabeth. I will keep Old Reliable's place warm." Vivian was right; this man liked to play games. He liked to play games because he was hiding something.

"As you wish." Annabeth was determined not to engage in the game.

Merry noticed Annabeth's look of indifference to whatever Will had said. She also saw how tired she looked. Annabeth had been out to the house almost every afternoon, helping in some form or another. She also noticed how tired Molly was. The pregnancy was taking a toll on her, and she was nearly dropping at the moment.

"Hud, take Molly home. Quinn can stay the night here." Molly tried to protest.

"That is a fine idea," Hud said as he helped his wife up from the table.

"But all these dishes." She looked at the table.

"But all these extra hands." Merry looked around the table. "The dishes will get done. Now go!"

"Yes, go, Molly. I will help with the dishes," Annabeth assured her.

"No, Annabeth, you are to rest too. You have huge bags under your eyes," Merry informed her.

"Maybe she is missing Rawly. I saw him get on the stage Friday night headed to his mother's." Franklin smiled across the table at his cousin. Rawly was a joke; everyone knew it.

"It's just that I didn't sleep well last night," she said rather quietly.

Thad noticed a light grin inching its way across Will's lips. He didn't like it.

Molly was ushered home, and Annabeth was banished to the porch. Will headed out there himself when he was stopped by Thad's hand on his chest—again. Another trip to the woodshed was coming, so to speak. "Not so fast. Come with me." Will followed Thad into the sitting room. "Don't trifle with her emotions," Thad Sheridan had the oddest color eyes. They were ice blue and at this time were piercing through Will's brown ones.

"I'm not."

"You are, and it needs to stop. Do I make myself clear?"

"Listen, I'm just trying to get Rawly to move this thing along."

"You are going about it the wrong way. You need to stay out of it." Thad's finger pounded on Will's chest. Thad wasn't one for getting involved, but this was his niece, and he wasn't going to let her get hurt by a man who had no intentions of settling down. Will thanked Merry for the meal and went home.

*****

"What was that private conversation you and Will had in the sitting room? He didn't seem too happy when he left." Merry was brushing her hair, looking at Thad in the reflection of the mirror. He was trying to unbutton his shirt. She went to help him.

"This reminds me of our first days together. This arm sure has seen better days. The gunshot wound hurt less."

She smiled. Thad had been dropped on her doorstep several years ago unconscious with two bullet holes in him. The strangers married a few days later, and the rest was history. "I asked you a question." She kissed him twice.

"Can we talk about it later?" He kissed her, not giving her the opportunity to respond.

"You're impossible," she mumbled.

CHAPTER 4

*W*ill continued to go to The Dowry. He wasn't going to let Thad Sheridan's far-fetched notions stop him. He wasn't toying with Annabeth. He liked to think of himself as her friend. "What's got you so blue, handsome man?" Vivian placed the daily special in front of him.

"I'm not blue, I just have something on my mind."

She followed his eyes. Rawly stepped off the stage, and Annabeth was there to meet him. "Hard for me to believe he ever kissed her passionately. I reckon she doesn't know what passion is. Somebody needs to show her the difference."

Will ignored the remark. "Where exactly does his mother live?"

"Far enough he has to take the stage. He doesn't say much about his mother to my recollection, but then again, I don't find myself listening to his and Annabeth's conversation. They are too dull. Oh, look, they are headed this way. You can ask him yourself."

Annabeth entered on the arm of Old Reliable. It was hard to think of him of anything else. When he spotted Will, his grip on Annabeth got a little tighter. "Hello, Mr. Stanton." Rawly nodded in Will's direction.

"Mr. Smith, Miss Lorton," Will spoke, looking directly at Annabeth.

"Will here was just wondering where your ma lives." Vivian smiled at the two men.

"She lives in Box Elder." Will nodded toward Annabeth.

"You should take Annabeth with you sometime." Rawly's face lost a little color. "You know, take her home to meet the family."

Rawly's face was now colorless. The man was speechless. Will wanted to laugh, but something in Annabeth's eyes stopped him. If looks could kill, he'd be a dead man. "Good morning," Will said as he passed through the door. Vivian was fighting a smile.

"I suppose, when Mother is feeling better, you could accompany me to Box Elder." He was fidgeting with his collar.

"I don't need to meet your mother, Rawly. That day will come when it is the right time. Just ignore Will."

Annabeth went behind the counter to retrieve some muffins for him. "I would gladly ignore him if you referred to him as Mr. Stanton instead of Will." This was the first sign of fight Vivian had seen out of Old Reliable. She stood with her back to the couple, just listening. You could gain a lot by using one sense at a time. The ear is as powerful as the eye.

"Oh, that's nothing. We practically live in the same house. I can't go around calling him Mr. Stanton all the time. That would be silly." She handed him a basket filled with goodies.

"Yes, I am aware of the living arrangements at the boarding house. Don't think for a minute I am fond of them."

Annabeth smiled. "I am flattered." She gave him a peck on the cheek.

"I don't trust Will Stanton." He frowned at her.

"Trust him in general or trust him with Annie?" Vivian piped up. She couldn't resist entering the conversation.

Annabeth turned Rawly toward the door. "Ignore her too," she whispered. "I will see you tomorrow night. I think Trudy is making meatloaf and peas. I know it is your favorite."

He returned her kiss on the cheek and exited.

"Well, well, well, it looks like Will Stanton has lit a fire under Rawly Smith. I have never seen him show that much emotion toward you. Wait until I tell Will about this." Vivian sashayed around the kitchen, humming some silly song.

"Vivian, this is none of Mr. Stanton's business."

"Okay, honey, but it never hurts to let a man know you have options."

Did she have options? She was too tired to think about it. If she was honest with herself, she really didn't care at this point. She only cared about her bakery. It was making a good profit, and she wanted to expand someday. She also would like to pay her parents back the dowry money or, better yet, give it to Patience for her wedding.

*****

Tuesday evening Rawly was punctual as usual. Will was walking by the door when the knock came. "Rawly, it's good to see you. Come on in. Are these flowers for Annabeth?" Will took them from Rawly's hand. "Annabeth, darlin', look at these pretty flowers." He burst through the kitchen door, Rawly on his heels.

Annabeth came from the pantry. Her face was flushed—almost as flushed as Rawly's. Will had embarrassed them both, but he just couldn't help himself. Rawly was an easy target. "Yes, Mr. Stanton they are beautiful." She went to reach for them, and he held them out of her reach.

"Mr. Stanton, is it? We're all friends aren't we, Miss Lorton? Is Will too informal, too intimate?"

Trudy saved all three of them by grabbing the flowers and handing them to Annabeth. "William Hodson Stanton, mind your manners and get cleaned up for supper." She gave him a good smack. He nodded at Rawly as he walked by, his smile stretching from ear to ear. Annabeth stood frozen, looking at the two men, the buck and the rabbit playing with the little field mouse. The mouse was ready to move on.

"Annabeth, will you take the roast out of the oven? I want it to rest a bit before I serve it to our guest. You three can eat in the kitchen if you think the boys will behave."

"I thought we were having meatloaf tonight." She looked toward Rawly.

"Oh, I found out Will doesn't like it—or peas."

Outstanding, Annabeth thought. Mr. Stanton had everyone doing his bidding.

At the table in the kitchen, Annabeth held her breath for most of the meal. She wasn't sure what was going to come out of Will's mouth. Most of the conversation was his doing. He spoke mostly to Rawly, but his eyes rarely left Annabeth's face. He was merely antagonizing Rawly. It was working; by the time the evening was over, Rawly was in a dither.

"When will he be moving on?" he asked with a hint of real anger.

"He is just trying to get a rise out of you. He likes to play games. He seems rather childish in that regard. Don't let it bother you." She smiled sweetly.

"Well, just so you don't get any ideas." He leaned to kiss her but was stopped by the sound of Will's voice.

"Oh, excuse me, I thought you had gone, Rawly. Annabeth, come find me when your company leaves. Carry on." Will gave Rawly's back a good slap and sauntered out of the room. Rawly immediate left in a huff.

Annabeth went into the kitchen. Will, Trudy, and Dan were sitting at the table. "Is Rawly gone?" Trudy asked.

Annabeth nodded. "My, and so soon. He isn't ill, is he? Did supper not agree with him? Oh, I do hope it's not catching. He seemed all right to me. Did he seem ill to you, Dan?" The whole time the muffin man just sat there drinking coffee, a silly half grin, half smirk on his face.

"He had to leave early tonight. He is fine." Annabeth eased her friend's fears. "You wanted to see me?" She turned toward Will.

He had a puzzled look on his face. "I did, but I can't remember now what it was about." He was a game player. She said her good-byes and exited out the back door.

Annabeth sat in the dark in her little abode. She was bone tired and cold. Winter was definitely on its way. She took down her hair. Too tired to rise from the chair, she curled up under a blanket. Will Stanton was a strange one. She wished he would stop messing with Rawly. She didn't need his help. Matter of fact, he was a hindrance to the situation. She decided the best course of action was to give it to the Lord. She still wasn't sure who or what Will Stanton was, and he certainly couldn't be trusted.

*****

Thad Sheridan had told Will two things. One was to stop trying to influence the relationship between his niece and her beau. The other was Owen Miller had something going on at his mill in the late-night hours. Thad speculated it was cards and whiskey, but he couldn't be sure. Tonight Will was going to have a look for himself.

Annabeth didn't know how long she had been asleep in the chair when something woke her. She stretched and stood up to look at the clock on the wall. It was midnight, and she caught movement as she looked out the window. Will Stanton was climbing out his window and dropped to the ground. "What is he up to?" she said aloud as she wrapped the blanket around her and exited her front door in just her house slippers. She didn't want him to hear her as she followed.

Will weaved through town until he could get a good hiding place just outside the mill's back entrance. There was a nip in the air; he rubbed his hands together, blowing on them. Winter was hastening quickly. Will was well hidden and had a bird's-eye view of the activities inside. There was a poker game in progress and drinks all around. He stood there until his feet became numb. Nothing more than a bunch of men losing their money and their decency.

Along with Mr. Miller, he saw Smithers from the bank, Mr. Jacobs, and the Randolph boys from the Feed and Seed. He watched a bit longer as Mr. Miller fleeced the group with some fancy card dealing. He would report this to Dan in the morning. He turned to move behind the building and make his way to the opposite side of the street. He got the distinct feeling someone was following him.

Will made a sharp turn and pressed himself up against the back wall of Tyler's Mercantile. When the person was within his reach, he grabbed them, pulling them into the tiny space. There was quite the scuffle, but something didn't feel right. This person was wrapped in a blanket, had no shoes on, and just bit him. He was certain this was a woman and pretty sure he knew which woman it was.

He wrestled to get a better hold. Her back was to him. "Let me go." He heard the familiar voice.

"Not on your life." His grip got tighter.

She wiggled to get free. "I demand you let me go!"

"No," he whispered in her ear.

73

She thrust her head backward, striking him in the chin. His grip momentarily loosened, but he reclaimed her as she tried to get away. "Annabeth, stop!" He jostled her a bit. "Annabeth"—he was much quieter—"stop." His voice was pleading, and she stood still.

The blanket wrapped tightly around her; he could feel her shiver. Letting her go, he removed his coat and draped it around her shoulder. He turned her to face him. "What are you doing?" He left his hands on her shoulders. She was such a mess she couldn't think. Her teeth started to chatter. His hands began to go up and down her arms to bring warmth. "Let's get you home. You'll catch a cold out here with just your slippers and that flimsy blanket."

"Not until you tell me who you are and what you are doing."

"You know I make rounds for Uncle Dan. That is what I am doing. Why on earth were you following me?" She couldn't speak; she was cold but hot all at the same time. "You keep showing up like this, a man could get the wrong idea." He pulled her a little closer, and she collapsed in his arms. "Annabeth!" He caught her before she hit the ground.

"Annabeth." He gently tapped her face. She didn't respond. He shook her just a bit. Nothing. He could see her chest rise and fall. He lifted her into his arms and gingerly made his way to Hawk's. Hawk heard the familiar sound of a knock on the door. Only this knock was a little different. This was someone kicking at the door. He buttoned his shirt as he went down the stairs, Avery following, tightening her robe. He turned on the light and opened the door. Will stood there with Annabeth in his arms.

"What happened?" Hawk placed his hands on Annabeth's face. "She is burning up. Bring her in here."

Will followed the doctor into a side room where he had a bed. He removed Will's coat and the blanket and started giving orders to Avery. Will stood quietly, looking at the little miss. Her body continued to shiver.

"What happened to her?" Those dark eyes of Dr. Sheridan were scorching Will with unmentioned accusations. "We were...we were talking, and all of a sudden, she collapsed."

Hawk didn't seem to believe the story. "She has a knot on the back of her head. How did she get that?" Hawk's voice was chilling.

Will took a deep breath. "I will tell you the whole story after you tend to Miss Annabeth. Please, just take care of her."

Hawk grabbed the man by the collar and dragged him into the room. He shoved him toward the chair. "Sit there and don't even think about leaving. You understand?"

Will understood. He understood more than Hawk realized.

Hawk further examined his cousin. The young girl was very ill. Under the bright lights, he noticed something he should have caught the last time he was with her: the yellow hue her skin had. He thought the color was the effects of the sun on the Southern belle skin. When he took a closer look at her eyes, the whites were yellow.

He pushed on her stomach, and she pulled away. The fatigue was more than overdoing it. "What are you thinking?" Avery asked her husband as she put a cool cloth on Annabeth's head.

"I'm not sure. It looks like yellow fever. They are not sure if it is contagious, so I need to keep her quarantined, at least until her fever breaks."

"Hasn't that been more prevalent in the South? Memphis, if I recall, was struck by an outbreak in the seventies." Avery stood looking down at Annabeth's frailty.

"Well done, Nurse Sheridan. Because I can't be sure, that possible diagnosis doesn't go outside this room."

The Sheridans were both looking at Will. "Of course not."

Annabeth stirred, and Hawk bent down to ask her a few questions. Will couldn't hear much of what she was saying, but he did make out the word *bakery*. "Don't worry about that right now. You know we will take care of that for you." Hawk stood and motioned for Will to leave the room. He followed.

"Is she going to be okay?" Will's mouth was dry. The little miss looked so small lying in the huge bed.

Hawk didn't answer. "I want to know what happened tonight. I want to know what she was doing out in the middle of the night with you. I want to know how she got a knot on the back of her head and where you got this fresh bruise on your chin." Hawk grabbed the man's chin, directing it toward the light. "And no vague answers."

Will told the doctor everything he could without telling him what his business was in Sheridan. Hawk never removed his piercing dark eyes from Will's face. "You better hope her story matches yours."

"It will," Will assured the young physician. "Is she going to be all right?" Will asked again.

"I don't know. If it is yellow fever, it has affected her liver. That is why she is tan looking. I will have Dr. Lapp take a look at her as well in the morning." Will nodded, and Hawk walked to the door. Opening it wide, he said "Good night, Mr. Stanton." There was no warmth in his gesture.

Will wandered around the town in darkness. The party at the mill had broken up; the city was, for the most part, a dry town. Where was Miller getting the whiskey? Was it being shipped from the South? This could be what he was looking for. He schemed his way to the back of the mill and picked the lock. Rummaging around, he found nothing that would suggest the whiskey was from a Southern distributor.

Will found himself in front of the bakery. Annabeth seemed to live for the place; it was like her child. He didn't know how serious her illness was. Dr. Sheridan did not seem to want to discuss her case in detail. Why should he? Will wasn't family. He was just one of Annabeth's many loyal customers. Will would like to think he was her friend. He knew after this early-morning escaped the Sheridans were less inclined to trust him.

He wished he could do something to help. He sat on the steps and prayed for the little miss. Through his prayers, he was given an avenue to help. Will went to the back of The Dowry and jimmied the door. It opened rather easily. "I'll have to fix that," he muttered to an empty bakery. He lit the lamp and turned it up high. Looking at the clock on the wall, he saw the time: four-thirty. The bakery opened at six in the morning six days a week. That wasn't going to change. While Annabeth was off her feet, Will was determined to see the bakery stayed open.

He wasn't a baker, but he could cook. He may have to temporarily change the menu, but he would keep The Dowry open. He looked through Annabeth's supplies and pulled out some recipes. Surely, with Vivian's help, he could pull this off. After the bakery closed, he could head to Tyler's and work in the afternoons. He found the apple cinnamon muffin recipe and decide to start in. Stoking all the fires first, he then donned an apron. He laughed at himself. If the Pinkerton boys could see him now, he would be drummed out of the agency.

At five o'clock, Vivian came through the back door. Her face registered shock when she saw the buck in the apron. She burst out laughing, and he flashed her a smile. "What is going on?" She looked around the room for her boss. "Where is Annabeth?"

Will took a pan of muffins from the stone oven and put another batch in. "She's sick, Vivian, really sick."

"Oh no, what is it?"

"Doc is not sure, but she has a pretty high fever. He will know more later today." Vivian's face showed her concern. "I thought you and I could keep the bakery open while she is out."

Vivian looked at the man with flour on his hands and an apron covered in muffin batter. "I think that is a grand idea."

The muffins tasted okay, but they sure didn't look like Annabeth's. She had a special touch with her cooking. "I thought we may have to alter the menu. We could serve breakfast. Flapjacks and eggs. I could see if I could get some meat from Tyler or maybe Thad."

"I say let's do it."

Vivian kissed Will's cheek. "You look awful cute in that apron. Sure will draw the women folk in here."

*****

Annabeth did indeed have yellow fever. Dr. Lapp confirmed the diagnosis later that morning. He and Hawk discussed how she could have gotten it. There had been medical reports that it was carried by mosquitoes. They thought it best to keep the diagnosis among just a few. No need to cause a panic.

Thad and Merry were notified that Annabeth was ill, and they promptly showed up. "She is resting," Dr. Lapp told the couple. "Her fever remains, and she still has a headache. She is very fatigued and has not said more than a few words. We need to keep her quarantined."

"We can take her home with us," Merry commented through the lump in her throat. "She shouldn't stay here with the children and others who may need Hawk's services," she added.

"That is right, Merry dear, but she doesn't need to be at the boys' home either." Merry started to protest, but Dr. Lapp stopped her. "Lydia and I are having her moved to our place above the store. She will be able to have continuous care." Merry didn't say anything. She was too overcome.

"Can we see her?" Thad asked.

"Yes, but you can't touch her or kiss her."

The door opened, and Hawk stood over his cousin, applying an herb paste to her feet. She had a cloth covering her eyes, and the room was dim. Thad knew about debilitating headaches. He had suffered with them for years. They looked at the lifeless body in the big bed, and tears streamed down their faces. "I need to telegraph Jackson," Thad said in a whisper. Hawk ushered them out.

"That is yellow fever," Thad said, looking at his son. Hawk's facial expression confirmed Thad's statement. Thad ran his hand down his face. "This could be the start of an epidemic."

"Not if we can help it. I don't want yellow fever mentioned until someone else presents with the symptoms. I do want to talk with Rawly, Vivian, Trudy, and Dan. They work and live with her. I want to make sure they have no symptoms and let them know to report to me if they have a fever, headache, or fatigue. But I want yellow fever kept out of the conversation."

Hawk was stern with his folks. This wasn't their son; this was the town doctor.

"You should include Will. He lives at the boarding house too," Merry added. Hawk's stoic face alerted Thad that something was amiss.

Thad and Merry went straight to the telegraph office and wired Annabeth's parents. Flurries added to an already dreary day. You never knew in the Dakotas when you were going to get snow. Any time after August, it was anyone's guess. They went past the bakery and saw people exiting. "What is going on at The Dowry?"

Merry and Thad made their way over. The Open sign hung on the door. They entered to find Vivian waiting tables and Will back in the kitchen. He nodded when he saw the couple come in. "Would you like some coffee? There is a table right over here. Just let me wipe it off for you." Vivian grabbed a wet cloth and wiped down the small table in front of the window. "It may be a little chilly here in front of the window, but with a hot cup of coffee and that sun coming through, you'll be warm in no time. Now, what can I get you?" She poured the couple a cup of coffee.

"You can get me the young man back in the kitchen."

Vivian turned and headed toward Will. "Papa Bear wants to see you."

Will removed his apron and headed toward the Sheridans. "Ma'am." He tipped his head in Merry's direction.

"What are you doing, Will?" Thad inquired.

"I am keeping this bakery open until Annabeth is back on her feet, sir." Will's face held no emotion. Thad Sheridan was not going to stop him. "And no one is going to stop me."

Merry's eyes went wide. She had never met a man so bold of speech. "No one is trying to stop you. What do you need from us?"

Will relaxed a bit. He told the Sheridans his plan.

*****

Jackson Lorton entered Laurel in the middle of the day, calling for his wife. Abby came from the kitchen. "Jackson, what is it?" She could tell by his face something was terribly wrong.

"Annabeth is ill. Very ill." Abby swooned a bit and leaned against the wall. He went to her, holding her around the waist. "Come and sit down." They entered the downstairs salon.

"She has a high fever and severe headache. They are keeping her quarantined until they make sure it isn't contagious."

"I need to go, Jackson. I have to go to her." She stood as if she could transport herself to her daughter's bedside.

He grabbed her hand. "I have already looked into it. Neither of us will be able to go. There is an early snowstorm blanketing parts of the Midwest. We can't get through."

Abby's face was pale, and she began to cry. "I was afraid something like this would happen. She has been working so hard. I know she is not taking care of herself. I can tell from her letters."

Jackson wrapped his arms around his wife. "We will take the first train we can get. I've sent word to let me know the minute train travel is available. Thad and Merry will take care of her as one of their own." He kissed the top of her head. "Thad's telegram said he would keep us informed." Jackson's words did little to ease the mother's heart.

"What's going on?" Patience entered the room. "Why are you home so early, Father?" When Abby looked up, Patience knew it wasn't good. She speedily went to her mother's side.

"Annabeth—" Abby choked on the words. Patience's head snapped to face her father.

"Annabeth has fallen ill," he supplied her with the information.

"When are we leaving?"

"We're not." Jackson saw the anger beginning to well up in his youngest daughter. "There is a snowstorm in the Midwest we can't get through." She plopped down beside her mother. "She will be fine. Hawk will take care of her. Between him and Dr. Lapp, she has the best care." Patience had all the faith in the world in Hawk Sheridan she always had.

*****

Avery bundled Annabeth up, and Hawk put her in the back of Thad's wagon. She was very weak, and her head wouldn't stop throbbing. She had had a bout of nausea, but Hawk had given her something to settle her stomach. They had told her she was to be quarantined. Annabeth couldn't wrap her mind around what was happening. She was just too tired to try to understand. What was happening to her bakery?

"I'm going to lift you out of the wagon now, Annabeth. I may jostle you a little bit, getting you upstairs and to your room," Hawk was saying as he lifted her in his arm, keeping her covered. They were getting more snow. Through an opening in the cover, she viewed her beloved bakery. She turned her face into Hawk's shoulder and silently cried. Was she going to die?

Hawk made his way into the dress shop and up the stairs to the Lapps' home. Lydia Lapp was waiting for them in the spacious room. The covers on the bed were pulled back and waiting to nestle the patient. Annabeth grimaced when Hawk laid her down. Her joints hurt as bad as her head. When was this nausea going to end? She asked herself again, was she going to die?

Hawk had told her everything. He left nothing out. He was never one for withholding any information he thought needed to be given. "Annabeth, I will be back to check on you. You know I learned everything I know from Dr. Lapp. You're in good hands."

Her neck hurt so bad all she could do was nod once. She did know she was in good hands, but she was still scared. She should pray, but the tea she sipped just before leaving Hawk's house made her too discombobulated to keep a thought in her head. She drifted off to sleep.

*****

After working at the bakery and then Tyler's Mercantile, Will was in no mood for Dr. Sheridan's interrogation. He was summoned from his room when the good doctor arrived after eight o'clock, wanting a word with him. He came down the stairs in a very foul mood.

"Oh my goodness, Will. Our Annabeth is sick. Dr. Sheridan thinks whatever she has may be contagious and wants to ask us all some questions. Check us over." Trudy was flitting around the room. "Let me get some coffee. I am just so nervous and worried about that girl. I told Dan she was working too hard."

Dan Bullock was so in love he just smiled at his wife as she created havoc around the three men. Will and Hawk wished she would just land somewhere.

"Mrs. Bullock, I can see nothing has slowed you down. You look very well. I just want you to be aware that if you start feeling tired or have a fever and a headache, come see me. Don't pass it off as a hard work day. You too, Dan." The sheriff nodded.

"I need to talk to you in private, Will." Hawk started up the stairs and entered Will's room. Will was a little miffed with the way the doctor was behaving. When Will closed the door behind him, he didn't give Hawk the chance to speak. "I told you the truth this morning. I can't possibly imagine why you would need to talk to me in private." Those dark eyes sparked anger.

"Annabeth confirmed your story. What she didn't say was why she was following you. Why would she do that?"

Will's eyes narrowed. "Does the answer have some bearing on her care?" Will wasn't about to be bullied.

"That depends on if her following you had something to do with her heart."

"What are you talking about?" Will plunked down in the chair it made a swooshing sound. That's about how he felt at the end of this day.

"It means you better not be—"

"Just stop!" Will demanded, his hand cut through the air. "I am tired of the assumption from the Sheridans that I am playing games with Annabeth. I am her friend, and that is the end of the story." Will rose to open the door. "And you can tell Hud, Tommy, and the rest of your family to save their breath. Good night, Dr. Sheridan."

Hawk left the room. To quote Shakespeare, the man doth protest too much, Hawk mused.

*****

Sometime around the third day, Annabeth's headaches decrease to a dull ache. Her temperature would go down in the morning and then back up at night. Nausea had slowed, and she was able to eat a little. The fatigue was unbearable. Hawk had told her it would take a while for her to get her strength back and she shouldn't push the process. When she stopped running a fever, the quarantine would be lifted.

The darkness of night had settled in, and Annabeth could hear the gentle snoring of the gray-haired man sitting in the chair beside the bed. Ezekiel Lapp had been the town doctor for years. He semi-retired when Hawk graduated from medical school. He and his wife were lovely people. They were kind and compassionate—just what Annabeth needed. She was missing her parents at a time like this, and her Uncle Thad and Aunt Merry not being able to visit made her situation more pitiful. She felt the tears mounting in her eyes. A soft sob escaped her lips.

"Annabeth, child, what is it?" Dr. Lapp laid his hand on her forehead. It was cool to the touch. "Are you in pain?" Her head went from side to side. He could see a tear stream down her face. He sat on the side of the bed and outstretched his arms. She sat up to wrap her arms around his neck and cried.

"Now, now, everything is going to be all right. You are getting better day by day." His voice was soft, and his hand patted her back. "You just cry all you want."

She did, holding on for dear life. After a few minutes, she leaned back. Dr. Lapp produced a handkerchief, and she wiped her face. "Will you help me sit up?" she asked, and he did without hesitation.

"Can I talk to you?" she asked in a quiet voice. He raised her hand and kissed it, bowing his head to start her talking. "Do you know what happened to me back in Charleston? I was left at the altar." He didn't say anything, just kept quiet. "It hurts. It hurts to think that I may die out here in the West, never fulfilling the dream of being a wife and mother. I say it doesn't matter, that I don't care, that I am better off, but those are empty words. It does matter, and I do care." She looked at the doctor.

"It certainly does matter, and you should care. I believe within every woman God placed the desire and longing to be a helpmate and a mamma. It is natural to wonder when that will happen. Can I say that it happens for everyone, no? God has plans and his ways or not our ways. You know his grace is sufficient for whatever happens in your life. You are still young, Annabeth. Give God some time." He winked at her, and she smiled.

"I will let you in on a little secret. Love at any age is something to behold. If I were to meet Lydia today, it would be the same as it was fifty-three years ago."

"That is sweet." Annabeth looked out the window.

"No, it's not sweet. That is just the way love is."

"My parents have that love. I guess I am afraid I will never find that strong of love."

"True love is that strong love. It is a love you can thrive on." Her lip twisted in contemplation. Wasn't the word *thrive* what Will used to describe love? There must be something to it.

Dr. Lapp kissed the top of her head as he rose. "You need to rest."

"As do you, I am sorry I woke you."

"Nonsense. I enjoyed stepping in a playing father for a minute or, at my age, grandfather."

She reached out her hand, and he clasped it. "I would be glad to have you as either."

The man was slightly overcome with emotion. "Sweet dreams Annabeth. Don't worry, that love can't help but find you. Maybe it already has." He left the room quietly. "I'll check on you in a little bit. Call out if you need anything."

*****

Will had been serving breakfast at The Dowry for the past three days. He hoped Annabeth wouldn't be too upset, but how could she? Will was making quite the profit. He wasn't none too happy when he saw Hawk Sheridan enter the bakery and stare him down. He could play that game.

"What can I do for you, Doc?" Will said without stopping his work.

"I need to speak with you."

Who was the lawman here, and who was the doctor? Will was beginning to wonder. "I'm a little busy right now."

"I can wait." Hawk grinned and leaned against the counter, snagging a cup of coffee and a muffin.

"That's two bits. You're not my kin," Will said as he headed to the pantry, Hawk following.

"What is it this time?" Will crossed his arms over his chest.

Hawk stood unbothered by the man's body language. "I need a favor."

Will was surprised. "And what's that?"

"I need a list of Annabeth's suppliers particularly any who may be from the border states. Do you know where she keeps that information?"

"I can find it. Why do you want it?"

"I'm trying to find out how she contracted her illness. Since no one else has gotten sick, it had to have been something strictly specific to her. If you find the list, can you bring it over?"

"Do I have a choice?"

Hawk didn't answer. He turned to go.

"How is Annabeth?"

Hawk noticed Will's voice took on a softer tone. "She is slowly getting better. If I told her you were running her bakery, I wouldn't be able to keep her quarantined."

"Don't tell her." Will's statement was more of an order. "If she asks, just tell her Vivian's taking care of it."

Hawk gave his word and left through the back door.

*****

"Annabeth, someone has left you a package." Lydia Lapp brought letters and missive to Annabeth daily. She didn't realize how much she missed people. Hawk told her when she could go twenty-four hours without a fever, he would lift the quarantine and she could have visitors.

Lydia placed the box on the bed; and it moved, scaring Annabeth. "Oh my," she said, and then the box moved again. "I am afraid to open it." Then she heard the softest yip. When she opened the box, a tiny puppy stretched its neck over the edge. "Well, aren't you adorable? Who sent you?"

The puppy jumped from the box right onto Annabeth's lap, licking her outstretched hand. Annabeth peeked in the box, looking for some type of note. It was empty. "Who?"

"I was sworn to secrecy." Lydia pretended to zip her lips. Annabeth frowned. "Enjoy him and don't worry about who was thoughtful enough to think of such a gift."

"You are okay with him staying here with me?"

"Yes, the person asked before they brought the puppy. What are you going to name him?"

"I will need to think about it. It has to be just right." Annabeth yawned.

"Well, the two of you can sleep on it." Annabeth fell asleep with the little pup snuggle in the crook of her arm. Her sleep was a peaceful one.

She awoke a few hours later with her new little friend staring at her. There was instant love. "Thrive—I am going to call you Thrive." The golden puppy tipped his head, then grabbed her sleeve, and gave it a good yank. For the first time in a long time, Annabeth felt joy again.

*****

Will went back to the bakery after he finished at Tyler's Mercantile. He needed to go through Annabeth's books, looking for a list of her suppliers. Her books were meticulous. Everything was accounted for. He noticed all her accounts had two sets of initials beside them: hers and the vice president of the bank, cousin Tommy.

She was smart in having Tommy double-check her work. The books showed a steady but marginal profit. The place had the potential to do better. He might put some thought into it if he wasn't in Sheridan to do a different job. He found her list. Most vendors were located here in town. There were a couple of companies she did business with in Rapid City and one in Charleston. He flipped through the requisitions. Every month she received something from Charleston, and it varied. One month, it was peaches, the next spices—the list went on.

"You are worse than Annabeth." Vivian's voice startled the man.

"What are you doing here at this time of day?" she asked.

"I could ask you the same thing."

"I came to drop off some things at the Lapps for Annabeth and saw the light on."

"How is Annabeth? I haven't heard any news the last day or two." Will closed the books, and Vivian caught the motion.

"Are you going through her accounts?" Vivian's voice had a protective edge to it.

"It's not what you think." "What do you think I am thinking?" She arched an eyebrow.

"I was looking at her list of suppliers. Do you know anything about this one?" He pointed to the one from Charleston.

"Sadler's Market is the company she contracted with for a discount. If she orders every month, she gets 25 percent off her order. Last month she got more than she bargained for. I never saw so many insects swarm a girl. Why are you so interested in Annabeth's suppliers?"

"Just wanting to learn more about the bakery."

Vivian screwed her mouth into a tiny knot. "You are an odd one, Willie boy. Forgive me, but you are too handsome to believe."

He smiled. "Trust me." He walked past her and kissed the top of her head. "And don't call me Willie."

She gave a hearty laugh and followed him out of the bakery.

"I think I know how Annabeth contracted yellow fever." Will entered Dr. Sheridan's office. "She has a supplier from Charleston, and last month, when she opened the shipment, Vivian said she was swarmed by bugs. If your research information is true, it could have been mosquitoes."

Hawk nodded. "I took her out of quarantine today, but I am limiting her visitors." Will started to leave.

"Avery should have supper about done. Why don't you stay and eat with us?"

Will was a little taken aback. Hawk didn't seem to care for him. Why was he invited to share a meal? His guard went up. About that time, River came in to tell his pa supper was ready, and he should get washed up. "Tell your ma Will is going to eat with us."

The little boy, who was the spitting image of his father, stood for a few seconds looking at Will. He had those same dark eyes and used them in the same manner as his father. Will thought he was on trial for something. "You are Annabeth's husband. How could you let her get sick? You should have taken better care of her."

The little boy turned and left. No one had the opportunity to set the record straight with the little tyke. When he left, Hawk burst into laughter. "You should see your face." He slapped Will on the back and nudged him toward the kitchen. Will enjoyed himself at supper. Hawk and Avery bantered back and forth a lot, all in good fun. There was an electricity between the two Will had never witnessed.

He contemplated this phenomenon as he watched Rawly Smith head into Lapp's dress shop. What was the opposite of electricity? Nothing! And that is what he saw between Rawly and Annabeth. A whole lot of nothing. He took himself over the dress shop as well.

"Dr. Sheridan dropped by to let me know you could have visitors. Do you feel up to it?" Rawly poked his head around the door.

Annabeth smiled. "Always. Come in. My aunt and uncle just left. They brought me some treats. Would you like a cookie or a piece of milk pie?"

"No, thank you." Rawly declined as he bent to sit in the chair beside the bed.

"I would love a piece of milk pie. My mom uses to make those all the time. Isn't that the pie you use your finger to stir the ingredients?" Will Stanton had nearly come in on Rawly's heels. The disgust was written all over Old Reliable's face. Will grabbed a piece of pie and sat on the window seat with his foot hiked up beside him.

"Hello, Mr. Stanton," Annabeth said with an appropriate smile. Will smirked and shook his head taking a bite of the pie. "Still Mr. Stanton, is it? Okay, Ms. Lorton. Hawk said you were able to have visitors. I thought I would check in and see how you are. When I carried you into doc's office the other night, you looked pretty bad."

"I'm much better. Thank you for your concern." She was seething almost as much as Rawly.

Mr. Lapp entered the room followed by Thrive. It wasn't proper for Annabeth to be left without a chaperone. Ezekiel didn't care how ill she was. He was not going to let anything tarnish her reputation. He thought she may need a little help when he saw Will enter the room.

Thrive immediately jumped on the bed for his share of the attention. He was Annabeth's number one, and he was going to let the other two gentlemen know it. "I didn't know you had a dog, Doc," Will said as he pilfered a cookie from the basket.

"Those are meant to be Annabeth's," Rawly growled at Will. Thrive gave a low growl at Rawly. "There's a dozen in there. Do you think Annabeth is some kind of hog?" Rawly's ears turned a burst of red. Will ignored him.

"Where did the dog come from?"

"Someone left it here as an anonymous gift for Annabeth." Mrs. Lapp had joined the guest with a tray of cups and a pot of coffee. She sat it on the bureau. "This came today."

She handed Annabeth a book. "*French Pastry Recipes*," she read the title aloud. She thumbed through it as coffee was served to her guest.

"I wonder who the mystery giver is. You, Rawly?" Will raised his eyebrows.

"The mystery giver would never own up to it. That would defeat the purpose. The gifts are meant to bring Annabeth cheer. It doesn't matter who gave them to her." There was a smugness to Rawly's comment.

"I bet it would matter to you, Rawly, if the gift giver were me." There was dead silence in the room. Even little Thrive stood looking from man to man. The field mouse had now gone into her hole, and the buck had just put the rabbit on the run. Will chuckled. "I will come back and see you when it's less crowded, Miss Lorton."

"He isn't really the one sending you those gifts, is he?" Rawly was very red-faced.

"Of course not. I am pretty sure it's Uncle Thad." Why did it seem when Will left the room he took all the oxygen with him?

"You mean you don't know for sure?" Rawly fidgeted in his chair.

"Only Lydia knows for sure who it is."

"You know?" her husband asked.

"Yes, and her lips are sealed." Annabeth looked at Dr. Lapp in bewilderment.

"Child, I have found I am very good at unsealing those lips." He winked at his wife, and she laughed. Annabeth gave a little giggle. Rawly missed the whole thing. He was stewing in the pot Will had stirred.

*****

"Vivian, we are getting low on cinnamon. Does Annabeth have some more somewhere?"

Vivian burst into laughter.

"What is so funny?" Will stopped to look at her. "You, a good-looking big man asking about cinnamon. Do you want a little vanilla too, sugar?" Vivian's face was lit up in mirth. Will shook his head. "Over there, darlin', behind the coffee. There should be a box of spices she received last week."

Will found the box. It was from Sadler's Market. He opened the strange wooden box and noticed something different with the base. The box had a false bottom. "Did you find it?" Vivian came around the corner.

Now wasn't the time to investigate. He would do that after Vivian left for the day. "I found it. Are all the crates from Sadler's this fancy?"

"Oh my, yes. I keep telling Annabeth she is paying for the fancy packaging."

"What does she do with the crates?" Will wanted to investigate them.

"Old Reliable gets rid of them for her. He takes them to his shop and uses them for something. This is the last shipment for a few months. They can't guarantee shipment during the winter months."

Will was itching to look into the box. He couldn't stand it anymore. "Vivian, why don't you take a few minutes before you head home and see Annabeth? I will finish up here."

She was happy to go. She had wanted to visit with her boss. She missed her something fierce. "Thanks, handsome. I will take you up on it." She grabbed her coat and headed next door.

Will barely waited for her to be out of sight to get the fancy wooden box. He carefully popped the false bottom. He wasn't surprised to find a stack of bills and a bag filled with two jeweled broaches. There was a scribbled note stating this would be the last shipment until spring and to wait for further instructions. Will poured a cup of coffee and sat on the counter next to the box. He never dreamed the bakery was involved. He was fairly sure Annabeth didn't know her deliveries were part of smuggling stolen goods. Or was he letting his friendship color his opinion?

As sure as he knew Annabeth was an innocent party, he knew Old Reliable was not. He was thinking about his next course of action. He wanted to talk things over with someone. He knew Thad Sheridan would give him sound advice. He would pick up Dan on his way out to Thad's.

*****

"Are you up for a visit?" Vivian poked her head in the door. Annabeth was sitting in the window seal. She rose to go hug Vivian.

"Yes, I am so glad to see you. I've missed working with you. I miss my bakery. Come sit with me." She led Vivian to the window.

"How are you feeling?" Vivian placed her hand on Annabeth's cheek.

"Much better. It will be a little bit longer before I can go back to the bakery. I hope the town will still come when I reopen." Vivian looked surprised.

"Viv, what is it? Has something happened to The Dowry?" Annabeth felt her chest tightening.

"Honey, your bakery never closed. It has been open for the last three weeks. Never missed a day."

Annabeth threw her arms around the older woman. "Vivian, thank you, thank you, thank you. I have been so worried about it. How did you do it?" Vivian stood and pranced around the room. "It wasn't me, sweet pea. It was that handsome big Will Stanton who has kept your bakery open. He is a regular little baker. We have expanded your menu to include more breakfast foods, steak and eggs, flapjacks, and biscuits and gravy."

Annabeth's mouth was wide open. She leaned against the window. Will Stanton kept her bakery open. Will Stanton. "That's right, honey. That man you keep dismissing is in the bakery every morning at four-thirty. When he is done there, he goes to Tyler's and then rounds at night for Dan. I don't recall Old Reliable kicking in to help."

Will Stanton working in her bakery—she couldn't picture it. "He is awful cute in that apron. If I was a few years younger, that man would be off the market."

"Will Stanton, in my bakery?" She finally got the words out.

"Will Stanton running your bakery and doing a marvelous job."

*****

Will went by the sheriff's office and asked Dan to meet him at Thad's. Dan had to stop by and tell the little woman he may be late for supper. Will chuckled inside. He made the trip to Thad's alone. Will was not sure if the little woman would allow Dan to go. Aunt Trudy was a gem. Will was glad she had found happiness with Dan Bullock. He remembered his mother telling him Gertrude didn't have the kindest husband, and that was all she would say. Dan treated her like a queen. Will reckoned she deserved it. Together, the Bullocks had treated him like a crown prince. He had no complaints.

Thad saw Will arrive from inside the barn. "We have company," he said to Hud, who was putting shoes on a very unwilling stallion. Thad was holding the horse's bridle with his good hand, trying to calm the animal. Will spotted the two and headed toward the barn. Without being asked, he grabbed the horse's leg and held it steady so Hud could finish the job.

"Are you doing all four?" Will asked. "If you are offering to help, I would just as soon get them done." Hud wiped the sweat from his forehead. Will moved to the other side, and Hud started the process again.

"What brings you out our way?" Thad asked, practically wrestling the horse's head into submission.

"I have something I would like to discuss with you." The two men made eye contact, and Thad knew it was business.

After a half hour, the horse was shod correctly. Dan had just ridden up. "I asked Dan to come out, so I could talk to both of you." The late-afternoon air was crisp, and you could see the men's breath. "Can we talk inside? I know Merry Sheridan has coffee on, and I sure could use a cup or two." Dan said, rubbing his hands over his cold ears. His hat didn't quite keep the large appendages warm.

The men walked into the warm confines of the house. Sure enough, coffee was on the stove. There was a note on the table stating Merry and David had taken some things over to Molly. Never wanting to be too far away from his wife, Hud said his good-byes and headed home. This left the three men alone, and that suited Will fine.

"What's on your mind?" Thad asked as he poured coffee for the gentlemen.

"I found out how the goods are getting to Sheridan," Will said as he took a drink of the strong brew. Dan and Thad looked at him with stoic expressions. "They are coming through the bakery." There was an emotion that flashed in Thad's clear blue eyes.

"I'm not saying Annabeth has anything to do with this." He put his hand up to cool Thad down. "Matter of fact, I am pretty sure she has no inkling. She also has no idea that her beau does have something to do with it."

Dan's eyes narrowed. Will filled them in on what he found.

"So what is your plan?" Thad leaned back in the chair and crossed his arms over his chest.

"I want the whole setup. No more shipments will come until spring. It will be interesting to see if Rawly continues to go to his mother's or if that is a cover-up. When the shipments start happening again, I will track them back to Sadler's Market in Charleston. When I have the entire route, the agency can close in on all sides. Nothing's going to happen until then."

Thad just stared at him. Dan set his coffee down. "I can wire the sheriff in Box Elder to find out what Rawly does there. He doesn't need to know why, just a little information. He owes me." Will nodded in affirmation.

"I could find out some information from my brother-in-law in Charleston about this Sadler Market."

Will gave a slow shake of his head. "I would rather not involve him. It may compromise the setup since they are going through Annabeth. I don't want her at any more risk than she already is."

"Yes, you are probably right. It may do more to hinder than help."

CHAPTER 5

*A*nnabeth was beginning to feel like her old self again. Thanksgiving was her favorite holiday, and it was just around the corner. Hawk had told her today she could return home and visit the bakery, but she wasn't to work! He said something about her cells needing time to build back up and her body to nourish itself. Whatever that meant. Because there were too many onlookers that would snitch on her, she had to abide by the doctor's order; but she let him know how she felt about it.

The back door to the bakery opened quietly. Annabeth peeked her head in. It was nearly closing time, and there was a sink full of dishes. Will was bent over the stove in a silly apron. Vivian was right; he did look cute. Her attitude toward him changed. He had proved he could be a good friend by keeping the bakery open. She watched as he inadvertently touched the handle of the iron skillet with his elbow. He flinched and mumbled something under his breath. He was trying to see the reddened area when he spotted her.

"Hey, Viv, look who's here." He wiped his hands and removed the apron. The burn was forgotten.

"Well, it sure is good to see you back, Annie. This bakery hasn't been the same."

"You can say that again!" a regular customer hollered from a side table. "The cookin's okay, but the bakin' ain't up to snuff."

Annabeth smiled, and the man did as well. One tooth was missing from the top, and one tooth on the bottom was gold. You didn't forget a smile like that.

"Thank you, Mr. Porter. I'll be back to baking as soon as Dr. Sheridan allows it."

The last customer left, and Vivian hung the Closed sign up. "Can I fix you something, Annabeth?" Will smiled as he lifted her up, setting her on the counter. It happened so quickly she didn't have time to react. "I have some eggs here. I can whip up some mighty fine scrambled eggs and ham." His eyes appeared to her to be dancing. Was he that happy in the kitchen? Her kitchen.

"What do you say?"

"Yes, please. I need to assess the damage that has been done to my bakery menu." She surprised him.

He chuckled. "Stand back and watch." He cracked the last two eggs in a bowl.

"I have been and saw you burn yourself." She hid a smile. He went to where she was sitting and placed a hand on each side of her. He bent over, looking her in the eye. Annabeth's breath caught momentarily. He was too close. "You think you're pretty cute, don't you, Miss Lorton?"

She shrugged her shoulders. She didn't want him to see how uncomfortable she was.

"Just remember, I know exactly how hard your head is. I haven't forgiven you," he whispered rubbing his chin. Not seeming to care that Vivian was privy to such an intimate moment, Will lingered until he heard Old Reliable clear his throat.

"Annabeth, what are you doing?" Annabeth sat up straight and tried to scoot off the counter. Will had turned his back to the counter and leaned against it next to Annabeth. His hand grabbed her elbow just as she nearly fell off the counter. Annabeth couldn't answer. What was she doing? Will had a smile that stretched from one ear to the other.

"What does it look like they are doing, discussing recipes?" Vivian mumbled only loud enough for Annabeth to hear.

"Never mind. I came to tell you I am leaving on the afternoon stage. I am going to see my mother and staying through Thanksgiving weekend. I will be back on Monday's early stage. When I return, we will have a discussion about your friendship with Stanton. I am too angered at the moment." Rawly's face was crimson.

"Don't worry, Smith. She'll be in good hands while you are gone."

Annabeth's mind caved. Did he just say that? She was angry, hurt, disappointed, and excited all at the same time. So many emotions were ripping through her she felt like she was going to crumble. Rawly left the bakery in such a rush he nearly knocked over the petite blonde coming through the door.

"Mother!" Annabeth had never been happier to see her mother than now. She needed her so much. Annabeth ran to Abby's open arms, tears streaming down her face. After a long embrace, Abby pulled away, putting her daughter at arm's length. Her hands cupped Annabeth's face. "You look so tired."

"I am much better, Mother. Honestly, I am so much better. Is Father with you?"

"No, he wanted to come. When we got Thad's telegram that you were out of danger, we felt it would be best if one of us stayed home because of the chances of inclement weather. We didn't think it would be a good idea if we both happen to get stranded here. Not that we would mind, but with the wedding in the spring, one of us had to stay with Patience. Believe me, we both want to be both places."

"I understand, Mother." Annabeth hugged her mother again.

"I did bring you something special." The beautiful woman stepped outside; and in a few minutes, she returned with a young man beside her.

"TJ." Annabeth tripped, running to her brother.

He caught her; and keeping her at arm's length, he reminded her of something. "You remember my rule. No kisses, Anna, just a hug."

She gave him a quick hug and sneaked a peck on the cheek. The fifteen-year-old groaned.

"Would you like a cup of coffee, ma'am?" Vivian's voice brought Annabeth back to the here and now.

"Oh, I'm sorry. Please, Mother, sit down. You too, TJ."

The duo sat at the nearest table. "Do you have tea? Abby Lorton removed her gloves and sat them on the table.

"Sure, we do." Vivian went to grab the tea kettle.

Will, who always had something to say, was just standing in the kitchen, silent. Annabeth's mother was breathtakingly beautiful and ageless. She felt Will staring and acknowledged him with a dip of her head. "Will Stanton, ma'am. I am a coworker of Annabeth's."

"Yes, you are the young man who kept The Dowry open while Annabeth was ill. That was a very kind gesture. I am sure she appreciated it."

Why did he feel he had been put in his place? Because, if she had been five minutes earlier, she would have witnessed Will Stanton trifling with her daughter's emotions, that's why. Mrs. Lorton was enough like her brother to take Will to the woodshed without raising a hand.

"How long are you staying, Mother?" Annabeth sat down next to TJ, handing him some leftover muffins. The boy ate them without taking a breath. "These are pretty good Anna. Better than they look."

Vivian and Annabeth both laughed, turning their heads to look at Will.

"Thanks, I will take that as a compliment." Will started on the dishes.

"You made them?" TJ looked surprised.

"See, son, it never hurts a man to learn how to cook. I am sure it has come in handy for Mr. Stanton."

"Yes, ma'am." Will went back to the dishes.

"This will be a whirlwind trip. I was told by your father not to take chances with the weather. He wants me home as soon as possible, and he would like for me to bring you with me." Abby sipped her tea.

"That's not going to happen." The man at the sink spoke but never looked up.

"I beg your pardon?" Abby sat the saucer down gently and turn to face Will.

"No disrespect, ma'am, but the way your daughter loves this bakery, she's not leaving."

Abby was a little astounded by Mr. Stanton's boldness. "We will talk about it later, dear. I want to hear all about the bakery." She turned the conversation back to her daughter.

Will finished the dishes and left for the day. He had another whole day of work waiting for him at Mr. Tyler's.

Annabeth couldn't leave. She couldn't go back to Charleston until he wrapped up this case. He needed her right here, and he could make it happen. He nearly ran Thad Sheridan over with his lack of attention to where he was going. "Where's the fire?" Thad asked with his usual smile.

"I had my mind on something. Sorry, I nearly ran you down."

Thad rubbed his chin. "It must be a woman to put a man that out of sorts."

Will frowned. "I can assure you it is not, and if you are looking for your sister, she is at The Dowry." Will continued walking.

Thad turned to watch the man, laughing to himself. Will Stanton was slowly but surely being wound around his niece's finger. Thad wasn't too sure he liked the idea.

Thad held his sister in his arms for a long embrace. He loved her so much and missed her terribly. "Merry and I are giving you until Wednesday to stay in town with Annabeth. Then you both are coming to the house for the rest of the week." Thad kept his arm around his sister.

"You better clear that with Mr. Stanton. He seems to think he has a say in what Annabeth does." Abby briefly looked at her brother and then turned to Annabeth. "Does he have a say?" She searched her daughter's eyes.

"No, he does not." Annabeth's response was difficult to believe, even to herself. In a small way, the man frightened her.

Annabeth took her mother to her home at the boarding house. TJ would stay in a room upstairs, and Abby would stay with Annabeth. "It may get a little chilly. Let me know if you are too cold. I can add more wood to the stove." Annabeth showed her mother around her small home. Thrive had jumped on the bed and curled up in a ball. Abby scratched the dog's ears as she watched her daughter look out the window.

"What is wrong, Annabeth?" Annabeth turned to face her mother, and a tear trickled down her face. Abby sat on the bed and patted the place beside her.

Annabeth sat down. Thrive immediately laid his head on her lap. She began methodically stroking the dog's coat. "I… I don't want to go back to Charleston. Will is right. I love the bakery. I couldn't leave."

Abby grabbed her daughter's hand. "Annabeth, we would never make you come back. Your father just misses you. You and he are so close. You leaving was hard on us all but especially him. After what happened between you and Jonathan, he feels particularly protective of you. To have you be so vulnerable and so far away bothers him."

Annabeth kept her head down. "I don't need protection, Mother. I can take care of myself. That is what has been so liberating about The Dowry. I feel I am accomplishing so much on my own. I know I have a whole host of Sheridans looking out for me, but they let me have the reins. Do you understand, Mother?"

"I understand, but does Mr. Stanton?"

"It's not what you think. Will—Mr. Stanton—is a regular customer who did a good deed in helping Vivian keep the bakery open while I was ill. It really doesn't go any further than that."

"What does Rawly think of your friendship with Mr. Stanton?"

"He doesn't like it at all." Annabeth was quick to respond. Her voice was raised just a bit.

"Why is that? I mean, if he is just a friend, I would think Rawly wouldn't be bothered."

Annabeth's chin dropped, and her mother lifted it up. She looked her daughter in the eye. "Will does things to antagonize Rawly."

"Such as?" Her mother kept her hand on her daughter's chin.

"When Rawly left today, Will told him not to worry, that I'd be in good hands."

Abby dropped her hand and raised her eyebrow. "Did he now?"

"Vivian says Will's a man that likes to play games. She is right. He is always saying or doing things to stir the pot. He can't keep his mouth shut." Annabeth wanted to change the subject. "I'm sure Trudy has supper ready. We better head on over."

Mother and daughter entered the kitchen to find TJ and Will setting the table. "That is a sight I have never seen, my son setting the table. You never offer to do that at home." Abby stood with her hands on her hips, looking at TJ.

"Man doesn't help, he doesn't eat," Will said as a matter of fact while pulling out a chair for Mrs. Lorton. She sat down, and he seated Annabeth as well.

"Mrs. Lorton, you are the most handsome woman I have ever seen. You are just a rare beauty," Trudy said as she placed her hands on Abby's shoulders. "We are so glad you came to visit. Annabeth is the best girl around. We love having her here with us. I hope you are not thinking of taking her back with you. My heavens, we couldn't stand that. Oh dear, no."

"Thank you, Mrs. Bullock, and don't worry, as much as I miss my girl, she belongs here."

Beautiful and smart, Will thought of Abby Lorton. Annabeth not only got her lovely eyes from her mother but also got her brains too. Except when it comes to Rawly. This made Will wonder what kind of man Mr. Lorton was. His mind went down a rabbit trail, trying to surmise what kind of family life Annabeth had. She never spoke too much about her upbringing.

Dan Bullock's knuckles rapping on the top of his head alerted him that he had not kept up with the happenings in the kitchen. "What's gotten into you, Will? Trudy said supper was ready."

Will looked up, and everyone but he and Dan were sitting. "Oh, sorry, I have something else on my mind." His eyes drifted to Annabeth. No, it wasn't a woman. Abby caught the gentle sweep of Will's eyes toward her daughter. She was determined to speak with her brother about Mr. Stanton.

Curled up in the small bed, Annabeth rested her head near her mother's. "I am so glad you came to visit." She placed a kiss on her mother's cheek.

"I am glad I came too. I am sorry I won't get to meet Rawly. I was looking forward to meeting him." Abby patted her daughter's hand.

"You mean you were looking forward to conducting a formal appraisal of him."

Abby laughed at her candid daughter. "I have already received a detailed report from your aunt Merry. She says he is pleasant enough."

"Yes, I suppose that is an accurate description." Annabeth sat up, leaning her back against the headboard. Her mother did the same.

"And Will—where does he fit into the picture?" Abby asked, watching her daughter's profile.

"Honestly, Mother, there is nothing there but a man who has the world by the tail. Or so he thinks."

Abby took her daughter's hand in hers. "That may be true, dear, but remember that currently, you are part of his world. Please be careful."

*****

Wednesday morning after breakfast at The Dowry, Abby, TJ, and Annabeth headed out to Thad's. The wagon was loaded with gifts and food. "Mother, can I stay behind and ride out to Uncle Thad's tomorrow?" TJ was standing beside Will. Abby wasn't sure, but she thought it had something to do with the man who had the world by the tail.

"Absolutely not," Abby replied, looking more at Will than at her son. TJ knew his mother well. When *absolutely not* was used, he could never persuade her otherwise. He had watched his father try over the years, to no avail, Will nodded toward TJ. It was an unspoken respect-your-mother nod.

"Why on earth would you want to stay in town and not spend time with Thad and Merry?" Abby asked her son on the way out of town. TJ was sitting in the back of the wagon. His mother turned to face him. The boy looked at his mother and then at Annabeth. He narrowed his eyes and shook his head no. Abby knew her son; something was up, and they would discuss it later.

Merry squealed as she flew off the porch toward her sister-in-law. They may not see each other much, but their constant letters had drawn them close. After some quick hugs, Merry ushered the group into her work kitchen. "Sit down and let me look at you. You haven't aged a bit. Still the most beautiful woman."

Abby flipped her hand. "You have spent too much time in the hot sun, sister dear."

They laughed as Thad pulled a chair out for his sister. He kissed her cheek. "I am so glad you are here even if it is for just a few days." He then kissed his smiling wife twice on top of the head.

Same sweet Thad and Merry, Abby thought. She turned to her daughter, who looked to be a million miles away. Annabeth's face was a mask of hurt and betrayal. Would she ever see the daughter she knew before Jonathan Taylor's deception? Thad's eyes met his sister's. He knew where her mind was. He saw the toll everything had taken on his niece. His heart ached for both of them.

The day was spent just visiting. That evening after supper, Abby found her son in the barn with Franklin, Gil, and David. "May I talk with you for a moment, son?" TJ left the group, following his mother outside. "What was all the secrecy this morning?"

"Mother, why do you and Father always have to ruin things?"

Abby was not taken aback by her son's statement. TJ was going through a very selfish stage and portrayed things slightly out of kilter. She gave him one of her looks, and he knew he better start talking. "Will was going to make a bed for Thrive as a surprise for Anna. He asked me to help him. Please don't say anything to her."

Abby scrunched up her nose. "I'm sorry, honey. That would have been fun for you. I guess I was too quick to answer and should have asked you why you wanted to stay. I'm sorry, TJ." She patted his arm. "Go on back with the others."

"You promise you won't tell Anna. He wants it to be a surprise for Christmas. Will would be mad for sure if she found out."

"I won't say a word."

"Will would be mad." Why would Will be mad, and who cares if he is? Abby thought as she went through the door. She wasn't sure she liked the man. He seemed too involved in her daughter's life and a little bit big for his britches. He exuded arrogance.

"What is that look for?" Thad asked his sister from his place at the sink. He was elbow high in turkey feathers. The bird was stripped of all its glory and lay pathetically in a baking pan. Thad did whatever needed to be done. It made no difference what it was.

Abby couldn't help but get lost in the life of her only brother. She supposed life had taught him the ropes to survival. If Abby knew how many times he was close to death over the years, she wouldn't believe it. She didn't like to think about it, yet her mind wondered. After the war between the states, she found him in a hospital back east nearly starved to death and a knife wound that traveled down his jawline to his neck. She shuddered at the memory.

"Abby, are you okay?" Thad's look was one of worry.

She walked over and kissed him on the cheek. "My mind is just going in so many directions right now I can't even begin to tell you. What I can tell you is how thankful I am for you. In case you don't know, it I love you very much."

He smiled. "I know."

It was late evening, and Merry was still preparing for dinner the next day. Thad was sitting at the worktable in the kitchen. He was there to help Merry if she needed. She rarely needed or allowed help, but they enjoyed being together no matter what the chore. Abby heard the gentle rhythm of conversation and slipped out of bed and entered the kitchen.

"Did we wake you, Abby?" Merry stopped chopping vegetables. Thad turned to see his sister exit the loft where she and Annabeth were staying. She had the same look on her face as earlier.

"What is bothering you, Abby?" he said as he rose to pull out a chair for her. There was a plate of cookies on the table, and Merry shoved them her way. She took a cookie and looked back at the loft. Her voice lowered.

"I'm worried about Annabeth." She nibbled the cookie.

"She is a lot better. Hawk says she will be back to full strength in no time." Merry smiled. They knew how sick Annabeth had been and how bad she had looked.

"I'm not worried about her health. I am worried about her heart." She turned to Thad. "Who is this Will Stanton, and what kind of man is he?"

Merry and Thad exchanged a look. "What? What does that mean?" Abby knew a moment of panic.

"It means nothing, Abby." Thad rose to pour himself a cup of coffee.

"Merry, I know what I just saw. Are you two keeping something from me?"

"What has you bothered?" Thad asked. "He knows Rawly Smith is courting Annabeth."

Abby turned to look at Thad. "Do you honestly think that would stop a man like Stanton?"

Thad had a hard time containing his laughter. Merry gave him a stern look.

"He is. He is just too much of a man." Abby looked at Merry. Thad nearly spewed his coffee all over the kitchen.

"What is that supposed to mean?" he asked his sister with merriment. "Oh, you know what I mean, don't you, Merry?"

Abby was looking for validation.

"Yes, I think so."

"Well, I guess you are going to have to explain it to me." Thad looked at the two women with perplexed expressions.

"I suppose I mean he is too much of a man for Annabeth." Abby sipped her coffee. "The last thing she needs is another broken heart. He pays her special attention, but I don't think he means anything by it. In my few brief encounters with him, I find I don't care for him. He speaks his mind without being asked, and he sometimes speaks for Annabeth. He is rather an imposing person. I am afraid she is too fragile for his games. There, I said it."

Annabeth had slipped on her robe and was headed to check on her mother. She didn't mean to eavesdrop, but her mother's words stopped her. She sat on the floor listening to the conversation. Tears streamed down her face. Was this the way they all saw her? A fragile, forlorn creature? She rose to go back to bed. She didn't care to hear any more, but her uncle's voice stopped her.

"Have you considered that maybe Will would be the one to suffer the heartbreak?" Thad leaned against the sink. "Speaking for the male population, if anyone could break a heart, it's Annabeth. And besides, she is a smart girl. I think she can guard her heart, especially after what she has been through. You are not giving your daughter enough credit."

Annabeth had to laugh; she was not a heart breaker, and she knew it. She couldn't break Rawly's heart, and she sure couldn't break Will's. She appreciated her uncle's faith in her, but there would never be anything more between her and Rawly than a comfort level of companionship. And there would never be anything between her and Will than a strange working relationship. Why was she still crying?

"You're right, Thad. I raised a strong, smart girl. I need to trust her. Can I help it if I don't trust Mr. Stanton? Maybe if I stayed around a little longer, that would change. I am counting on you to protect my precious girl." Abby was near tears.

"I can only protect her so much. We need to leave the rest in the Lord's hands." He gave his sister a big hug. She clung to him, knowing he was right. She prayed for her daughter.

Annabeth exited the loft early Thanksgiving morning. Determined to be light and joyous, she wanted everyone to know that she was back to her old self. She wanted no more conversations regarding her like she heard last night. She thought of telling her mother she had overheard her concerns, but that would only make her mother upset.

Merry had just put the coffee on and the bird in the oven. "Good morning, Aunt Merry. What can I do to help?" Annabeth's smile was over the top.

"Good morning, honey. Did you sleep well?" Merry patted her niece's cheek. She didn't think Annabeth looked as if she had slept a wink.

"I tossed and turned quite a bit. I think I am just excited about us all being together today. I have missed my family. I wish Patience and Father could have come."

Thad came from the bedroom. "Good morning, ladies," he said as he put his coat on, heading out to do the chores. "If Merry doesn't need you at this moment, you can accompany me to the barn." His smile was always so infectious.

Annabeth smiled and retrieved her coat. She loved spending time with Uncle Thad.

Once in the barn, Annabeth felt the urge to thank Thad for his kind words he had spoken on her behalf. "I overheard my mother's concerns last night."

Thad turned to face her. "Please understand your mother is just worried about you."

"Oh, I do. I am not upset. Well, I was a little last night, but I gave it some thought and prayer, and I understand. Your take on the situation made me laugh, and that made me feel better."

"What part of my statement did you find funny? If I recall, none of my words were meant as a joke." He looked displeased.

Annabeth's head went to one side. "A heart breaker, please." She moved to rake some hay into a stall.

"Annabeth, you are not standing where I am."

She turned to look at him. "What do you mean?"

"You are very much like Merry. Neither of you see the beauty and attraction you have. You both have something very alluring to a man. You think it is all in what the eye can see. You're both fortunate to have great physical beauty but also an underlying inner attractiveness that makes a man sit up and take notice."

She gripped the handle of the rake. "My experience with Jonathan causes me to dispute your argument, counselor."

Thad shook his head. "How many jurors are on a case?" She was silent, and he waited. "How many?" he asked again.

"Twelve," she answered.

"Exactly. Your focusing on one man instead of looking at the others."

"We'll see." She continued her work.

"Yes, we will." She could hear the mirth in his voice. "And you are going to be surprised."

*****

The wagons began to roll in. Hawk and Avery with the children were the first to arrive. Hunter and River followed their father straight to Merry. Hugs and kisses were exchanged, and they were out the door. As Hunter passed Annabeth near the door, he stopped and looked around. "Where is your husband?" he asked with the sober face that accompanied all of Hawk Sheridan's children.

"I don't have a husband, honey." The boy stared and walked out of the door.

"Who was he expecting to be here?" she asked Hawk, who was nibbling some turkey.

The man just smiled and shrugged his shoulders. He looked like the cat that ate the canary. It wasn't long until Molly waddled in with Hud and Quinn. The Kennedys had also arrived on the heels of Jonah, Hannah, and Tommy. The family was complete.

The group sat around the table and held hands. Each one was to tell what they were thankful for. Just before starting River whispered in his mother's ear but not so quietly that everyone couldn't hear. "Will's not here yet. We can't start." Everyone seemed to be looking at Annabeth. "Will is eating with his Aunt Trudy and Uncle Dan." Avery helped the boy get seated. "But—" he tried to continue. "That is enough, son." Hawk gave the youngster a stern look. "Why don't you tell us what you are thankful for?" Merry addressed her grandson. "I'm thankful for…for—" He looked at everyone staring at him. "I'm thankful for Hunter," he said as he buried his head into his mother's arm.

And so it went around the table each telling what they were thankful for. After the meal, everyone began to migrate to different parts of the house. The weather was reasonably tolerable, so the children went outside. The men went into the front room to play chess or checkers, and the women stayed at the table. Franklin, Gil, Annabeth, and Tommy cleaned up the dishes. Hud was just about to head into the front room when he saw Molly frown.

"You all right, Molly?" About that time, she inhaled sharply, and her hand went to her swollen abdomen. "Oh!" She clenched the edge of the table, and Hud went to her side. "I… I think I need to go home." She tried to smile at the group now staring at her. Avery went to get Hawk. Hud assisted her to stand and another pain hit doubling her over. Hud lifted her into his arms and headed toward their home. Hawk and Avery followed.

Laying Molly gently on the bed, Hud stepped back to allow Hawk and Avery to tend his wife. He knew he would be of little use for the next several hours. When Quinn was born, Hud just sat at the head of the bed and did whatever Molly asked. She was very stoic when it came to pain, but she gripped his hand so tight he thought he would lose a finger or two.

"It's going to be awhile, Hud." Hawk looked at his brother. Hud shook his head. "Please go back and enjoy the day," Molly said to Hawk and Avery, who were standing at the foot of the bed. "We will take care of Quinn, so don't worry about him." Avery placed some water and towels beside the bed. "We will check on you frequently. Hud, you come and get us at any time." Avery rested her hand on Hud's arm.

"Unless he wants to deliver this baby on his own. Let us not forget he has done it before." Hawk's smile caught Hud's surprised look. "That was a once-in-a-lifetime event for me. One I don't care to repeat." He frowned at his brother. Hud had delivered Lach and Jamie's son, Michael, eight years ago during a snowstorm. It was frequently brought up when a Sheridan was expecting.

It was late evening and still no baby. Hawk and Avery made trips back and forth from Thad's to Hud's. They would be staying the night for sure. On one walk back, Avery stopped. "She has progressed very slowly. I would have thought with this being the second one, it would go faster. Remember how quickly I delivered River?"

"Yes, and I remember Piper's arrival seemed to drag on. This is probably a girl as well. You females have a tendency to keep the world waiting."

"Is that so?" Avery was a little miffed at her husband. He grabbed her around the waist and pulled her to him.

"I didn't say it was a bad thing. Matter of fact I have always found the wait to be worth it." His voice was soft, and his lips passionately met hers. After a few seconds, she leaned back looking him in the eye. Taking his hands, she placed them on her abdomen. "I can't believe you missed this one. Number four is on the way, Dr. Sheridan."

Dr. Hawk Sheridan could tell if a woman was pregnant before she knew herself. He always told Avery she was expecting before she could confirm it. Molly laughed at him when he said she was pregnant with Quinn as well as the one they were waiting on now. It was some sort of gift or knack he had. It always amazed Avery. Tonight she got to surprise him. "How did I miss this?" Hawk said as he pulled her back in for another kiss. "I am losing my touch."

"I don't think so." Her hands rested on his chest.

Abby, Merry, Thad, and Annabeth were sitting at the table eating a midnight snack. No one wanted to go to bed until Molly had her baby. They could sleep tomorrow. Tommy came from his room. "W-what's taking so long?" he asked as he poured a cup a coffee and cut a wedge of pie. "Y-you don't think s-something is wrong do you?" He looked to his ma for an answer. "No, Hawk said she was fine. Sometimes it takes a while." Tommy looked worried like something more than the birth of the baby was on his mind.

"Son, you look like a man with the weight of the world on his shoulders. And it's not just Molly?" Thad watched his son massage his forehead. Everyone was looking at him. "I-I have something I need to tell you." He looked at his parents. "And something I need to ask you." His eyes shifted to Abby. Abby looked a bit shocked but nodded her head. "You can ask me anything, Tommy."

"I would like to go back to Charleston with you on Saturday. I was wondering if I could stay with you until I can find a job." Merry was stunned. Where had this come from? Thad, for the first time in his life, was speechless. He knew there was more his son needed to say.

"Of course, Tommy, our home is your home." Abby took in the expression of the young man's face.

He sat down at the table. "Josie and I were married Wednesday evening. She will be coming with me." Everyone at the table was a little shocked. They knew Tommy and Josie were in love, but her father made it almost impossible on the young man. Ever since Jonah stole Hannah away, Owen Miller had been determined to keep his youngest daughter on a tight leash. Tommy did not have the temperament of Jonah, and this is what made those at the table look so stunned.

"I take it Mr. and Mrs. Miller aren't aware of this?" Thad asked his son.

"No one knows except Pastor Grey and now you, not even Jonah and Hannah."

"Why now, son?" Thad asked.

Tommy's body became stiff. "B-because h-he h-hit her for the last time!" His voice was raised in anger. If those at the table were stunned before, they were now knocked off their feet.

"Whoa, what?" Thad hadn't a clue Owen Miller could be abusive.

"Since Hannah eloped Owen, Miller has been determined to keep Josie from me. He took to using his hand anytime he thought she was inclined to see me. I tried to obey his rules. I even stayed away from her. If she were late coming home from the bakery, he would assume we were together, and he beat her."

Annabeth felt sick inside. Josie had been helping out in her absence at The Dowry. "You need to go get her this instance, Tommy." Merry stood, rage in her face at the injustice Josie was receiving. "Settle down, Merry. It seems Tommy has a plan. Let's hear him out." Merry paced a little, letting the steam escape from the top of her head.

"I-I really like C-Charleston, and I think I can g-get a job there. I will b-be able to provide for Josie."

"I'll say you can get a job in Charleston," Abby said with authority. "Jackson knows a lot of people. If he doesn't have an opening, he will help you find something, and you can stay with us until you are on your feet."

"I h-have some money saved up. I-I think we will be fine. I will m-miss all of you." His eyes met his mother's. They were filled with tears.

At two o'clock in the morning, baby Nora Elizabeth Sheridan quietly entered the world. The tiny baby didn't have a lick of hair, not even a little peach fuzz. She was the ugliest baby Hawk had ever delivered, but he would never mention it out loud. The tiny baby looked even smaller in the arms of her father who cradled her close and kissed the top of her bald head. Molly was grinning from ear to ear as Hud swayed the baby from side to side cooing.

"May I see her?" Molly asked. When Hawk handed the baby to Hud, he assumed he would give the infant directly to her mother. Hud looked shocked. "Oh." He handed the baby to Molly. She pulled the blanket down to inspect the baby then wrapped it tightly and held it to her chest skimming her lips over the baby's head. Nora kicked up a little fuss; it was time to eat.

The next-day plans were put into place to see that Tommy and Josie got to Charleston successfully. The Sheridan family was still in shock of how quickly they were going to lose Tommy. Between that and the emotion of the new baby, Merry was in a constant state of tears. It didn't help when she overheard Avery telling Molly another baby was on the way. Her world was changing at a rapid pace. She entered the barn and went right into Thad's arms. "I can't take it," she cried resting her face on his chest. His arms went around her, and his lips brushed her temple. He said nothing but let her cry; his heart was breaking just a little bit as well. He wanted all their boys to live around them. Never did he dream Tommy would be the one to go.

*****

The stage was scheduled to leave at eight. Annabeth was not going to be all gloomy. She instead would be thankful her mother and brother came to see her. After all, it would be just a few short months, and she would be headed to Charleston for Patience wedding.

"Sure you won't come with us?" Abby asked her daughter while lifting the girl's chin to look into her eyes.

"I'm really happy here, Mother. Truly, I am. It has been so good for me. I don't know if Uncle Thad told you, but The Dowry is doing quite well."

"It is not the bakery I am worried about." Abby dropped her hand. "I know I contracted yellow fever, but I think that was just a rare happening. For the most part, I am hale and hearty."

"It's not your health. I am worried about currently either." Abby now frowned.

"Mother, please." Annabeth's voice held a bit of contempt. "I can handle myself. I am not worried about catching a husband. It is the furthest thing from my mind."

"But it might not be the furthest thing from his mind." Abby finished packing.

"Rawly has made no attempt to speak of such things, and I don't expect him to in the near future or the future in general. Please don't worry, Mother." It wasn't Rawly she was concerned about. It was the man leaning on the doorframe looking at her daughter with pure mischief in his eyes.

"Annabeth, why don't you go see if TJ is all packed before we sit down to breakfast?" She was looking at Will.

Will knew TJ was packed. He also knew Abby knew the fact also. She wanted a word with him; it was obvious. Annabeth moved past him. Her toe caught, and she fell against him. He steadied her, and she smiled. "I am so awkward." She sighed. Will held her eyes with his. She did have a tendency to trip a lot.

Top heavy, he thought. He turned to find Abby's eyes on him. *Here it comes*, he mused, *another lecture from the high and mighty*.

"A word with you, Mr. Stanton, if you please." Abby closed her suitcase and sat in on the floor.

"Do I have a choice, ma'am?"

Abby's eyebrows were so high on her forehead; they almost disappeared under her hat. "I don't know you very well, Mr. Stanton, but I find you to be somewhat pompous." His look was one of indifference. "You are right. You don't know me very well, so why don't you say what you aim too, and we can move along?" Abby was seething inside. Never had she been so irritated. "Stop dallying with my daughter."

"I am not wasting time with your daughter. We make an excellent team," he replied.

Abby's eyes narrowed. "Isn't that the correct meaning of the word *dally*, to waste someone's time?"

"I hardly think Annabeth or I have wasted one another's time, do you?"

113

"All right, how about the word *flirt?* Does that drive my meaning home?"

"I am familiar with the word, but I don't flirt." Will remained in the doorway. "What do you call the interaction that just transpired between the two of you?"

"I call it an interaction, nothing more." Abby was beyond frustrated. "I see the way you look at her."

"Yes, and if you stuck around, you would see every man in town look at her."

"I don't understand the Sheridans' obsession with protecting someone who doesn't need protecting. Annabeth is level-headed and able to think and reason things out. Just because one male idiot misbehaved toward her doesn't mean that every man is out to annihilate her."

"I know my daughter, thank you very much, and I know you are pushing your luck." In all her anger Abby never once saw any from him.

He shook his head. "I understand you fully, Mrs. Lorton. Be assured my intentions are not to woo your daughter." He bent to pick up her travel bags.

"Make sure she knows it," Abby said as she followed him out the door.

CHAPTER 6

*R*awly Smith laid the law down when he returned from his mother's. Annabeth needed to be aware that Will Stanton was nothing more than a Casanova who would be gone when the town held no more allure for him. If Will were to continue working at the bakery, there would be rules put forth by Rawly that Mr. Stanton and Annabeth would have to follow.

"You're being silly, Rawly." Annabeth was standing outside The Dowry, the wind whipping at her coat.

"I am not, and tonight I plan to lay out those rules to Stanton after supper." His face was red, and his hands were clenched in a fist. He looked like a little boy ready to fight the school bully, knowing full well he would be sent home with his tail between his legs.

"Please, Rawly, don't make a scene."

He huffed and stepped off the boardwalk. "I will see you tonight," he said with affirmation.

Vivian and Will watched from inside the bakery. "He has a lot of nerve keeping her out there in the cold like that." Will had a hint of disgust in his voice. "I have never met a man poorer at courtship than Old Reliable. Look at him."

Vivian wasn't watching Rawly and Annie. Her eyes were fixed on Will. "What color did you say your eyes were?"

"Brown. Why?" He turned at her boisterous laugh. He caught her meaning. "Funny." He turned to clear the tables.

"You ought to be in a vaudeville show." Her laugh got even louder.

"What's so funny?" Annabeth entered. Taking off her hat and coat, she looked at Vivian. The now-giggling woman removed the dirty dishes from Will's arms and sauntered into the kitchen. Annabeth faced Will with a quizzical look.

"She's touched in the head, you know, off her rocker."

His expression made Annabeth smile, and what a smile it was. He didn't remember her ever smiling like that before. Something had changed since the visit with her mother. Annabeth was healing from a deep hurt.

"My daughter here?" Owen Miller stormed in the Closed door of the bakery. His eyes landed on Annabeth.

"No, sir." Her mind whirled. Did he not know Josie, by now, was in Charleston? "We have been closed since Thanksgiving. We reopened today."

His eyes were so cold it was eerie. "She spent Thanksgiving with her sister. She was supposed to come home last night. There is no one home over at Hannah's." The man looked like he was about to explode.

"I would say your daughter is probably in Charleston by now," Vivian piped up. She was headed to stand face-to-face with Owen Miller.

"What are you talking about, woman? Charleston?" He looked to Will as if Vivian Ascot had lost her mind.

"That's right. That sweet baby girl of yours got on the stage Saturday morning headed South."

The man's rage was about to erupt. He turned to leave the bakery. "No need heading over to the bank. Tom Sheridan is gone as well. In your ignorance, you've managed to lose both your daughters and run off a fine young man. The only one who will end up miserable in this story is you."

"That is enough, woman." The stocky man used his booming voice of authority.

Vivian laughed. "Your tantrums don't work on me. Nor would the back of your hand if you thought of using it. That seems to be your chosen method of negotiating: ignorance and violence."

For a split second, the bakery was filled with silence. A hard breath came from Mr. Miller, and he left.

Annabeth moved toward Vivian, but the look on the woman's face stopped her. Her eyes were filled with tears. "Not now, Annie," she said as she left the bakery through the back door.

Annabeth turned to face Will. "She sure let him have it," he said as he made his way to the sink and began doing the dishes. She stood next to him.

"In a way, I feel sorry for Mr. Miller." Annabeth began drying the dishes.

"Maybe you're touched." He gave her a quick side glance.

"No, Vivian was right. He's lost both his daughters and possibly his wife's affection as well. He will be a miserable man."

Will shrugged his shoulders. "Every man has to learn his actions have consequences. Miller is learning the hard way."

Annabeth said no more. She was too busy trying to figure out Will Stanton.

*****

Tuesday night supper at Trudy's kitchen table was a painful one. Dan had something come up and couldn't be home for the meal. There were four boarders Trudy was serving. This left Will, Rawly, and Annabeth to eat alone in the kitchen. Rawly and Will seemed to be in some sort of contest as who could stare the other one down while devouring the contents of the food placed on the table. It was a tedious meal as Annabeth picked her way around her plate.

"Are you not hungry, Annabeth? You've barely touched your food." Will smiled her way.

"There is nothing wrong with Annabeth." Rawly snapped.

Will turned in his chair to make sure Annabeth was in his full view. A warm smile graced his lips. Without looking at Rawly, he agreed. "There is definitely nothing wrong with Annabeth."

She blushed under the scrutiny of both men.

"That's it." Rawly's chair skidded across the floor as he stood. "May I have a word with you outside, Stanton?"

If only it could be just a word, Will thought. He was getting tired of these little confrontations he was having, but this one might be entertaining. He rose and followed Old Reliable out the back door. Rawly took no time getting in Will's face or at least trying to. Will was a good three or four inches taller. Annabeth watched from the window.

"I don't know what you're up to, but this game playing with Annabeth stops tonight. Any simpleton can see she is spoken for. I have been calling on her for a good six months."

Will just listened. Any simpleton could see Rawly was going nowhere with Annabeth whether Will Stanton was in the picture or not.

"And now that Annabeth's health is improving, you are not needed at the bakery. I demand you quit working with her." Rawly's words were final, and he looked expectantly at his nemesis.

"No," Will said and headed back inside.

"What?" Rawly followed.

"You wanted a word, and that's what you got. No." Will walked past Annabeth standing in the kitchen. "See you in the morning." He winked. Rawly left as well.

Will would be glad when this case was over; he didn't want to tip his hand and expose the whole operations. He also had a moral obligation to protect Annabeth Lorton. Will was using her bakery, and he was using her. It was complicated; he needed Rawly to continue to use Annabeth's bakery for delivery of the stolen goods. It wasn't big items, but it was high-priced items. Someone had set up a pretty elaborate racket.

Rawly's arrival a few months after Annabeth gave him time to scout the town. A pretty young entrepreneur arrived with ties to the very Southern states where things began to go missing. It was like a gift for him. All he had to do was woo the little miss and just let the setup take hold.

Will would be glad to put Rawly and his cronies away. He wasn't looking forward to Annabeth getting hurt again. He figured that was why he flirted and teased with her. She needed to know there were more men—better men—than Rawly who would love her wholly and honestly. He frowned. All she had known in regard to men was dishonesty including himself. The thought lay heavy on his chest. It stole his sleep.

Will overslept the next morning, giving Rawly and Annabeth the feeling he was abiding by Rawly's request. Old Reliable was disappointed when he witnessed Will entering The Dowry. Will waved to the blacksmith as he opened the back door. Rawly pounded his anvil a little harder.

"We were beginning to get worried about you. You look just horrible." Vivian put a cup of coffee in his hand.

"I had trouble sleeping last night," he mumbled as he took a drink of the coffee. "What do you need me to do today?" He yawned.

Go home, Annabeth thought. His unruly dark hair was distracting her. She wanted to run her fingers through it. His lips were in a sleepy smile. His brown eyes were dreamy and looking directly at her.

"Something wrong, Annabeth?" She heard him ask softly.

"Uh, no, what did you say?"

"He asked what you needed him to do today," Vivian said as she walked by and whispered into Annabeth's ear. "If he could read your thoughts right now, you would be in some kind of trouble."

The woman sashayed to clear tables, leaving Annabeth mortified. Could he read her thoughts? And where had those thoughts come from?

"I was thinking." She regained some self-preservation. "I was thinking that I probably don't need all that much help anymore. Vivian and I can manage as before." She went to pull some treats from the oven. "So you could go back to working for Mr. Tyler full-time."

He stopped her with a hand to her upper arm, pulling her, so they were eye to eye. "I could, but I am not going to. I have made a place for myself here, and let's face it, Annabeth, you would miss me." The last phrase was barely a whisper. His hand remained on her upper arm, and his eyes were intense.

"Boy, this kitchen sure does heat up fast," Vivian commented as she passed by the couple with an armful of dishes. Will let out a little chuckle in spite of the rock in his stomach. He was doing what he had promised Abby, Thad, and Hawk he wouldn't do. He was playing with Annabeth's emotions.

Annabeth closed up the bakery. She was going to drop off some cookies to Rawly and the schoolchildren and then head home. She peeked inside where Rawly was working. As cold as it was outside, his shop was nice and toasty. She watched a moment while he worked, forging and bending a metal piece into a farming implement. He spotted her, and she lifted the bag of cookies. He smiled and nodded for her to have a seat on a nearby stool. In a few minutes, he joined her.

"I am on my way home and just stopped by to drop off some cookies."

"That is mighty kind of you. I love your cookies." He opened the bag and took one out. Sinking his teeth into it, he smiled, offering her one.

"No, thank you." She looked around at some of the projects he was working on. "You and Jonah should get together and make some furniture. Iron and wood would make sturdy and beautiful pieces."

"I suppose." He neared her and, taking her hand, helped her off the stool.

"Annabeth, I need to know something." He looked very serious. She nodded for him to continue. "I need to know that Will Stanton isn't coming between us." His hands had gripped her upper forearms. He pulled her close. "I need to—" He didn't finish. His lips ever so softly met hers—warm and passionate. She felt like she was falling, and he kissed her again and then a third time.

"Will who?" she asked, and he released her with a smile.

"I think I have my answer. You better head home. It looks like snow."

Annabeth left on a cloud. That was the second time Rawly had really kissed her with any feeling. The other times had been sweet pecks on the cheek or forehead. It confused her. Before Will Stanton's arrival, she was happy with the pace her relationship with Rawly was on; but now it seemed she felt an urgency within her. One thing she was sure of was the fact she needed to decide what role each one of them would play in her life.

Annabeth had to admit to herself she was attracted to them both. She reasoned that Will's spontaneous flirtations awakened the realization that she wanted more from Rawly. Will was a man with the world by the tail, and her mother was correct; she was in his world currently, but Rawly would be permanent.

From now on, she would concentrate on being Will's friend and Rawly's future. She prayed the Lord would direct her thoughts and path to do just that. Perhaps she should have a conversation with Will. The thought made her queasy. What if he wasn't flirting? What if he was just nice? Maybe he was her friend and just trying to get Rawly to move along. No, she could never speak to him about it. The what-if of yet another humiliation stood in the way.

She was so lost in her thoughts she wasn't paying attention and ran headfirst into a two-by-four sticking out of the back of Tyler's Mercantile. She fell backward and slid off the sidewalk. The alley behind the local business didn't have all that much traffic; only one person saw her mishap. Her settled-upon friend saw the whole thing as he was stocking the back room. Will speedily made his way to help her up.

"I have meant to fix that," he said as his hand went out to lift her up. "Are you okay?" She couldn't talk; she was too embarrassed. "Annabeth?" His hand lifted her face. A trickle of blood ooze from the gash on her forehead. "I better get you over to the doc's." He first led her into Tyler's back room and sat her on a stool. He grabbed a handkerchief from the stockroom and pressed it to her head.

"Too much on your mind today?" he asked. "You know that two-by-four has been there as long as the building has." He smiled at her with charm. She shook her head in self-disgrace. "That's probably going to need to be stitched. Can you walk, or do you want me to take you in the wagon?"

I don't want you to take me at all, she thought. "Well, it is obvious I can't walk, but I am afraid with my history, I may fall out of the wagon as well." She tried to smile, but it was weak. He took her elbow and escorted her to the doctor's office.

Hawk had caught a glimpse of the two from his office window. He met them at the door. "What happened this time?" He directed his stern tone toward Will.

"I butted heads with a two-by-four." Annabeth lifted her head, and the blood traveled into the corner of her eye.

Hawk put the handkerchief back over the wound. "Come in the treatment room. It is going to need a few stitches." Will helped her up on the table.

Avery and Piper had lain down for an afternoon nap. Hawk didn't want to wake them. "I hate to wake Avery. She usually helps me with instruments if I need them. Do you mind, Will, staying around and helping?" He looked to Will, certain the man would stay.

"Oh, please don't wake Avery. If Will has to go, I can wait until she wakes up."

Hawk shook his head. "Lay down."

Hawk instructed Will as to what he wanted him to do. In just a few minutes, Annabeth had six stitches in her forehead. The V-shaped wound was going to be an eyesore and would probably leave a scar right between her eyebrows.

"I will see you home, Annabeth," Will offered.

"If you don't mind"—she was speaking more to Hawk than to Will—"I would like to stay here for a little while and visit. If that is okay with you, Hawk."

"I am not exactly overrun with patients this afternoon. I would love to have you stay."

Will said his good-byes and went his way.

"What is bothering you, Annabeth?" Hawk motioned her into the kitchen, where he poured himself a cup of coffee. "Want some?" he asked as she took a seat at the table.

"Yes, please."

He poured and sat across from his cousin, taking a long sip of coffee. She played with the rim of her cup.

"Is there a medical reason why I am so clumsy?"

He knew this wasn't what was really bothering her. "No, there is not." Unless she wanted the excuse of top heavy, which Will seemed to think was her problem. He suspected Will was what was bothering her.

"Now that we have that settled, what is really bothering you? Will?"

She looked up. Was she that obvious? "Yes, Will, but—" She didn't finish. Avery had come through the door.

"Annabeth, how did you get that, and why didn't you wake me?" She turned to Hawk.

"I didn't need you." He rose and got another cup of coffee, kissing his wife as he sat the cup in front of her.

"Annabeth was just about to tell me why Will is bothering her." Annabeth was caught off guard. She thought Avery's arrival would delay the conversation if it were to happen at all.

"It doesn't take a physician to know why Will Stanton would bother a woman," Avery said most emphatically. Hawk gave his wife a most comical look.

"It is not what you are thinking. It isn't that way at all." Annabeth pleaded with the two whose looks were skeptical. "He is a friend. I am not sure Rawly understands. I am not sure I understand myself. Can a man and woman be just friends?" There was a knock at the door, and Hawk left.

"Of course they can, Annabeth. I know a lot of people don't believe that. I was one of them. Then I met Molly."

Annabeth wasn't understanding. "Do you know who is one of the closest friends Hawk has? Molly. They were friends before I met him. They have a bond that both Hud and I had to come to understand. There have been times I have sent him out to see Molly because I felt she and Hud could help him more than I could with something. It doesn't mean I am any less of a wife or woman in doing so. I think it means I understand my husband more than most."

Annabeth was taking it all in. She couldn't see Rawly letting her go to Will when it was something that involved the bakery. He would try to provide the answer within his own knowledge. "But, Annabeth"—Avery broke her train of thought—"if you think this triangle of you, Will, and Rawly involves a mere friendship, you are wrong."

Annabeth started to speak, and Avery threw her hand up. "Hear me out. Will Stanton's actions are more than a friendly gesture here and there. He overtly flirts with you in front of Rawly. Don't talk yourself into thinking that man wants to be your friend. Some men like the idea of being able to steal another man's girl. It is a challenge. A game. Now, I am not saying that is Will's motives, but it is obvious to a six- and seven-year-old that there is more there than what meets the eyes. If my sons see it, we all see it. The question is, do you see it?"

"What am I supposed to do? I have feelings for Rawly. We have been courting for several months. I know Will is playing with me. I think he is doing it to prod Rawly along. I am not exactly sure what to do about it."

"You don't do anything." Avery's answer surprised her. The look on her face had Avery smiling. "Enjoy the attention. Either Rawly will take the next step, or Will Stanton will shake you free from a relationship that isn't going anywhere. You don't have to do anything but be true to yourself."

Piper's tears ended Annabeth's conversation with Avery. Avery started to stand. "Let me go get her." Annabeth made her way to Piper's room. The dark-headed girl with hazel eyes smiled when she saw Annabeth. She lifted the tot out of her crib. The little girl snuggled in close, sucking her thumb. This is what she wanted: a home filled with children. She fought back a tear.

*****

Christmas was just a few days away, and Annabeth couldn't help being a bit sad. This would be another Christmas away from her parents. She was looking forward to spending the holidays with her uncle Thad. She had purchased a few gifts but wanted to make some fancy pastries for everyone to try. It was a big group, and she hoped to get some honest feedback on the creations. Trudy was letting her use her kitchen of an evening to experiment. Will and Dan were more than happy to sample the products.

"Girl, you're gonna make me so fat I won't be able to get around town." Dan Bullock grinned as he took another "one of those fancy little things."

"They are called petit fours." Annabeth smiled.

"Well, I have had more than four." They all laughed.

"These are excellent, Annabeth. The best I have ever eaten," Will said as he took another one. Her mind wandered on what occasion had he had such a delicacy. "I've lived a life before here, Annabeth. Don't look so surprised."

After she cleaned the kitchen, she went to her little home. She gathered in some extra wood. It was chilly, and the whipping wind made it even colder. Thrive was on her heels. He was allowed in Trudy's house but only in the back room. He would lay at the entryway into the kitchen and watch Annabeth work; he was a great source of companionship to her. She often asked who bestowed the dog on her, but Lydia Lapp would never tell.

A few days after Thanksgiving, a dog bed with Thrive's name carved on it was left at her front door. The bed had a straw mattress covered in red-and-black plaid flannel. It was adorable, and the dog napped there often. It was an early Christmas present from Will. She stoked the fire and readied for bed. She read her Bible and spent some time in prayer.

She had a peace about her life after talking to Avery. She was always trying to figure out what she should do. She was always worrying about what Rawly thought or what Will did. She felt relief in giving up the idea she had to respond. Annabeth had begun to do nothing, just be who she was to both men. She did, however, disagree with Avery that Will wanted to be more than a friend. She was confident in his own way he felt he was helping her in her relationship just as Vivian was, although Vivian seemed to be pushing her toward Will.

Thrive let out a giant yawn and cuddled up at the end of the bed. She dimmed the light and snuggled under the down quilts. She woke an hour later. The wind was lashing fiercely. The room was frightfully cold. She made her way into the kitchen where the fireplace still had the piece of wood, but the log had gotten wet. The wind had blown a chunk of snow down the chimney, causing the fire to go out. She lit the lamp and removed the wood. Grabbing another log, she tried to burn it. Just as she did another, bluster of wind blew another chunk of snow down, hitting her and Thrive in the face.

Will rarely got cold, but tonight was different. The wind outside had made the house harder to heat. One log usually got him through the night, but tonight he needed more. His feet were like ice. He threw another log on the fire and searched for his socks. In doing so, he noticed a light at Annabeth's. He peered out his window just in time to see the snow hit her in the face. The action elicited a quick response from him. In just a few seconds, he was fully dressed.

The knock on the door started Thrive barking. Annabeth peered out the window. Seeing Will rubbing his hands together and the wind nearly knocking his hat off, she opened the door. "What on earth! Get in here." She opened the door wider, and he stepped in.

"I see you are having issues with the fireplace. It's too cold for you to stay out here. Come into the main house."

She looked shocked, but her teeth were chattering too much to respond.

"Now, Annabeth," he said to spur her on. "Come on, Thrive." The dog obeyed Will better than he did Annabeth. Thrive stuck his nose outside and turned to look at Annabeth. She followed with her coat and blankets draped around her. Once inside, the three were very quiet. "Go sleep in my room," Will whispered. Annabeth shook her head no. "I said go sleep in my room. I just added more heat. Now go." He turned her and shoved her toward the stairs. "Thrive and I will sleep down here." The dog stayed at his feet.

The two were quite the pair. She couldn't argue with either. Trudy would have a fit if she knew Thrive had slept in a guestroom. She made her way to the first step and then turned to remove the blankets that were wrapped around her; she handed them to Will. "You may need these." Her hand brushed his as he took the blankets.

"Thank you, Will Stanton." She made her way up the stairs.

*****

Heavy snow had accompanied the blustery winds. No one was going anywhere for a few days. Dan and Will trudged through the snow to survey the town. Everyone was safe and sound in the confines of their homes. There were a few of the elderly in town who needed help with hauling in a supply of wood. A couple of families required a few food staples; but other than that, the town of Sheridan was weathering the storm.

Back at Trudy's, Annabeth looked out the window. Her heart was heavy. As much as she loved Dan and Trudy, she longed to be with Thad and Merry. It was vital for her to be with her family. Especially at Christmas. She couldn't hide her disappointment when the men returned, stating the small town was shut down. Annabeth poured the gentlemen some coffee and placed a plate of muffins on the table.

"Looks like we are going to be snowed in here for a little while. I sure am glad we house the town baker." Dan smiled as he slathered the honey butter on his muffin. Will was quiet as he watched Annabeth's face produce a weak smile. She was sad.

"Missing Old Reliable?" He wiggled his eyebrows at her.

"William Hodson Stanton, stop teasing that girl." Trudy stood behind Dan, her hands resting on his shoulders. "And stop calling him Old Reliable. That isn't very kind. Rawly is a perfectly good man," she added.

Will had a smirk on his face. He faced Dan. "If you were courting Annabeth, would you let a snowstorm like this stop you from seeing her?"

Annabeth wished she could crawl in a hole. She hated being discussed like this. "You have a point there, son." Dan patted Trudy's hand.

Annabeth went into the back room with Thrive. She had been teaching the dog tricks, and he was a fast learner. After putting Thrive through his paces, she gave him some much-needed attention. The dog sensed her sadness and laid his head on her lap. She didn't hear Will approach.

"If you bundle up real good and only take a few things, I think I can get you to Thad's." Her head went up.

"It's too bad out. The snow is so deep."

"I wouldn't have offered if I didn't think we could get there. I would like to leave now, so I won't be traveling in the dark when I return." She sat, just staring at him.

"Get a move on." He reached out his hand to help her up. "I can't ask Dan and Trudy to watch Thrive." The dog was looking from Will to Annabeth. "That dog is no problem. I already spoke with Dan. He will take care of him until I return. You are out of excuses. Either you want to go, or you don't." She shot up; and in mere minutes, she was ready to go.

It was a slow and cold ride on the back of Will's horse. Annabeth felt sorry for Will. At least, she had his back to block the wind from her face. He had instructed her to bury her face in the back of his coat and lean into him. It would keep her warmer. He also had draped a blanket over her legs before they took off. Why was he doing this for her, and why did she let him? It was risky. And the poor horse, to put him through this. "You okay back there?" She heard him say through the scarf around his face. She wrapped her arms around his stomach and gave a little squeeze. She thought she heard him chuckle. She loosened the grip around his midsection, and she heard him full out laugh. She head butted his back.

"Hey now," he said as he continued to laugh. It took double the time, but they finally made it to the Sheridans. Will gave a hearty knock on Thad Sheridan's door. It took a minute; and the door opened, letting in a swoosh of cold air and snow. "Special delivery," Will said. Standing behind, Annabeth he had a wide grin on his face.

"Get in here." Thad opened the door wider. The house once again was full. All the Sheridan boys came home for the Christmas holidays, except for the newlyweds; but they had sent gifts and a telegram detailing their happiness in Charleston. They hoped next year they would be able to make it home.

"Get those cold wet coats off and go stand by the fire." Merry was helping Annabeth off with her coat. Avery poured some coffee and handed it to the couple. "You two are crazy. I had a difficult time getting out here yesterday. I can't imagine what it was like after the wind last night." Jonah, who rarely spoke much, was looking at Will in disbelief.

"If it is one thing I can't stomach, it is a woman with a sad face. You should have seen her. Between her and Thrive, I am not sure who can look the most pitiful. I wasn't going to have that ruin my Christmas," Will spoke to the crowd.

For such an endearing gesture, he made it sound like such a chore. The women of the Sheridan household were offended on Annabeth's behalf. The men in the room comprehended his full meaning. They also knew it was a cover-up for "I love this woman, but I just haven't realized it yet."

"Find a seat somewhere and relax. I think Merry was going to make some ornaments with the children. I was about to beat Franklin in backgammon."

Franklin looked at his pa. He was the most competitive of his seven boys. "Not today." Franklin flew past the men into the front room, Gill following. Hud and Hawk were playing chess at the kitchen work table. Nora, nestled in her father's large arm, was sleeping soundly.

"I need to be heading back. I just came to drop Annabeth off." Will drained his coffee cup.

"Why doesn't he ever want to be with his wife?" Hunter whispered to his father but not quiet enough that Will or the other men didn't hear. Thankfully, Annabeth had gone into the larger dining area to help Merry and the others with the children.

"I don't know, Hunter. Why don't you ask him?" Dr. Sheridan had a shrewd look on his face.

The little boy marched right over and tugged on Will's shirt sleeve. "Can I have a word with you?"

Will was taken by surprise. The seven-year-old was approaching him like a grown-up. River had come to stand with his brother as if he were about to embark on some tedious job that needed reinforcements.

The men in the room were trying to hide their smiles. Will Stanton was about to be ambushed by a very cunning enemy. "Uh, sure."

The youngsters went into the boys' quarters and motioned for Will to follow. They wanted a private word with him. Hawk Sheridan was about to bust. He was trying so hard to keep from laughing.

"You should stop them," Hud commented to his brother.

"They need to hear it from him. Avery and I both have spoken to them about the relationship between those two. They still have their minds made up."

"What can I do for you, fellows?" Will started, but he was pushed to sit down on the bed. He was now eye level with the children. "Why don't you ever want to be where your wife is? You married her. You should be with her whenever you can," Hunter asked, and River just stared a hole through Will.

"Annabeth and I are friends. We are not married," he said direct and to the point.

"You live together." River commented.

"And you work together," Hunter added.

"We don't exactly live together, and it is true we work together, but that doesn't make us married." Will looked at the boys to gauge if they understood what he was saying.

"Our pa and ma work and live together. They are married, and don't try to tell me they ain't." River was defiant; and for a moment, Will contemplated whether or not he should continue or summon the boys' father.

"Besides, we see how you look at Annabeth. Just like Spotted Hawk and Swirling Wind look at each other and Night Wolf and Morning Dove," Hunter continued.

Will was confused. "Who?"

"No wonder you don't know you are married," Hunter lamented. "Spotted Hawk is our pa, and Night Wolf is our grandpa. Are you beginning to see the light?"

If Will had any sense, he would leave now. He had just been dressed down by children. "There is more to being married than just those things." Will noticed Hunter rolling his eyes.

"Yes, you have babies. We know."

Will's thoughts were tripping over themselves on how to proceed. "There has to be a ring and a ceremony first, and Annabeth and I haven't done that. Nor is it likely we will do so. Like I said, we are just friends. Now, Rawly Smith and Annabeth may have a ceremony and have rings but—"

They cut him off. "You would let Rawly Smith marry your wife? That's not right."

Will fell back on the bed. He didn't know how to continue.

"Where are the boys? Merry is ready to get started." Avery entered the work kitchen, looking at her husband. He pointed to the bedroom.

"They wanted a word with Will." He smiled at his wife.

She didn't look pleased, and she lowered her voice. "Is this about Will and Annabeth?"

Hawk shrugged his shoulders and moved the chess piece. "Hawk Sheridan, you know this has been an ongoing thing with the boys. Hard telling what they are putting him through. Go get them." Her hands were on her hips, and her husband wasn't about to move.

"We have both tried to tell them. They need to hear it from him and maybe even Annabeth."

"Hunter, River, get in here now!" Rarely did Avery yell. She was yelling for her boys, but she was yelling at her husband. Hawk was grinning.

Will was relieved to hear Avery summoned her boys.

"We will be watching you," River promised as they followed their mother's command.

Will flopped back on the bed. Annabeth had been taking up too much of his mental strength. He was walking a tightrope; he couldn't get out of Sheridan fast enough. Sadly, he had a few more months to go.

The door opened, and Dr. Sheridan's figure filled the opening. "Did you survive? Any wounds need to be treated?"

Will sat up. "You set me up. I won't forget it."

Hawk laughed. "You set yourself up, bringing her out here in a blizzard. If that isn't love, I don't know what is."

Will's head went from side to side. "A man and woman can be friends. I would do the same for any of my sisters."

"I agree, and I am sure you would, but Annabeth is neither, and my boys know it. If you want to change their mind, you better change your ways."

Will came out of the bedroom. "I need to be heading back to town. Thanks for the warm-up."

He made an effort to seek Merry out. "Oh, are you sure? We have room if you'd like to stay." Thad came from the other room.

"No, I promised Aunt Trudy I would be home for Christmas. She is counting on it."

"I don't think your coat and scarf are dry yet. It will be awfully cold with these wet garments." Merry was handling the wet wool fabric.

"I will be fine, Mrs. Sheridan."

"Here, take my coat, and we can switch when I bring Annabeth back to town." Thad held his coat in an outstretched hand toward Will.

"Thanks."

Annabeth came from the other room. "Here." She wrapped her scarf snugly around his neck. "Thank you, Will. Please be careful."

Out of the corner of his eye, he noticed Hunter and River watching.

"Will?" Annabeth had a puzzled look on her face.

He leaned in a bit. "While you are here, would you explain to Hawk's boys that we are not married or anywhere close?"

She turned to look at the two angels who had their arms crossed over their chest, staring powerfully. "Yes, of course," she promised.

The ride back to town was colder. It shouldn't be. The wind was to Will's back now. He pulled the scarf around his nose and face. Annabeth's scarf. It smelled like the bakery, cinnamon and sugar, and every warm and homey smell. It was her. He didn't need this type of distraction. He did need to change his behavior. Hawk was probably right. He needed to distance himself from flirting even if he could justify his motives as part of his cover in the case.

CHAPTER 7

*I*t was New Year's Eve, and there was an ever-present blanket of snow on the ground. The town of Sheridan didn't let that stop them. The Dowry seemed to be the place to congregate this morning as every table was full. Vivian, Annabeth, and Will could barely keep up. Annabeth was baking as fast as she could. She seemed to be running out of everything. She endured the whole thing with a smile on her face. This is what she wanted.

The only thing that wasn't making her happy was Will. Something had changed since their Christmas ride out to the Sheridans. He seemed to be keeping his distance. He wasn't his annoying self. It had only been a few days, but even Vivian noticed.

"What's gotten into you, Will Stanton? You haven't pulled one prank or made Annabeth blush one time since Christmas. Did you get coal in your stocking?"

He smiled, but it seemed a little strained. "I've been hard on Annabeth. I just thought I would give her and Old Reliable a break, quit picking on the lovebirds."

Vivian gave him a stare as if she didn't believe a word he said. Vivian was about to challenge him when she noticed he was not paying attention. Something at Tyler's Mercantile had caught his eye. She followed his gaze. It landed on a lovely female entering the store. "I'll be back in a minute," Will shot out the door, barely putting his coat on. She watched as he followed the woman into Tyler's.

"Annabeth, you have competition." Annabeth frowned.

"What are you talking about?" She brought a tray full of dirty dishes and sat them on the counter. Joining Vivian at the window, she saw nothing. "You missed her." Vivian peered closer to the window as if she could somehow see more than was there.

"Missed who?" Annabeth put the dishes in the sink and headed back to clear more tables.

"The woman who just made Will Stanton dart out of here like his shirt was on fire."

"Are you going to stand there all day or help me get this place cleaned up?" Annabeth was just as curious as Vivian, but she had work to do. The bakery came first. Will Stanton's shenanigans were not going to distract her. When he returned thirty minutes later, he looked guilty.

"Who is she?" Vivian made no attempt to be coy.

"What?" he asked, taking off his coat. "Don't try that with me. Who is the woman that made you leave us in a cloud of dust?"

"I thought it was someone I knew."

The look on his face told Annabeth he thought for an instance it was Christina. She kept quiet and willed Vivian to do the same. A useless task.

"But she wasn't. Did you find out who she is?" Will scratched his neck just under his chin. Annabeth never noticed him do it before, but it looked to be a nervous motion. He did it until she thought he'd break the skin. As if he was suddenly snapped back to reality, the old Will returned.

"Not only did I find out who she is, I am having supper with her tonight."

Annabeth was a little shocked. She hoped it didn't show. Vivian laughed. It showed.

"You are a fast worker. Are you going to tell us who she is?"

Will began cleaning the other tables. "Vivian, I never thought you were this nosy."

She put her hands on her hips. "Who is she?" She wasn't moving until she got her answer.

"She's Mr. Tyler's niece. She is visiting with him for a while. She is going to be staying at the boarding house." He looked at Annabeth.

This should be good. Now Annabeth has some competition, Vivian thought and for once didn't say it aloud.

Jayne Hanson was, to say the least, beautiful. Auburn hair that shined as if the sun were continuously bestowing its light upon it. Her brown eyes were set perfectly apart with a slender nose in between; her rosy lips popped against a creamy complexion. Her stature was flawless, just the right height and weight. Her curves were precisely where they were meant to be. If this wasn't enough, her voice had a perfect pitch and her speech a natural cadence. Annabeth couldn't help but stare from her spot in Trudy's kitchen. In her periphery, she could see Will Stanton staring as well.

Jayne Hanson was, to say the least, average looking. Her auburn hair had too much red in it; and to be honest, it was too perfect, almost like a wig Will saw at Tyler's. Her eyes held no spark, and she was pale looking. Will didn't mean to be taking a survey of her, but a man couldn't help it. She was too thin, and her voice to him seemed monotone. There was no excitement in her speech. In his opinion, there wasn't much to get excited about. Oh, she would have no trouble being courted while she was in Sheridan if that was why she was here, but it wouldn't be him. He laughed within himself. That's because she wouldn't have him.

*****

Mr. Tyler joined the Bullocks for supper. Jayne was the only guest, so they all ate in the dining room. Over fried chicken, Jayne Hanson relayed that she was traveling from the district of Alaska back east. Five years ago, her father, Mr. Tyler's brother, took his son and daughter to the territory in search of adventure in the wild north. Jayne always surmised her father wanted away from his in-laws. When his wife, Jayne's mother, died during childbirth along with the infant, they blamed her father.

Three years ago, Jayne married a surveyor from Europe. Eighteen months ago, her husband perished in a fishing accident along with her only brother. Her father, being overwrought with grief and a friend of the bottle, sent his only daughter packing, back to a better life.

"My goodness, child, you have been through a lot. How long are you staying here in Sheridan? I hope some time, at least enough to heal from all this tragedy. You know, Sheridan is just the place to do that for you. Well, you should stay at least until winter is over. You can stay right here. Isn't that right, Dan?" Trudy was in action. It was as if things had to be settled right this very minute. Dan just smiled and nodded at Mrs. Hanson.

As it turned out, Jayne was a delightful person. She was easy to talk to and pitched right in at Trudy's. She took some of the load off Annabeth, which gave her more time in the bakery. It also gave Jayne more time with Will. Just about every evening, the two could be found playing a game or discussing what was in the latest newspaper. When Rawly came for supper, Will barely acknowledged. He was too intent on making sure Jayne was not neglected.

Annabeth had been the object of play for Will and Rawly for so long she had gotten somewhat used to it. To have Jayne thrown in the mix gave Annabeth something to think about. Why did it bother her when Will and Jayne would sit for hours talking about everything under the sun? She knew Will was easy to talk to and could talk about anything. Her conversations with him offset the lack of depth when she and Rawly conversed. She decided she missed Will's friendship, and that was the extent.

*****

"What have you done to Will?" Vivian interrupted her thoughts.

"I haven't the slightest idea what you are talking about." Annabeth was truthful. She hadn't a notion as to what Vivian was driving at.

"He is awfully quiet here at work. It is like the wind has gone out of his sails. I got great enjoyment out of watching him distract you. Now it's as if you aren't even in the room. Something has changed him." Vivian began to place pastries on display platters. The bakery would be opening soon. Will had yet to arrive.

"Perhaps he is preoccupied with Jayne Hanson. They spend a lot of time together in the evenings after supper. She is a lovely person." Why did Annabeth feel like she had to justify the statement by sharing the admired attribute of Jayne?

"Does it bother you?" Vivian asked with a sheepish grin.

"Why would it bother me?"

The rolling of Vivian's eyes could almost be heard. "Because every female likes the kind of attention Will Stanton gives. When it is gone, there is a draft in its place. Don't tell me you don't feel cold."

Annabeth shook her head. "Vivian, you are too much. Mr. Stanton can flirt, court, or woo anyone he wants. It makes no difference to me. I will tell you this. I pity the woman who falls into that kind of trouble."

Annabeth turned to see the object of conversation standing in the kitchen. His arms crossed over his chest, leaning against the kitchen counter. If he hadn't heard the whole discussion, he heard Annabeth's declaration. He stared at Annabeth doing a lingering appraisal of her. He pushed himself away from the counter and came toward her. Standing in front of her, he bent very close to her face. They were nearly nose to nose. "Some women enjoy a little trouble," he whispered as his lips grazed her cheek on his way to open the bakery door.

"I reckon you feel that draft now, Annie." Vivian did one of her sashays as she walked by. "Willie boy, you're an ornery one."

*****

The snow was slowly melting a good sign that spring was on its way. With that came Patience's wedding. When Abby Lorton visited over Thanksgiving, she brought with her Patience's request that Annabeth make the wedding cake and delicacies for the ceremony. All winter long, Annabeth had been going through recipes. She wanted Patience's wedding to be perfect, but there was a problem: she had used all her unique recipes for her own wedding. She couldn't repeat the menu.

"What are you doing here so late? The bakery closed hours ago." Will entered The Dowry from the back door and found Annabeth sitting at one of the tables with papers everywhere.

"I'm working on finding just the right recipes for my sister's wedding."

He pulled out the chair across from her and sat down. Thumbing through the papers, he leaned back.

"All these and you can't come up with something?" She looked at the stack he was holding.

"Those are what I used for my wedding." She wrinkled her nose. "I don't want to jinx her wedding." He gave her a that's-nonsense look.

A rap on the door startled the two. Old Reliable stood peering through the glass. Will rose to unlock the door and let him in. Rawly's frown for Will still being at the bakery was the least of how he was feeling. He would like to kick Mr. Stanton right back where he came from except no one knew where he came from.

"The bakery is closed," Will said jokingly.

"Then why are you here?" Rawly snapped.

Will threw both hands up. "I'm just menu planning with Annabeth, that's all."

"Menu planning for what?" Rawly was beyond annoyed.

"You know, Patience's wedding," Annabeth supplied.

"Who?"

Who? Will thought. *You are supposed to be in love with her, and you don't know who Patience is?* Will mentally wanted to crush Rawly. He knew all to soon the blacksmith's true colors would come out. He just hoped Annabeth could survive it.

"My sister, silly, you remember?" Annabeth didn't seem as bothered by Rawly's lack of attention to detail as much as Will.

Rawly turned to Annabeth and schooled his features. "Yes, of course. I am sorry, Annabeth. I came by to see if you have received anything from the company in your hometown. The one with the fancy boxes."

Will stayed still and pretended to be looking at recipes. "No, I won't get anything for weeks." Her smile was warm and inviting.

He really hated what was about to happen to Annabeth's world. Those boxes would be the beginning and the end for Rawly Smith. The man left after getting the only information he cared about.

Annabeth sat back down and let out a sigh. "I should have just told my mother to hire someone else to do this."

"Why don't you use that French recipe book someone dropped at your door?" Will's suggestion made Annabeth think.

"Those recipes take practice and more hands than I have."

"So practice. I will help you. You know Trudy and Dan will eat whatever you fix."

"That is all well and good, but that will not help me in Charleston. There will be no one there free to help me."

"I will be there."

She had a disparaging look on her face. Before she could answer, he stopped her. "You will need someone to escort you home."

"I didn't need an escort out here." He raised his eyebrows. "Well, my father did see to it one of his business associates accompany me as far as he could."

"And how far was that?"

"Never mind. Whatever happened on the way out here, I don't need an escort back." Her words had an air of finality.

"Do you honestly think that overprotective uncle of yours or your persnickety mother is going to let you travel alone?"

Her eyes were wide. "My mother is not persnickety."

He shrugged her reprimand off. "Can you realistically see Thad letting you travel alone?"

"I will talk to him." Annabeth began rearranging her papers.

"No need. He thinks my accompanying you home is a good idea. It is planting season, and all the menfolk will be in the fields. I am expendable, you see, the perfect choice. Besides, I have some business to attend to in Charleston."

She was losing a battle she didn't even know she had. "I was in hopes you would be here to help Vivian keep the bakery open."

He heard the defeat in her voice. "Jayne will help her," he supplied.

"Jayne! Jayne—she doesn't know anything about the bakery."

"She will be starting Monday." Annabeth looked at him in disbelief.

"I can't pay her." There was an edge to her voice. His high-handedness had gotten her feathers ruffled.

"She knows that. She is doing it as a favor to me."

Annabeth rose and gathered her recipes. "Lock up when you leave *your* bakery."

It all happened without her input. She was angry every time Jayne stepped foot into The Dowry. It wasn't Jayne she was mad at. It was Will and Vivian and her Uncle Thad, who all seemed to agree Will had arranged things nicely. She didn't take it out on Jayne. No, Jayne was a very kind woman. Annabeth merely let Vivian and Will show Jayne the job responsibilities. Annabeth, however, was very curt with her two counterparts.

Rawly was the only one who seemed upset with the fact that Will was traveling with Annabeth. "I don't like him being the one to escort you." Rawly had taken Annabeth's arm and pulled her away from the well-wishers who flanked the two travelers.

"He is the reasonable choice if I am not to be allowed to travel by myself. That is the true travesty."

"I would go, but this is my busiest time of year. I need to be here to mend equipment." His hand was running up and down Annabeth's arm in what some might call a loving way. It plain annoyed Will. The stage driver called the *all aboard*, and Annabeth tripped right into Will's arms as she approached the door.

Will held on to her a little snugly, and he smiled at Rawly as he assisted her in the coach. Instead of sitting across from her as might be customary, he sat next to her. Rawly stomped off the depot platform. Will felt vindicated anytime he could make the crook angry.

*****

"You are not going to marry him." Will had stowed their belongings in the overhead compartment of the train and took his seat next to Annabeth.

Across the way, the woman' ears perked up. "I beg your pardon?" Annabeth had lowered her voice, hoping Will would do the same.

"Rawly—you are not going to marry him. I don't care who you marry, but it is not going to be him."

The lady not only had her ears perked but also leaned to hear more. So be it. Let them all hear. "What makes you think you have a say in who I marry?"

He plopped down beside her, putting his elbows on the armrest and interlocking his fingers.

"Has he even mentioned it?"

"As a matter of fact, he said when I returned, we should start thinking about the future."

Will laughed out loud; and turning to the woman casually trying to eavesdrop, he spoke, "Are all women this naive?" The woman looked stunned.

Annabeth leaned up in her seat to address the third party. "Are all men this obnoxious?" The woman grinned and shook her head no to both of them.

Annabeth lowered her voice to a whisper. "Just what am I naive about?"

"He doesn't love you, Annabeth. It is obvious. What kind of good-bye was that at the stage? It wasn't a sweetheart's good-bye. It wasn't even close."

"It was good enough for me." She rested her head back and closed her eyes. She could feel him staring at her.

"Oh, Annabeth, you deserve so much more." His voice was soft and tender. *Was he right?* Annabeth asked herself. "That's why you are not marrying him," Will added as if he was the final say.

The couple chose to travel nonstop. They had to change trains twice, and sleeping on the train was an experience. Annabeth had never slept sitting up, and it was most uncomfortable. It did not seem to bother Will. He was stretched out with his legs underneath the seat in front of him and his head on her shoulder. It was very inappropriate, but it was dark, and no one seemed to notice. She tried to nudge him to get him to move, but he just hunkered down. She got very little rest.

Annabeth practically jumped out of the train when she saw her father and mother standing on the platform. Jackson Lorton lifted his daughter off the ground. "Father, I have missed you so very much."

She kissed his cheek and then went to her mother. "You look so much better than when I last saw you, dear. I am so glad you could come home."

Abby's eyes narrowed a bit when she saw Will headed her way with Annabeth's valise.

"Mrs. Lorton." Will removed his hat, nodded, and replaced the hat.

Abby nodded in return. "Mr. Stanton, this my husband, Mr. Lorton."

"Please, call me Jackson." Will shook the man's hand.

"Call me Will."

"It was nice of you to escort our Annabeth home. We appreciate it. Do you have a place to stay while you are in town? You are welcome to stay with us. We have plenty of room."

Jackson was very cordial. It was obvious by the look on the women's faces he had not discussed this with his wife or daughter.

"I was just going to find a boarding house. It is what I am used to." He grinned at the women who were plastering smiles on angry faces.

"You can stay with us, right, dear?"

Jackson was giving his wife a hearty grin. "But of course, our home is your home, Mr. Stanton." Abby was all Southern charm.

"It's Will, ma'am."

Will did most of the talking on the ride out to Laurel. This was not surprising to Annabeth or Abby. Jackson conversed easily with him it was as if the females weren't present. TJ had found a friend in Will in just a few days. Would her father be the same?

When they arrived, the big talker was speechless—briefly. "This is one beautiful home," he said as he helped Annabeth out of the conveyance.

"I would like to move it to Sheridan among the Black Hills," Annabeth confessed as she took his outstretched hand for assistance.

"You look very tired, Annabeth. You should rest."

Abby was irritated. Who was he to help Annabeth out of the carriage and tell her she should rest? He wasn't her guardian. He was just supposed to make sure she got here safely and see to his own business until the trip back. But no, her husband had to invite him to stay. She would have a talk with Jackson as soon as they were alone. She didn't have to wait all that long as Annabeth confessed she was fatigued and wished to lie down. TJ insisted on giving their guest the grand tour of the house and grounds.

"A word with you, Jackson." Abby's stern demeanor tickled Jackson. He knew what lay ahead. He gladly followed his wife up the stairs to their private room.

"I told you what kind of man he was. Why on earth would you ask him to stay here?" She pointed to the floor below her. "How could you?"

He went and put his arms around his wife's waist. "I would like to get to know this man who has forced himself into my daughter's world. I can't very well do that from a distance, now can I?" He leaned in to kiss her, and she pulled back.

"Three weeks—he is going to be here three weeks. This could get ugly." He released her.

"Why are you so all fire sure he is a bad person?"

"I don't think he is a bad person. I just think he is not the person Annabeth needs in her life right now." Abby moved to put herself back in Jackson's arms. "At least here, I can keep an eye on him," she said in concession as she reached up to kiss her husband.

*****

TJ had told Will which room to put his things in and then meet him at the back of the house. Will had just unloaded his bags and walked down the long hallway when he overheard the Lortons talking about him. So he wasn't the person Annabeth needs in her life right now. Will wondered if the persnickety—yes, persnickety—Mrs. Lorton would say that if she knew what Will did. He was most certainly the right person Annabeth needed at this time.

"Who are you?" A lovely girl had caught Will by surprise.

"Who are you?" he asked, knowing full well this was Patience Lorton.

The petite brunette lifted her chin "You, sir, are in my home. I am not required to tell you who I am but rather demand an answer in knowing who you are."

"I, my dear lady of the house, am a figment of your imagination."

He turned and jaunted down the stairs.

Jackson and Abby exited the room and found Patience gazing at Will's back. "Who is that?" She turned to face her parents.

"That, dear one, is Will Stanton." Abby looked at her daughter. They both shared the same expression.

"The one who helps Anna with the bakery? That is not at all how I pictured him from her letters. He is somewhat on the brash side, don't you think?" Patience could be just as brash, Jackson mused as he watched his daughters' reaction. "I need to speak with Annabeth." Patience turned on her heels and headed in the other direction.

"You don't suppose he heard us talking. The door was nearly wide open." Abby looked at her husband.

He frowned. "I have a feeling he did. Men like that are always in the right place at the wrong time."

"Well, he already knows what I think of him. It probably wasn't a surprise."

Patience opened the door to her sister's room quietly. Annabeth was sitting at the window facing the grounds of Laurel. Will and TJ were standing near the carriage house talking intently. TJ was doing most of the talking, and Will looked to be hanging on to his every word.

"So that's Will." Patience had snuck up on her sister.

"Patience! You look wonderful." Annabeth grasped her sister's hand and pulled her to the bed. They plopped down, causing a whoosh of air to escape the feather mattress.

"Thank you. It is the look of love, or so I have been told. You, on the other hand, look like a woman in distress. You and I need to talk and talk now." *Good old Patience cuts right to the chase. Just like—* she stopped herself. She was not going to compare her sister to Will.

"Nonsense. I want to hear all about your wedding. How did Preston propose?"

"If I tell you all the romantic details, will you spill the beans about the handsome man in our courtyard?"

"There is nothing to tell."

Patience went to the window and looked at the "figment of her imagination."

"Could you at least make something up? That is too good not to have a story."

She grinned at her sister. "I will try to spin you a yarn, but you first."

Patience told in detail about the romantic walk down by the water in Charleston. The moonlight was just right, the setting perfect, and then the question. It was all fairy-tale style, just as hers and Jonathan's had been. She hoped Preston Middleton was of better character than Jonathan.

"We need to talk about the cuisine for the wedding and your cake. Will and I have been talking over some ideas."

Patience lay back on the bed, resting her hands under her head. "You and Will have been talking over ideas. Seems to me there is something to talk about."

"He helps me in the bakery, and he offered to help me with some fancy French recipes. They are complicated and take more than one person. I find we work well together in the kitchen." Annabeth tried to curtail what her sister may be surmising.

"And outside the kitchen, do you work well together?" She was fighting a smile.

"We are just friends, Patience, and that is the end of it."

"I will be the judge of that after I have watched the two of you. I can say my first meeting with him didn't go very well."

"You've met him?" Annabeth fidgeted a little bit.

"Yes, in the hall. I asked him who he was, and he answered by asking me who I was."

Annabeth's eyes slid shut. "Don't worry about it, Anna. Mother gave me an idea of what kind of man he was when she returned from seeing you in November. One thing she didn't say, nor did you, was how handsome he is. By far better looking than any of the Charleston men, Preston excluded, of course."

*****

Since the Depression was beginning to ease, the Lortons had retained a cook to assist Abby. The two had laid out a sumptuous meal for Annabeth's return. When the call for supper was given, the family made their way to the dining hall. Abby watched in awe as Will gave a single nod to TJ, prompting the young boy to seat his older sister. "Why, thank you, TJ. That is very sweet of you." Will seated Patience, and she gave him a smug look. Jackson seated his wife. The two shared a look. Never had their son made the gesture before.

"I thought Mr. Middleton would be joining us tonight," Will spoke to Patience, who sat directly across from him. *Joining us—my, but he has the nerve.* Both Abby's and Patience's thoughts were running in the same vein. "He will be here later. He had a meeting."

"And what is it that Prince Charming does for a living? No, wait let me guess."

Annabeth was cringing inside. Why do his manners always seem so abrasive? Patience put down her fork and raised one eyebrow. Will smiled. "Lawyer?" Patience's eyebrow remained raised. "Banker? Businessman?"

"He happens to be a combination of all three. He works in the front office of the railroad company."

Will simply nodded and continued eating.

"And what is your trade, Mr. Stanton?" Patience had a proud smile on her face.

"I split my time between a bakery and mercantile." His eyes locked with hers.

"I meant when you are back home, and where is back home exactly?" Everyone at the table just sat there. Jackson should probably stop Patience from interrogating their guest, but she was saving him time, so he let it continue.

"Back home is wherever I was last."

TJ snickered. He liked Will Stanton. He was keeping his annoying older sister on her toes. "I consider each place I currently am home for the time I am there."

Annabeth wanted to stop the conversation, but she realized how little she knew about the man practically running her bakery.

"And you go from town to town just working here and there? No real direction or goals?"

"Oh, I have goals and direction." Will put a forkful of savory meat in his mouth.

"May I ask what some of them are? I am genuinely a curious person. Please forgive me." She was using her Southern charm.

"You forget Miss Patience I am not from the South, so the cunning way in which you wish to get information has no effect on me. But out of respect for your mother, who appears to have the same concerns, I will share my main goal. I aspire to become a full partner in The Dowry."

Both Abby and Patience were stunned and mortified. Will almost couldn't keep a straight face.

"He is teasing, Mother." Annabeth attempted to quell the emotion playing on her mother's and sister's faces. "He tells me that all the time. It is a running joke between him and Vivian." She looked to Will, and he had a very mischievous grin on his face.

"I'm teasing," he said as he nudged TJ. "I think I took it too far, TJ." The boy was trying to contain his mirth.

"You took it too far," Jackson stated with neither censure nor delight.

Abby looked a little miffed, and Patience looked downright mad. "I don't care for you, Mr. Stanton," Patience said with finality.

"That doesn't bother me in the least, Miss Patience." He winked as he raised his glass to take a drink.

The meal was eaten in relative silence. With small talk here and there. Annabeth was relieved when her father scooted back his chair and thanked Abby for the meal. He rose to give his regards to Gretchen as well. Will and TJ immediately stood and began clearing the table. This happened all the time at the Sheridans, but to happen here was something different. The two helped Gretchen with the clean-up, and Will suggested the women go in the salon and have a long discussion about his poor manners.

"You are not making friends, Mr. Stanton," Abby said as she walked past him.

"I know, ma'am, but you didn't like me to begin with."

She stared at him for a moment. Handsome and full of himself, he was a drifter who left chaos in his wake—she looked again—and many broken hearts.

The next morning after breakfast, Will and Annabeth headed into Charleston to procure needed supplies for the upcoming wedding. They also planned to visit Thomas as he was referred to in Charleston and Josie. Traveling down the main boulevard, Annabeth spotted Sadler's. "I would like to go in and introduce myself. Do you mind?"

This was exactly what Will was looking for. He wanted a reason to be in the shipping store without causing suspicion. He escorted her across the street. The store wasn't a massive operation, but it was busy enough. Will took inventory. He spotted two men in the back packing up supplies. It looked innocent enough. One of the men turned to see Will staring. Thankfully, it was someone he knew from the agency. They had placed someone undercover in the store. When everything was lined up, the whole ring would be busted. It would be Will's word that set the plan in motion.

"When will you begin shipping to Sheridan again?" Annabeth asked the man behind the counter. She had yet to receive any catalog or complimentary item that was their signature start to a new season.

"It probably won't be for another four weeks or so. I can send you a telegram if you wish."

She didn't have time to respond. Will did it for her. "That would be appreciated."

The man looked from Will to Annabeth. "Yes, thank you, Mr. Sadler."

"Annabeth." When she heard her name, her eyes slid shut; and her facial expression turned grim. "I would recognize that voice anywhere." A man was approaching from the side. A tall blond man with green eyes and wire-rim glasses. Will knew by Annabeth's posture Jonathan Taylor stood before them.

"Jonathan, it's good to see you. How are you?"

"I am well. It is wonderful to see you. I heard you had been ill. You would never know. You look as lovely as ever."

"Will Stanton."

Will stuck his hand out toward Jonathan. Jonathan grasped the offered hand.

"How is Lillian?" Annabeth asked as was proper etiquette.

"I don't know. You see, she never married me."

"Oh." Annabeth couldn't hide her shock.

"Well, you reap what you sow," Will said as he put his arm around Annabeth's waist. "I personally can't thank you enough for sending Annabeth my way."

Annabeth remained speechless. Jonathan's eyes never left hers, and Will's words were ringing in her head. She mentally shut down.

"Good day, Annabeth, Mr. Stanton," Jonathan said as he left the store, turning back briefly to look at Annabeth.

*****

After finding all ingredients for Patience's wedding feast, Will and Annabeth ate lunch with Tommy and Josie. They were doing well. Tommy had taken a position at the bank, and Josie was expecting their first child late summer. Annabeth was sworn to secrecy. The couple had not written the news to anyone. They wanted to wait a few more weeks. The visit ended much too soon as Tommy had to return to the bank. The group said their good-byes, promising to see each other again at the wedding.

Will sent Annabeth home. He had business in Charleston. "I won't be home for supper tonight. Please give my apologies to your mother and Gretchen." With that, he turned and went down a side street.

Annabeth wondered what kind of business he could have in Charleston. She didn't think about it very long. Her mind went back to the meeting with Jonathan. He and Lillian hadn't married. Why? And what did Will say? She appreciated his gesture of softening the humiliating situation she found herself in, but she wished he hadn't. It was all false pretenses, and it wasn't fair to her.

She found herself in front of Madame Norma's dress shop. She needed to get her dress fitting completed. She might as well do it now. The doorbell echoed over her head. It sounded loud in the quiet store. Norma appeared from the back. "Miss Anna, are you here to get your dress fitted for your sister's wedding?"

"Yes, ma'am, if you have time. If not, I can make an appointment and come back."

"Nonsense. I have time. Come to the back."

Annabeth followed the woman. Each step reminded her of a happier time over a year ago when she entered Norma's to have her own wedding dress fitted. There was an emptiness in her soul she thought she had filled. Seeing Jonathon today brought back everything.

"I think I will have to take this dress in. I used your measurements on file, but that was a year ago." Madame pulled on the fabric at the waist. "Your mother said you have been ill. Are you feeling better, dear?"

"Yes, ma'am, I am, thank you."

"Such a shame, that beautiful wedding dress, and such a tragedy. What did you do with the dress? If you don't mind me asking." She did mind the woman asking, but she couldn't say so.

"I am not sure. I left it for my mother to take care of. She may still have it somewhere. Would you like to have it back?"

"Oh, no, dear, you keep it. Now, turn around and see what you think of this dress Patience picked out for you. She has such a keen eye for these things." Annabeth looked at her reflection in the full-length mirror. The dress was an exquisite color. It looked like shimmering champagne Annabeth saw once at a friend's wedding. Her family was teetotalers. The dress had straight lines and a delicate neckline. The garment was beautiful. The woman wearing the apparel felt she didn't do it justice.

*****

"Where is Mr. Stanton this evening?" Patience asked as the family sat down to dine. "He had business in town and said he wouldn't be with us this evening."

Patience frowned. "What business can you have after five in the evening?" She looked to her fiancé and father for confirmation.

"Some people hold business dinners, Patience," Jackson answered his inquisitive daughter.

"Yes, but they rarely take place on Friday evening. They are usually reserved for the weekdays."

"His business is none of our business, Patience." This came from TJ, who seemed to have become Will's champion.

The moon was full and extremely bright. It lit up Laurel in grandeur. Will was walking up the path to the front door when he passed Preston leaving. "Good evening, Mr. Stanton. We missed you at dinner."

"Good evening, Mr. Middleton. I missed being here." Will smiled.

When he slipped in the door, Patience was just turning down the lights. "Your parents don't set a curfew? It is awfully late."

"My parents trust me implicitly."

Will turned to look at the closed door. "Do they trust Prince Charming?"

"Completely." Her tone was laced with pride. "No business dealings last this late into the night unless they are unsavory," she added, looking down her nose at their guest.

"Correct, Miss Patience, but not all of my day was spent in business affairs. I have an acquaintance here in Charleston." He started to move past her when a noise outside caught their attention.

Patience went to open the door, but Will stopped her. He got in front of her and quietly opened the door. Scanning the yard, he saw Jonathan throwing pebbles at the upstairs window he knew to be Annabeth's. Patience gasped. She had followed Will out.

"That's Jonathan, and he is—" She tried to push past Will, but he stopped her with his hand. Putting his finger to his lips, he motioned for her to be quiet. The two moved around to the corner of the porch behind the magnolia bush. They heard Annabeth's window open.

"Jonathan, what are you doing?" From where he was standing, Will could see Annabeth bathed in the moonlight. She looked stunning. Jonathan was at a loss for words. "Jonathan," she whispered again, "what do you want?"

Will knew exactly what Jonathan wanted. He wanted her, and that was not going to happen.

"I want to speak with you. I need to explain." His throat was dry.

"I would love to hear what he has to say," Patience whispered from behind Will. "The scoundrel," she added.

"There's nothing to explain. It is all water under the bridge." Annabeth started to close the window.

Jonathan motioned for her. "Yes, and you're all wet. Jonathan Taylor," Patience's whisper got a little louder.

Will turned and gave her a stern look. If they were discovered, it could be disastrous. She put her hand over her mouth. About that time, Annabeth appeared on the porch. Her dressing gown wrapped tightly around her.

Jonathan sat on the lowest step and patted the seat next to him. "She won't do it," more whispering. This time, she was so close to Will it made him uncomfortable. He could just see Jackson Lorton appearing out of nowhere to find one daughter in the bushes with a man and the other on the front step kissing another. Wait, what? Yes, right there in front of his eyes was Annabeth and Jonathan kissing. He felt Patience move, and he grabbed her around the waist.

"Don't do it," Will admonished Patience. He wanted to break them up as badly as she did, but it wasn't the right thing to do. Patience took hold of Will's hand and dragged him to the back entrance. "If I can't put an end to it, I certainly am not going to watch it." Will nodded his head in agreement. "I will talk to her in the morning," she added.

"Please don't, Patience. It might make things more difficult for her. If she wants you to know, she will tell you."

"You are infuriating. Do you know that?" She stomped in the house and nearly flew up the stairs.

Will hadn't found time to eat supper in town. He had met with a few of the men from Pinkertons to get a better idea of who in Charleston was part of the corruption. He found now he was starving. It was either that or anxiety over what was happening on the front porch. He made his way to the kitchen, sure he could scrounge something up. He was shocked to find TJ leaning against the counter, drinking a glass of water.

"Couldn't sleep?" Will asked the young man. TJ shrugged his shoulders. "I often have trouble sleeping. I thought I would come down and read for a while. Sometimes it helps."

"I guess for me that would depend on the book. I have had books that I couldn't put down."

Will opened the icebox. "Hungry?" He looked toward TJ. He had an inkling the boy had something on his mind. Will pulled out some cold pork and looked around. "Don't tell me there is none of Annabeth's bread around here." TJ went to the bread box and pulled out a half loaf. "Slice," Will commanded, and TJ did as he was told.

"So what's really keeping you up nights, a girl?"

TJ laughed. "No, not that."

Will forked some of the pork onto the thick slice of bread. Reaching for the cherry preserves on the counter, he slathered it on the pork. TJ turned up his nose. "Don't discount it until you try it." He fixed another sandwich and shoved it the boy's way. "If you don't like it, I will eat it." Will took a big bite out of his and smiled while he chewed. TJ took a small bite. To his astonishment, it was tasty; and he took a larger bite. Will poured a couple glasses of milk.

"So are you going to tell me what's bothering you?" TJ wasn't sure if he could share, but he was tired of keeping everything in. First, Annabeth was getting married, then all that hullabaloo, followed by Patience's grand engagement and wedding preparation TJ was left by the wayside.

"I guess you would say it's school trouble." Will stayed quiet and let the boy continue. His eyes remained on the young man playing with his glass of milk. "Would you believe my teacher actually ask me *not* to participate in class as to give the other students the opportunity to catch up? Even when no one answers, she tells them to find the answer and return the next day with it. I know the answers, but she doesn't want me to say. When I do ask her a question, she will tell me she doesn't know the answer. She directs me to speak with my father."

"What kind of questions are you asking her?" Will fixed himself and TJ another sandwich.

"Science mostly. I've read every book in our library, and I just have a lot of questions. I would like to go to a boys' school in Washington DC to learn more than the school here. Lachlan Kennedy suggested it to me when we visited over Thanksgiving. Do you know Lach?"

"Yes, a little. I heard he was a professor at the college here. Have you mentioned it to your parents?"

"They talked about it and said no." The boy looked truly dejected.

"Did they give you a reason?"

TJ sighed. "My mother didn't want me to go."

"That really isn't a reason, but I understand why a mother wouldn't want her son to go away to school." TJ looked at Will, and there was something more in his eyes.

"She always refers to me as her melancholy child. To be honest, sometimes I don't want to live." It cost the boy to admit his feelings. He started to leave the kitchen.

"Hold on, TJ. We need to talk a little bit more." The young man stopped, and Will put his hands on TJ's shoulders, leading him to the table. The two sat.

"I assume you know what *melancholy* means."

"Yes, and it is true. I am sad most of the time for no reason. But it was the word used to describe my aunt Jenny. She was eighteen when she died, and I get the feeling she had some sort of mental frailty that caused her demise. No one really said what the cause of death was. I know her dying crushed my father. They were very close. She and my mother were best friends. All they say is she was very melancholy. It makes me wonder if something runs in the family."

The young man was looking to Will for answers—answers that should be coming from his parents. Will supposed having two debutante daughters would cause one's time and energy to be consumed. It would be easy to assume TJ was doing well because of his demeanor.

"Have you ever considered talking to your folks about the way you are feeling?"

"They have so much going on with the girls I would feel silly going to them with such trivial emotions."

Will just looked at TJ. Then it hit him. He knew what TJ's problem was. "I think I can help you, TJ, but you need to trust me to talk to your parents on your behalf." The boy looked uncertain.

"You, son, are much more intelligent than your surroundings. You're bored. Why, there isn't enough around here to keep you on your toes. That is why I think you are so melancholy if you are, in fact, melancholy." TJ looked astonished. "You think on it. Pray on it. And let me know in the next day or two if you want me to talk to your folks. It has to be your decision. Meanwhile, let's eat this cake your sister made today and almost threw it out because it wasn't perfect."

Annabeth was listening at the door. What could be going on with TJ that he would need an intercessor, especially one such as Will? She was glad Will suggested her brother pray about whatever it was. When she heard the two laughing, she entered the kitchen.

"What are you two doing?" They looked like six-year-olds who just got caught with their hands in the cookie jar.

"What are you doing?" Will asked. Annabeth was confident she was the one who looked as if she had been caught. Did he know? The look on his face told her he knew something. Those eyes held so much mischief.

"I think I will be able to sleep now, Will, thank you."

"Anytime." As TJ passed his sister, he gave her a hug and a kiss good night. This behavior was very much against her brother's nature.

When he left, she looked at Will. "What is going on with TJ? Is he all right?"

"He is fine." Will pulled out a chair for Annabeth.

"There is some mighty fine cake here. Can I cut you a piece? A glass of milk perhaps."

"I hope it tastes better than it looked."

He cut her a slice and poured her a glass of milk. "You are too hard on yourself, Annabeth. There was not one thing wrong with that cake. At this rate, nothing is going to be good enough for the wedding." He watched her closely as she ate.

"This is wonderful," she said of the bite she just put into her mouth.

"Yes, it is." Somehow, by the way he said it, she didn't think he was talking about the cake. She couldn't stop the blush creeping up her neck, and he couldn't keep the knowing smile off his face. "Pleasant dreams, Annabeth," he said as he kissed the top of her head and left the kitchen.

*****

The next morning after breakfast, TJ cornered Will in the foyer. "You can talk to them. I would appreciate it. It doesn't have to be today, whenever you have time."

Will patted the youngster on the back. "Have a good day at school and remember what I told you." TJ left with a smile on his face.

"What did you tell him?" Patience was standing next to Will. He twisted his head a little bit and frowned.

"Not everything concerns you."

"Nor you," she answered back quickly. They had a little staring contest.

"I waited until well after midnight for Annabeth to come to bed. I must have fallen asleep. I peeked in this morning, and she is sound asleep, all curled up with a smile on her face. It makes me ill to think that that worm has gotten his toe in the door. What are we going to do about it?"

Will looked at her again strangely. "I am not going to do anything about it. Annabeth knows her own mind. She is sensible. You better leave it alone, Patience."

She frowned at their visitor. "You seemed rather bothered by it last night. I saw your face."

"You saw nothing." He started to walk away, but he saw Abby standing on the stairs watching him and Patience going toe to toe. Her look told Will she misunderstood.

"What seemed to bother you last night, Mr. Stanton?" This whole family was a mess, he deduced. Everyone listened in on everyone's conversations. For such a big house, the world inside was awfully small. Jackson now joined his wife. This was perfect timing.

"Do you two have a minute?" Will asked his host.

"It seems to me this may take more than a minute." Abby glanced at Will with a woodshed look on her face.

"I have all the time you need," Jackson answered and pointed to his study. Will headed that way. Patience tugged on his shirt sleeve. In low tones, she spoke, "What are you doing? You can't speak to them until you talk to Annabeth."

He removed her hand from his sleeve like he was removing a beetle inching its way up his arm. "Will you leave me alone?" His voice too was quiet but full of anger. "And stay out of it," he added.

Mr. and Mrs. Lorton was not pleased. Once in the study, Abby sat in the straight-back chair. Jackson was perched on the edge of his desk. "What was that all about?" Abby began the conversation.

"That…was nothing, honestly." She gave him an I-don't-believe-a-word-you-are-saying look. "And that is not why I want to speak with you. This is about your son." Abby's eyes flashed to Jackson.

"Our son? What about him?"

For the next hour, Will relayed all of TJ's fears and disappointments. "I believe your son is more intelligent than anyone realizes. His teacher more or less told him he has surpassed her. Higher and a more robust education will do wonders for him."

Tears streamed down Abby's face. "All those years, I called him my melancholy child. I had no idea he equated that with Jenny." She shook her head and covered her face.

Jackson had a stunned look on his. He tried to spend as much time with his son as he could. Now it seemed as if Jackson didn't know him at all. He went to stand beside his wife. Placing his hand on her shoulder, Jackson thanked Will. Turning to Abby, he suggested they go get their son and begin opening his world.

As they passed, Abby placed her hand on Will's. "this doesn't answer our questions about your conversation with Patience, but I will take your word for it that it was nothing."

"It was nothing, ma'am, I promise."

She smiled and patted his arm. "Thank you, Mr. Stanton."

"Will." His hand covered hers.

"What happened? What did you say? Were they upset? Are they going to confront Jonathan? You really should have spoken to Annabeth first."

Will was walking too many tightropes. Things didn't seem to be this complicated back in Sheridan; but then again, Patience Lorton wasn't in Sheridan to muddy everything up.

"Talk to me first about what?" Annabeth's eyes were on Will.

Will turned to Patience. "She's all yours." He made a sweeping gesture Annabeth's way. "I haven't said a word to anyone," he spoke to Patience first then turned toward Annabeth. "Remember that I haven't said a word to anyone." His words were cryptic, and she watched Patience and him exchange a strange glance.

Patience frowned. "Oh, never mind, it doesn't matter now. Come and help me in the parlor. I have wedding things to attend to." She grabbed Annabeth's arm and nearly dragged her into the other room.

That evening his sisters had never seen TJ so happy. He talked nonstop with his parents about possible school options for the next term. His lively spirit was far from melancholy. This was Will's doing, Annabeth thought, and she loved him for it.

CHAPTER 8

*A*bby and Annabeth spent the morning doing some last-minute errands for the wedding. It was just a few days away, and they still had a list of things to get done. They returned home midafternoon. From the entrance hall, they could hear the piano melody of Beethoven's "Moonlight Sonata."

"Patience has really gotten good." Annabeth headed toward the salon that held the grand piano. "Yes, she must be practicing when I am away. Let's just sit out here and listen. I don't want to disturb her." The two ladies sat with their eyes closed as the music switched from one piece to the next. Vivaldi's "Spring" followed by Strauss's "Blue Danube Waltz." When the first notes of Pachelbel's Canon in D began, tears streamed down Abby's face. It was her sister-in-law Jenny's favorite.

"Who is playing such beautiful music?" Patience's voice startled the two lost in the soothing music.

"We thought it was you."

Patience let out a snort. "I could never play that well."

When the door cracked, open Will's head went up. He had been caught. The three women came swiftly toward the piano. He changed the melody to Mozart's fast-paced "Rondo Alla Turca" ("The Turkish March"). It was fitting for the way they came toward him. "That's not funny." Annabeth smiled.

"You should see the three of you headed this way. The tune was most proper."

"You play extremely well, Will, very accomplished." Will could hear a hint of sadness in Abby's voice.

"You are playing for my wedding," Patience said decidedly.

"I am?" Will went back to playing.

"Preston and I have not been able to come to an agreement on music. I am sure we can agree on you. I am assuming you know Mendelssohn's 'Wedding March.'"

Will took on a contemplative look as if he wasn't sure. Then he played the tune as if he was playing it in a local saloon. Abby and Annabeth snickered. Patience turned to leave. "I still don't like you, Will Stanton, but you will play at my wedding."

Abby followed her daughter. "Play anytime you wish, Will. I've never heard more beautiful music."

Will scooted over a bit and motioned for Annabeth to join him. He continued to play. Some of the songs Annabeth had never heard. "Your mother looked as if she had been crying."

"She was. Canon in D was my aunt Jenny's favorite."

"I will be careful not to play it at the wedding." He didn't want to make anyone sad on such a happy occasion.

"I think you should ask her and my father. They may want you to play the song in remembrance." They sat in silence for a few seconds. Annabeth was caught up in a memory.

"Were you close to your aunt?"

"Oh no, she passed on before my parents were married. She actually brought them together."

"How so?" It amazed Annabeth how he could play and look at her at the same time. Whenever she played, she had to concentrate on the music. Will had no music in front of him.

"Aunt Jenny and my mother were best friends. They were in school together. My aunt had just turned eighteen when she fell ill. She developed pneumonia, and it weakened her lungs. She became very despondent and never recovered. My mother was by her side nearly every day, helping my grandmother take care of her. It was during that time my father got to know my mother. When Jenny died, they were a great comfort to each other. My father said when he lost Jenny, he knew he couldn't lose my mother. She was just as much a part of him."

"A love he could thrive on. They are blessed" Will winked at her.

"Very. I hope Patience and Preston have that kind of love."

*****

Annabeth lay quietly in her bed. The sun had just broken through the sky. Today was Patience's wedding day. Undoubtedly, the day would start perfectly and end perfectly. There would be no chance of this wedding convening the way Annabeth's had over a year ago. She couldn't help but feel a little—what was the right word? She was happy for her sister; but deep in the recesses of her heart, there was an emotion she couldn't describe.

Jonathan's arrival the other night took her by surprise. He came to apologize for the hurt he had caused and to confess he hadn't stopped thinking about her. He said he felt fate had stepped in and stopped his marriage to Lilly. Perhaps they were meant to be together. Then he kissed her, and she allowed him to do so more than once. She reprimanded herself for allowing not only Jonathan to kiss her but Rawly as well. She was unsure of her feelings. To yield to their kisses wasn't helping her plight. It was like she was an orphan, not looking for parents but looking for that one heart where only she was the reason it thrived. What a mess she was making of things. Where had she gotten off track?

"Hey in there. Are you going to sleep the day away? We have a lot of work to do." Will's voice accompanied the loud rap on the door.

"When I get down to that kitchen, you better have the coffee and an apron on," Annabeth responded as she threw back the covers. She heard his hearty laugh as he retreated down the hall. He was right. They had a lot of work ahead of them.

Abby watched as Annabeth and Will worked like a well-oiled machine. Their mechanics precise, their timing impeccable, and it was all done with laughter and smiles. As much as Will Stanton promised he was not out to hurt her daughter, it was evident he could. "Everything looks beautiful, Annabeth. Patience will be so pleased." Abby kissed her eldest on the cheek. She knew how hard this was for her daughter.

*****

From his seat on the piano bench, Will had a bird's-eye view of the whole event. He had a list of songs Patience wished to be played to which he did flawlessly. When Annabeth came into view, Will was mesmerized. Never had he seen anything as lovely as her. She stood just outside the entryway, smoothing her shimmering gown. When she lifted her head, it was as if Will's breath left him. Whatever he was playing transitioned into the first movements of Beethoven's "Fur Elise."

Annabeth glided to the front on the melody of the love song. If there was one thing Will knew at that moment, it was that he didn't want to live if Annabeth wasn't in his life. He loved her. When she reached her stopping point, she smiled sweetly at him and turned to face the bride.

On cue, Will's hands began the familiar wedding march; but his mind was engaged on the revelation before him. "Fur Elise," if he remembered correctly, was composed by a man who was in love with a woman who wasn't in love with him. The melody fit his feeling, but the end result very well could be the same.

The wedding went off without a hitch, and the cake was perfection in appearance and taste. The accompanying food pleased those gathered immensely. Will insisted Annabeth enjoy the evening while he and Gretchen took care of the guests. She surprisingly agreed and disappeared into the crowd. When he could, Will watched her intently.

The customary thing at weddings was to have a dance. Patience was anything but customary. She merely wanted to visit with the guests without the tiring ritual of dance. Too bad for Will, he would have loved nothing more than to hold Annabeth in his arms, gazing into those mystical blue eyes. Just as he wished to be holding her, he noticed several other gentlemen who could possibly be feeling the same way.

He watched as one by one the men made their way to Annabeth, kissing her hand or laying their hand on her forearm. *Go ahead and try,* Will thought. *That one is mine.* Just then, she turned to face him; and he realized she was not his or likely to be after all the mess in Sheridan was over. He smiled and turned his gaze to her parents. They certainly wouldn't allow it even though he found a little grace in regard to TJ. Patience certainly wouldn't have it.

"Well done, Mr. Stanton." Preston stood at the table, getting a glass of punch. Patience was standing next to her husband.

"Especially Annabeth's entrance, that wasn't what we decide on, but it seemed to fit your mood." She raised a questioning brow.

"I don't know what came over me," Will said in a dismissive tone.

"Don't worry, we all know what came over you." Preston grinned as he escorted Patience away from the fray and back into the thick of things.

If Hunter and River Sheridan could pick up on the emotion, why would he be surprised if all of Charleston could see it? Did Annabeth see it? She wasn't acting like it. One thing he honestly liked about the little miss was the fact that whether here or in Sheridan she was the same. There was no facade in either place. The genuine good nature of Annabeth Lorton was ever present.

The well-wishers stayed until late in the evening. It was after eleven when Preston and Patience were sent on their merry way. The pair had stars in their eyes and smiles on their faces. They would stay the night at the Pavilion Hotel and leave for the coast of Maine the following day. Everyone said their good-byes to the couple with promises of meeting for brunch before their departure. Patience held tight to her sister. She knew Annabeth well enough to know her sister was happy for her but carried a painful loneliness. Rawly, Jonathan, and now Will were destined to cause her sister much turmoil. In its own way, it dampened Patience's happiness.

Will couldn't sleep. Every time his eyes closed, there was Annabeth. What was he going to do? His future was not going to be pleasant. When Annabeth finds out her pride and joy was the front for laundering stolen merchandise, she will be devastated, not to mention Rawly Smith using her in the process. And what about him, using her in a different way? When it is all said and done, will he have a chance? And what about Jonathan? What if she decides to stay and work things out with him? He couldn't take it anymore. He had to have a plan. He headed back to the salon where the wedding had taken place.

Will sat at the secretary in the corner of the room and pulled out a sheet of stationery and a pen. He looked around the place that remained decorated. His eyes went to the piano, and he once again saw Annabeth making her way down the aisle. He began to write:

Dearest Annabeth,

> Tonight, April 10, 1898, I realized I have fallen in love with you. If you are reading this, it means you have found out about what has been going on at The Dowry almost from its infancy. You are now aware that Rawly Smith was a cunning and evil man and is getting what he deserves. You also, at this time, are probably pretty angry with me. Please understand I did not mean to withhold information from you. I only meant to protect you and complete the job I was sent to do. In the course of all that, I met the one woman who caused me to thrive as a man. I know the real risk of losing you. I am writing this letter tonight as proof that I am honorable and trustworthy. This letter that will be mailed to your uncle Thad will be my only saving grace. Whatever happens between us will be your choice.

> All my love,
> Will

Will sat for a moment and allowed the ink to dry. It was a gamble, but he knew he needed insurance. He hoped it worked. Will folded up the letter and put it in an envelope. He would write a short note to Thad explaining he wanted him to hold the letter until the operation was all said and done. Will put the envelope in his shirt pocket. When he turned, he saw Annabeth enter. She didn't see him at first. When she noticed, she turned to go.

"Don't go, Annabeth." He was making his way to her.

"I'm sorry. I didn't know anyone was in here." She sounded doleful.

"No, I will go. You came in here for a reason." His words were soft and gentle. When he was about to pass her, his hand reached out and touched her cheek. Her eyes were lonesome. Cupping her face in his strong hands, he kissed her. Then he kissed her again and again, his hand sliding through her thick soft hair. She barely moved, but her lips moved in motion with his.

Jackson Lorton cleared his throat. Annabeth dropped her head. Will's hand rested on her waist. "Annabeth, why don't you head on up to bed?" Jackson's voice was calm and reassuring.

Annabeth started to move, but Will's hand detained her. His lips skimmed her temple, and he whispered in her ear. "Pleasant dreams. I know mine will be." He released her.

As she shamefully passed her father, he grasped her hand. "I will be up in a minute." He kissed her trembling hand. He knew he had to handle this situation delicately. The last thing he wanted to do was cause friction between his daughter and himself. Annabeth practically ran up the stairs.

"I make no apologies. I am not the least bit sorry," Will spoke to the man standing in the doorway.

"No, I wouldn't expect you to be. But you better not leave this spot until I return. Do I make myself understood?" Jackson didn't have anger in his voice; it was more like a forcefulness. Will began to fold and stack the chairs, indicating he wasn't going anywhere.

Annabeth felt like she was in some form of shock. What kind of person was she? She was pacing with nervousness, not so much as to what her father might say but of what just happened between Will and her. There had been a few times she felt he was going to kiss her, but it was all game playing. Tonight it was different. It was like nothing she had ever felt before. It was as if his kiss was drawing something from her soul.

There was a soft knock before her father entered. She flew to him hugging him. "I am so sorry, Father. I shouldn't have let that happen."

He led her to her window seat. "You didn't let that happen, sweetie. You made that happen, and it is nothing to be sorry for."

The look on her face was pure confusion. He laughed. "Oh, Annabeth, what man wouldn't want to kiss a beautiful woman as moonlight spills on her face? And you, my dear, are lovely and intelligent and most certainly have the personality that makes a man fall in love."

"I can just see Mother's face if she had been the one to witness my actions. She would be mortified." She hung her head.

"You think so? Don't underestimate your mother. It seems to me she had more than one stolen kiss in that very parlor."

Annabeth's mouth went into an oh. She was aghast. Jackson nodded and wiggled his eyebrows. "Nothing inappropriate, mind you." She smiled widely. "Don't lose any sleep over this, darling. It will all figure itself out. You just remember to be true to yourself." Jackson slipped out the door. He had business downstairs.

Will had stacked all the chairs but two. He had untucked his shirt and unbuttoned the first few buttons. It had suddenly become hot in the room. It seemed like forever before Jackson returned and sat on the lone chair.

"I know you're not sorry, but I do need to know what your intentions are?" Jackson leaned back and waited for Will to speak.

Will let out a long sigh. "This is very complicated, and I am going to have to ask you to trust me." He made eye contact with Jackson.

"That doesn't sound like your intentions."

"I love your daughter, sir. I didn't intend to fall in love, but how could I stop myself?"

"What happens now?" Jackson never changed positions. "Your vagueness is not impressing me, and it sure will not impress my wife."

"Let me ask you a favor and a question." Jackson didn't look too happy. He stayed quiet.

"Do you trust Thad Sheridan?"

What kind of question was that? Jackson thought. "Yes," he answered a little skeptically.

"Thad knows all the important things about me, and he trusts me."

"What is the favor?"

"In the next few months, things are not going to be as they appear. I need you to trust me and know I will always fight for your daughter and have her best interest at heart. Even if it means walking away."

"It is in your best interest not to disappoint me," Jackson said as he reached his hand out to Will.

Will grasped it firmly. "I won't."

Jackson made his way upstairs. He had gone into his study after Patience left to spend some time in prayer. Abby had initially joined him, but he sent her up to bed when he saw how fatigued she was. It was a good thing she didn't catch her daughter in the arms of Will Stanton, a man she didn't care for. Should he tell her? He had to tell her.

"Have you been praying this long? You always told me to say what's on my mind and leave it to the Lord." Abby yawned, leaning up on her elbow.

"I did, but then I got sidetracked by the magic that takes place in the south parlor." Jackson removed his shirt and sat on the edge of the bed to remove his shoes.

"What are you talking about?" He turned and kissed her.

"You remember how conducive that parlor is for kissing." He kissed her again.

"Yes, I remember, but the study is at the other end of the house. Why did you end up in there?"

"I ended up in there because I saw my daughter go into the parlor."

"Oh, Jackson, is she okay? I have worried about her all day."

Jackson laughed, "I am not sure how to answer that. You see, she wasn't alone."

"Mr. Stanton," Abby said it with a hint of agitation. "What bit of information is he going to enlighten us with about our daughter? He seems to know our children better than we do. It is most distasteful to me." She scooted up to lean against the massive headboard. She placed a pillow behind her back.

"He is in love with her."

"You heard him tell her? What did she say?"

"He hasn't told her although I suspect she may have got a hint by the way he was kissing her. And let me add she takes after her mother." Abby blushed. Abby Sheridan never once tried to stop Jackson Lorton from kissing her in that same parlor many years ago.

"Game playing—that is all this is. Will is not in love with her." Abby adjusted the covers around her. "Jackson, how can you be so naive?" She gave her husband a hard stare.

"After I followed Annabeth upstairs to make sure she was all right, I had a talk with Will. He told me he didn't realize until tonight he had fallen in love with Annabeth."

Abby just shook her head. Jackson relayed his conversations with both his daughter and her suitor to his wife. "How can I trust a man like that?" Abby asked her husband.

"Don't think of it as trusting Will. Think of it as trusting Thad."

*****

Will indeed had a pleasant and peaceful rest. His first order of business was to speak with Annabeth about what happened last night. He wanted to make sure she understood it was not a game. He dressed and headed downstairs he looked everywhere for Annabeth but couldn't find her. He didn't want to be too obvious, but he had to get some things settled—today!

It was if Annabeth was intentionally avoiding him. Didn't the tender moment make her want answers? He found her and TJ just as they were headed out the door for brunch. "Are you coming, Will? You know you are welcome." TJ was all smiles these days.

"No, I have some errands to run. Annabeth, I hoped we could have time to discuss—"

She cut him off. "We really should be going." She turned swiftly and exited the house.

Will made his way to Sadler's. He needed to do a little more investigating. He also needed to mail the letter to Thad. The post office sat across from Sadler's. Will was able to survey the comings and goings of the building. He watched for a good thirty minutes before he made his way over. Just before going in, something caught the elbow of his jacket.

"Mr. Stanton, may I speak with you?" He turned to face Jonathan Taylor. Jonathan led the way to the space between two buildings. "I want to tell you I plan to do everything in my power to make amends with Annabeth. My goal is to have her as my wife, and nothing will stop me." The man had a determined look on his face.

Will smiled widely and stuck out his hand. "From now on, Mr. Taylor, you can just refer to me as *nothing* because I will stop you."

The men dropped hands. "I guess we understand each other," Jonathan said as he turned and went behind Sadler's.

Will tried again in the afternoon to speak with Annabeth, but she was in her room with a headache. He doubted her head hurt to the point where a conversation would make it worse. Will corrected himself. Annabeth did have bouts of headaches. Who was he to judge the extent of them?

At supper, she seemed herself. After the meal, Will popped his head into the kitchen to ask to speak with her. "After I help Gretchen clean up, I promised TJ a game of chess. Perhaps tomorrow." It couldn't be tomorrow. After his conversation with Jonathan, he knew he had to get the record straight.

"As you wish." He sounded resolved to the fact it would have to wait another day. Annabeth knew her mother had planned an all-day outing for her, and the conversation would never take place if she had her way.

Jackson, Abby, TJ, and Annabeth were all in the library. It was late evening, and Jackson was reading the *Post*. Abby was working on her needlework. TJ had just beaten Annabeth in chess, and she had picked up a book.

Will entered and went directly to the settee where Annabeth was seated. "I am glad I finally found you in leisure. Since you have been avoiding me, I have no recourse than to speak with you here in front of your family."

Abby's needlework stopped, Jackson's paper came down, and TJ was all ears. Annabeth was livid. She tossed the book on the side table and rose. Storming out of the room, she gathered Mr. Stanton with a firm grasp of his arm. Jackson pulled the paper up. He was about to burst out laughing.

Annabeth dragged Will into the abandoned kitchen. Her arms crossed over her chest. "What?" She stood there like a simmering volcano.

"Don't you want to talk about what happened last night?" Will was his usual calm but irritating self.

"Nothing happened." She turned to leave.

"Nothing, Annabeth? Are you sure about that? It sure felt like something to me."

"The only thing that happened last night was a sensible woman lost her head!" She turned and stormed toward the door. "And a sensible man lost his heart!"

Will was now angry. His words stopped her. He quietly stepped behind her and put his arm around her waist, drawing her back to him. She stayed facing the door. His cheek rested near her ear. He whispered, "Annabeth, I've fallen in love with you. Please don't tell me nothing happened." His lips skimmed her temple. He rested his chin on her shoulder. "Say something." His grip grew tighter. "Anything."

"I don't want to play this game. Please let me go." Her voice was so soft, so hurtful Will couldn't do anything but let her go.

What was he going to do? Will was fighting an uphill battle. He decided to let her have some time. They had a long way home with plenty of time to talk. The next morning Annabeth was up early and gone. It was apparent she wanted to be nowhere around Will.

When he found out she was gone, he decided to head into town himself. There was a lot to see and do in Charleston, and he wasn't going to miss this opportunity. He would also make one last investigation of Sadler's. He needed to keep his mind clear and on point.

He would find a way to make Annabeth understand the depth of his love.

His love currently was sitting in a local eating house sipping tea and watching him stroll down the boulevard. More than one woman gave him a look. How could he possibly confess his love for her when he so obviously is not the marrying type? He didn't stay in one place very long, and he has no steady employment. Love indeed.

"Good morning, Annabeth." Jonathan Taylor slipped into the seat across from his ex-fiancée. "Do you mind if I join you?" He raised his fingers to the waitress and ordered a cup of coffee.

Annabeth rose. "I was just leaving."

"Now, Annabeth, you were not. You were lost in thought, looking out the window." His eyes followed the direction in which hers had previously been. "Ah, Mr. Stanton." He motioned for her to remain seated. For some reason, she did as he asked.

"Are you happy, Annabeth?" He leaned up to look into her eyes.

She couldn't look away. She was, at one time, willing to commit her life to the man in front of her. She found she couldn't speak. His eyes caressed her face. "I thought not." His hand clasped hers. "Annabeth, we are meant to be together. I made a huge mistake. Am I not worthy of a second chance?"

She still couldn't speak. She decided maybe she should just listen. He raised her hand to his lips and kissed it softly.

Will Stanton headed to the small cafe. He had spotted Annabeth sitting near the window. He also watched Jonathan Taylor slip in. Will made his way to a corner table where he had a full view of what was taking place. He felt like he was playing a chess game. His queen was in danger, here and back in Sheridan. He slowly sipped on his coffee and blatantly stared at Annabeth. He watched every emotion play on her face. He figured between Old Reliable, Jonathan, and himself, she must be pretty confused.

Annabeth felt strange. Like someone was watching. Who wouldn't be watching a man kissing a woman's hand in broad daylight? Her eyes drifted to the corner table. There sat Will. He raised his cup of coffee in her direction in acknowledgment. Annabeth left the place immediately. Jonathan left money on the table and went after her. Annabeth disappeared into the crowd. Will finished his coffee and even ordered a bite to eat. He was satisfied that if Annabeth had more regard for Jonathan than himself, she would have stayed. Yes, he was satisfied with this move.

Annabeth felt sick to her stomach; she was confused to no end. Her mind and heart were in constant turmoil. She never thought of herself as being such a fickle person, such a ninny about things. She walked briskly about the town, her mind racing. Twice she was nearly run down when she wasn't paying attention. She found herself outside of her father's office. She hoped he would have a moment to speak with her.

"I have been waiting for you to come and talk to me," Jackson said as he closed the door to his office and pulled out a chair for his daughter.

"What do you mean?" She had a perplexed look on her face.

"In the last week, I have had three young men express to me their love for my daughter." Her eyes grew wide. "First was Will, of course. Then Jonathan paid me a visit day before yesterday, and today I got this note in the mail from Rawly. Not even your mother, as beautiful as she is, had three men in love with her at one time."

"I wish they would all go away," she said in a huff.

Jackson smiled. "It doesn't work that way. They are all very determined. Annabeth, I would like to hear your thoughts."

"My thoughts are mush. I thought I was deeply in love with Jonathan. He was the one. Then he wasn't. He wants a second chance. He says he made a mistake, and he deserves forgiveness."

"He does deserve forgiveness, but the gift of forgiveness isn't necessarily your love or your life. It is simply to forgive." Her father always saw all the angles. Jackson held up the letter from Rawly. "And this young man, that neither your mother nor I have met—what about him?"

"After I moved to Sheridan, it was like a clean slate. But what Jonathan did had me feeling less confident about my future. Rawly started courting me, and it made me feel relevant again. I know that sounds petty, but it brought back a little bit of life to me. He is charming and has taken things slowly. I am a little surprised he would write to you so soon."

"I'm not, which leads us to gentleman number three. I suspect Will has something to do with Rawly's haste."

"Will plays games. Every action he does is simply for playing the odds on what the reaction will be. Trust me, Father, that declaration has a catch."

"He seemed pretty smitten the other night in the parlor. I wouldn't count him out, Annabeth. He could be the most sincere."

Her father apparently hadn't spent enough time with Will to see his wily ways. Her mother and Patience had him figured out. Poor TJ and her father—they just didn't understand. "I know that look. I have seen it a thousand times on your mother's face. That is the 'Jackson, you just don't understand' look. Annabeth, I am a man, and if I know one thing, I know how a man's mind works when he is in love. It doesn't."

She laughed. "I love you, Father, so very much." She was determined then and there to hold her three suitors to the standards she found in her father. Whichever one came the closest would be her choice. She doubted any of them would come close, and she could end this season of her life.

*****

The time had come for Annabeth to head home. At the train station, her mother tried desperately not to cry. It was hard enough letting her go the first time, but something about the look on her daughter's face caused Abby alarm. Jackson had relayed all the young men's intentions to his wife. She was confused as her daughter, but no one could make the decisions in Annabeth's life but Annabeth.

"Are you sure you won't stay?" Jackson said as he squeezed his daughter tight.

"If I could be two places at once, wouldn't that be nice?" She kissed her father. "I will be back soon," she promised. A promise he knew would not be kept.

Will stood behind the trio, speaking with TJ. "You keep me informed about what you're doing in school. I want to hear all about what you are learning," Will said as he shook hands with the young boy.

"I will."

By this time, Jackson had joined them. "Will, it was nice to meet you. Don't make me regret allowing you into my parlor," Jackson said with a face void of emotion.

"You won't, sir." Will stuck his hand out, and Jackson gave it a good shake.

"Take care of my girl." Will looked to Annabeth. He wanted to do nothing more.

Annabeth was sad as she made her way to her seat on the train. As the locomotive inched out of Charleston, Will felt a little relieved in not seeing Jonathan at the station. Perhaps part of Annabeth's sadness was Jonathan not making one last attempt at the train station. And why didn't he if he loved her so much? *Weakling.* Will smiled to himself.

"Why on earth would you be smiling in that manner?" Annabeth's words took him by surprise. She had not spoken to him since the night in the kitchen except what propriety demanded.

"Can't a man in love smile?" He kept the smile on his face. She huffed and turned her face to peer out the window.

"Annabeth, I confessed my love for you. That is probably the hardest thing a man like me can say, and you are treating me like I called in the bank loan on The Dowry." There was a roughness in the way he said it that put Annabeth on guard. Why would it be so hard for him to say?

"And what kind of man are you? What does that statement mean? It doesn't appear to me that you are any different than any other man," she continued to look at the passing landscape.

He jerked her chin around to face him. "Because it is not something I say a lot, unlike Jonathan who seems to think you can say it, deny it, then say it again. If it comes that easy for a man, it isn't real."

She slapped his hand away. "You know nothing about Jonathan."

"I know he could only love you so much. I know what that means."

"Yes, you do, which makes you and him about the same type of man." She stared at him.

"All right Annabeth, have it your way. Juggle three men at one time and boost your ego. When it is all said and done, only one will be standing, and it will be me."

"Boost my ego!" she nearly screamed. "If anyone continually needs their ego boosted, it's you!"

"Really? I don't have a string of helpless females in my wake now, do I? And you say I play games." He turned his head to face the passengers on the other side of the car.

"What about Jayne? Before we left, the two of you were pretty chummy."

"Only a woman in love would make a mountain out of that molehill." He smiled at her, leaned his head back, and put his hat over his eyes.

"Do you honestly think I would give a man, who both my mother and sister do not like, the time of day?" She fidgeted in the seat beside him.

"You better pay attention to what the men in your family think. Women know a woman's mind. Men know a man's. You better think on that, miss high and mighty."

She turned not just her head but her body toward the window in total rejection of Will Stanton. He wasn't going to have that. He reached over and rested his hand on her forearm; he caressed it. She didn't move.

*****

Once again, the long train trip home was overtaxing. When Annabeth stepped out of the stagecoach at Sheridan, Thad and Merry were there to greet her. Standing just behind them leaning up against the building was Jonathan Taylor. Annabeth did not initially see him, but Will did. He made eye contact, and Jonathan nodded with a smirk on his face. *Nice move,* Will thought. He didn't expect this, and neither did Annabeth.

When Thad sat Annabeth back on her feet, she noticed Jonathan. She had to take a double look. Watching her face, Thad turned. "Do you know him, Annabeth?"

Jonathan sauntered over. "Jonathan Taylor, sir. I assume you are Annabeth's uncle, the one she speaks so highly of." He extended his hand, and Thad shook it. Merry's face showed her annoyance with the man who caused Annabeth such heartache. "And you must be Merry." He tipped his hat. Merry only stared.

"What are you doing here, Jonathan?" Annabeth found her voice.

"Why wouldn't I be here? How else am I going to win you back? I certainly couldn't accomplish the task miles away."

"You can't accomplish the task at all," Will spoke as he picked up his luggage and smiled at Annabeth and Jonathan. "Merry, Thad, it's good to see you. I take it you'll see Annabeth home since Rawly isn't here." Thad gave Will a you're-on-thin-ice look. Will went his way.

Annabeth wanted to seclude herself in her tiny home. She was thrilled to see Thrive. The dog nearly knocked her over with his greeting. "We are so glad you are home, Annabeth. How was the wedding? I bet you had a grand time. Now, I want to hear all about it after you rest. Are you hungry? We have a new boarder, Mr. Taylor. He is from South Carolina. Oh my, is he handsome. You'll meet him at supper."

When Trudy took a breath, Annabeth spoke quickly. "Trudy, if you don't mind, I am going to get some rest. I am truly worn to a frazzle."

"Heavens, no, you rest. I will send some food over after a bit. There were some packages left for you. I put them on your bed."

Annabeth was surprised. "Thank you, Trudy."

When Annabeth and Thrive entered their humble abode, Annabeth was mesmerized. On the table was a large bouquet of spring flowers with a card that said, "Welcome home, sunshine." There were also three packages on her bed. Since her illness, she had been getting random gifts. Thrive was the first and then followed a few others. They came at various times. Only Lydia Lapp and, by now, Ezekiel Lapp knew who the secret gift giver was. She couldn't be sure, but she thought her uncle was behind it. He and Merry would orchestrate something of this nature.

Why wasn't Rawly the first to come to mind? He was supposed to be in love with her. Wouldn't he be the obvious one? Her mind jumped to the stage office. And shouldn't he have been there to greet her? He knew what day she was coming home. Instead, there was Jonathan. He had to have taken the train a day or two before her to get here first. Her head was spinning, and it hurt.

Thrive jumped on the bed and began sniffing the packages. They did temporarily take Annabeth's mind off what was going on around her. She tore the paper away from the first gift. When she opened the small box, she found cake decorating tips. There were six different patterns. Her mind whirled at how she could use the culinary finery in the bakery. Someone understood her passion.

The next package was soft and not in a box. When she carefully removed the paper, a beautifully embroidered apron fell out. It was white with golden-yellow and bright-blue flowers lining the edges. Someone had excellent taste.

The last box was tiny. She opened it to find an exquisite gold broach with a watch face. The elegant timepiece was scrolled with small vines intertwined with rosebuds. All she could do was stare at the lovely piece of jewelry resting in the palm of her hand. She must talk to Lydia and find out who was giving such gifts.

CHAPTER 9

*A*nnabeth wasn't sure what time it was when she awoke under the quilt Merry had made her. Thrive was snuggled at her foot in a tight little ball. Her movement caused the dog to start wagging his tail. Annabeth stretched. It was dark out, and only the moonlight shone through her bedroom window. She had missed supper, and her stomach was letting her know about it. She put on her shawl and walked to the backdoor of the boarding house. A light was burning in the kitchen. Trudy probably left it on for her. There was undoubtedly a plate of food tucked away as well.

Annabeth entered the kitchen with Thrive on her heels. "No, boy, you stay here." The dog gave a little huff and lay down on a rug just outside the kitchen. Annabeth was tickled with the dog's apparent agitation. When she turned, she found Will sitting at the table. His feet were outstretched, his head was back, and his eyes were closed. On the table in front of him was an open Bible. A cup of coffee sat near his hand. She wasn't sure if she should turn and go or send him to bed. Suddenly one of his eyes opened.

"I'm sorry I didn't mean to wake you," Annabeth whispered.

"I wasn't asleep. I was praying." Will straightened up. "I think Aunt Trudy left a plate for you in the oven." He started to rise.

"I can get it." Annabeth headed to the stove. "You continue your Bible study and prayers. I will just take this back to my house and eat."

"Nonsense." He pulled out a chair for her. "Would you like some coffee?" Will had refilled his cup.

"Yes, please." She smiled. It was the first time since his declaration of love that she sincerely smiled for him. "Where are you reading or studying, if you don't mind me asking?" She began to eat the huge plate of food left for her.

"Are you familiar with the passage of Psalm 37?"

"Isn't that the one that starts out admonishing us not to fret and continues with words like *committing* and *delighting*?"

"Yes, that is the one. It holds the verse that God has given me as my favorite, the verse that guides me."

"I like how you refer to it as the verse God has given you. I have one of those as well."

Again she smiled, and Will knew he was headed down the right path. "What is your verse?" he asked her.

She sat up a little straighter as if she was reciting the verse in front of the congregation. "Proverbs 3:5, 6: 'Trust in the Lord with all thine heart and lean not unto thine own understanding. In all thy ways acknowledge him, and he shall direct thy paths.'"

He smiled at her, and she found a warmth she didn't know. Why did it make her blush? "Are you going to share your verse?" She wanted him to stop staring at her. "Psalm 37:23: 'The steps of a good man are ordered by the Lord, and he delighteth in his way.' You found me praying about my next step with you, Annabeth. I am a good man, no matter what you think. Perhaps I fell in love with you without checking to see if it was ordered by the Lord. It happened so suddenly and so splendidly I have to believe it was in his plan. Maybe he didn't want me to announce it at the time and place in which I did but nonetheless, it is out there, and I am praying." She was speechless.

"You worry too much, Annabeth. Trust in the Lord. He will direct your path. Just don't be surprised if you find me walking beside you."

She gave him an astonished look. He moved his Bible to face her and tapped the page. "You want to know more about me, it's all here." He turned to leave. "Do yourself a favor and get a piece of that cherry pie. It is outstanding. Good night, precious."

Why did she feel like she was on the verge of tears? She sat there for a few minutes looking at the door he just walked through. Her eyes were drawn to the Bible in front of her. The book lay open to reveal Psalm 37. There were several notations in the margin of the Bible. She began to read them. She thumbed through the pages and found a lot of markings, not to mention pieces of paper with thoughts and notes written on them. It was evident Will Stanton studied the word. The Bible reminded her of her father's.

Annabeth turned to the front of the book. The Bible was given to him by his parents, Benton and Catherine Stanton, on January 5, 1883, for his twelfth birthday. She tried to picture Will as a boy. It wasn't hard. She doubted he was much different than he was currently. She turned the paged. "Family" was the title. Under Mr. and Mrs. Stanton's name were the following: Rebekah Stanton, born August 1, 1861; Emily Stanton, born December 19, 1862; Rosemary Stanton, born May 21, 1864; and Ben Stanton, born January 5, 1871. Will has a twin brother. He never mentioned any of his family. She shamed herself. She never asked. Something caught her eye. Next to Ben's name, in shaky writing, was "died September 3, 1882." She stopped.

The urge to cry was replaced with actual tears. Poor Mr. and Mrs. Stanton to lose a child so young and poor Will to lose his twin brother. They had to be very close. The next page had all his sisters' wedding dates with their spouse's name and birth date. In the back of the Bible, there was a list of dates and towns. The last year was 1897 with Sheridan out beside it. She studied the list. Had this been all the places he had traveled? Many different towns and states filled the page. She wondered at the traveler she knew as Will Stanton. She realized she knew very little about the man, yet Annabeth felt she knew more about him than she did Rawly or Jonathan.

Thrive whined from the doorway as Annabeth finished a piece of cherry pie. She closed Will's Bible and placed it in the center of the table. She started to rise when Jonathan entered. She jumped when he said her name. "I didn't mean to scare you, Annabeth. I am sorry. I just kept thinking about the cherry pie I had for supper. Is there any left?"

Annabeth moved to get him a piece, and he stepped in front of her.

"Are you angry with me for coming all this way?" His hand had hold of her wrist.

"I think it was a waste of your time and money, Jonathan. I told you back in Charleston I forgave you, but there will never be anything more between us than an empty promise. I am sorry if that hurts you, but it is the best I can do."

"I don't believe you, Annabeth." He gazed into her eyes; his hand now stroked her hair. "Annabeth, how many times do I have to tell you what a fool I was?" His hand swept her hair from her forehead, and he kissed the spot where the hair had been. "You're my love," he whispered. "There will never be anyone who compares to you."

"Where exactly is Lillian these days, Jonathan?" Annabeth felt him stiffen.

He let out a sigh. "All right, Annabeth, what do you want? All the gory details. It turned out she and I were on different paths. She wanted a lot from me, things that all required a pretty high price. I found out just in time what she was after." He stayed relatively close to her throughout the conversation. A little too close for comfort. Annabeth attempted to move, but he circumvented her.

"You and I have always seemed to have the same goals, the same wants, and the same desires," he said as he leaned in. "We were made for each other." The words were spoken softly as he looked into her eyes. His thumb stroked her lips, and he bent toward them.

"No, Jonathan, don't." He didn't heed the warning in her words. From the doorway, Thrive began to growl and let out a bark. It startled Jonathan, and he moved away. Annabeth went to the dog, and she and Thrive left the kitchen.

From his chair in his room, Will watched Annabeth enter her home. She shut the door and leaned her back against it. He had heard Jonathan exit his room, and he had heard Thrive bark and then Jonathan return. Will needed to speak with someone he could trust about everything going on in his life. He decided tomorrow he would seek out the only man in town he trusted entirely: Thad Sheridan.

*****

The next morning, Will was the first to arrive at the bakery. When Vivian came a half hour later, she was all smiles and hugs too. "Boy, it has been the dullest time around here without you and Annabeth," she said as she jerked on Will's collar to bring him down to her level. She placed a big kiss on his cheek. "Now, don' get me wrong. Jayne has done an excellent job, but you were missed."

"Thanks, Vivian. I can tell you I was more than ready to come home."

"Where is Annie? I figure she would be here bright and early." Vivian's started making the morning fare.

"She was pretty tired. I hope she takes another day to rest." Will began putting the chairs around the tables.

"We all can't help but worry about her, can we? All but Rawly, that is. I didn't see him at the stage depot to welcome her home." Will made no comment. The fact made him mad and glad all at the same time. Vivian gave him a side glance.

"He sure did spend a lot of time hanging around the bakery while she was gone."

That got Will's attention. His eyes narrowed. "Why would he be doing that?" He wanted more information. He suspected Rawly wanted to snoop while he and Annabeth were gone.

At that time, Jayne came through the door. Vivian raised her eyebrows and motioned toward Jayne. Will caught her meaning. Rawly was interested in Jayne, at least while Annabeth was gone. Again, he was mad and glad all at the same time. The pathetic man would get his reward.

Thirty minutes after the bakery opened, Annabeth came rushing in. "I am so sorry. I overslept." She looked at her bakery running smoothly. She got a little choked up. It would be open whether she was present or not. It made her mood more melancholy.

"Annabeth!" Mr. Porter came from his seat in the corner. He lifted her up and swung her around, his gold tooth gleaming. "There hasn't been a muffin compared to yours for weeks. Don't ever leave again!" He accentuated his sentiment with a kiss on her forehead. The bakery erupted in cheers. No one's smile was more significant than the man who loved her. Will stood in the kitchen, taking it all in.

After everyone settled down, Old Reliable waltzed through the door. Will watched Rawly's eyes go first to Jayne then to Annabeth. He noticed a blush on Jayne's face. "Annabeth, how was your trip?" he asked as he took a seat at an empty table. Jayne poured him a cup of coffee. Vivian's eyes met Will's, and she made a face.

"It was good, thank you. How have you been?"

"Good, do you have any muffins left?" Annabeth smiled and went into the kitchen where Will was waiting.

Will lowered his voice and leaned into her space. "Annabeth, I won't press you about what happened in Charleston between us, but I will point out my observations along the way. For instance, if we were apart for three weeks, I would be the one to open that stage-coach door, and my first words wouldn't be about muffins." Her face heated.

Will went to the sink and began to wash dishes. Annabeth brought Rawly a muffin and poured him a cup of coffee. "Won't you sit down a minute, Annabeth?" Rawly took a bite of his muffin. Annabeth was about to sit down when Jonathan arrived on the scene.

"Annabeth, you look well rested." He took her hand and kissed it softly. Vivian poured herself a cup of coffee and settled in. A herd of buffalo couldn't move her from her spot. She had heard a Jonathan Taylor from South Carolina was staying at the Bullocks' boarding house. She knew it was Annabeth's Jonathan Taylor.

"And who are you?" Rawly asked the man kissing Annabeth's hand.

"I am Jonathan Taylor, and you must be Mr. Smith."

Jonathan, always the gentleman, extended his hand. Rawly stood. "You have some nerve coming here." Rawly didn't mince words.

"Yes, I do, and you need to know I am here to steal Annabeth from you."

Rawly was taken aback. At this time, Will walked between the two men and began to clear the nearby table.

"You can just go back where you came from. Annabeth wants nothing to do with you." Who did Rawly think he was, speaking for her? Annabeth fumed. *What a half-wit,* Will thought of Rawly. It was a big mistake to speak for Annabeth in regard to Jonathan.

"If you don't mind, I will defer until I hear from Annabeth," Jonathan responded and stood a little taller in his tailored suit.

Annabeth was about to explode. They were acting as if she wasn't even in the room. "Tell him, Annabeth," Rawly demanded as the two turned to face her. When they did, Will emerged from between them with arms full of dirty dishes, a broad smile on his face. With elbows out, carrying his load, he bumped both men.

"Will you get rid of him, Annabeth?" Rawly motioned his head toward Will. Jonathan was brushing debris from the elbow of his suit coat.

"You've gotten jam on my coat." He frowned at Will's back. "Will this come out?" Jonathan was looking at Vivian as if she was his hired help. That irritated Will just a touch, so he walked over with a wet dirty rag and began scrubbing the spot. Jonathan drew his arm to himself. "You're making it worse. Annabeth, get rid of him."

"He does work here, and at the moment is the only one doing anything productive. Now, The Dowry will be closing in ten minutes. If you wish to order anything else, I suggest you do it and get out." She turned and headed toward the back pantry. Rawly followed her, but he was stopped by Will's large hand on his chest. "I wouldn't if I were you," Will said low and slow.

"Well, you're not me," Rawly said as he forcefully shoved Will's hand away.

Jonathan took a seat. He wasn't leaving as long as Rawly was in the pantry with Annabeth. He sipped on his coffee and watched Will and Vivian work. "This is what you do for a living?" he said as he continued to mess with his coat. Will didn't answer.

"Perhaps when I take Annabeth back to Charleston, she can sell it to you."

Will continued to work. He couldn't care less what Jonathan thought. Once a cad, always a cad.

In the pantry, Annabeth was shocked that Rawly followed her. "I asked you to leave, Rawly." He gripped her by the arm.

"We need to discuss Jonathan being here. I thought he married someone else."

"They obviously didn't go through with it. He said he made a mistake. I told him it was water under the bridge and I had moved on. I made it clear there could never be anything between us."

"Well, you didn't make it clear enough. I don't know if it is because you're too nice or just not smart enough to know how to tell a man you're not interested. Neither Jonathan nor Will, for that matter, has seemed to get the message."

Not smart enough? Not smart enough! Annabeth's mind whirled. She slapped his face. Old Reliable was shocked. For a split second, he just stared at her. She was so mad tears started to form in the corner of her eyes.

"Oh, Annabeth." His voice was soft. "I'm sorry, honey. I didn't mean it." He placed his arms around her and drew her to him. "I didn't mean you weren't smart in the manner you are thinking. Oh, love, what man would give up on you? I can understand those fellas being persistent. It's not your fault. It's mine. I haven't staked my claim very well now, have I? They will keep trying until I put a ring on your finger. I have been saving up, you know." He pulled back a little so he could see her face.

She swiped at a tear trickling down her face. "I am sorry I slapped you." She placed her hand on his face, and he covered it with his own. He leaned in and kissed her. "Soon, Annabeth, it will all work out like you want. I promise." He kissed her again. This time a little more passionately. It happened so quickly she didn't have time to stop him.

*****

Will left the bakery and headed out to Thad Sheridan's. He knew the man was still planting his crops. Will would help the family just as he had with last year's harvest. He knew there would be an opportunity to speak with the man after the day's work was done.

185

Merry was kneeling, doing a little of her own planting around the porch. She had smudges of dirt on her face, and her hair was slipping out of the ribbon that held it loosely. She was a beautiful woman; but more than that, she was a smart woman. Perhaps Will should speak with her about Annabeth. He was considering the notion when she noticed him.

"Will, what are you doing out here? Is Annabeth okay?"

"Yes, ma'am, she is fine. I came out to see if you all needed help with the planting." He dismounted his horse.

Merry rose from the ground quickly. "Will Stanton, I could just kiss you. How did you know that both Gil and Franklin are down sick? They can't even get out of bed without their stomachs protesting."

"Do I need to ride into town and get the doctor for you?"

"No, I had David stop by there and tell Hawk to come out this evening after he was done in the office. I also told him to stay with Lach after school, so he didn't get sick as well."

"Good thinking. Where are the men working?"

"They are in the south pasture. I would go and help, but I didn't feel I could leave the boys. You are a godsend."

Will smiled. "I'll get right out there."

"Just a minute." Merry whirled into the house and came back with some food and water. "Thad won't stop if things are going well." Her smile was radiant. Will hoped one day Annabeth's face would light up when she talked about him. He wanted to make her proud of him. If he could see her face at this moment, he wouldn't like what he saw.

Annabeth needed to speak to someone. She needed advice on the situation at hand. She knew her uncle, and probably her aunt as well was in the field. Avery was about ready to deliver, so she didn't want to bother her. Vivian was too entertained by it all, and she didn't know Jayne well enough to divulge such intimate details of her life.

Annabeth left The Dowry with her basket of leftovers and nearly ran into Dr. Lapp. He was headed into the dress shop through the back door. "Annabeth, child, you look like you've seen a ghost. Are you all right, dear?"

She closed her eyes. He and Lydia were just what she needed. "Do you have time for a chat?" She smiled at her surrogate grandfather. He stroked his short clipped silver beard. "Only if there is something in that basket to go with it." He smiled and opened the door to the shop for her.

Inside Lydia was altering a dress, and her face lit up at the sight of her husband. "It's about time you got back. I sent you to Tyler's over an hour ago. Did he have the thread I needed?"

"He did, and I wasn't gone an hour. I wanted to stop in and check on Avery. That is why I was delayed. I found Annabeth looking bewildered and offered to chat with her in exchange for some of her baked goods." He winked at Annabeth and handed his wife the thread.

"I will put some coffee on, and we will have that chat. Do you drink coffee, or do you prefer tea?" The doctor was making his way into a small kitchenette behind a curtain.

"I drink both, so whichever you choose," Annabeth replied.

"Honey, he drinks nothing but coffee, and I can't stand the taste of it." Lydia turned her head toward the curtain "Will you fix me a cup of tea, Zeke?"

"Sit right down and tell us what is on your mind." Lydia moved a dress she was working on to make a place for Annabeth to sit.

"Don't start without me." Ezekiel Lapp's baritone voice sounded behind the barrier.

Lydia shook her head. "Worse than any of the gossips in town."

Her husband appeared with her cup of tea and two cups of coffee. Annabeth handed him her basket.

"I will get right to the point. Will Stanton, Jonathan Taylor, and Rawly Smith are on my mind. I don't know what to do. All three of them have spoken with my father about marrying me. Not one has seriously sat down and talked to me. They all have inferred it but no discussion. More like they are telling me it is going to happen." She felt such relief in getting it all out she just flopped back on the sofa. The Lapps both chuckled.

Dr. Lapp took a doughnut out of the basket and dunked it in his coffee. "You have come to the right place, Annabeth. You see, before you is a woman who endured the same dilemma. Lydia is an expert."

"You are? What, how, how did it all work out?"

"I had been courted off and on by the young man who lived next to us," Lydia began her story. "Well, it seemed as things progressed we would eventually marry. Then the preacher's son returned from school only to take an interest."

Annabeth's eyes grew wide. "You?" She looked at Dr. Lapp eating a second doughnut. He shook his head no.

"The preacher's son was a little pushier. He thought I was the perfect one, and there would be no doubt he would win me over. I was in a quandary. Then a young physician came to town to study with our town doctor. And let me tell you, he wasted no time in stirring up trouble. He was bold and went about things very uncharacteristically. He wreaked havoc for me everywhere he went." Lydia looked at her smiling husband. He looked as if he held some sort of secret.

"In what way?" Annabeth wished to know. "He just seemed to always be at the right place at the right time. I don't like confrontation, so I did my best to be nice to them all without giving any of them false hope."

"How did you finally decide?" At that point, Dr. Lapp went to get more coffee.

"Two things actually happened. The first was something Zeke said. He told me he was eventually going to leave town, and if I was satisfied still playing with boys, I could stay; but if I wanted to see the world with a man, I had better change my ways." Annabeth had a shocked look on her face.

"I was pretty upset with him at that point, so he left me alone. I figured getting back to normal would be the best thing. He planned to leave and head West, and I was not interested in leaving my family. That is when the second thing happened. Normal didn't feel normal anymore, not without him. That man had disrupted my whole world. Things didn't fit together anymore. It seemed as if I was a square peg trying to fit in a round hole. Unless"—she emphasized the word—"unless I was with him. When we were together, I never felt more complete."

"The best man will always win if the woman is smart like my Liddy." Dr. Lapp bent and gave his wife a loving kiss. "And you, Annabeth, are smart," he added.

"You will figure all this out. I encourage you to make it a matter of much prayer," Lydia added as she grabbed Annabeth's hand. "We will be praying earnestly for you."

*****

The sun had begun to fade. Merry knew Thad wouldn't be in until the last scrap of light was gone. It had been a flawless day, which made planting easier. She was startled by the presence of her eldest son. Hawk had arrived to take a look at his brothers. "Do you like sneaking up on people, Hawk?" Merry stood with her hand over her heart.

He smiled. "I am sorry, Morning Dove." He kissed her on the cheek and headed to assess his brothers' condition.

"Will you stay for supper? Your pa, Hud, and Will aren't in yet."

He nodded. Hawk loved Avery more than anything, but she was not a great cook. Average but nothing like his mother. Of course, he would stay for supper. "Will is helping?" He had a questionable look on his face.

"He just showed up after the bakery closed. He said he needed to talk to Thad and thought he might need help with the planting. He couldn't have come on a better day, that is for sure."

Hawk left his brothers. There wasn't much he could do for them. They needed rest and frequent but small amounts of water. He instructed his mother on some tea that could help and assisted her in brewing it. When Franklin and Gil had drunk sufficient quantity, they were left to rest.

"I would keep David away for a day or two, so he doesn't get it and keep Quinn out too. The last thing I need is for Nora to pick up this illness." Hawk gave his suggestions. "David is going to stay at Lach and Jamie's. I will suggest Quinn go too."

Merry heard the men talking with some gentle laughter and went out onto the porch. "How much more do you have to do?" Merry asked her husband as he kissed her not once but twice.

"We're done, thanks to Will here. For a bakery man, he is outstanding in the field."

"Yeah, thanks. Will, I don't know what caused you to come out today, but it sure was a blessing. I appreciate it." Hud slapped him on the back in appreciation. "I enjoyed myself."

Will acted as if he were going to leave. "I have supper waiting, and you will eat with us, Will."

Will seemed to have no choice. He remembered past meals at the Sheridans and realized he didn't want a choice. Merry Sheridan was a fine cook. "Yes, ma'am."

"Hud, are you staying? Hawk is here." Merry turned to her son.

"No, Ma, I'm going down to the creek and get some of this grim off and then head home. I'm sure Molly has something waiting for me."

Thad smiled. Rarely did Hud Sheridan want to be away from his wife. It was not because she had weak legs that needed crutches and braces to help support them. It was because she was his world. He just wasn't happy being anywhere else when he had the option of being with her. Thad's eyes turned to his own wife. He knew the feeling well.

"I suppose getting the grim off wouldn't hurt any of us," Thad surmised and looked at his wife. "Can supper wait a few more minutes?"

"If it means cleaner men at my table, yes, it can wait."

Thad, Merry, Hawk, and Will sat down to supper thirty minutes later. Will knew everyone was tired, but he needed to discuss Annabeth with them. He pushed right in. "The main reason I came out today, I was in hopes of getting a few minutes to speak with you about Annabeth." Everyone stopped and just looked at him.

"Is she all right?" Merry asked.

Will's head did a slow nod. "Yes, she's all right."

Hawk burst out laughing, an uncommon occurrence for the stoic doctor. "You owe my boys an apology." The whole table erupted, except for Will. He just had to sit there and take it. It had been evident to everyone but him and apparently Annabeth that he had fallen in love with her.

"I suppose you want to know what to do about it?" Hawk had stopped laughing, but his face didn't know it. He was grinning from ear to ear. "You are on your own. You have to figure it out just like the rest of us." Hawk stood and kissed his mother's head. "I'm headed home. It's where I belong. I'll have to tell Avery what astute children we are raising."

"You can tell Avery, but that is as far as it goes, Dr. Sheridan." There was no need for the whole town to know his troubles.

"I'm in a mess, Thad, and you know it." Will's eyes met Thad's, and he nodded. "Does she know?" Will asked as both his eyes and Thad's turned to Merry.

"No," Thad answered. "You ask me not to say anything."

Merry sat quietly for a moment and then rose. "I am going to check on the boys and then head to bed. Will, it is getting late you are welcome to stay the night. The loft is always ready for guest."

"You are the kindest woman I think I have ever met, Merry." Will grasped her hand and kissed it. "Thad will explain everything to you later. I will ask you to keep it in confidence, and this is going to sound harsh right now, but I am asking you to stay out of it."

Will and Thad talked for a while. Will wanted Thad's advice on how to proceed with his plan to catch Rawly and the gang of robbers. He wanted his thoughts on how and when he should tell Annabeth the truth about what has been going on at her bakery. He wanted his thoughts on how to get Jonathan out of the picture. He just needed to talk everything out. Thad's advice was sound, and he encouraged Will to be cautious and follow his gut instincts. He most importantly advised him to continue praying with each step.

*****

Annabeth headed to the bakery in a very nasty mood. She reprimanded herself. Why should she be in a huff just because Mr. Stanton had stayed out all night, and as of early this morning had not returned to the boarding house? Trudy surprisingly was not bothered by this. Nor was the sheriff. Taking her cue from them, she said nothing. Where could he have gone? He left the bakery yesterday, and that was the last she saw of him. She was still stewing over this when she hung the Open sign in the window and saw him trotting from the sheriff's office to the bakery. He came through the front door.

"I am sorry I am late," he said to his coworkers. Annabeth's face held some irritation. "You weren't by chance staring out the window looking for me, were you, Annabeth?" His words were said for only her. "Just another observation," he added as he went to join the women in the kitchen. She wanted to scream, but a customer came through the door, and she seated him.

*****

The boarding house had four guests: Jayne, Jonathan, and two men from Missouri on their way to Washington. Trudy had a rule. She and Dan ate with their guests in the formal dining room. Any other time, they all ate in the kitchen. Jayne and Jonathan requested to eat in the kitchen. They felt since they were long-term boarders they could eat with Annabeth and Will. Tonight was Tuesday, and Rawly would be coming for supper. Annabeth was dreading it.

Will entered the kitchen, whistling. He went straight to the cabinet and pulled out the plates, stopping only to smile at Annabeth. He went into the dining area; she could still hear him whistling. Then it dawned on her what the tune was: "Fur Elise." He came back in, still caring the familiar melody and still smiling. "Will you whistle something else?" she asked as she pulled the bread from the oven.

The aroma made Will close his eyes and take a deep breath. When he opened his eyes, she was staring at him. "Nope," he answered her request and continued whistling into the dining area.

The five younger guests sat at the kitchen table. Rawly sat in between Annabeth and Jayne. There was a time or two Will thought he saw Rawly reach for Jayne's hand under the table. He couldn't be totally sure, but he would not put it past the man. He was wondering if Jayne and Rawly could possibly know each other from a previous encounter. Could Jayne be part of Rawly's debauchery? Will was lost in thought.

"So what, or who might I asked, kept you out to all hours of the night last night, Mr. Stanton?" Jonathan had no more begun eating when he posed the question.

Will's first inkling was to tell Mr. Taylor to mind his own business, but that would imply guilt. His silence brought all eyes on him except for Annabeth, who kept eating.

"I am just curious. Aren't you curious, Annabeth?" Jonathan looked to Annabeth for a response.

"Mr. Stanton's actions have no bearing on my thoughts or pique my curiosity."

Will almost snickered. She was bothered by it, and she was curious. "So we're back to Mr. Stanton, are we?" Will shook his head.

"Anyone else interested in how Mr. Stanton spends his time?" Will asked the other two at the table.

Jayne hid a smile. "You annoy me, Stanton. I couldn't care less where you go or who you were with."

"You would care if it were Annabeth."

Annabeth's head shot up. "Will!" She was looking at him with daggers.

"So we are back to Will now? You need to make up your mind if I am a friend or just an acquaintance."

"I was at home last evening and all night," she said rather loudly toward him, but her eyes captured the three onlookers.

"Yes, you were, and I was at Thad and Merry's. It was late when we finished planting, and they invited me to stay the night. So you see, Annabeth, how mixed up things can get if you don't get the facts, and you don't give a person the benefit of the doubt."

The rest of the meal was eaten in silence. When everyone was finished, Rawly took Annabeth into the parlor. Jonathan followed. Will began working on the dishes. Jayne stayed back to help him.

"You shouldn't treat Annabeth so cruelly. It isn't very fair."

"In what way do you think I am cruel?" Will asked.

"I think she is very devoted to you as a friend and coworker. It is obvious there is something more there that I am not sure she understands. Your little jokes aren't helping."

She had nerve, Will thought. *Now, how to reply?* "Tell me, Jayne, which is more cruel? What I am supposedly doing to Annabeth, or what you are doing to her?" She let out a slight gasp and nearly dropped the plate she was drying.

"What I am doing? Whatever do you mean?"

"I know all about you and Rawly and what went on in Annabeth's absence."

"That Vivian talks nonsense." Jayne was quick to respond.

"Oh, you think Vivian told me?"

"Well, I, you…" she began to stutter.

Will reached and grabbed the plate in her hand. "Why don't you go collect yourself? I will finish the dishes." She started to leave. "And, Jayne, before you start meddling in other people's affairs, perhaps you should clean up your own."

That sent her over the edge. With a red face, she flew out of the kitchen.

Will did some collecting of himself. It was getting difficult fighting the battle on two fronts. There was Rawly and all his weapons and Jonathan and all of his. Will was getting worn out. He finished the dishes and headed to his room. He needed to spend some time in the word. It was the only way he could win.

He heard everyone retire for the night and watched through the window as Rawly walked Annabeth to her door. This was probably the most challenging thing he was fighting. When should he tell her the man courting her was a villain. He watched as the enemy placed a kiss on the lips of the woman he loved. His gut clenched. He knew when Annabeth found out who he was and why he was in Sheridan, she would have the wrong idea about him as well. She would feel duped for the third time. Hopefully, when it was all said and done, his letter written the night of Patience's wedding would help her understand.

Annabeth felt guilty. She had been upset with Will for staying out all night. What a nice thing he had done helping her uncle with the planting. She had heard from Avery that Franklin and Gil were sick. She didn't think about how that might affect the farm. She never dreamed Will had gone out to lend a hand. She felt the urgency to apologize. For some reason, it couldn't wait until tomorrow. She put her shoes back on and stepped out on the boardwalk. Noticing his light still on, she took a move from Jonathan's playbook. She found a small rock and hurled it at his window. Much to her surprise, it landed where it should. No response. She picked up another one and threw it with a little bit more force.

"You're going to break the window if you throw it any harder." Will startled her. "You know you don't have to throw rocks at my window to get my attention. You already have it. It is an amateur move, something Jonathan would do."

Annabeth was having trouble finding her words. He had startled her so badly.

"Come into the kitchen. It is rather chilly tonight." Thrive bounded toward Will in search of attention. Annabeth had yet to move. What did he mean it was something Jonathan would do. Did he know? "Annabeth, honey, come inside." She made her way into the kitchen.

"Did you need to see me about something?" He pulled a chair out for her and sat in the one next to her, bringing it as close to her as he could get. Thrive was on the other side of her. "Were you headed out?" She finally found her voice.

"Yes," he answered with a smile. "You do recall from time to time I patrol the town for Dan. I believe we have met on more than one occasion while I was doing so." He placed his arm on the back of the chair she was sitting in and leaned in to face her.

"What is it you needed from me so desperately that you would throw rocks at my window?" She momentarily got lost in the way his eyes looked directly into hers. There was just silence between them. Even Thrive was quiet, placing his head on Annabeth's lap, looking at Will.

"Well, I can see you do your best work at night, Mr. Stanton. You certainly are keeping me on my toes." Jonathan interrupted the potential tender moment. "Does Rawly know about these late-night kitchen rendezvous? I am rather surprised at you, Annabeth. I am certain your mother and father would be." He was leaning against the door, facing.

"They might be if there was anything more than conversation going on. I can't believe you would insinuate anything else was occurring." Annabeth stood, and Will did too.

"Go home, Jonathan. There is nothing here for you." She turned and whispered the apology she had initially set out to give into Will's ear and tenderly kissed his cheek. "Good night, Will. Good-bye, Jonathan." Annabeth started to leave.

"I'll go, Annabeth, when I am ready and not one minute earlier. I don't mind losing you to the blacksmith, but I will do everything in my power to stop this vagrant from having any claim on you."

Annabeth looked at her one-time fiancé. She didn't even feel like she knew the man in front of her. She shook her head. "Let's get one thing straight. You can't lose something you don't have. And I am not something you can stake claim to. I am sorry you were ever part of my life, Jonathan." Thrive started to growl, and Annabeth took him home.

"You'll never have her. I'm wiring Charleston for an investigation on you. I will find a way to ruin you," Jonathan said as he stood face-to-face with Will.

"You can't ruin a man who doesn't care. I am not afraid of you, Jonathan. Stage leaves at ten." Will left to make his rounds.

*****

A week had passed, and Jonathan remained in Sheridan. He spent half of his time at the telegraph office and the other half practically stalking Will. It was if he was building some sort of case against him. Will was confident in his covert responsibility. The agency has no record on him. To them, he doesn't exist. Jonathan's investigation will only lead him all across the country, starting and ending in Will's home state of Indiana.

Will had done some of his own investigating of Jonathan. It was purely accidental. On his nightly patrols, Will found Jonathan liked to frequent Owen Miller's poker games. He watched as Jonathan would intentionally lose a few hands and then wind up taking home a massive haul. He also knew Owen Miller was onto Jonathan's game. Will didn't care if the two gamblers came to blows. What he did care about were Annabeth, Hannah, and Josie. The three women would be immensely hurt if they knew these shenanigans were going on. He took a moment to pray for the gentlemen.

Late one evening, there was quite the ruckus. A boarder from Trudy's had come to play as well. When Jonathan was suspected of cheating, the two men nearly came to blows. Chairs were knocked over, and the man had Jonathan by the collar. Just as he was ready to level the aristocrat from Charleston, a woman stepped in. Will was shocked to see Jayne step in between the men. She laid her hand on Jonathan's chest and pushed him back. Standing there, Will watched as Jayne defused the potential scuffle; and they all sat back down. Jayne was dealing the next hand. Mr. Tyler would be crushed if he knew his niece was involved in this type of behavior. She was laughing and cavorting with the gentlemen in Owen Miller's backroom saloon.

Will needed to speak with Dan. These types of meeting places can slowly tear up a town. Maybe when he finished with his case, he could stay long enough to help Dan clean up a little bit of what was going on. He hated the thought of Sheridan having even a small mark on its name.

Rawly was happy to have Jonathan dogging Will's every move. He was in hopes both gentleman would move on. Annabeth had told him she was in no hurry to marry any man. Which meant she was unsure of her feelings. Darn that Will Stanton. None of this would be happening if it wasn't for him. He pounded a little harder on the anvil. He watched as the object of his hatred bounded up the steps of the bakery and knocked on the closed door. It was the middle of the afternoon, the bakery was closed, yet there was Annabeth to let him in. If Rawly weren't right in the middle of something, he would head over there and have it out with Mr. Stanton.

CHAPTER 10

*A*nnabeth had just put a cake in the oven when she heard a knock on the front door of the bakery. "Why didn't you come in the back door? You know it is always open," she asked Will as she let him in.

"Rawly can't always see me coming in the back." Will turned and waved in the direction of the blacksmith."

"There are times I don't think you are very nice."

"And the other times, what do you think of me?"

She ignored him and moved into the kitchen. "What did you want?"

"I came to see if you needed any help. You know we make a pretty good team when catering an event."

"This is just a surprise birthday party for Aunt Merry. It is hardly an event."

"I bet Merry thinks it is an event." He reached over and stole a bit of frosting. "Not bad."

Annabeth frowned. "Does it need something else?" She sampled a little bit herself. "No, Annabeth, it is perfect. I am just teasing you."

Will poured himself a cup of coffee and looked in Annabeth's basket. There was one lonely muffin. "May I?" he asked.

She nodded. There was a knock on the back door. Hunter and River Sheridan stood stoically waiting. "Hello, boys, what can I do for you?" Their eyes drifted to Will eating the muffin, and they frowned most disgustedly.

"We were wondering if you had any do-overs." Their eyes never left Will. "Or did he eat them all?" River said as if Will had single-handedly ate every cookie in the world.

Will felt as if he had been sentenced to death by staring. The muffin was stuck in his throat. He usually was pretty good with children but not these two. They were protective of their cousin as they should be. He wondered how they treated Rawly; but then it dawned on him, Rawly was probably not around them much. He never seemed to want to be around Annabeth's family. Will wondered if Rawly was going to the surprise party at Hawk's this evening. He would have to watch how the boys reacted—that is, if they could curb their surveillance of him.

"I do have some for the children. Let me go get them." Annabeth moved to the back where she had a tin full of sugar cookies. "Not as good as your grandma's, but I think you will like them."

The boys rendered their thank you, and River tugged on her sleeve and whispered, "If he ain't your husband, why do you let him hang around and eat up all your muffins?"

She bent over and whispered back, "Doesn't the Bible say if your enemy is hungry feed him?"

"He doesn't look like no enemy to me. He looks like a husband," Hunter added as he pulled his brother away and headed back to school.

Annabeth had to laugh. Will had not heard the conversation, and he didn't want to ask what was discussed. He knew it had been him. "Those boys," she said as she sat across from him. "Do you mind if I ask you something?"

"Go ahead. Ask me anything." Will leaned back in his chair.

"I would like to ask about your family."

Will leaned up, putting his elbow on the table and resting his cheek in his hand. "Now, that sounds like something a woman who's thinking about a long-term relationship would ask." She should be used to this by now. The look on her face said forget it. He folded his hands on the table. "I suppose in particular you want to know what happened to Ben." He searched her face with his eyes. Annabeth stayed quiet.

"We were much like Hawk's boys: inseparable. I don't reckon any brothers were closer. We fought some but, for the most part, got along. One afternoon, on the way home from school, Ben collapsed on the road. I tried to wake him up, but he wouldn't. I didn't want to leave him, but I knew I needed to get help. We were closer to town, so I ran back.

"The first person I saw was the town drunk. I told him what had happened, and he sent me to get the doctor. He would go get Ben and head that way."

Annabeth had tears in her eyes. More so because of the pained look on Will's face than anything. The story was horrid, but his retelling of it after all these years was taking its toll. She rested her hand on his. "I am sorry I asked." Her voice was soft.

He continued, "I ran to Doc Crowder's and told him what happened and that Old Whiskey was bringing my brother. Old Whiskey was all we ever called the man. I don't think anyone in town knew his real name. It wasn't very long until he came running through town with Ben in his arms. I can still see the old man with tears in his eyes.

"Dr. Crowder tried to send me home to get my parents, but I wouldn't leave. The town sheriff had seen Old Whiskey running through town and followed him. He rode out to get my folks. I don't know how long I sat there, but I do remember Old Whiskey staying by my side. We were always taught to keep our distance from him. But that day—I will never forget that day—those strong arms carrying my brother and then cradling me as I shook uncontrollably. Ben died a few hours later."

Annabeth had a stream of tears down her cheeks. "Did they know what happened, why he died?"

"They weren't sure. They thought it could have been a heart or brain ailment. The doctor suggested I get seen by a special doctor in Chicago, just in case. So a week after we buried Ben, my mom and I spent two weeks in Chicago. I was poked and prodded by more than one person. The only thing they could tell my mother was to keep a close eye on me. That turned out to be futile. I was determined to do everything I wanted. If I was going to die too, so be it. I presented my parents with a real challenge."

Will took a deep breath. "Smells like your cake is done."

Annabeth rose, knowing full well Will wanted to change the subject. What emotion it had cost him to relive that tragic day. She pulled two perfect round cakes from the oven and set them to cool. Will joined her in the kitchen.

"Perfection yet again, Miss Lorton."

She moved into the back room. "I ordered a stack of bakery doilies just for such occasions and some fancy candles." She pulled a box from Sadler's and put it on the counter. "This came yesterday."

Will's heart lurched. Did Rawly know it had arrived? He couldn't ask. Annabeth opened the container and removed the contents of the small box and noticed a crack in the bottom and saw something shiny underneath. She placed her hand inside the box and felt the flooring move. A false bottom. She worked as she removed the board. Will watched as his heart fell into his stomach.

"Oh my," Annabeth said as she saw some jewelry and cash. Her eyes turned to Will. The look on his face told her he knew all about this. "You...you know about this?"

The astonishment was on her face. "Don't let your mind go down all types of rabbit holes." He took her hands and held them. "Hear me out, Annabeth, completely." She didn't say a word.

"I work for—" He couldn't tell her everything. "I'm working for someone who is trying to bust a smuggling ring." Her eyes were huge. "This type of merchandise, as well as cash, has been transported from the South to Western towns in Colorado."

"Via my bakery! For how long?" She pulled her hands from his.

"Annabeth, please listen." It was like she didn't hear him.

"You have been spying on me, working here under false pretenses. Do you think I am part of the ring? The trip to Patience's wedding—it was all part of this?"

He gave up and sat on the counter. He let Annabeth reason and rationalize all her thoughts. In a burst of anger, she threw the box across the room. Luckily for Will, it didn't break. He went to her, putting his hands on her shoulders.

"This isn't what it looks like, Annabeth. I know you had no clue the goods were coming through The Dowry."

"How long have you been keeping this from me?" she said in quieter tones, shrugging her shoulders to free her from his hold.

"I found out while you were ill."

"Why haven't you gone to the sheriff? Isn't this his jurisdiction? Does this person you are working for have the authority to overstep the action of the town sheriff?"

"Not exactly, but Dan has agreed to let me make the decisions. We want the whole setup, from Sadler's in Charleston to Sheridan and into Colorado." She stood perplexed, just staring at him. "Annabeth, you do understand who the person is that's seeing the merchandise and cash are getting out of Sheridan, don't you?"

She nearly fainted when it occurred to her that Rawly too had been playing her as a fool. She turned and leaned against the counter, her head down. Will went to stand behind her. He put his hand on her back. "I am sorry, Annabeth. I couldn't risk telling you." She straightened but didn't turn around. The air seemed to have become very cold.

"You can go, Will. I have work to do." She moved to get around him, and he stopped her.

"Annabeth, I need your help in this. You can't act like you know. You can't confront Rawly. I need you to continue letting the shipments come here. A lot of people have put their lives at risk to take this outfit down. I need your promise you won't interfere."

She picked up the box and put the stolen items back in and placed the false bottom on top. She handed it to Will, and he sat it on the counter. "Give it to Rawly." He tapped the top of the box. "Yes, now please go."

Will hesitated, but he knew nothing he could say or do right now would help how utterly victimized Annabeth Lorton was feeling at the moment.

*****

Merry Sheridan was surprised *and* thrilled when she walked into Hawk's living room. All the people who mattered the most to her was wishing her a happy birthday. "You're behind this, aren't you?" She turned to her husband, who was grinning widely.

"I had some help." He winked at Avery and Annabeth who had put the party together.

Merry's sons each came and gave their mother a kiss and wished her many more. Her grandchildren clung to her, jumping up and down, vying for her attention.

"You have got to see the cake Annabeth has made. It looks too beautiful to eat," Molly said over the heads of the children.

Annabeth had used the decorating tips she received from her secret friend. The cake was covered with flowers and scrolling vines. "Annabeth, it's beautiful. How did you get such intricate detail?" Merry asked, looking at the cake.

"You know how I got them. I used the decorating tips you gave me."

"Tips I gave you? I didn't give you any tips." Merry looked to Avery as if she could help explain.

"This apron." She smoothed the apron as if drawing attention to it would jog her aunt's mind. "This timepiece, the tips, and recipe book, Thrive—didn't they all come from you and Uncle Thad?"

Merry looked a bit shocked. "No, honey, they're not from us."

Lydia Lapp overheard the conversation and smiled to herself. She had kept a pretty good secret, not even telling her husband.

Annabeth turned to see Lydia smile. "You are not going to tell, are you?"

The woman just shook her head no. "If the person wanted you to know, they would tell you themselves."

Annabeth wanted to ask more, but River had tugged on her hand. "Where's your husband?" This was getting old.

"Yes, where is Will? He was invited, wasn't he?" Hawk looked to Avery. She made no effort to hide her irritation with her husband.

"Yes, he was invited," she said to her husband but bent to address her son. "River, we have told you that Will and Annabeth are friends, and you need to stop referring to him as her husband. Do you understand?" She looked at her son in the eye.

"What's *referring* mean?" The boy curiously looked at his mother.

"It means stop calling Will Annabeth's husband."

"Can I call her his wife?"

"No." Avery turned the boy and shoved him toward the other children.

"Where are Will and Rawly? I just assumed you would let Rawly know he was invited," Avery mentioned to Annabeth as they were serving the cake.

"Rawly should be here any minute, and I don't know where Will is."

Avery thought there was a bit of sadness in Annabeth's tone.

"Will is right here." The man himself had come in the back door and was standing behind Annabeth. All of a sudden, there was excitement as Merry rushed toward her. Annabeth wasn't sure what was going on until she turned to see Tommy and Josie standing beside Will.

"H-happy b-birthday, Ma." Merry flew into Tommy's arms; there was a lot of hugging and kissing going on. Josie and Hannah embraced for a long time with tears trickling down their faces. It was more than evident that Josie was expecting, so more congratulatory sentiments were shared.

The evening was a big hit except for Annabeth. Thad knew his niece was a bit uncomfortable for some reason, and he wondered if it had something to do with Will or Rawly. Will's eyes rarely deviated from her whereas Rawly seemed to be enjoying the evening a little too much. He dreaded what lay ahead for his niece and wanted to protect her in every way possible. Thad knew he could not, but he knew who could, so he quickly said a prayer.

"You're in deep thought." Merry linked her arm through her husband's.

"Yes, I am. I am sorry. Here it is your birthday, and you should have my undivided attention."

She moved to stand in front of him, putting her arms around his neck. "I don't mind sharing your attention a little bit here and there as long as it eventually comes back to me." She smiled.

"Well, that my dear, is a given." He pulled her close and kissed her—twice. It didn't matter to Thad who was watching. It never did. Will happened to be the only one that caught the tender moment between the birthday girl and her love. His eyes drifted to Annabeth. He wanted to be her husband more than anything.

Dan Bullock was glad Tommy had brought Josie back to town. He needed to talk to both girls. He wanted to let them know what their father was up to and that Owen Miller might be in a little trouble. Some of the money exchanged during the late-night poker games was counterfeit. Dan spoke with both Jonah and Tommy, asking to see them and the girls first thing Monday morning. He gave the young men a brief word about what he intended to discuss. The Sheridan boys didn't seem all that surprised about their father-in-law.

*****

Annabeth sat in her usual place beside Rawly Sunday morning. Why did she feel like the hypocrite? She had done nothing wrong. "Guilt by Association" was the compelling title of Pastor Grey's message. She was thinking maybe the message was going to be for her specifically. The pastor began to teach how even though we were not there on the day Christ was crucified, we were guilty of putting him to death. Our sins sent him to the cross. He became our sacrifice and mediator to reconcile us to God. It was our free will that allowed us to be with the Lord or against him.

The pastor's final words were "Your decisions, folks, will send you to heaven or send you to hell." Rawly had never squirmed so much. Annabeth hoped the Lord was dealing with his heart. He could turn things around by repenting.

Will exited the church without much conversation. He waited for Thad to come down the steps and head for his wagon. "Can I talk to you for a moment?"

Thad knew it was serious by the look on Will's face. "Sure, why don't you come out to the house for lunch? We can talk after." He watched as Will's eyes went to Annabeth's. "Annabeth will be there," Thad provided the information.

"It can wait. I will get with you sometime this week. Tommy's in town, and I know you want to spend time with him and Josie."

Merry approached the wagon, and Thad helped her up. "You go on home, Merry. I will be there directly. Whenever dinner's ready, go ahead and eat." Merry looked at Will walking away. "It's that father's heart you have." She smiled at her husband. "Getty up," she commanded the team and headed home.

Thad followed Will, calling for him to come back. He motioned, and the two headed into the church. Will wasted no time. "Annabeth found out. She stumbled on the false bottom boxes and found the goods."

Thad sighed. "What are you going to do?"

"I want to get this over with. I am wiring headquarters first thing in the morning that with the next shipment I'm closing in."

"And how did Annabeth take it?"

Will shook his head. "She's so hurt, first Jonathan, now Rawly, and me. I think she is the angriest with me. She won't even look at me nonetheless talk to me. She thinks I have been using her."

"Do you want me to give her your letter?" Thad didn't like seeing the man in agony, but he certainly didn't like the thoughts of Annabeth in any distress.

"No, it's not the right time. There is more to come, and I want every inch of my last year cleared up and out in the open."

"What do you mean there is more to come?"

"The last few nights I have been making my rounds, I found Jonathan involved in the games at Miller's as well as Jayne Hanson. I can tell you both surprised me. There is counterfeit money coming from those games, and Miller's in trouble.

"What's Annabeth going to do when she realizes neither of her would-be husbands were committed to the Lord, only playing games in the church house? She'll start to question her own spiritual discernment. That will hurt her most of all."

Thad just sat there, taking it all in. His mind was on Annabeth. "Let's pray for the Lord's guidance," Thad finally spoke. The two men spent the next few minutes in prayer.

"I'll get some time with Annabeth today. See how she is doing. Do you want me to tell her about Jonathan and Jayne?"

"I think Dan was going to talk to Jayne and tell her it was time to move on. The counterfeit money surfaced before she got in on the games. He didn't think it was necessary to tell Mr. Tyler."

"Dan is a good sheriff and a good man."

"We probably don't need to tell Annabeth just yet." The men stood to leave.

"I better start home. Merry's gracious, but when it comes to one of the big family meals, she has her limits."

Will laughed at Thad's expression. "In that case, I will drive you home."

Merry pleaded for Will to stay and eat lunch with them. Annabeth had turned toward the stove when Will entered the house. this motion was not missed by the two knights of Queen Annabeth who were setting the table. Will didn't want to deal with the young men today. If Will stayed, he'd be questioned. If he left, he'd be maligned in their little minds. Either way, he was doomed; and why was he so worried about a couple of children?

"Thank you, Merry, but I am going away for a few days, and I need to be getting on the road. I have some things I need to take care of."

She didn't push it. "Very well, but wait just a minute before you go." In true Merry fashion, she packed some food for his journey.

"Thank you, Merry. This is much appreciated."

Thad followed him out. "You didn't say anything about leaving."

"I just got this notion I had better do my telegraphing from a different city. I don't want the town knowing who I work for. I am sure the telegraph office is confidential, but I can't take any chances."

Thad nodded. "Be careful, son."

"Thanks for everything, Thad. No matter how all this turns out." His eyes drifted toward the house. "I'm glad I met you."

Is Will running away? Will some other person come in and take over the operation? Annabeth was in a world of her own, and everyone at the table knew it. They asked for something to be passed, and she never heard them. She dropped things and looked as if she was near tears. Everyone had the good graces to just let her be. That was until Thad decided he needed to intervene.

Thad and Merry took her aside for a walk and told her that they knew about what was happening at her bakery. They listened as Annabeth poured her heart out about everything. From Jonathan leaving her at the altar to Rawly's debauchery to Wills willingness to use her and her emotions to sustain his secret operation. She felt like a fool; and when it was all said and done, she would be a fool. She would more than likely lose The Dowry.

"Slow down, honey." Thad stopped her tirade. "First, no one blames you. This is devious men doing devious crimes. Rawly could have very easily used Tyler's Mercantile, the mill, or the bank he knew he could have more control over your smaller business. Who would suspect the bakery? He is very cunning." She wasn't buying what he was saying. She was too busy running things around in her own head.

"Don't play the poor victim in all this, Annabeth Lorton. You are better than that." Merry's words was stern and caught Annabeth by surprise. "You had nothing to do with this. You are an honest, sweet, loving girl, and that does not make you a fool. And I don't expect you to change. Jonathan will move on. Rawly will most definitely move on, and only time will tell if Will's actions are sincere. He too may move on. I realize you don't trust yourself in matters of the heart right now, but don't wall yourself off. Life can get pretty miserable if you shut all the doors. Very few men are willing to try to break down barriers in a woman. So don't build them."

Annabeth began to cry. Merry put her arms around her niece and held her tight. "It will be all right, love. Everything will work out as it should. You just need to trust in the Lord and look for him to guide your path. You know we are always here for you and will love and support you no matter what direction the Lord leads you."

Annabeth grabbed Merry's hand, and the two went on to walk a little farther. Thad headed back to the house. He figured Annabeth needed the ear of a mother for matters of the heart. He thanked the Lord that he was able to break down the barriers Merry had so many years ago. God did indeed direct the path of those who trusted in him.

*****

Sunday evening Jayne Hanson announced she would be leaving on the Monday stage. It didn't seem to be a surprise to Dan or Trudy. *I wish Jonathan would be on the stage*, Annabeth thought. Where was he anyway? She hadn't seen him since Saturday afternoon.

"Where is Jonathan?" Trudy asked as if she had been following Annabeth's thoughts.

"I was just thinking the same thing. I haven't seen him since Saturday afternoon."

"I wonder if he is sick." Trudy rose and went to Jonathan's room. She knocked on the door; and when there was no answer, she opened the door. Jonathan was not in his room.

"He isn't in his room," she reported.

"Are his things still there?" Dan asked his wife.

"Yes, all his belongings are still here."

Dan didn't say anything. He just got up, kissed his wife, and headed out the door. Jayne retired to her room, and Annabeth and Trudy did the evening dishes. Annabeth couldn't help but wonder where Jonathan was as well as Will.

Dan made rounds. There was no game going on at Owen's place. He looked the town over. Nothing out of the ordinary was happening. He circled back and fourth down the sides of the buildings in town. No sign of Jonathan Taylor. He noticed activity at the doctor's house, but that wasn't anything out of the ordinary. He saw Hawk get in his buggy and head his way.

"I'm on my way out to Lach's. Michael just rode in to get me. Seems Lach found Jonathan Taylor out in the brush near his house."

"Mind if I ride with you?" Dan didn't wait for an answer but climbed in. "What condition is he in?"

"Michael didn't say. Just said it was bad and his ma was beside herself."

When the doctor arrived, it was too late. Jonathan Taylor was dead. The man had been in a struggle. There were several cuts, bruises, and swelling; but the fatal blow was to the head. There was a large gash to the temple with some skull depression.

Hawk examined the body with Dan in attendance. They concluded a murder had taken place. Jonathan had no money on him, and his watch was missing. All the appearance of a robbery but Dan wasn't so sure. Since Will's report on Jonathan's involvement in the poker game, this could have been more than a petty theft gone wrong.

Dan began his investigation starting with where Lach found the body. Carrying two lanterns each, the men headed out to the scene. It did look like a struggle had taken place in the brush. There was blood on a nearby rock. Could this be the murder weapon? Dan would have to come back in the light of day. He also needed to shut down his town. No one was leaving on tomorrow's stage.

Dan arrived home late to find Annabeth and Trudy waiting up for him. "Where have you been? Did you find Jonathan?"

He looked exhausted, and Annabeth didn't like the look on his face. Something was terribly wrong. "I found him." Dan pointed to the kitchen.

Once in the kitchen, the two women began to fidget. "He is dead." Dan caught Annabeth right before she hit the floor. Trudy scurried to get a chair to put her in and got a cold cloth for her head.

"What happened?" Trudy asked her husband as Annabeth began to stir.

"It looks like he was murdered."

"Murdered!" Annabeth, Trudy, and Jayne, who had now entered the kitchen, spoke in unison.

"Yes, and you are not leaving on tomorrow's stage. No one is."

"You don't think I had anything to do with this." Jayne seemed shocked.

Trudy and Annabeth were also taken aback by Dan's tone. "Miss, after what I have found out about you, I don't take anything for granted."

The woman returned to her room in a huff.

"Dan, what is going on? What did you mean about finding something out about Jayne?"

"This is an investigation of more proportions than even I am aware of. I am going to ask you, ladies, not to question me. You'll find out information as I release it. I suggest you both get some rest. And tomorrow go about your daily business." They both just looked at him. "Annabeth, I know Jonathan was a friend of yours, and you have my condolences. I am sorry this happened."

Annabeth was numb. When she felt steady enough, she headed to her little cottage. She was devastated.

Sheriff Bullock was quick to get started on his investigation. His first order of business was to speak with Josie and Hannah Sheridan. He felt he owed the girls the courtesy of telling them before the town found out about their father. They were shocked, humiliated, and angry. The sheriff informed them that there would be a lot more come out as the investigation progressed.

Tommy wasn't sure he could be away from his job any longer than what he had planned. His heart wanted to remove Josie from this horrible situation as soon as possible, but that had to be her heart's desire as well.

Josie had known Tommy all her life. She knew she could trust him. With a pale face, she turned to him. "Take me home as soon as Sheriff Bullock gives the okay."

"To see Mother?" Hannah asked, her voice shaky.

"No, Hannah, I am sorry. I want to be far away from the situation. I am not strong like you."

Jonah was a little irritated at his sister-in-law. It wasn't fair to his wife. She would be left to carry the burden. His hand gripped tighter around his wife's. He wanted her to know he supported her without causing more hardship by speaking his mind.

Tommy saw the look on his brother's face and the tears in his sister-in-law's eyes. "H-how long to w-wrap this up, Sheriff?" he asked.

"I'm headed there now." The sheriff moved to get his hat.

"We will be out at m-my f-folks until we are n-no longer needed." He turned to his sobbing wife and bent down to face her. "It is the right thing to do, Jo."

She buried her face in his embrace. "I know," she whispered.

Hannah took her sister out to their in-laws. Jonah and Tommy wanted to accompany the sheriff. The scene wasn't pretty as Owen Miller was taken into custody for questioning. Dan Bullock was a good man and tried every way to keep the matter confidential and protect the innocent. Word in a small town spread quickly. Gambling wasn't illegal, but counterfeit money was, and Dan needed to get to the bottom of this problem.

Pretty soon, the murder of Jonathan Taylor was discovered; and the town nearly lost its mind. What was happening in their small community? Were the two crimes connected? Everyone became some sort of private investigator in a matter of minutes.

Those who were involved in the games at Miller's brought their winnings to the sheriff along with their alibis. Speculation was rampant, and it was difficult to wade through all the stories. There was a definite undercurrent. Jonathan Taylor was a card shark, and so was Owen Miller. The two had quarreled on more than one occasion.

There was also a well-known fact that Jonathan Taylor and Will Stanton had a near altercation late one night outside The Dowry. There was no fisticuffs, but the two were nose to nose, and there was a little shoving. This was all witnessed by none other than Jayne Hanson as she was leaving Miller's after winning quite the tidy sum.

*****

Will was traveling back from the neighboring town. He had planned to leave right after he sent his telegram and received confirmation. When the confirmation came, it brought a whole new situation. Sadler's had declared it was going out of business. The last shipment to Sheridan would be this week. The key player would be pulling out of the deal and moving on.

Will rode as fast as his horse would take him. He had set his plan in motion quickly, and he needed to alert Annabeth. When he made it to town, he noticed a lot of unusual activity. Something was going on.

He headed to the bakery first. He entered through the back door and found Annabeth sitting at a table, looking out the window toward the street. She turned when she heard someone enter. When she saw it was Will, she turned back around. She looked horrible. For the first time in a long time, he felt fear.

"Annabeth, are you all right?" He made his way to the table and sat beside her.

"Did you need something?" she asked, never looking at him. Yes, he needed something. He needed her. He looked around. "Are we alone?" He didn't want Vivian to hear them talking.

She looked at him strangely. "Yes."

He desperately wanted to know what was wrong, but it was apparent she was not going to divulge anything to him. "I came to tell you there will only be one more shipment from Sadler's. They are closing. The operation has been halted and possibly compromised. We have to close in with your shipment this week. It is due Thursday or Friday."

"Very well. Just tell me what you need me to do and when you need me to do it." She rose and left the bakery, not saying another word to him. This was all Will needed. Something was definitely wrong with her. He couldn't be worried about her during this time. He had a job to do.

Will headed over to Hawk's. Perhaps he could pay a house call to Annabeth to make sure she was all right. When he opened the door to the doctor's office, he noticed several patients sitting in the room. The little bell above the door notified Hannah Sheridan another patient had arrived. She had taken to working for her brother-in-law a few hours a day.

"What can we do for you, Will?" He leaned over and spoke quietly. "I just need to speak with Hawk for a moment. I need to give him a personal message." She looked at the room full of patients and then back at the closed exam room door.

"I understand, Hannah. Would you just tell him I would like for him to see Annabeth sometime today? She doesn't look very well."

Hannah rose and knocked on the door. When she heard Hawk say, "Come in," she entered quietly. It was a few minutes, and the patient in the room was released, and Hannah showed Will in.

"What makes you think Annabeth is unwell?" Dr. Sheridan asked.

"She is very pale and stoic. I don't know. Something is wrong."

"When did you get into town, Will?"

"Just now. I went straight to The Dowry. Why?"

"Jonathan Taylor was found dead Sunday evening. That's what is the matter with Annabeth."

Will was speechless. "How?" Will asked when he found his voice. He didn't wait for an answer. "You're busy, I'll head over and talk to the sheriff." He didn't wait for any comment from the doctor. He left, walking briskly to the jail.

"What happened?" Will asked his uncle as he burst into the sheriff's office. Dan gave him the same information he gave everyone else in the town. Will frowned.

"You know I can't tell you any more than what I tell the town. The investigation is ongoing." Will understood.

"I'll let you get back to work," Will said as he started to leave.

"Don't leave town," Dan said to Will's back.

The man turned slowly. "What?" Will chose not to hold his anger.

"I have had more than one witness say you and Taylor got nose to nose in the alley between Tyler's and The Dowry. Maybe a little shoving match, raised voices?" the sheriff questioned.

Will left without saying a word. Yes, he and Jonathan had more than one set of words since Jonathan's arrival. He didn't like the man, but he wouldn't kill him. Anyone of the poker-playing party would have the motive to kill him. Jonathan was pretty good at fleecing, even Mr. Miller, who was pretty good at it himself.

Will hoped his uncle was combing through all leads appropriately. He didn't need the suspicion of murder cast on him at this time. He trusted Dan to do the right thing, and he trusted the Lord. He had to find Annabeth.

*****

Annabeth wanted out of town. People would stare and whisper, shaking their heads. Surely, they didn't think she killed Jonathan. She put on her bonnet called for Thrive, and the two headed out to the Sheridans. She knew there she would feel safe. She knew she could trust them with her whole heart.

When she arrived, Merry, Molly, and Jamie Kennedy were sitting under a big oak tree, quilting. Molly was the first to spot her and waved her over. "Come and help us, Annabeth. We are making a quilt for Avery's new baby."

This would be a good distraction, Annabeth thought.

Merry rose. "Here, take my spot. I was just going to go in and fix lunch."

"Why don't you let me fix lunch? I am better at cooking than sewing."

Merry sensed Annabeth's need to keep busy, so she sat back down.

*****

Will felt like he needed to tell Thad about the plan he had put into place. He also needed to keep busy. He couldn't do that in town. Word had gotten out that he was a suspect. Strange looks were sent his way as he went into Tyler's to tell the man he wouldn't be in for a day or two. Mr. Tyler trusted Will and told him not to worry and to come to work when he was able. After all, he wasn't paying the man for his work. Will rarely needed anything in exchange for his labor.

Will tied his horse to the railing of the corral and went into the barn. Thad wasn't there. Nor was any of the boys. He looked to the fields—nothing. Will made his way to the front door and knocked. He was shocked when Annabeth answered. For a moment, he just stared at her. There was an emotion in her eyes that ripped his heart out.

"Are you following me?" she asked in a cool tone.

"No, I didn't know you were here. I wanted to speak to your uncle. He is not in the barn."

"He and the others are helping Lach at his place." She turned and headed back to preparing lunch.

"I didn't kill him, Annabeth." Will was now standing behind her. She continued working. Never flinching. "So just like that, your offering of friendship over the past months is rescinded." Still no movement. "I understand, Annabeth. It all has to be your way." He turned to leave.

"You lied to me, just like the others." She turned with the knife in her hand she used to slice some cheese.

"When did I lie to you?" He stepped back toward her.

"Your whole reason for being in Sheridan, working at my bakery, every interaction has been based on a lie." She was wheeling the knife while she was talking.

"Can we put the knife down?" Will asked, trying to diffuse the situation.

She stabbed the knife into the cutting board. "You lied, just like Rawly and Jon—" A sob caught in her throat. "I can't take any more of this." Her grip eased on the knife handle.

Will put his hands on her shoulders and turned her toward him. "I never lied to you. I just didn't confide in you." She wouldn't look at him. He gave her a little shake. "Annabeth, look at me." Her face turned up, her eyes full of hurt. "I never lied about loving you."

"Everything okay in here?" Thad had entered through the back door. He had returned to the house for some supplies and heard Annabeth's voice raised in emotion. Thad watched from the back porch before entering. He didn't want to interrupt at the wrong time.

"No," Will answered as Annabeth answered, "Yes." Will did not ease his grip until Annabeth wiggled out of it.

"He is here to see you." Annabeth wouldn't look at her uncle.

Will exited the front door, Thad following behind. "Save me one of those." Thad pointed to the stack of sandwiches on the plate next to the knife.

Will was untying his mount. "Hold on, son. You came out here to see me. What is it?"

Will cooled down a fraction. "I came out to tell you it will all be over this week."

He wasn't going to say any more. "What is your hurry? You know Dan has a murder investigation going on."

"How could I not know? I am his number one suspect." Thad's expression showed he didn't know that piece of information. "I was out of town. When do they think Jonathan was killed?"

"Sometime yesterday afternoon. He was found off the road near Lach's. When did you get into Keystone? I am assuming that is where you went to telegraph the agency."

"I got there around four. Since it was Sunday, the telegraph office was closed. I wanted to be there first thing this morning, so I could get things in motion. It took longer than I thought. Sadler's is closing their business. One of the stakeholders in this operation has pulled out. The shipment coming in on Thursday will be the last. It has to be this week, or I've lost the whole case."

"Does Dan know?"

"Not yet. I wanted to tell Annabeth first. She was so stoic I thought she was ill. I went to tell Hawk so he could check on her, and that is when I found out about Jonathan. I knew now was not the time to tell Dan about what I found out in Keystone. He has a murder to investigate, but I needed a few answers, so I headed there. That is when I found out I was a suspect. I was told not to leave town."

"You need to tell Dan. You can't stop what is going to happen this week." Thad looked back at the house. "And you can't stop her from feeling hurt, lied to, and used." Will mounted his horse. "Do you want me to give her the letter?"

"No, it wouldn't make a difference to her now. I don't know if there will ever be a right time." He turned his horse and headed back to Sheridan to talk to Sheriff Bullock.

Thad made his way into the house. Annabeth sat at the table her head in her hands; he sat across from her. "Do you want to talk about it?"

She shook her head no. "Annabeth, I know you are a mess right now, but I want you to know when the smoke clears, it will all make sense."

She blew her nose. "I know."

"Do you?" he asked her.

She looked puzzled. "Do you know how much he loves you?"

"Please, Uncle Thad, not now."

He rose. "Don't make a mistake you'll regret based on things you don't fully know."

CHAPTER 11

Sheriff Bullock methodically worked his case. Owen Miller was held on charges of racketeering. He would be held at the jail until further notice. Mr. Miller was encouraged to get a lawyer. His wife and daughters were supported by the town. Jonah offered to keep the mill going until Mr. Miller's fate was decided. It angered Owen Miller, but he could do little about it behind bars. Eve Miller gave Jonah full rein of the business.

Jonathan's murder was going to take a little more time to solve. He knew Will didn't do it, but he didn't think it was as cut and dried as robbery. He questioned the two men from Missouri. Both had alibis, albeit shaky alibis. The sheriff was leaning toward the two men as being the distributors of the counterfeit money. He had wired Denver and Rapid City for a check on the two travelers.

Jayne Hanson was allowed to leave town after detailed questioning. Jonathan Taylor's body was being sent back to Charleston. Annabeth had barely spoken to Will since the meeting in Merry's kitchen on Monday. He came to work each morning and tried to act normal, but Annabeth only talked to him about work details.

"What is going on with you two?" Vivian approached Will near the back entrance. "It's obvious she is mad at you. What did you do?"

Will was antsy. The shipment from Sadler's had yet to be delivered. He was losing his window of opportunity. "I said what did you do to her?" Vivian asked again, nudging him.

"I guess nothing makes a woman angrier than a man professing his love," he said it so Annabeth could hear loud and clear.

"I knew it. I knew the first day you walked in here you were the man for our Annie. She's playing hard to get, is she? That is customary." Vivian cackled, "Old Reliable is going to pitch a fit."

Annabeth excused herself and left the bakery. Will watched as she headed to the blacksmith shop. What was she up to? He followed her. Trying to be inconspicuous, he circled back behind the blacksmith shop.

"Did you kill Jonathan?" Annabeth asked Rawly.

It caught him by surprise. "I think you should be asking Will Stanton that question. Isn't he one of the suspects? Why would you ask such a thing anyway, Annabeth? I am not a person who could kill another human being."

"You've been lying to me. I know what you have been up to."

No! Will's mind screamed. She was going to destroy his whole operation.

"Is this about Jayne? Annabeth, it was nothing. You were gone. We just had dinner together a couple of times."

Annabeth had no idea Rawly and Jayne had been cavorting while she and Will were in Charleston. She noticed Will peeking through the crack of the back door. He shook his head no. "We are through, Rawly." Annabeth turned to leave, but Rawly grabbed her arm.

"You don't mean that, Annabeth. Let me explain." His grip was a little tighter than Annabeth could stand. She tried to get free from him.

"Let go of me!" She pulled her arm from his. "I don't want you stepping foot in my bakery. I don't want to see you again."

He moved to get in front of her. "You mean to tell me nothing happened in Charleston between you and Stanton? Or here, living practically under the same roof? Jonathan told me about finding you and him together more than once."

"This isn't about you and Jayne or me and Will. This is about me not wanting anything more to do with you." She started to leave again, and he shut the door in front of her.

"What are you getting at, Annabeth?"

"I am not getting at anything. I just find I can't trust you, and I don't want to be a part of your life anymore."

He grinned an evil grin. "You know, don't you?"

"Know what?" She tried to hide the fear in her voice.

"The shipments from Sadler's. You got more than you asked for, didn't you?"

Her face couldn't hide the fact that she knew. "You'll never get away with it," Annabeth said boldly.

"Sit down, Annabeth, and let me tell you a story about how you are going to help me get away with it." He shoved her onto a stool near the anvil.

Will wanted to move in, but he first wanted to hear what Rawly had to say. "If you go to the authorities, I will pin this on you. You knew all along the goods were being moved through your stupid bakery. After all, isn't that why you came out here? Wasn't that your plan from the beginning? Yours and the lately departed Jonathan Taylor?" He was trying to blackmail her. Her eyes were wide.

"That's right, honey. Jonathan Taylor was in on this from the start. You are such a gullible little fool. You were so in love with Mr. Taylor. You couldn't help but tell him about your lifelong dream to own your own bakery. Do you remember telling him if you hadn't started courting you'd be out West with your uncle? That started old Jonathan thinking. It took a year to come up with the perfect plan.

"Jonathan and Lilly hatched the wedding debacle to drive you West. Lillian then persuaded Mr. Sadler to be the catalyst to get the merchandise to Denver via the little Dowry. My cousin Lilly is quite the jewel thief. You see, Annabeth, it would be effortless to make you a likely part of the whole setup. So when the next shipment comes, you're going to bring it to me like a good little girl. I would hate for something unfortunate to happen to you."

Annabeth was livid. She prayed silently that the Lord would give her wisdom. "Something unfortunate like what happened to Jonathan?" she asked.

"Yes, Annabeth, I killed him. He came here unloading those counterfeit bills. He wanted to put an end to our goldmine and start a new racket in California. He seemed to think to stop and relocate a business like this was the way to go. We had a difference of opinion. If I get lucky, they'll hang Will Stanton for the crime."

"That is not going to happen." Will slipped through the door to stand behind Rawly. He turned with a smug face. "And what are you going to do, run and tell Uncle Dan? Please, I can implicate you just as much as Annabeth. You both knew all about it from the beginning. I certainly can shed some light on your dislike for Jonathan." He then turned to look at Annabeth.

"You'll go to jail knowing three men fought over you, but none of them were in love with you." He laughed; and Will punched him, knocking him to the ground. Rawly scrambled to get up; and when he did, he pulled a gun. He fired three shots into the body of Will Stanton.

Will dropped. Annabeth screamed. Running to kneel beside him, she watched as the blood oozed from his chest, shoulder, and leg. His body twitched. He coughed, and blood trickled out of his mouth. Stunned, she looked up to find Rawly saddling his horse. He was going to get away. Reaching for Will's gun still in his holster, she aimed the gun and fired. She heard Rawly cry out in pain and fall to the ground.

The doors of the blacksmith shop suddenly opened, letting light flood in. Annabeth couldn't see who was coming through the door. "Get Hawk—now!" she screamed with an emotion-laden voice.

Jonah had heard the shots and headed over to the blacksmith shop. He took off running as Dan entered hurrying over to Will.

Annabeth had the hem of her skirt on Will's chest, trying to stop the bleeding. He was growing paler as the moments ticked by. "What happened?" Dan asked as he placed his fingers in the crease of Will's neck.

"Don't do that," Annabeth said in anger. "He is not dead. He can't be."

Dan wasn't so sure. The boy's pulse was so weak he could barely feel it. When he thought he did feel it, it was awfully erratic.

Rawly moaned from across the shop. Dan went to assess his injury. The man had been shot in the seat of his pants. Dan was a little confused but would have to wait for answers.

Hawk burst onto the scene, and he too put his fingers to Will's neck. He looked at Annabeth. Her eyes pleaded with him. He lifted her hand off the chest wound and heard the gurgling sound the injury made. The bullet had penetrated the lung. "I want you to go get Dr. Lapp and Lydia. I am going to need all the help I can get." Annabeth was dazed. "Now, Annabeth!" The sternness in his voice got her to move.

Jonah had arrived with a wagon to carry Will to the doctor's. Once they got Will inside, Avery began preparing for whatever her husband would need. He was going to have to explore just exactly where the bullet was and what it hit on its way.

Hawk helped Avery cut away Will's clothes. The chest wound was by far the worst, but the other two were bleeding continuously as well. Will only made the sound of a wet bloody cough now and again. He was cool and clammy to the touch. "Good heavens!" Lydia Lapp exclaimed when she saw Will's lifeless body. She began helping her husband remove his coat. He and Hawk were scrubbing their hands with the warm soap and water Avery had supplied. Lydia wrapped the men in clean aprons and stood at Will's head. A cloth was draped over his face, and the four adults began to work. No one in the room had very high hopes that Will Stanton would live through the process. But they all were going to give it their best try. And pray with all their hearts.

Annabeth sat in the doctor's outer office in a dress covered in blood. Her face was streaked with tear stains, and she was shaking uncontrollably. Hannah had gone to watch the children in the main part of the house, leaving Annabeth alone. She should go tell Trudy, but she couldn't move. The room was quiet, and the clock ticking in the hallway was so loud it was making her nervous. She bowed her head and began to pray.

When Annabeth lifted her head, she was startled to see Hunter and River sitting motionlessly beside her. Without a word, both boys entwined their hands in hers, their little heads resting on her shoulder. A fresh set of tears trickled down her face.

It didn't take long for the room to begin to fill. Trudy chattered more when she was upset, and it made Annabeth more agitated. Vivian stood near Trudy. This was an odd occurrence as the two were not the best of friends. The duo was making things worse.

Annabeth sat transfixed with the boys beside her. At last the two people she really needed had arrived. Thad and Merry quietly made their way to Annabeth on the settee. "Annabeth, come with me." Merry's voice sounded a lot like her mother's. "You need to get out of those clothes. Come upstairs. I know Avery won't mind you wearing something of hers."

Annabeth was reluctant. The door to the treatment room opened, and Lydia popped her head out. "Thad, we need more help in here."

Thad immediately headed toward the room. Annabeth stood to follow. Merry grabbed her by the arm. Looking at Lydia, Merry raised her eyebrows in question. "He is still alive, child, and that is all I can tell you. Keep praying."

Thad entered the room and was astonished. Blood was everywhere. "What do you need me to do?"

Hawk had his father scrub his hands and forearms and put on a surgical apron. "Help Avery with the leg wound. I've sewn up the nicked artery, but the bullet still needs to be removed. I've got a number of intricate problems with this chest wound."

Upstairs, Merry helped Annabeth get cleaned up. "What happened, Annabeth?"

The girl was still shaking. "I... I shouldn't have gone to Rawly like I did. I didn't mean to let him know I knew about the smuggling operation. I meant only to tell him we were through. I wanted to know if he killed Jonathan. He did, Aunt Merry. He killed Jonathan, and now what if Will dies?" An onslaught of fresh tears poured down her face.

"Now we need to have faith, Annabeth." Merry hugged her. "Did Rawly say why he killed Jonathan?"

"Oh, Aunt Merry, Jonathan was all part of it. He and Lilly staged my whole courtship and wedding mishap to drive me West to open the bakery. They wanted a place to run the goods through. I couldn't believe the detail they went to set the whole thing up.

"Rawly was going to blackmail me if I went to the authorities. He said he could make it as if I was in on it. I never knew people could be so devious, so methodical, and so calculated with their schemes. I put Will in an awful position."

It took Merry a minute or two to grasp what all Annabeth was saying. She knew Rawly, but the whole added element of Jonathan was a little difficult to take in. She was sure Jackson and Abby would be flabbergasted at the thought of someone they have known for years weaving their daughter into such a plot. It makes one lose their confidence in the human race.

"Where is Rawly?" Merry asked, and Annabeth stopped in her tracks. Her face went white.

"I… I… I shot him." Merry was surprised to hear this bit of news. "Aunt Merry, what if I killed him? I was so worried about Will that I never checked on Rawly. I don't even remember anyone mentioning him. They haven't brought him to Hawk's. He must be dead. Aunt Merry, I killed a man."

It was a good thing Annabeth was sitting on the bed because she fainted—again. Merry stretched her out on the bed and got a cool cloth and placed it on her head. She went to the stairs and called for Hunter, knowing River would be right behind him. The two boys appeared in no time. They didn't say anything, just waited for instruction. "Sit here with Annabeth until she wakes up." The boys stationed themselves on either side of the bed.

Merry made her way downstairs. Vivian and Trudy stood when she arrived. "How is Annabeth?" Trudy began.

Before she could get another question or comment out, Merry stopped them. "I have gotten her to lay down. The boys are going to sit with her. I know she would be appreciative if you would let her know of any changes with Will. I need to step out for a moment."

Merry left before they could say anything else. Merry saw Sheriff Bullock head into the jail. She called out, stopping him on the step, "Dan, a moment if you have one to spare."

He stepped into the street. "How's Will?" was his first question.

"Still alive, for the moment. They have Zeke and Lydia and even Thad in there helping."

"And Annabeth? How is she holding up?"

"Did she…did she kill Rawly?" It was hard for Merry to get out.

The sheriff chuckled. Merry didn't know whether to be relieved or disturbed at the sheriff's reaction. "No." He smiled. "But I think he wished she had."

"She said she shot him, did she?"

"Oh, she shot him all right, right in the—" he paused. "Let's just say he won't be sitting in a saddle or a chair for a spell."

Merry gathered his meaning. She smiled. "Good, she thinks she killed him since he hasn't been brought to Hawk."

"I dug the bullet out myself an hour ago. A lot of fat back there but it sure was painful for him."

"You know he killed Jonathan Taylor." Merry wanted to make the man aware if he didn't already know the bit of crucial information. "I didn't know. I suppose Annabeth told you. I will need to question her when she is up to it."

Dan removed his hat and scratched his balding head. "I got to piece this all together. I will be over to check on Will in a little bit. Sure hope the boy makes it. It didn't look to promisin' in the black-smith shop."

Hunter came running toward his grandma. "Pa says go get Uncle Hud and Uncle Tommy as soon as you can."

She was surprised. "Did he say why?"

Hunter shook his head. "He said he would explain later."

"Take my horse, Merry. She's all saddled and ready to go." He gave her a leg up, and she tore through town like a whirlwind. Dan watched as Hunter went into the mill. He was speaking with Jonah. It must be pretty bad if Hawk is calling for all his brothers. The sheriff needed to check on his wife. He knew she would be beside herself; but at the moment, duty called. He made his way into the jail to question his prisoner.

With the help of River, Annabeth made it downstairs to return to the vigil being held in the parlor. The sun was slipping behind the Black Hills. How many hours had they been working on Will? It was almost dark when Merry returned with Hud and Tommy. Everyone seemed to be in a quandary as to why they were summoned. It didn't take long until Thad and Hawk exited the room. Everyone stood. Hawk, who never minced words, got straight to the point.

"He is very unstable and has lost a lot of blood. I can't say whether he will make it or not." There were some sobs from the women in the crowd. "He needs blood." The group just stared at the physician. "Dr. Lapp and I have talked it over. I have seen it done and think it is worth a try. I need a healthy male donor near the same age. That is why I called for all of you. I want to give Will the best chance with the procedure."

Trudy swooned at the thought. "Trudy, snap out of it! This is Will we are talking about!" Vivian gave the woman's arm a sharp rap with her own. Trudy straightened up.

"How does it work?" Hud asked.

"I take blood out of the donor a few ounces at a time and inject it into Will's bloodstream. It was used in the Civil War, and they have continued to perfect the procedure. There is no harm to the donor."

"But there is a possibility it will hurt Will?" Merry questioned.

"Yes, his body could reject it."

"What will that do to him?" Vivian piped up.

"The worst thing is death, but we are already staring that in the face." Hawk looked at the crowd.

"Who do you think would be the best c-c-andidate? The cl-closest m-match?" Tommy asked as he began rolling up his sleeves. "I-I'm willing to do it."

"I'll be honest. I thought of you first."

"W-we're w-wasting time. What d-do I n-need to do?"

"Go to the kitchen and find Lydia. She will get you ready."

There was one thing all the Sheridans knew: Tommy Sheridan got squeamish at the sight of blood. This was a huge thing he was doing. As he walked by, Hawk tapped him on the top of the head. "I'll make sure you don't see anything. You're a good man, Thomas Sheridan."

Hawk turned to follow Tommy when Avery appeared. Hawk changed directions to face the crowd again. "I need a bit more help. Though she won't admit it, Avery is in labor, and she needs to lie down. Ma, can you help her?"

Avery frowned at her husband. It was true her labor had begun, but it wasn't to that awful stage where she couldn't stand it. This was her fourth child, Avery knew it would be a few more hours before the work would begin. She also felt it was another girl. They seemed to take longer.

"Of course, Avery, let's get you upstairs."

"I'm fine!" she lamented, but her husband would have none of it.

"You've been on your feet all day. It is not good for you or the baby. Now do as the doctor says." He kissed her. "Hud, stick around. I may need your delivery skills." He winked at his wife and turned toward his brother; Hud gave a disgusted look. The banter eased the tension in the room.

"This baby won't come until her father can deliver her." Avery headed up the stairs with Merry at her elbow.

*****

Tommy lay on a cot next to Will Stanton, a sheet hung between them. Lydia had scrubbed the daylights out Tommy's arm. His flesh was so red it looked burned. "You ready?" Hawk eyed his brother with concern.

"Yeah, I am ready."

Hawk inserted the needle and drew out some blood. Tommy was instructed to keep his head turned away.

"Don't worry, I won't take out too much. Your body will replenish what I have taken. You might feel a little tired." When he thought he had sufficient amount for the first injection, he moved around the drape. Will lay still. His breathing was some better, but his pulse was weak and rapid. The blood would help. His body needed the fluid.

Hawk injected Will with a clean needle and transfused the blood from Tommy to Will. He did this three times. If there were no improvement in Will's pulse, he would do it again tomorrow. Hawk made sure Tommy drank some water and ate. He wanted him to stay the night on the couch so he could watch him. Tommy insisted on going back to Jonah's. Josie was there with Hannah. He didn't want her to worry. Hawk conceded with the promise that Jonah would keep an eye on him.

In all this, Annabeth sat in a daze. Waiting. Everyone had gone home except Thad and Merry. Thad was still in the room with Will and Hawk. Merry was upstairs with Avery and Lydia. Annabeth was all alone with her harrowing thoughts.

"I think it would be helpful, Annabeth dear, if you could fix us all something to eat. It has been a long day, and I know Hawk hasn't eaten since early morning." Dr. Lapp was standing in the doorway.

It was if Annabeth all of a sudden found herself. "Yes, of course. Why didn't I think of that?" She rose to go into the kitchen.

Dr. Lapp put his big arms around her and held her close. "You're a blessing, Annabeth. Don't ever forget that."

Lydia came into the kitchen. She wanted some fresh water for Avery. "How is Avery?" Annabeth said as she filled the pitcher.

"She is progressing slowly. You never know when that might change." She smiled at Annabeth. "Something sure smells good."

"I have made some stew and cornbread. I know it is almost midnight, but I doubt anyone has eaten much. I could send some up for you and Merry, but I don't think that would be fair to Avery."

"No, it wouldn't. I'll send Merry down. You try to get Hawk and Zeke to eat." Lydia scooted up the stairs.

Everyone took turns coming into the kitchen to eat. Annabeth got to spend just a few minutes with each one. The fatigue was evident on everyone but Hawk. How did he do it? He came downstairs after cleaning up and seeing Avery as if he had just awakened from a full night's sleep. She fixed him some food and sat across from him.

"Is—"

Hawked stopped her. "Don't ask me if he is going to live or die. I don't know." She looked hurt. "I do know it may help if you would go in and talk to him. I have always believed no matter what state the patient is in they can hear." Hawk also knew Annabeth needed to be kept occupied.

Annabeth slipped into Will's room just before two in the morning. Dr. Lapp rose from the chair he had been dozing in. "You don't have to leave," she whispered. He moved the chair closer to Will's body. Taking Annabeth's hand, he laid it on Will's. She felt the coolness of his skin. Her heart was pounding. Zeke stepped to the other side of the bed and felt Will's pulse. It continued to be fast and weak. He left the room.

Annabeth didn't think she could say anything. Her throat was so tight. "I'm sorry, Will. Sorry I went to talk to Rawly. None of this would have happened if I had waited for you." She picked up his hand and cradled it to her face. It was lifeless. "I should have trusted you. Please don't die. You are the best friend I have ever had." She couldn't say any more.

She sat quietly with her hand on his. In the dim light, she saw the color of the bandage on his shoulder change. She rose to see blood seeping through. "Dr. Lapp!" she said loud enough to summon the man. When he walked in, she pointed to the bandage.

"Get Hawk." He moved to the other side, and she hurried up the stairs. Knocking on the bedroom door before she opened it, she poked her head in.

"He is bleeding again."

Hawk made his way quickly down the stairs. Thad was coming from the parlor. He had made Merry lie down for a little while; and when she was asleep, he was going to find his niece and see she do the same. He saw Hawk coming down the stairs heading into Will's room. Annabeth wasn't far behind him.

"What is it?" he whispered, taking hold of Annabeth preventing her from going into the room.

"He is bleeding again."

She sank down on the bottom stair. "Did Aunt Merry tell you I shot Rawly? I assume he is dead. No one has called for the doctor." She rested her head on the staircase railing. Thad sat down beside her.

"Rawly is going to be fine."

She turned to look at her uncle. "He is alive?"

"Yes, in all this going on, Merry forgot to tell you. The bullet struck him in the posterior." He stopped. She wasn't understanding. "You shot him in the seat of his pants." Her eyes went wide. Thad let out a chuckle.

"Who taught you to shoot?" She leaned her head on his shoulder.

"Vivian showed me how to hold a gun properly and pull the hammer back. Her pistol was a lot smaller than Will's gun."

"Yes, I imagine so. When all this is over, I should probably teach you how to defend yourself, although you didn't do too poorly."

"Will I go to jail?" She felt bad for even asking. Of course, she should go to jail; she could have killed Rawly. If she had to do it over, she would have done no different. Every time she shut her eyes, she saw Will's cold, lifeless body lying on the ground oozing blood. She shivered, and Thad put his arm around her.

"I don't think Dan will do much about it. After all, Rawly admitted to killing Jonathan and"—he stopped and looked toward the closed door—"and shooting Will like he did. I doubt he will worry about one bullet to a killer's backside."

A low moan came from the upstairs bedroom. It was the first anyone had heard from the laboring mother. "Probably won't be long now. Maybe I should go in and see if I can help Zeke and free Hawk up." Thad started to stand. "You need to rest Annabeth." He cupped her chin. "Go into the parlor and lay down." He helped her up and sent her on her way. She didn't want to leave her post. "Go, I will come to get you when Zeke or Hawk says it okay." He went behind the closed door.

*****

Hawk made his way upstairs. To say he was exhausted was an understatement. He repaired the bleeding vessel in Will's shoulder and went to clean up again before seeing his wife. The last thing he wanted to do was cross-contaminate when delivering his baby. With the birth of his other three children, he was with Avery throughout the whole process. This time, he had been in and out. He didn't like not being with her.

He was thankful Jonah and Hannah had taken his other children home with them. He was thankful for a lot of things. As tired as he was, he wouldn't change one thing. He loved being a doctor, and he loved Avery and the life they had created. He said a prayer before he entered the room.

Avery lay on her left side, her knees drawn toward her chest. She was trying to relieve the pain in her lower back. Hawk sat on the side of the bed and rubbed the spot where she hurt. "It's all in my back this time." She panted. He continued to massage the area. Lydia slipped out of the room. Hawk didn't say anything for a few moments, just letting her rest before the next pain hit. It wasn't long until she was sitting up, panting harder with tears in her eyes. Hawk put his arm out, and she grabbed it. He felt her belly with his free hand.

"This baby is about ready to greet the world. It won't be much longer, Avery." When the contraction subsided, Hawked helped her get in position to deliver. Another contraction. This one was fiercer than before. Hawk could see the head. "I am afraid this one has lots of black hair as well, Avery."

All the doctor's children had their father's dark hair and eyes; not one had blond hair and light eyes like their mother. He saw her stomach muscle contract again. "Okay, I want you to push, Avery."

She did and no baby. She relaxed for a split second and then pushed again. The infant glided into his father's waiting hands. Hawk cleaned out the baby's mouth and stimulated him to breathe. The child let out a wail, and Avery immediately cried with joy.

"You and Piper are outnumbered." Hawk smiled at his wife as he wiped the baby off and handed him to Avery. Four babies and the whole process never ceased to amaze her. The feeling of holding a baby in your arms was something to cherish.

"I love you," she said when her eyes made contact with her husband's. "I hope you know. I don't say it near as often as I should."

He winked at her as he finished cleaning up the mess. Yes, he knew it; and after all this time, he still couldn't believe it.

Hawk knew everyone downstairs was wanting to know about the new arrival; but just for a moment, he wanted to cradle Avery in his arms as she snuggled their son. He kissed her temple as they admired the tiny boy. "What are we going to name him?" Avery never took her eyes off the child as she stroked his soft skin.

"Did you have something in mind?" Hawk asked his wife.

"No, you seem to find a name that fits our children." She smiled up at him.

They watched their son as he stretched and kicked his leg. All newborns kick, but this little guy seemed to be running in place. "Look at his little legs. He is going to outrun you one of these days," Avery said to her husband, who was known for the speed at which he could travel by foot.

"He will always be chasing me," Hawk said smugly. "That would be a good name for him."

Avery looked up in dismay. "Runner?"

"No, silly. Chase. Chase Sheridan."

"I'll have to think about that."

There was a knock on the door, and Merry poked her head in when she heard the "Come in." Merry and Thad cooed at the baby, and Merry briefly held her grandson. It was four in the morning, and everyone was tired, so they didn't stay long. Annabeth was the last to peek in and see the new addition to the family. "I'm going to sit with Will. Is there anything I need to know?" She was speaking to Hawk in the hallway.

"I'm still not sure he is going to make it, Annabeth. I don't want to give anyone false hope. I am praying just like everyone else. We just have to trust that God does all things well." She nodded her response and headed downstairs.

*****

Trudy returned at seven to check on Will. She had developed a sick headache the night before, and Dr. Lapp sent her home with some medicine. Will's aunt appeared pale, but the headache had subsided. She didn't see anyone in the parlor but heard whispering in the kitchen. Thad and Merry were sitting at the table, drinking coffee.

"Any word on Will?" The woman dabbed at her eyes. "Dan has telegraphed his folks to let them know what is going on," she added.

"There has been no change. I think Hawk wants to give him more blood today." Thad stood to give Trudy his chair.

"I know Hawk is doing everything he can to save Will and I do trust him, but taking blood from one to another—I just don't know about that."

"I saw it a time or two during the war. It worked for some," Thad added around a yawn.

"My goodness, but you and Merry must be exhausted. Why don't you head over to the boarding house and get some rest? There is a room available ready for company."

Thad looked at Merry. She was worn to a frazzle. Trudy followed his eyes to his wife's. "Now I insist. You go on."

"I am pretty worn out." Merry stood and took her husband's arm.

"Come and get us if we're needed or there is any change," Thad said as he escorted his wife out of the kitchen.

All night, Annabeth had watched the slow and shallow rise and fall of Will's chest. Several times during the night, she leaned up to make sure his chest was moving. It was that hard to see. She had finally given in to the sleep that overcame her. She didn't arouse when Hawk entered the room. He gently touched her on the shoulder.

"Please, Annabeth, go home and get some sleep."

"How is he this morning?" she whispered as if she didn't hear his plea for her to get some rest.

"If I tell you my plan for him today, will you go home as I asked?" She nodded her agreement. "His pulse has slowed a little but not as much as I would like. It is still weak. Tommy is coming by late morning, and I will give Will another transfusion. Then we wait." Bewilderment was on her face. He was going to die; she just knew it. "Home," Hawk said as he helped her up. "And no stopping by the bakery." The bakery—she had totally forgotten about the bakery. "Vivian is taking care of it." Hawk read her mind. How did he know Vivian was running the bakery? To Annabeth's knowledge, Hawk had not left the house since Will was brought in. "Go, Annabeth." He steered her toward the door. "I'll send word if anything changes."

She stepped out of the room to find Trudy pacing in the parlor. Trudy went to her and wrapped her arms around Annabeth. "All we can do is pray, Annabeth. He is in God's hands. Now you head home and rest." Annabeth was silent.

When she stepped out on the stoop, she met Tommy. "Any change?" He held Annabeth's hand.

"Maybe a little. Hawk wants to give him more blood today if you are willing."

Tommy squeezed her hand "I-I'm w-w-illing." Tommy made his way into Will's room. "Annabeth says he needs more blood. When do you want to do it?"

"First, how are you feeling? Are you tired?" Hawk looked at his brother with concern.

"Yes, but only because Josie w-woke me up e-every hour to make s-sure I was all right." He rolled his eyes.

Hawk had a soft laugh. "Better take advantage of the attention. Once the baby is born, she won't give you a second thought."

"Seeing as how I hear baby number four has arrived, you are speaking on a professional level, not personal level, I presume. You seem to have gotten a second thought and a third and a—"

"Okay, go up and see your nephew then come back around ten."

*****

Thrive was happy to see Annabeth. Dan had seen to the dog in between his investigating duties. The dog wouldn't stop circling her and licking her outstretched hand. "I've missed you, boy."

Thrive, sensing her sadness, whimpered. She bent to snuggle the pup. She turned down her bed and changed into her nightgown. Yes, it was the middle of the morning; but she was exhausted. She crawled under the quilt and began saying her prayers. She barely started when she drifted off to sleep. Thrive curled up at her feet with his muzzle resting on her leg.

*****

Three more tubes of blood were taken from Tommy and given to Will. When Hawk inserted the last injection, Will flinched. It was the first movement he had witnessed. Hawk couldn't be sure if it was voluntary or involuntary movement. When he was finished, he placed a bandage on the site. Will flinched again.

"Will," Hawk spoke in a louder-than-normal tone. Will's eyes twitched. "Will, look at me." With Hawk's command, Will's eyes opened briefly and then shut again. A sound came from the man, but it was incomprehensible. This was a good sign, but Hawk wasn't ready to pronounce Will out of the woods—far from it.

Will was fuzzy. The last thing he remembered was hitting Rawly. He smiled just a little. Then his mind went to Annabeth. Was she okay? He opened his eyes. He knew instantly where he was. Not because the room was familiar to him but because of what stood before him. Hunter and River Sheridan were peering down on him. *Please don't start asking me about Annabeth,* Will's mind pleaded. Hunter looked to River and gave the nod. The boy left instantly.

"Speak if you can," Hunter said as he lifted Will's wrist and found his pulse.

"What?" With the first word, Will realized how dry his throat and mouth were. He coughed, but that shot pain across his chest. "What do you want me to say?" Will got out in a hoarse voice.

"That will do." Hunter dropped the man's arm and laid his hand on Will's head.

"What is the verdict, Doctor?" Will was trying to focus his eyes.

The boy frowned. "To soon to tell."

Will would have laughed, but he feared the boy may be correct. "Is Annabeth all right?" It was Will's first concern.

"She is fine. She is at the bakery." This news should have made Will completely happy, but part of him was sorry she was not here with him. He genuinely thought she might care for him. It was too much to ask for a woman to fall in love so many times in such a short period. Who was he kidding? He wasn't the kind of man the type of woman like Annabeth could love.

Hunter was looking at his bandages, inspecting for any blood. The door opened, and Hawk walked in. "How is our patient?" he asked his young son.

"To soon to tell." the boy proclaimed again.

"His heartbeat in his wrist is better."

Hawk walked to the bedside and timed Will's pulse. "It is much better. Down to ninety. Do you feel like you could drink some water?" Will croaked out a yes, and Hawk sent Hunter to get some water for the patient.

"Can you fill in some of the details for me?" Will tried to lift his head and look at his body. The action caused a lot of pain.

"Rawly opened up on you. A bullet to your chest, shoulder, and leg. I am most concerned about your chest. You bled a lot. I had to give you a transfusion." Will wasn't sure he heard the doctor correctly.

"A what?"

"A transfusion. I took blood from a donor and put it into you."

His head was spinning. He had heard of this procedure but to have it performed on him outside of the confines of a hospital seemed barbaric. "Whose blood did I get?" He wasn't sure he wanted to know. He rubbed his face with his left hand.

"Tommy," Hawk said. "Hud and Jonah also offered, but I decided on Tommy."

Will was humbled. The Sheridans had been nothing but nice to him. He would have to do something to repay Tommy. How do you repay someone for saving your life? Will felt like he was on the verge of tears. He closed his eyes.

"If you keep some water down, I will let you eat a little later this afternoon. Is there anything I can get you?"

"I need to see Dan," Will answered after he drank a bit of water. He needed to find out what all happened. "What day is it?" he asked Hawk as he started to leave.

"Saturday." He was shot on Thursday. Did the operation get exposed, or had the whole thing gone up in smoke? Only Dan could answer those questions.

Dan was making his way over to see Will. He stopped by the house and gave his wife the news that Will was awake and had asked to see him. Annabeth was relieved. She knew he was probably still in a critical phase, but it was good that he was awake.

Trudy began to cry. "I am going with you, Dan," Trudy said as she blew her nose and wiped her eyes.

"I thought you might want to." Dan smiled at his wife.

"Are you coming, Annabeth?" Trudy asked the girl peeling potatoes.

"No, I will stay here and get supper ready for your guest. You stay as long as you need. Will needs his family right now." She gave her best smile. She was hurt that the first person Will wanted to see was Dan. But of course, he would. He needed to make sure his job was completed. She took a moment to pray for Will's continued recovery.

After Trudy had fussed over Will and informed him his parents were on their way, she left the room. "Notifying my folks wasn't necessary," Will said to Dan.

"Son, you almost died. Of course, your aunt was going to notify your ma."

Will frowned. He didn't like the fuss. "What is the word on Rawly and the operation?"

"I just got a telegram before coming over here they wrapped everything up very neatly. The whole line was shut down, and everyone is in custody. Rawly was extradited on yesterday's stage by one of your fellow agents. A telegram of commendation was also sent." Dan pulled the missive from his pocket and laid it on the table next to Will.

"How did you let someone like Rawly ambush you? And I thought you were going to notify me when you went in to arrest him," Dan stated factually, not condescendingly.

"Annabeth had headed over to Rawly's, and I followed. It wasn't supposed to go the way it went. Rawly found out that she knew and was going to blackmail her. I confronted him, and the next thing I knew, bullets were flying. He confessed to everything for the whole year-long plan. He murdered Jonathan. Did you know that?"

"Yes, Annabeth gave me a full statement."

*****

"Trudy tells me Will is doing much better. He is sitting up and able to eat. Why don't you take him some of what you've baked this morning?" Vivian said as she watched Annabeth take another pan of goodies from the oven.

"So you and Trudy are friends now?" Annabeth continued working, not looking at Vivian's stern face.

"This isn't about Trudy and me. This is about you and Will Stanton. Why haven't you been seeing him now that he is back among the living?"

"If Will needs something from me, we both know he will ask. And as of yet, he hasn't."

"So that is it. He hasn't asked for you, so you're not going."

"That is not it at all, Vivian. I am not the type of person to make myself a nuisance."

Vivian laughed. "Honey, you are anything but a nuisance to that man."

Annabeth ignored Vivian. How could she go see him? She almost got him killed. She fought back the tears. Annabeth felt as if her life was one big mess. She knew at any moment Dan Bullock would be in to arrest her for shooting Rawly.

Annabeth was trying to wrap her head around the whole plot Jonathan and Lilly had hatched. She had confided in Jonathan her dream of heading West and opening a bakery early in their relationship. Even before they started courting. They had been friends for years, and she often talked to him about life goals. So many men in the South thought a wife was chosen to better the man's situation in life. Either monetarily or politically. Jonathan always appreciated Annabeth's independent thinking. Now she knew why.

Will was sitting up in bed. The very act seemed to tire him out. Why hadn't Annabeth come to see him? The bakery closed hours ago. Yesterday, when his aunt Trudy came, she stated Annabeth had stayed back to take care of the guest. It was as if she was avoiding him. Okay, he was no dummy. She was avoiding him. Well, by golly, when he could walk out of this room, he was walking right over to the bakery, and she was getting an earful from him.

The problem was it would be a while before he could walk out of here. First, his lung had to heal. Then he had to worry about his right leg and right shoulder. Hard to use crutches when you can't move your right arm very much. Hawk had told him it would be a long slow healing process. He bowed his head and prayed. He knew he would need a lot of strength from the Lord to help him in the upcoming days.

The door creaked open, and Lydia popped her head in. "There is someone here to see you, Will."

Finally, he thought, thinking it was Annabeth. When the door opened wider, it was his parents. Ben and Catherine Stanton rushed into the room. Catherine covered her mouth to stop the moan from her lips. Her baby looked so pale.

"How are you feeling, son?" Mr. Stanton moved his wife closer to the bed and helped her sit down.

"You made the long trip for nothing. I am going to be just fine." Will smiled at his mother. "Ma, I'm fine," he said again to make sure she knew it was true.

"I knew this would happen, you going from town to town, a drifter, working here and there. You were bound to get into some type of trouble." "When are you going to settle down, son, stay in one place, get a real job?"

Usually, this would make a man mad but not Will. His parents—none of his family—knew what he did for a living. He was strictly undercover for the Pinkerton Agency. He had been very good at his job. No one knew at age sixteen he had worked for an agent right in his hometown. He was good at blending in, and he was sneaky. At least that was what the agent told him so many years ago. When he turned eighteen, he joined the agency and had traveled around for the last ten years.

He was done, tired of it. He worked enough odd jobs; he knew he could find steady work. With the decision to quit Pinkerton's, he felt he could now tell his folks the full story. For the next hour, he told them everything.

Annabeth couldn't stand it anymore. She loaded her basket full of goodies and headed out the door. Vivian was relieved as she watched Annabeth march out the front door headed for the—the sheriff's office. Vivian thought sure she was going to heed her advice and go see Will.

"Annabeth, come on in. What brought you in today?" He smiled then looked at her basket. "Is that cinnamon I smell? I just made a pot of coffee. I sure hope there is something in there for me."

"There is." She smiled and put the basket on his desk he peeked inside. "But first I need to ask you something."

He motioned for her to sit, and she did, on the edge of the seat. In a low voice, she said, leaning toward him, "I shot Rawly. Shouldn't I be"—she swallowed and bent her head toward the cell—"in there?"

Dan Bullock wanted to laugh, but he knew he couldn't. He rubbed his face to hide his mirth. "I have done my investigation and written my report. A concerned citizen of Sheridan witnessed the shooting and tried to stop the perpetrator and did so with exemplary shooting as to not render the man unable to stand trial." Annabeth's mouth dropped open. "Rest easy. You are not in any trouble."

Dan reached in the basket and took out some muffins. "Take the rest of these over to Will. That is an order from the sheriff's office."

Annabeth's mind was eased. She had asked the Lord's forgiveness and felt she had received it. She needed to ask Will's forgiveness. She put him in this awful predicament, and he had the right to lecture her. She slowly crossed the street and headed to Hawk's.

She would also take the time to peek in on Chase. He was the cutest baby she ever saw. He could donate some hair to poor Nora who was still just as bald as she was eight months ago.

Annabeth knocked on the door to Will's room. A man who looked much like Will answered the door. "Well, it's about time," Will said, barely propped up in the bed. "I have been craving one of your muffins since Hawk gave me the go ahead to eat. Please tell me you brought some."

To be honest, he didn't look that much better. He was pale and had dark circles under his eyes. Annabeth smiled, but it wasn't a genuine smile, Will thought. Something was troubling her. It was as if she didn't want to be there. "Yes, I have some muffins and some cookies. Would you like some coffee?" She turned to look at the couple who had to be Will's parents.

"Annabeth, these are my parents, Ben and Catherine. This is Annabeth, the woman who has allowed me to work in her bakery for the past several months and has kept me on my toes."

"It's nice to meet you, Annabeth. We have heard wonderful things about your baked goods. Everyone in town suggested your

place for a good cup of coffee and a treat when we got off the stage."
Catherine clasped Annabeth's hand. Ben nodded and smiled.

He smiled like Will. Like the cat that ate the canary. "That is
kind of them to say. Let me get that coffee, and you can judge for
yourself. You may find the town of Sheridan is a bit biased." Annabeth
exited, tripping over a rug in the room and falling into Mr. Stanton.
He helped her right herself. With a red face, she left the room.

"If that doesn't keep you in Sheridan, nothing will." Ben Stanton
eyed his son.

"It's a little complicated right now." Will messed with the sheet.

"Yes, I bet it is." Catherine snickered.

"Mother, for the record, I don't need any help."

"You obviously do, or she would have been right here when we
arrived." His mother pointed to the chair she now occupied.

"You are getting the wrong idea." Will was glad when Annabeth
returned. Annabeth had the feeling she had been the topic of conversation while she was gone. She served the Stantons and moved
to leave. "You're not staying?" Will asked around the muffin in his
mouth.

"You need to spend time with your folks. I want to see Avery
and Chase while I am here, and then I promised Trudy I would be
home to help. With your folks here, she has a full house." Annabeth
gave her best smile.

"We look forward to getting to know you, Annabeth." Catherine
smiled. She had an adorable expression. "And if anything, the town
did not do your baking justice. These are extraordinary."

"It was a pleasure meeting you, Annabeth." Will's father opened
the door for her. "Thank you for the muffins and cookies. I have
never had an oatmeal cookie this good." He held up the half-eaten
cookie in his hand. "I bet you have secret recipes."

"I do. It was nice meeting you. I look forward to seeing you at
Dan and Trudy's." She left this time without tripping.

Annabeth made her way upstairs to speak to Avery and cud-
dle the newest addition. As she was coming down the stairs to go,
Tommy and Josie were making their way into Will's room. "Will,

w-we will be leaving first thing t-tomorrow, and we just wanted to s-stop in and say good-bye." Tommy made his way to the bedside.

"I can't thank you enough, Tommy. I wouldn't want anyone else's blood running through my veins. You saved my life."

"You would have done the same for m-me."

Will had tears in his eyes. He put his left hand out. "I'll never forget you. If you ever need anything, you get in touch with me. I'll move heaven and earth to get it for you."

Tommy gripped Will's hand. "Godspeed, Will."

"Godspeed, Tommy."

Josie leaned over and kissed Will's cheek. "We will keep you in our prayers."

"I appreciate that, and thank you for supporting Tommy in his decision to donate his blood."

She smiled and put her arm around her husband. "It was the right thing to do." She looked at her husband in awe. The couple turned to leave. "If I am ever fortunate to have a son, his name is Thomas."

Tommy turned and smiled. "Better secure yourself a wife before you make that kind of statement."

Everyone laughed, and the Sheridans left.

Annabeth heard the whole conversation. It was a pretty special thing Tommy had done for practically a stranger. She said her good-bye to the couple and was following them out when she heard Will call her name. "Annabeth, come back when you can stay longer. You and I need to talk." It was pretty hard for him to get the whole sentence out with much force, but she had heard him. She kept walking. "Don't make me take the action I had to in Charleston." He watched her back stiffen, and she exited the door.

"And you say you don't need any help. You most certainly need help." Catherine stared at her son.

CHAPTER 12

*T*hree days had passed, and Annabeth had not returned to see Will. He was now sitting up on the side of the bed. Hawk had given him exercises to help get his leg strength back. His shoulder still hurt, but the thing that bothered him the most was his chest. He couldn't do anything without getting winded and pain shooting across. Hawk told him that he would get better in time. The scar on the right side of his chest just above the muscle was more extensive than what Will expected. The bullet had lodged in his lung; and to repair the damage, Hawk had to make an incision.

Will was going stir crazy. Almost all the Sheridans had either stopped in or dropped off a note. Vivian had stopped by every chance she could. He perked up when he heard her voice outside his door. "Well, look at you, up on the side of the bed all cleaned up and shaved. Were you expecting me?" she said in her saucy manner.

"Always," Will smiled.

"You're a liar, Will Stanton. You were expecting Annabeth, and she ain't coming." She had her hands on her hips.

"And why is that, Vivian?"

Vivian sat in the chair and stretched out her legs. "Think about it. In the last year, year and a half, she has had two suitors who played her for a fool. One is six feet under, and one is in jail. And you think she is going to wade into those waters again with you? She is a little water shy. I can't say as I blame her."

Will hung his head. He knew Vivian was right. It was just that everything was over now, and Will felt like he could give Annabeth his undivided attention. He wanted a relationship with her at any cost. He had to have it. It was like he couldn't breathe.

"Are you willing to take a step back, start at the beginning?"

He looked at Vivian. Her face showed concern, a real concern for Annabeth and himself. "I am so in love with her, Vivian. I'm not sure I can go back to the beginning and start over."

"You are a lot like my James. That man was bold. He took on anything. When he came into my life, it was like a big wind blew me over. When he said, 'Let's get hitched,' I threw caution to the wind, and I went. Annabeth is a more cautious person than me and more so since all this has happened. You are going to have to start over. You get yourself better and come back to the bakery and turn on the charm. She'll come around."

"I guess I should trust your experience on these matters." He grinned at his friend.

The door opened, and Hunter Sheridan came in and stood before Will. "How are you feeling? Any dizziness or feeling like you are going to faint?"

Will turned his gaze to Vivian and motioned with his head toward Hunter. "My personal physician," he said as he turned to answer the boy. "No dizziness, no notions of fainting," Will responded in a professional manner.

Vivian rose to leave. "I see you are in good hands." She winked at Hunter. "I will be back to see you when time allows." She bent and kissed Will on the top of his head.

Hunter continued with his examination. Lifting Will's hand, he felt his pulse. "Doesn't it bother you that your wife has not been here to see you except to bring your parents some muffins? She was here when she thought you were going to die, but now she does not come." Will would never cease to be amazed at how obsessed the Sheridan boys were with his relationship to Annabeth.

"She is not my—" he couldn't finish because Hunter was giving him the let's-not-go-through-this-again look. "When was she here?" he asked the boy to repeat it.

"When they brought you in. She stayed all night and day boohooing like the rest. My ma and Liddy are the only two who kept their wits about them." The young physician apprentice laid his hand on Will's chest to check his breathing.

"Maybe she is hidin' from Sheriff Dan." The boy was mimicking the actions of his father it was almost comical.

"Why would she be hiding from Dan?" Hunter shook his head and pulled Will's eyelid up.

"Because she shot the blacksmith." Hunter acted as if Will should have known this. This was the first he heard about it. He put an immediate stop to the boys' assessment.

"Wait, she shot Rawly?"

The boy nodded and tugged his hand free of Will's grip. "How many fingers am I holding up?"

"Two. Was he hurt bad?"

"Naw, they didn't even bring him to Pa. Sheriff Dan dug the bullet out at the jail. If they had brought him here, I bet I could have dug it out and maybe put in a stitch or two."

The boy tapped Will's knee with a small rubber hammer he pulled from his pocket. "Where did the bullet end up?"

"The gluteal maximus."

"The what?" Will leaned a little closer to the child.

"He had no idea where that was." Hunter sighed. He was getting tired of the interruptions in his work. "The gluteal maximus."

"Where is that?"

Hunter let out an even longer sigh to emphasize that the patient was a moron. He turned and pointed to his own behind.

Will wanted to laugh. Annabeth had shot Rawly. He wished he could have been awake for that. What a trooper she was. He could start over. He would start today. "When we are finished here, will you do me a favor?" Will bent his elbow so Hunter could check the reflex.

"I suppose. What is it?"

"Will you go over to The Dowry and ask Annabeth if I can have a do-over?" Hunter slapped his own forehead in disgust. "Please?" Will pleaded. "I'll let you practice splinting and bandaging this evening." Hunter hated bartering for this kind of experience, but he stuck out his hand, and the two shook on the deal.

"Maybe you should worry more about your heart than your stomach."

The messenger hightailed it out of the room headed to the bakery. Annabeth was startled when she turned to see Hunter and River standing directly behind her. She even let out a little shriek. "You boys scared me half to death. You should announce yourselves."

"We're sorry." The two took her by the hand and led her to one of the chairs.

"Is something wrong?" She felt a little fear creep up her spine.

River leaned on the edge of the chair, his cold dark eyes looking at her profile. "We have a message from Will." Hunter frowned. "Your husband."

"Boys, we have had this discussion. He is not my—"

River put his hand out to stop her. "We've heard it all before."

Annabeth was taken aback by the attitude of the younger brother. Hunter gave his sibling a stern look.

"Well, what is the message?"

"He wants a do-over."

Her head went back just a bit as if she didn't believe the boys had gotten the message straight. "He wants a do-over?" Saying it out loud, she grasped the full meaning of the message. He wanted to start over. Annabeth rose and went to the cupboard and pulled out a few remaining items and put them in a basket. "You tell him I don't have much to offer right now." The duo just looked at her strangely. She handed them each a cookie and sent them on their way.

Annabeth returned to her chair watching the boys make their way home. Lydia entered the back of the bakery. She found Annabeth in a daze, so much so that she didn't hear Lydia come in. "Annabeth, honey, are you okay?" Lydia approached.

Annabeth let out a huge sigh. "What am I going to do about Will?"

Lydia sat across the table. "Have you prayed about it?"

Annabeth looked her straight in the eye. "Yes, just as I did about Jonathan and Rawly. Look where that got me. Somehow I misread what God was telling me."

"I don't think that is correct. Annabeth, you were genuine with both men. Many people were fooled by these gentlemen. It wasn't just you. Can you look at it as God spared you from two perilous situations?"

Annabeth turned back to look at the doctor's house. "He says he loves me. How can I trust any man ever again?"

"It only takes a small measure of trust to make something out of nothing. You need to give yourself some time, dear. No one says you have to get back into the courting circle. Matter of fact, I think you should just focus on the bakery. Where do you want to take it now that you're free from any distractions?" "Eventually, I would like to expand it. I would like to do something for the community, to help the less fortunate." Annabeth's mind was racing.

"Why don't you take a moment and jot down some goals for your business and work toward those? And take your hands off the reins."

Annabeth smiled. She needed the clear vision of Lydia Lapp to set her on the right track. She took some time to pray before she began writing her goals.

Hunter delivered the goods and the message to Will. He had to disagree with Annabeth. She had a lot to offer. He understood. He would need to have some patience. Will leaned back in the bed. The pain also reminded him of the same need for patience his body was requiring. He grimaced with the movement.

"Are you in pain, Will?" Hawk stood at the door.

"Not any more than usual. I thought I would be better by now. It has been a week."

"It has been a week since you were shot, but you have to remember it's only been a few days since I consider you to be on the mend. You are going to have to relax for a while and let your body heal."

Will frowned and turned his head toward the window. It was a beautiful day—a day he should be spending with Annabeth. Hawk laughed from his post at the door. "You have Annabeth written all over your face." Will's frown deepened. "You can deny it if you want, but I know what I see."

"I'd like to rest now, Doctor, if you don't mind."

Hawk grabbed the wooden chair in the corner and brought it over to the bed. Flipping it so he could straddle it, he faced Will.

"You better dig your heels in and show some resolve. The men are going to come out of the woodwork now that Rawly is gone."

"You're not helping."

"What is your plan?" Hawk asked his patient.

"I don't know yet, but I'll figure it out."

"Can I give you a little advice."

What did he have to lose? Will mused. "Sure, spew your wisdom."

"Do not underestimate Annabeth and trust her."

"I never mistrusted her, and I've never underestimated her."

Hawk got up and replaced the chair. "From the outside looking in, I would say you have done both."

Anger flashed in Will's eyes. "You're going to have to prove that to me." Will wanted to know what Hawk meant.

"When you found out her bakery was part of a crime ring, did you tell her? No, you didn't think she would be able to handle it. Did you trust her to keep your secrets? You used her."

Will started to fidget. He was getting angry because it was true. "Whether you intended to or not, it happened, and you have to take ownership of your choices." Will subdued, and Hawk left.

*****

For two weeks, Will had been convalescing at Hawk Sheridan's home. Daily he was subjected to the late-afternoon inquiry as to why his wife had not come to see him by the two youngsters that would put any Pinkerton detective to shame. His folks had returned home, and Will himself wanted to return to the boarding house. He would at least get to see Annabeth and begin to build the trust he needed to win her heart.

Hawk wanted him to stay until Monday. He wanted to make sure Will could walk up and down the stairs without getting short of breath before he sent him back out into the world. Although several people had come to visit him, some even daily, Will missed the life he had established in Sheridan. He missed going to church. It was kind of Pastor Grey to give Will a copy of his sermon notes and visit him when he could. Thad was a spiritual help to him as well. Thad and Hawk would consistently ask Will if he needed anything spiritually. Never had Will had such friends.

It was the first Sunday Annabeth had made it to church since the shooting. She felt condemned when she walked into the building. She had shot a man, been involved in a crime ring, and had a dead ex-fiancé. What does the town of Sheridan think of her? It didn't take long as the church folks behaved toward her just as they always had. Some whispered a quick "I am praying for you" or "You did the right thing." It gave Annabeth a warm feeling during a cold time of her life.

She saw her uncle motion for her, and she made her way to his pew. She sat next to Merry, and soon the Lapps joined them. Annabeth was swept away with the message Pastor Grey had delivered. It was "Be still and know that I am God." The pastor spoke to know God, you must first become still before him.

"You can't hear a knock on the door unless the knock is louder than what is going on inside," the pastor spoke convincingly. "There comes a time when the noise inside must diminish so the knock can be answered. That is what happened when we become saved. Jesus calls, and we silence the ruckus going on inside of us long enough to hear the savior extend the invitation. Then comes the point of decision: do I open the door to a life of peace and contentment, or do I raise the ruckus to drown out the knock?

"Some weeks ago, I watched a young man in the congregation come to that decision. I could tell there was a moment of choice in his heart when he silenced one to hear the other. It was all over his face. That young man chose to ignore the knocking. That young man's body went home in a pine box." Jonathan—Annabeth's eyes closed. "You may think I am bold this morning in my message calling out someone we all knew, but, folks, this thing is serious, and I am too old to care about the feelings of people when hell is enlarging its borders every day. If you are saved, continue to walk in the light, pointing others to Christ. If you are lost, and you hear the knocking in your heart and life, make haste to answer. Choose to live for him and find peace and contentment in life."

The closing hymn was sung, and the pastor gave the opportunity for people to pray. As Annabeth sat quietly in her pew while people were praying, she too was searching her heart. Her mind went to Rawly and how nervous he was the weekend of Jonathan's death. He had murdered Jonathan, and God miraculously still extended mercy. She felt compelled to write to Rawly. The words of the letter were forming in her head as she felt God was instructing her. It was indeed a good sermon. Be still. She needed to be still about everything in her life and listen for God's direction. And he was telling her to reach out to Rawly one last time for the sake of his soul.

"Annabeth, are you joining us for lunch?" Merry asked her niece.

"Yes, I would love to."

"I need to stop by Hawk's and get the boys. They wanted to ride home with us but first had to change their clothes."

"And I need to check in on Will. I know he is going stir crazy," Thad added, and Annabeth's face faltered a bit. She didn't want to go to Hawk's. If she did, she would feel obligated to see Will. "Are you never going to see him again, Annabeth?" Thad lifted her drooping chin. She looked so distraught. "I think it would do you both good to talk about all that happened."

"Not today," she said in a sad voice. "Can you pick me up outside of the sheriff's office? I need to speak with Dan."

Thad nodded, and Annabeth went to find the sheriff. She needed Rawly's current information. She had a letter to write.

Will was always glad to see Thad Sheridan. He turned out to be a good friend. "How was the service today?" Will asked from the comfy chair in the parlor, his Bible open on his lap.

"It is always good, but today was extraordinary."

Will smiled and held up the notes Pastor Grey dropped off Saturday evening. "I can just imagine. I've been reviewing his notes."

Thad took a seat as Merry helped the boys change out of their clothes. Avery slipped in and handed Thad his youngest grandson. He cooed at the bright-eyed child. "I tried to get Annabeth to come to see you. She is coming out for lunch today." Thad's eyes traveled from the infant to Will. He half smiled.

"Give her my best." He knew Sheridan was a small town, and very soon she would be coming face-to-face with him.

"I haven't given her the letter yet. Would you like for me to give it to her today?"

Will scratched under his chin, and Thad could see he was weighing a decision. "No, not yet. I have some work to do."

"How come Annabeth had to go to the sheriff's office on a Sunday?" River asked his grandfather as he rubbed Chase's head like he had seen his father do countless times. This piqued Will's interest.

"I don't know, son, but I wouldn't ask her about it if I were you." Thad raised his eyebrows at the boy in a stern warning. River turned and looked at Will, then walked out of the house, and got into the wagon. Hunter and Merry were coming down the stairs.

"We are ready to go," she said as she came to take the infant from Thad.

"Not so fast." Thad withheld the child from his grandmother. "You practically held him all through church." She leaned toward her husband and smiled trying to get the baby. He raised the baby a little higher and bent and kissed his wife twice. There it was again: that happy look a couple has when they are secure. His heart ached.

"Will?" Merry had said something, but he was lost in his own thoughts.

"Huh?"

"Never mind." She smiled; and taking hold of Hunter's hand, she exited. Avery took Chase to change his clothes, and Piper scampered to sit on Will's lap. She had become quite attached to the resident patient.

Annabeth obtained the address for the jail Rawly was housed. She would write the letter today and mail it first thing. She was waiting outside the jail when she saw Thad's wagon. Thad started to exit to help her up, but she waved him off. She put her foot up; and sure enough, she fell flat on her back in the middle of main street. Before Annabeth knew it, Hunter, River, and Thad were all helping her up. Would she ever see a day when she didn't do something detrimental to draw attention to herself? She laughed off the mishap and climbed in the back with the boys.

Sunday evening Will showed the good doctor that he could walk not once but four times up the stairs without becoming short of breath. It had been over two weeks, and he was feeling much better. His chest was now down to just an ache at times, and his shoulder and leg only gave him trouble if he overdid it.

"Okay, you can go home tomorrow." Will let out a little whoop. "But with restrictions. I don't want you lifting anything heavy for another two weeks." Hawk grabbed his daughter from her play area and put her in front of Will. "Lift her," he commanded. Will effortlessly lifted the child and stationed her on his hip. She looked at her father and then to Will as if she had done something significant. "Nothing more than what she weighs."

"Okay." Will started to put the child down, but she wouldn't allow it.

"Why don't you carry her upstairs? It will be a good test. It's time for her to go to bed."

Will carried the girl up the stairs, talking to her the whole way. The toddler just kept messing up his hair. He never knew how badly he wanted to be a father.

*****

The Dowry was busy. Annabeth couldn't be happier; with the help of Vivian, she had made a few changes. Mrs. Lapp had encouraged her to set goals, and she had. She started with little ones; and in time with hard work, she could accomplish the bigger ones.

"Well, will you look at that?" Vivian's voice had such glee.

When Annabeth looked up, she saw Will enter. She swallowed hard. He was a little thinner, but he looked...he looked. "Just when you think a man can't get any more handsome, well, there you go," Vivian practically spoke Annabeth's thoughts.

Will sat at the corner table where he had the first day he entered the bakery. He smiled at Vivian and waited. "Go wait on him." Vivian nudged Annabeth.

Annabeth moved to the oven. "I have to take these muffins out of the oven. You wait on him, Vivian."

Vivian frowned at Annabeth's back and picked up the coffee pot. She headed over and poured Will a cup.

"It sure is good to see you up and around. You look as good as new."

Will smiled. "I have missed you, Vivian. Now can I have whatever smells so good, and I would like to see the owner."

Vivian snickered. "Yes, sir."

"He wants one of those." Vivian pointed to the cinnamon roll she pulled from the oven. It was a recipe Molly had given her and had quickly become a favorite. Annabeth put one on a plate and shoved it toward Vivian. "Oh, no, honey, he wants to see the owner."

Annabeth turned to look at Will. There it was—that mischievous big old grin. He raised his cup toward her, and the smile grew wider. Vivian was full-out laughing. "It is good to see you, Will. You look well."

For a moment, he didn't say anything. He just looked at her intensely. She sat the roll in front of him and turned to go.

"I came to see if my old job had been filled." She stopped in her tracks but didn't turn around.

"No, it's been here waiting on you," Vivian piped up. She wasn't about to let Annabeth mess this up. Annabeth frowned at her coworker.

"I work real cheap. Just a muffin now and again and a daily supply of coffee. You can't get any cheaper labor than that," Will said to her back. "We make a good team, Annabeth."

She started to walk away. "I'll think about you, I mean *it*. I'll think about *it*." She felt horrified at the way she misspoke.

"A man can't ask for more than that." He saw her shoulders slump.

Trudy was overjoyed at the prospect of Will coming home. When Annabeth returned from the bakery, Trudy had already begun to prepare. "Annabeth, dear, would you make a cake for Will's homecoming?"

"Sure, I can do that. What is his favorite?" Trudy pondered for a moment.

"I don't reckon I know. Now that is a shame." She looked guilt-ridden. "You have spent a lot of time with him. Do you have a clue?"

Annabeth wanted to scream. She didn't have any clue about anything pertaining to Will. Trudy stood waiting for an answer. "I'll think of something. Now if I was Will Stanton, what would be my favorite cake?" Annabeth sat down at the table. Nothing came to mind, except him.

Her mind went back to Charleston and what a contradiction in character she saw. The way he played the piano flawlessly was hardly what anyone would expect here. There was a finesse about him that added a particular layer to his mystique. He was complicated yet uncomplicated. He made his presence known wherever he went, yet everyone seemed to embrace him.

"Did you come up with something, Annabeth?" Trudy interrupted her. It was a good thing she did. Her mind was just about to relive his lips on hers.

"Yes, I came up with something." She rose and went to the pantry.

"I knew you would." Trudy left, and Annabeth began to do what she did best: bake.

Will entered the front door and walked through the boarding house. He stopped and inhaled. The aroma was making his mouth water. He entered the kitchen and found both his aunt and Annabeth working away. Trudy was peeling potatoes over the sink, and Annabeth was frosting a cake.

"I don't know if I have ever smelled anything so good." He put his arms around the two women. "I am very grateful to Dr. and Mrs. Sheridan, but Avery is not the best cook. Great nurse, wonderful person, but not a cook." His hand was resting around Annabeth's waist. It made her uncomfortable. Surely, he felt the extra inch or so of fluffy fat. In Charleston, she didn't give it a second thought because of the corset. The apparatus was a mainstay there, but here it just wasn't practical.

Will bent to kiss both women on the cheek. "What is the occasion?" he asked sincerely.

"Why, it is your homecoming, silly." Trudy gave him a quizzical look. "I wanted to do something special for my favorite nephew."

He turned his head to face Annabeth. The grip around her waist tightened. "I'm not your nephew." His eyes sparkled.

"You're my good friend, and I'm glad you are hale and hearty again." She quickly turned her attention to the job at hand.

"If you think I am settling for a good friend, you're going to be happily mistaken." He had lowered his voice and was practically whispering in her ear, "And you're going to frost the icing right off the cake if you don't stop." His hand caressed her back as he removed it. The gesture made her shiver.

"Is that one of the cakes you made for Patience's wedding?" She about choked on the gulp of air she inhaled. She had made Will Stanton a wedding cake—kind of. He snitched a bit of the frosting. "I think TJ and I ate all the leftovers. This was my favorite."

Annabeth excused herself after supper and declined dessert. Will was a bit put out with the little miss. She can't avoid him forever. If she didn't let him back to work at the bakery, he would still be there every day, sitting in the corner. He eventually would have to get a paying job to support himself and the family he planned on having; but for right now, he had enough to sustain his way of life.

Will retired early but not because he was tired. He and Annabeth needed to talk; and until the conversation happened, things couldn't progress. Seeing her light still on, Will headed back downstairs. As he went through the kitchen, he cut a large piece of the white cake with rich boiled frosting and grabbed two forks. He headed to Annabeth's front door. He didn't have to knock as he heard Thrive yipping. He knocked anyway, and Annabeth came to the door with Thrive whirling around the two of them for attention.

"I brought you some cake." Will was poised to enter.

"You can't come in here at this late hour." Annabeth thought she sounded like her mother.

"Either I come in, or you come out." She frowned as he spread out his arm to hold the door for her. "How about the front porch?" he said as she passed.

The only furniture currently on the front porch was a swing for two. She could sit on the step, but she knew he would never allow it. Annabeth sat in the swing, and Thrive jumped up beside her. Will sat down and handed her the cake and pulled the forks from his shirt pocket. Thrive looked expectantly at Will and the cake. Will gave the pup a sad look. He took a forkful of cake and savored it. He focused on Annabeth, who was looking down at her lap.

"You're not going to eat any cake. Did you put something in it? Annabeth, are you trying to kill me?" There was laughter in his voice. She choked back a sob. "Annabeth, I was only teasing." He stopped the motion of the swing, reaching to turn her face toward him. Her eyes were filled with tears. "I'm sorry," he said. "I know you would never do anything like that. I was only having some fun."

"But I did almost kill you. I never should have gone to see Rawly. I just wanted to tell him we were through, but in the back of my mind, I wished I could confront him, and it happened. He shot you, he aimed to kill you, and he almost succeeded. Will, I'm sorry. This is all my fault."

Thrived nestled his mistress, laying his head on her shoulder. She buried her head in his fur. *Sneaky dog,* Will thought. Didn't he know that kind of loving support should come from him? "Annabeth, this was not your fault. It was a strange turn of events that just happened to no fault of anyone except Rawly. If you think you need forgiveness, I forgive you, but it isn't necessary, and we need to move on." She just looked at him.

"Or can we move on?" he asked with a little edge to his voice.

"I can't do anything right now." She stroked Thrive's head. "I don't know if I can ever—"

He knew what Annabeth was going to say. She was going to say she didn't know if she could ever love him. He stopped her by putting a forkful of cake in her mouth. "We will talk about it later," he said to her, gazing at her lips covered in frosting. Thrive quickly took a swipe with his tongue to get the frosting.

"Eww, Thrive." She wiped her lips. Once again, the dog had circumvented a privilege Will thought should have been his.

"Did you ever find out who sent the dog and all the other gifts?"

Annabeth had quit trying to figure it out. She thought it was Rawly then her uncle. She contemplated Will at one time, but he just debunked that theory. "I haven't a clue anymore. The two people

I thought might be responsible have denied it. Only Liddy Lapp knows for sure, and she is not telling."

"You don't think it is Liddy herself, do you? Maybe she and Dr. Lapp are doing this for you."

Annabeth had never thought of that. It very well could be. "Don't think on it too hard. Just enjoy it, Annabeth. You deserve every good thing you get." He stood to leave, leaving her to think on the things they discussed. He rubbed Thrive's muzzle. Bending, he brushed a soft kiss across Annabeth's lips. "Pleasant dreams," he said as he whistled his way into the house. It was a familiar tune. Annabeth closed her eyes.

*****

The next morning, Will showed up at The Dowry a little after it opened. He entered through the front door and went straight to Annabeth. "So can I have my old job back?"

Vivian threw an apron at him. "Of course you can. If she says no, I will quit, and that will be the end of the bakery."

"The corner table needs to be cleaned," Annabeth said as she turned to put the finishing touches on one of her pastries.

Will smiled at Vivian and went to work. It felt good to have the burden of the agency off his back. He had turned in his resignation last week; and it was accepted, much to his bosses' displeasure. He hated letting anyone down; but after all that happened in Sheridan, he knew his path was being directed away from Pinkerton.

Hawk's prediction had come to fruition: every eligible bachelor had made his way to the bakery for one thing or another. Some poor chump would approach Annabeth and begin the common pleasantries that came with asking for a date. Will would just stand behind her with a smile on his face, arms crossed over his chest, shaking his head no. Most gents got the hint; other hardheads were met with a physical disruption. Will had to literally step in front of one man on his way to clear the table, forcing the man to forget what he was about to say. It was getting to be a full-time job stopping the nonsense. Annabeth didn't seem to be the wiser, or maybe she didn't mind him throttling the plans. Vivian got great amusement watching the theatricals.

Liddy Lapp slipped in the back door of The Dowry and placed an intricate teapot on the counter. Will watched her slip back out with neither Annabeth nor Vivian noticing. Annabeth almost walked past the gift. "Where did this come from? Has it been here all morning?" She looked at Vivian.

"I don't remember seeing it earlier. Look, there is a little card attached."

Annabeth removed the small note. "Relax and enjoy the life you are meant to have," she read the note to herself and smiled. That is exactly what she planned to do.

"Does it say who it is from?" Will asked as he made his way over to look at the gift.

She handed him the card. "I think you are right. I think it is the Lapps."

To the side of the teapot, Will noticed a piece of paper with several items listed. He picked it up, and Annabeth tried to grab it from him. "What's this?" He raised it above his head.

"Just give it to me." She stood on her tiptoes, trying to get it. He handed it to her.

"Keeping secrets from your coworkers are you?" He turned toward Vivian with questioning eyes.

"She is making plans for the future of the bakery," Vivian supplied.

"Did you figure me in those plans?" he asked.

Vivian cackled. "Will Stanton, I sure am glad Rawly's aim was off."

Annabeth sucked in her breath. *What a thing to say*, she thought.

"Oh, Annabeth, you are too sensitive. We can joke about it now. Will doesn't mind, do you, Willie boy?"

He frowned at Vivian. "Don't call me that, and if we are talking about aim, who taught you to shoot, Annabeth?"

"She got Old Reliable right in the britches." Vivian was more than cackling now. "And didn't he deserve it." Will and Vivian seemed to be getting great enjoyment out of Annabeth's malicious action toward another human being. Every time she thought about it, she got nauseous.

"Show him your plans, Annie. I think they are excellent." Vivian had moved to wash dishes.

Annabeth handed Will the list. She might as well let him have another good laugh. He perused the list. "I like them, especially the first one about using The Dowry to help the community. I have a thought on how you might accomplish that. would you like to hear?" He was serious. He leaned both elbows on the counter and bent over to rest. She wondered if his chest wasn't hurting. She had witnessed him rub the area earlier.

"Why don't you get with Hawk or Avery and find out who in the town or on the outskirts are in need? Hawk makes rounds and seems to know. You could package up what is not sold and put it in some sort of container and deliver the goods." He was eye level with her. "You could do it anonymously if you wanted, and we could get Jonah to make special boxes up. Only a few people would need to know. We could be sneaky about it." He grinned at her.

"What is this we talk?" Vivian asked with a coy smile. "You planning on hanging around?" She nudged him.

"I have made no secret of my desire to steal Annabeth's heart as well as her bakery." He winked at his coworker.

Annabeth ignored his remark. She didn't ignore his idea; it was a good one. Her mind was playing the suggestion over and over.

"I bet Mr. Tyler would even donate some things. He is a good man. You could start out just doing it a few times and see how it goes." Annabeth looked at him, but his eyes had drifted to the front window. "Uh, I'll go talk to him now, see if it is something he would be interested in." The man was practically running out of the bakery.

Annabeth turned to see Hunter and River Sheridan headed up the steps of the bakery. "Chicken," she threw over her shoulder at the vanishing man.

"Hello, boys, what can I do for you?" Annabeth went to greet her customers. They both scanned the room, undoubtedly looking for Will. "The telegraph man sent us over here with this." Hunter handed her a telegram. It was from her father. She ripped it open. Her heart was beating fast. She was afraid something had happened.

"Not bad news, I hope." Vivian went to stand beside her. Annabeth let out the breath she had been holding.

"No, he and my mother are on their way here. They heard about Jonathan."

"What is that?" Annabeth pointed to another telegram in Hunter's hand.

"It is for your husband. Where is he?" The boys had smug looks on their faces as if they knew he was running from them.

"He isn't here." She decided not to have the discussion yet again with the boys. "Would you like for me to give it to him?" Annabeth smiled.

"No, we were told to give it to him directly. Do you know where he is?" Both boys had narrowed their eyes, searching as if Will had been hiding somewhere in the bakery.

"He is over at Tyler's," Vivian spoke up. "He went in the back door. You go on over, and here take these muffins to Mr. Tyler, and you tell him they are from Vivian."

"Is Mr. Tyler your husband?" River asked.

"Not yet," Vivian replied to Annabeth's shocked face.

Will saw them coming. The two boys had determined looks on their faces. He knew they were coming for him. "Boys," he greeted.

They just stuck the telegram out and went marching into Tyler's store. "These muffins are for you, Mr. Tyler. Vivian sent them and said to tell you they were from her and you're not her husband yet."

The look on Mr. Tyler's face was priceless. Will just shook his head as he opened the telegraph.

He was requested to appear before a judge in Rapid City along with Annabeth Lorton in the case of Rawly Smith. They needed more than just Dan's account. He and Annabeth would have to testify in front of a judge. They were expected to appear in three days.

Once the Sheridan boys had gone, Will made his way back to the bakery. He wasn't sure how Annabeth was going to take having to speak with a judge. He found her with her own telegraph. "They sent you one too?" he asked, holding up his telegram.

"Of course, but I don't understand why my father would tele-graph you about their arrival." Annabeth had an unpleasant, puzzled look.

Will looked a little confused. "Let's exchange telegrams." He handed his to her and watched her face drop.

"How far is Rapid City from here?" She handed the missive back to him.

"Not too far. We can take the stage and come back the same day. There might be a chance we'd have to stay the night, but I doubt it."

She didn't ask any more questions, but Will saw the worry on her face. "Close up for me, Vivian. I am going out to my uncle's. They will want to know about my parents' arrival."

Will wanted to go with her but sensed she needed to be alone. He watched as she and Thrive headed down the road.

CHAPTER 13

*M*erry was headed into the house with a basket of laundry when she spotted Annabeth and her companion coming down the road. Ulysses, the Sheridans' dog, made a dash for Thrive; and the two canines went scampering into the high clover.

Merry waved to her niece. The pathetic return gesture was a sure sign this wasn't an ordinary visit. Merry wasted no time. "Come in and help me fold these clothes and tell me what has put worry all over that lovely face."

Annabeth loved Merry from their first meeting several years ago. Next to her mother, she was the woman Annabeth looked up to the most.

Annabeth pulled the first garment from the basket and began to fold. "My parents are coming. I got a telegram today. I am not sure when they will arrive, but I expect it to be any day."

"You don't seem to happy about it." Merry gave a surprised look.

"I am. It's just I am afraid they are coming to try to get me to return home. They heard about Jonathan. Wait until they find out I shot Rawly, which is another reason I don't want them to come right now."

"What do you mean?" Merry pulled out a bedsheet and handed Annabeth one end.

"Will and I have to go to Rapid City in three days to appear before a judge. I may not even be here when my parents arrive. They will love that. 'Where's Annabeth?' 'Oh, she had to appear before a judge because her boyfriend killed her ex-fiancé, and she shot him.' Jackson Lorton will have me on the first train to Charleston quicker than you can blink."

"I think you are overreacting just a bit and not giving your folks enough credit."

"I feel like my life has spun out of control. The only stable thing is the bakery. I don't want my parents to come and take that away from me. Not that they would intentionally do so, but out of their care and concern, they might make it difficult."

Merry stacked the folded sheet on the chair. "As I said, you're not giving them enough credit. They love you, and they trust you. Why wouldn't they want to come and support you during this difficult time? I can't think of two better people to have in your corner than your parents. Now, about appearing before this judge, tell me more. I thought Dan took care of all that."

"I thought so too, but Will got a telegram today saying he and I needed to appear before the judge. I was hoping to speak with Uncle Thad about it. I was wondering if he thought Rawly would be present. I don't want to see him again after what he did to Will." Annabeth looked forlorn.

"How is Will?" Merry asked.

Annabeth was caught up in a memory. Several seconds passed, and Merry took the shirt Annabeth was holding and folded it. She lifted a pile and handed it to Annabeth. "Put these on my bed, then come back, and help me plan for supper. If you want to speak with your uncle, it will have to be at the table."

Annabeth did as she was told and laid the stack of clean clothes on the bed. As she went to leave, something caught her eye. Her name was scrawled across an envelope lying on her uncle's chest of drawers. She walked over and lifted the letter. She stared at the script; it wasn't familiar. Should she open it? It wasn't sealed, and it did have her name on it. Curiosity got the better of her, and she slipped the note from its confines. She read the letter and then reread it. As if things couldn't get more complicated. She sat on the edge of the bed.

"Annabeth, did you get lost?" Merry entered the bedroom and knew in an instance what Annabeth had found.

"Your uncle isn't going to be too happy with you." Merry approached her niece.

"Well, I'm not too happy with him!" There was anger in her voice. "When was I supposed to receive this letter addressed to me?" She grasped the letter tight in her hand, her eyes full of hurt.

"I believe Thad was the keeper of the letter until Will thought it was the right time."

"And when he was near death, wasn't the time to give it to me?"

Her aunt did not answer. "Have you read it?" Annabeth's tone softened a bit.

"No, nor has Thad. Will did let us know it was an explanation of what brought him to Sheridan."

"Why didn't—" Merry put her hand up to stop Annabeth's question.

"Any questions need to be directed to your uncle or Will. Now come on and help me in the kitchen."

The sun was just beginning to dip toward the horizon, and supper had been neatly laid out on the large table when Franklin came storming into the house. This was never a good sign. Franklin was undoubtedly mad about something. Thad, Gil, and David followed. Thad looked at his wife, and she knew in an instance the two had quarreled. He went directly to Merry and, kissing her on the cheek, gave her a little extra squeeze.

"Annabeth, it is good to see you. What brings you out our way?" He pulled the chair out for her as he had done for Merry and kissed the top of her head. The tension in the room had her second-guessing her desire to speak with him about the court appearance and Will's letter.

"Annabeth has a couple of things to discuss with you." Merry smiled at her husband and watched as Gil and David took their seats.

"Go get your brother. Tell him I said we have company, and he will be a gentleman and come to the table," Thad directed this at Gil.

The redheaded boy did as he was told. It was only a minute before Franklin arrived at the table and sat next to his pa.

"Annabeth, will you say grace?" He reached for her hand and the hand of his son. This was the tradition whenever they prayed. She nodded and said a quick prayer. "What did you want to speak with me about?" Thad turned toward Annabeth as he passed the platter of meat to her.

"Good news. My folks are coming for a visit. They should be here any day. I got the telegram this morning."

Thad's smile was huge. "That is wonderful news. I haven't seen your father in a while. Is TJ coming too?"

"I am not sure. The telegram didn't say. I also got another telegram. Well, I didn't. Will did. He and I have to go to Rapid City in three days to give testimony to a judge there about Rawly." Thad's brow wrinkled. "Is this a bad thing, Uncle Thad? You don't think I am in trouble, do you?"

Thad quickly schooled his features and smiled. "No, I just thought Dan's report would have been enough. I am sure Will filed his report with the agency." Thad looked at his niece. "Don't fret. It will be fine."

Agency? What was he talking about? Will never told her who he worked for. She figured it was some private person. *Agency,* she kept saying it over in her head.

"What agency?" Gil asked.

"I don't think it's common knowledge, and it doesn't go out of these four walls, but Will was an undercover agent for Pinkerton."

"Now that is something." Franklin, who had not spoken, looked up with his eyes wide. They were not nearly as wide as Annabeth's open mouth. "You didn't know?" Thad deduced at Annabeth's expression.

"No, it would seem no one tells me anything." she said with a huff. "Am I thought of as a child that I can't be trusted with pertinent information that basically affects my daily living?" She stood and took her plate to the sink, dropped, it in and stormed out of the house.

Thad started to rise. "She found Will's letter on your dresser." Merry let him know as he walked by.

Annabeth had just stepped off the porch when Thad caught up with her. "Do I get a chance to explain?" His pace matched hers, and she turned to call for Thrive.

"I don't know. Do you think it may impugn my delicate constitution?"

He smirked at her, not liking her tone at all. "I know you and Franklin are too old for the woodshed, but that is precisely what you both need." He lifted her and put her on the fence rail so they could be eye level.

"I am going to set you straight on a few things, and you may not like it, but you need to hear them."

She wanted to turn her head, but that would be disrespectful. She fixed her gaze on his. "No one thinks you can't handle what comes your way. Annabeth, you have to understand that a man's nature is to protect. Now, I am sorry Jonathan and Rawly were men who chose to override that natural instinct for money. Their motives were to destroy. But Will's inherent nature was to protect you at all cost, and that is what he did. It may have not been done in the best way, but it got the job done. Even to the point of him nearly losing his own life."

Her eyes never left his as they filled with moisture. She was shaking, and Thad lifted her off the fence rail to cradle her in his arms. "Your father, me, and Will—we love you, Annabeth. Please let us do our job without interference."

Will slowed his steps when he saw Thad and Annabeth near the fence. It sure looked like Thad was giving Annabeth a talking to. In a way, it riled Will up. What could be going on that anyone would take her to task? He also knew Thad Sheridan was not given to tirades for no good reason. When he saw her put her arms around him, he knew everything must be all right. He continued his leisurely pace. The pair stopped when they saw him headed their way.

"You're too late for supper." Thad smiled at the man.

Will also smiled at Annabeth, not at Thad. "I just came to check on Annabeth. I thought she might need to be escorted home."

Her heart clenched. He was protecting her; it came naturally.

"Not before I've had a piece of Aunt Merry's cobbler and some coffee." Annabeth turned to go back to the house. Thrive was confused. Were they going or staying? That was the look on the pooch's face. Will bent to scratch the dog's head. He grimaced with the movement.

"How's the chest?" Thad asked as Will straightened up.

"Movements you wouldn't think would aggravate it does. I can't mount a horse yet. I tried this afternoon, and it sent a ripping pain through this leg and shoulder. Hawk said it will be weeks before I will be able to do much manual labor. I am confined to the bakery."

Thad chuckled. "Which suits you just fine, I am sure."

"Did Annabeth tell you about going to Rapid City?" The two men were walking intently slow.

"Yes, I wonder why your report, as well as Dan's, wasn't enough."

"This judge is very thorough. He doesn't like surprises and wants every loop closed. I suspect it won't take long."

"Do you want me to go with you?" Thad offered.

"I appreciate the gesture, but I don't think it is necessary unless you think Annabeth would be more comfortable if you went."

"I don't think it matters to her. We can ask her." Thad opened the front door and let Will in.

*****

Will and Annabeth walked in silence for a while. They had stayed a little too late at the Sheridans, and it was nearly pitch black when they left. There wasn't a cloud in the sky, and every star looked as if it was polished gold. "How come you never told me you were working for the Pinkerton Agency?" Annabeth spoke, turning to look at Will's profile. He was scanning the surroundings.

"One, I was undercover, and two, I didn't think it mattered."

"Am I the only one who didn't know?" Annabeth placed her hand on his arm to stop him.

"No one knew. I just told my parents when they came to visit." He wanted to wrap her hand in his; but for some reason, it didn't feel right. He kept walking.

"You kept it a secret from your folks? For how many years?" Why did she want to know all this? It was fast becoming his past, and he was leaving it behind.

"Yes, it is better when you are working undercover not to alert anyone. The agency would even deny I worked for them. I have been doing it since the age of sixteen." Annabeth stopped in her tracks. "And I stopped last week. I turned in my resignation. This job was going to be my last no matter how it turned out." He kept walking. She started to speak, but he stopped her. "I'm not saying any more, Annabeth," he said it with such finality that the only thing she could do was shut up.

Merry stood on the porch, watching her niece and Will stroll down the path to town. She felt her husband's arm around her waist and lips sweeping across her neck. "If those two don't end up married, it will be a big mistake. Stubbornness sure runs in your family." Merry reached up and stroked her husband's face.

"It sure does, and aren't you glad of it? Just think, Merry, if I hadn't been stubborn when it came to winning your heart, look how miserable you would be." His arms grew a little tighter around her.

"Speaking of stubborn, what has our son all bristled up?"

Thad laughed. "Can't you guess?"

"A girl." Merry leaned her head on Thad's chest.

"A girl who needs a break from Franklin's charm. He wasn't happy when I told him he needed to stay home tonight." The couple shared a laugh and a couple of kisses.

*****

Annabeth exited her little home in her pink traveling suit. She thought it looked smart and may help when she went before the judge. Will was waiting for her. He too had a suit on. He was a fine figure of a man whether he was in a suit or an apron. She couldn't stop staring. He met her halfway up the walk.

"You look lovely, Annabeth. The judge will forget all about Rawly Smith when he sees you." She just smiled. He offered her his arm, and they went toward the stage office. The coach would be leaving in a half hour. They stopped by the bakery.

"I have never seen a more handsome couple. I do declare, Will Stanton, you sure can clean up nice. And we know how striking our

Annie is." Vivian circled the pair. "Those look like wedding clothes to me," she added.

"We will be sure and wear them to your next wedding to Mr. Tyler." Will was quick with the retort, and Vivian blushed.

"What on earth are you talking about?"

"You do know Hunter told Mr. Tyler the muffins were from you."

"Yes, I told him to say that." Vivian looked a little put out.

"Did you also tell Hunter that Mr. Tyler wasn't your husband yet, because that is what Hunter told Mr. Tyler."

Vivian's eyes slid shut. "Oh, heavenly days. Well, at least he knows where I stand, what my aim is."

Will and Annabeth were speechless. They knew Vivian was bold but not this bold.

Will fidgeted with his tie. The warm sun was already making the garment feel like he had been lassoed. Annabeth reached up to straighten it but instead untied it and removed it. She placed it in his pocket and then unbuttoned the top button of his shirt. "No need being uncomfortable the whole day over a little piece of string. No one cares if you have the thing on or not."

He was a little stunned but was very thankful the albatross was removed from his neck.

The stage arrived on time; and with it came Jackson, Abby, and TJ. As the Lortons exited, they were surprised to see Will and Annabeth on the platform. "How did you know we would be coming today on the early stage?" Abby smiled as she hugged her daughter.

"We didn't," Annabeth replied as she went to hug her father. His embrace was extra long. He had been apprehensive about his eldest.

"What do you mean?" TJ stuck out his hand to Will.

"We are actually on our way to Rapid City for the day." His eyes met Jackson's. "We've been summoned to present testimony to a judge in the case."

"How long will you be gone?" Jackson asked Will. "And do you need my assistance?" The two men talked as if Annabeth and Abby were nowhere around.

"If all goes well, which I don't expect it to go any other way, we will be home this evening. If Annabeth feels she needs you to come, it is all right with me, but I think we can handle it."

"All aboard!" the stage driver announced, and the Lortons moved so Will could get in the coach. He waited inside for Annabeth. She needed a few minutes with her parents. Once she assured them she was fine, Jackson gave her a hand into the coach.

Annabeth tripped over Will's large foot and nearly landed on her head. Will caught her just in time. When she was in her right mind, she stood up straight and adjusted her jacket. She raised her arms to fix her hat; and as she did, the stagecoach lunged forward, throwing her on to Will's lap. She scurried to stand, but he wouldn't let her. Instead, he helped her get seated beside him.

"For the sake of both our safety, I think you should stay seated next to me instead of chancing a move to sit across. Don't get me wrong. I would love to sit for a few hours just looking at you, but I just can't risk you getting hurt."

She elbowed him in the ribs and heard the sharp intake of air. She had forgotten his injuries were still very much healing, and she had just caused him pain. She bowed her head and shook it slowly. "I'm sorry." She let out a sigh.

"I will live, Annabeth. It is just a little tender. Don't worry about it."

Annabeth was pretty quiet on the ride to Rapid City. They were due to arrive by noon, speak with the judge at one, and then take the three o'clock stage home. She prayed it would go that smoothly. She wanted finality to this whole ordeal, and she was hoping today would do just that.

They appeared to be right on schedule. Will helped Annabeth out of the stagecoach without incidence. They stopped and inquired direction for where the meeting was to take place. It was just down the street. Once they found the building, they crossed the street to get a cup of coffee until it was closer to one.

Will tried to engage Annabeth in small talk, but her mind was preoccupied. "I don't believe Rawly will be here today if that is what has you so worried," Will offered.

"I was afraid he might be," she confessed.

"We are just going to go in there and tell what happened and answer any questions. We know the truth, and it will clear up any misconceptions held by any involved." He sipped his coffee and frowned. "This is awful." She had to agree it did taste like last week's grounds.

Before mounting the steps of the judicial building, Will clasped Annabeth's hand. Neither said anything as they made their way toward the door. Will opened the heavy wooden door and allowed Annabeth to precede him. The hallway was massive, and the ceilings were high and arched. Annabeth felt extremely small as she looked up at the painted ceiling. Lady Justice was with her blindfold, and scales was perched on a pedestal just to the side of the double doors.

Will approached the clerk and told them why they were there. They were asked to take a seat on the nearby bench. Again, Will clasped Annabeth's hand as they waited. It was his way of protecting her, Annabeth deduced. She didn't mind. It seemed to calm her nerves. They waited a good fifteen minutes before they were summoned in.

The room was empty except for three people: the prosecutor, the defender, and the judge. Annabeth was asked to tell her account of the shooting. Will and Thad had instructed her not to mention anything, just directly answer the questions. She did as she was told; and in only a few minutes, all seemed to be satisfied. Will was interrogated a little longer and a little more forcefully by the defense attorney. In the end, they gained no new knowledge; and Rawly's fate was sealed.

Will and Annabeth sat in the empty room for a moment in silence. Finally, Annabeth spoke, "I thought after this there would be a sense of relief, but I feel as troubled as ever. I just want to go back to Sheridan and have my life return to normal."

Will sat up on the edge of the bench and faced her. "I want you to close your eyes, Annabeth, and when you do, ask yourself, what is the first thing you see in regard to life in Sheridan?" Her eyes closed. "If it is not me," Will whispered, "I will leave Sheridan, but if it is me, I will expect you to become my wife."

The door of the room suddenly opened, and the judge returned. Annabeth stood, calling out to the man, "There was something, sir, I wanted to ask you but didn't. May I approach the bench?"

The judge smiled. "I adjourned court, so there is no need to ask for permission. What is it you wanted to know?" Annabeth shot toward the man.

Will sat disappointed. He had just put everything on the table, and her mind wasn't even on what he had said. How could she have any question concerning the event of the past hour? He couldn't hear their conversation; he was too busy deciding what to do next.

Annabeth had a rather lengthy discussion with the judge before the little miss returned to sit beside Will. "What did you want to ask the judge?" Will thought his best course of action was to forget what just happened. She put her hand on the side of his face.

"I wanted to know if he would marry us." She looked at his surprised face. "Today, right now, this very minute. When I close my eyes, you are all I see. When you ask me to think about my life in Sheridan, I realized it is not Sheridan. It is you. With that, my troublesome feelings left. It wasn't all that had happened that was troubling me. It was you. In a good way, mind you." She kissed him tenderly on the lips.

"But, Annabeth, you deserve a big fancy wedding." Will's head was down, looking at their hands entangled. "And a beautiful ring and all the things women like to plan and do before the big day."

"I had all that once. I really don't care to go through it again. I am not leaving Rapid City without being Mrs. Will Stanton. If it makes you feel better, you can whistle 'Fur Elise' in my ear." She snuggled her face close to his. He didn't whistle. His lips were otherwise happily engaged with hers.

The door opened a second time, and the judge returned with the bailiff. "I don't have to ask if you're ready. You're ready," the judge said as he motioned the two forward. In less than five minutes, Will and Annabeth were married. Will kissed the bride, and they stepped out into the sunshine.

"I better head to the stage office. Do you want to leave on the four o'clock stage or the six o'clock stage?" Will asked his wife.

"How about the noon stage?" She smiled. "You can wire Dan and tell him we got held up here in Rapid City and have to spend the night." Will wasted no time placing the telegram or finding the hotel to secure a room for the night.

"Are you hungry, Annabeth?"

"Starving. I was too nervous to eat this morning."

"I need to have something to get the taste of that rancid coffee out of my mouth."

They both laughed and started to stroll leisurely down the boardwalk hand in hand. They window-shopped a little before Will spotted a church. He led her there. The door was open, and they went in. He motioned for her to sit in the pew.

"Our wedding vows had little if any spiritual meaning. There are some things I would like to say to you here before God." He sat next to her angling so he could face her. "All my adult life, I held the belief that God would continually mold me to be the man I should be for his glory. He intentionally left places void that only you could fill. I have never felt more alive than I have since I met you. I have never known the kind of love a man can have for a woman until you settled in here." He laid his hand over his heart. "I love you as Christ loves the church, and I will give my life for you."

What could she say to that? No one had ever spoken so powerfully about love to her. "You expect me to say something that wonderful and endearing back? I have so much love for you, but I don't think I can put it so breathtakingly beautiful," she said with emotion-laden words and a trickle of tears. To say she felt the same somehow wouldn't be enough. "I give you everything, Will Stanton. I am yours, and I will do my best to fill all your days with unfailing love." He crushed her in an embrace. "But let's keep that giving of your life to the spiritual and not the literal. You've already come a little too close to that for my taste." Annabeth rubbed his left arm. "I never want to go through that again."

He smiled. "Me either." He kissed her forehead, and they sat in the church house for a few moments.

The minister saw the young couple head into the church. He gave them a few minutes before he went to see if he could be of assistance. "Hello, I am Pastor Dawson. I saw you enter and wondered if there was anything I could assist you with." He knew the young lady had been crying, and it looked as if the young man might have been as well.

The couple smiled. "We just got married this afternoon at the municipal building by a judge, and we wanted to step in here and talk about the spiritual aspect of the sacred vows."

"I see, or maybe I don't see. Why didn't you come to the church? I would perhaps have married you after a brief discussion. Your actions seem to suggest you have a relationship with the Lord."

Annabeth smiled at the man. "Are you familiar with the phrase spur of the moment?"

"Ah, yes, I am very familiar with the phrase and the action. I married on a whim twenty-seven years ago."

"We would appreciate some words of advice going forward, as well as a prayer." Will took Annabeth's hand when he made the request.

Pastor Dawson quoted some scripture made a remark or two and then prayed for the newlyweds.

"We appreciated your words, Pastor. Can you recommend a place worthy of a wedding supper?" Will asked.

The man of the church gave them directions to a nice, wholesome restaurant in town with delicious food. "Tell them I sent you." The pastor smiled as he followed the couple to the sidewalk.

*****

After they ate, they did a little more window-shopping. Annabeth saw lots of things she could add to her wish list for the bakery. The sun would soon be sinking behind the horizon for good, so they headed to the hotel. Will stood outside the hotel room door and looked at Annabeth. He slipped the key in the door.

"No seconds thoughts, no change of heart?" he questioned her. "This will be your last chance to reconsider our hasty actions today. Once I open the door, there—"

"Open the door," Annabeth said emphatically.

The heat of the day had led to some pretty severe thunderstorms during the night. An early morning blast of thunder awakened Annabeth. When she moved, she did not feel Will beside her. She felt a twinge of fear. Had he left her too? Sitting up, she looked to find him standing at the window peering out.

"Is something wrong, Will?" Even as dark as it was in the room, she could see him smile.

"How could there be anything wrong?" He dropped the curtain back but remained by the window. "I was just thinking about you. How thankful I am for you. In all the excitement of the day, I felt I needed to thank the Lord. You found me praying, Annabeth."

Annabeth's heart smiled. She remembered her husband's favorite verse and knew he was praying over every step of the journey, the journey they were taking together. He made his way back to bed and settled Annabeth in his arms. It was indeed the safest place she had ever been. "Won't Vivian give us what for when we get back to Sheridan?" Annabeth spoke in a low tone.

"You know who is going to be livid?" Will asked his bride, answering before she could. "Your persnickety mother and sister. Neither one of them cares for me."

She leaned up, putting her face directly in front of his. "The only thing that matters is if I care for you. And I most assuredly care for you." Annabeth made sure there was no doubt in his mind.

CHAPTER 14

*T*he storms in Rapid City had hovered over Sheridan. When Will and Annabeth hit the platform, they hurried into the station. Thad and Jackson were waiting inside. "How did it go?" Thad asked the couple. He sensed something was going on. He couldn't quite put his finger on it.

"Things went better than I expected," Will commented.

"Then what was the delay in keeping you an extra day?" Jackson was looking to Will for an explanation. Annabeth looked at her husband who was focused on his father-in-law.

"We got married," Annabeth said in a happy tone.

"You what?" Jackson's question had a bit of anger in it. His eyes stayed on Will. "I said we got married, yesterday afternoon."

Jackson ran his hand through his hair, landing on the back of his neck. He half turned his back to the couple. "Annabeth, why now?" he said in a calmer tone.

Thad stood quiet as did the groom. Annabeth was dumbfounded. She thought of all the people her father would be the least affected by her announcement.

Jackson turned and gently grasped Annabeth's elbow, attempting to lead her to the other side of the room for a private conversation. "Nope." Will stopped the man. "Anything you have to say to Annabeth on this matter, you can say in front of me." Jackson looked affronted.

"Let's all just take a breath," Thad suggested. "Will, why don't you and Annabeth take a little time and then head out to the house where we can sit down and have a discussion? Is this okay with you, Jackson?" He still had a hold of his daughter's elbow.

Leaning in, he kissed her cheek and exited the stage depot. "Okay with you two?" Thad moved closer to the couple. They nodded. Thad leaned to kiss his niece and then put his hand out toward Will. "Congratulations." His tone was low as if he didn't want Jackson to hear him. Annabeth smiled. She felt she and Will had an ally.

"I didn't expect that reaction from your father," Will said as he put his suit coat around Annabeth to keep her dry as they walked back to the boarding house.

"He is very protective of me. I think he is more hurt than anything."

"I don't know why he would be hurt. I told him back in Charleston how I felt about you. He seemed to be okay with it. Can you imagine what your mother is going to say?"

"It doesn't matter now. We are married. I really would like to shout it to the world, but that is not my personality." She smiled up at him from underneath his suit coat. The rain was pelting his face. She really wanted to kiss the look off his face, but they were walking down main street. It simply wouldn't be proper. She giggled at the thought. The rain began to get heavy; and putting his arm around her waist, Will picked up the pace.

Annabeth opened the door to her little home and went in, leaving the door open for Will. "I am going to my room to get some dry clothes." He started to shut the door. "You're coming back, aren't you?" Annabeth went to the door.

"Of course, I am coming back, silly." He kissed her forehead. "We need to tell Dan and Trudy. She will have heart palpation if she finds you in my house in the morning." Annabeth giggled.

"I'll be back for a dryer, Mrs. Stanton, say, in twenty minutes?" Will asked, his face nearly touching hers, his arms wrapped tight around her.

"Make it ten." She kissed his laughing face.

"What have I gotten myself into?" He put some space between them and ran down the boardwalk to his room.

Ten minutes later, Will arrived with an umbrella. He didn't knock just walked right in. "Look what I found." Annabeth handed Will a package. "It was resting on my pillow."

Will frowned and handed it back to her. "Open it."

She opened the package, and inside the small box was a gold ring. She held it up.

"Annabeth, do you have something you need to tell me? This definitely isn't from the Lapps, and somebody has gone too far."

"I have no idea who this could be from. I am at a loss." Her face was one of perplexity and astonishment.

"You sure you don't know who the admirer is?"

She moved her mouth from side to side in contemplation. "Honestly, I don't."

"This sure isn't getting our marriage off to a very good start." His frown was dreadful.

"You seriously can't believe I have any part in this?" She looked a little panicked, and Will couldn't hide his smile. He took the gold ring and put it on her finger. "It's been me all along, Annabeth. And it will always be me. I was going to ask you to marry me when we returned."

She leaped into his arms, wrapping her arms around his neck and hanging on for dear life. The movement caused a twinge of pain in his chest, but it didn't seem to matter in regard to what he was holding.

He sat her down on her feet and unwrapped her arms from his neck. "Let's go tell Aunt Trudy so we can get out to see your folks. The sooner I endure your mother's very calculated Southern dress down, the sooner we can get on with being married."

"Mother is good at politely telling someone she is highly disappointed in them."

They stepped out on the stoop, and Will opened the umbrella. "Annabeth"—Will stopped her—"I don't want you to be disrespectful to your parents. Whatever they say to me, I can take it. Just let it go."

"I always give my parents the respect they deserve, but if they start picking on my husband, I am not sure I can hold my tongue. I make no promises." She tugged him toward the wagon.

*****

Jackson and Abby sat in the front room at the Sheridans. It wasn't that they disliked Will; as a matter of fact, Jackson liked him a lot. They just thought it was too soon. Annabeth, and Will also, had been through so much. They rushed into something on a wave of emotion.

"Who are we kidding, Abby?" Jackson finally stopped his wife from pacing. "They are married. It was going to happen. We both knew it."

She closed her eyes and bent her head, her hand resting on her forehead. "She deserves a proper wedding. I deserve to fuss over her, and you deserve to walk her down the aisle and give her away to a man who will—" she stopped.

"Love her," Jackson filled in the missing words. "Isn't that the end result we want, that our daughter is loved and cherished? If Will is that man, does it matter when, where, or how they are married? I think our pride is hurt just a smidgen." He smiled at his wife. Why was he always right?

Will pulled the buggy as close as he could to the Sheridans' porch. He popped out and assisted his bride up the steps. TJ met them on the porch. "I'll take care of the mare." He grinned at the couple. "They have been waiting for you."

Annabeth looked at her little brother. He wasn't so little anymore. He was nearly as tall as their father and was the spitting image of her uncle Thad: same dark hair, same stunning blue eyes. Handsome—that is what he was—and growing up way too fast.

"For the record, I am glad you two got married." TJ then did something so out of character. He hugged the couple. First, his sister then his new brother-in-law. "Don't mess this up, Annabeth. Will is the best thing to happen to this family in a long time."

"Now, TJ, Preston is a good man too." Annabeth didn't want any disparaging reference to her sister's husband.

"Oh, I like Preston, but he doesn't have anything interesting to say. He just works and does Patience's bidding."

"As he should," Will said with a sarcastic tone. The three shared a snicker.

"It's the kind of man Patience needs," TJ admitted.

Will opened the door and allowed Annabeth to enter. The Sheridan house was always warm, cozy, and inviting. Thad and Merry were sitting at the table drinking coffee and talking when the two entered. Merry rose and gave Annabeth a hug. "Congratulations, sweetheart." She gave a wide smile to Will.

"Jackson and Abby are in the front room." Thad pointed to the room off the kitchen.

The newlyweds headed into the small parlor. Abby moved to hug her daughter and then sat on the settee. She motioned for Annabeth to take a seat in the chair across from her. Jackson had sat in the other chair. This left a spot open next to Abby for Will. He somehow thought they were trying to separate the couple for this important talk that would go nowhere.

"Please, have a seat, Will." Abby politely patted the seat next to her. "I'll stand," he said as he took his place next to Annabeth's chair.

He could tell Abby was trying to hide her ire. "As you wish." Abby gave a brief dip of her head and turned toward her husband. He nodded for her to continue.

"We want you to know, Will, we are not upset because we disapprove of you." She paused, which caused Will to ask, "Are you sure about that?"

Abby frowned. "Will you please sit down somewhere?" she said indignantly.

"With all due respect, Mrs. Lorton, I am not going to bend to your every whim." Jackson about burst into laughter. His wife was not accustomed to anyone but him telling her no.

"Please sit down, Will." Annabeth looked up and smiled. Will took her hand and assisted her up. Taking her seat, he settled her on his lap. *Nice move,* Jackson thought. He really couldn't help liking his new son-in-law.

"You are not helping your cause, Mr. Stanton." Abby frowned. "It's Will, or I will allow you to call me William if you wish." Abby turned again to her husband. She wanted him to take over.

"We want the two of you to understand we were a little shocked at the speed of your wedding. We concede we knew it would eventually happen, but we felt Annabeth and perhaps you too, Will, needed a little time before you rushed into things." Jackson was very skilled at negotiation, but what was he negotiating? Nothing.

"We do have some questions for you, Will. You don't have a form of income presently, no home per se. How are you going to provide for our daughter?" Jackson asked.

"Please don't tell us you plan to take over the bakery," Abby added.

"It's true I am out of a job. It is also true I am living with family currently. I do have money safely in the bank and can take care of Annabeth. Until Dr. Sheridan says otherwise, I can only do certain things. When I am given the go ahead, I will get a job. I would never take from my wife something she loves so much. The Dowry belongs to her and her alone. She made it what it is. If she allows me to work alongside her, I'll do it, but I would never take it from her." He could feel Annabeth practically melting in his arms.

"Have you considered moving to—" Abby did not get the word out of her mouth.

"Charleston?" Will supplied. "No more than we have considered returning to my home in Indiana."

"There is more opportunity in Charleston than there is here or Indiana. It is just something to consider, Will." Abby was getting tired of the battle she was having with her headstrong son-in-law.

"We need to get one thing straight." Will looked his mother-in-law in the eye. "I'm not Preston Middleton. I like my new brother-in-law, but we are not cut from the same cloth. I'm not in this union to please you, Abby." Her face was one of astonishment.

"Now"—Will rose from the chair—"I will leave you to visit with Annabeth, and you can try to convince her what a mistake she has made. I've known her long enough to know she is like her mother and will not be persuaded." Will grinned and winked at his mother-in-law and bent to kiss his wife. He headed out to find TJ.

"I think the mare has a rock in her shoe," Will said as he approached TJ. Gil had joined the boy in the barn.

"You two want to hold her while I get it out?" The mare was known to be on the rambunctious side, and Will didn't trust her. TJ and Gil took their places, and Will began trying to remove not one but two stones in the horse's shoe.

"Tell me what has been going on with your schooling, TJ," Will said as he stroked the horse's hind quarter, trying to get her to settle down. Jackson was watching from the barn door opening. Will took a particular interest in his son. If it wasn't for Will, they might have never known of TJ's trouble in school and the unnecessary fear the boy was experiencing.

Since Will's visit in April, TJ was a different young man. His daughter certainly had changed for the better. Yes, he had to admit Will Stanton had impacted his family most uniquely. Will caught a glimpse of Jackson and raised his eyebrows in question.

"I'd like to speak with you when you're done with the horse if you don't mind." Jackson made his way to the back of the barn. The boys took the mare into the stall and headed to where the new goats were dancing in their pen. Will proceeded toward his father-in-law. He leaned against the tact table, giving Jackson his full attention.

"Imagine how I felt when I found out the man I handed my daughter over to had planned her demise. He was willingly leading her on for his gain. The plot that Jonathan concocted still leaves my head spinning. Then I meet another man who is shrouded in mystery but tells me he loves my daughter, but I need to trust him. And there was a third, faceless man, who was also set on the destruction of my daughter. Don't you think, Mr. Stanton, I am a little uneasy at the thought of not being able to protect my own daughter? If Abby and I have been harsh, it is only because we feel we failed Annabeth most miserably."

Will felt sorry for the man standing before him. In no way was any of this the Lortons' fault any more than it was Annabeth's. It just happened.

"I love your daughter, sir, and I will protect her with my very life, but we can't always see things coming. I still need you and Abby to trust me. Trust me to seek God's will and do the best for Annabeth. If he is first, the rest will work out."

"How can a man argue with that logic?" Jackson put his hand out, and Will grasped it in a hearty shake. Jackson pulled him in for a hug. "Welcome to the family." Jackson leaned back with a smile on his face. "You are going to have a time winning my wife over, but I think you have just enough charm to do it." The two men laughed for a few minutes and then transitioned into some serious discussion.

"I know what you are going to say, Mother. I already know how you feel about Will. He is too much of a man for me. I somehow see that as an insult to both of us, but I love him very much, and I didn't want to wait. He asked me to marry him. It was my idea to do it right that moment, so if you're going to be angry, be angry with me."

Annabeth stood looking out the window as her husband made his way into the barn. Abby joined her daughter at the window as they watched Jackson standing at the barn door entrance. "I did say I thought he was too much of a man for you, but it was not an insult. You have to admit he is pushy. I just felt he would roll right over you. When I heard of the wedding, I assumed he had made the decision, and that was to marry quickly." Annabeth turned to face her mother.

"He wanted me to have a proper wedding. He said I should have the fun of planning the event. I had that, Mother, and it was a disaster. In no way did I want my wedding to Will to resemble anything associated with what happened in the past. I wouldn't have it any other way."

Abby stroked her daughter's face. "I am happy for you, Annabeth. I do like Will, but his ways will take a bit of getting used to."

Everyone begged the couple to stay the night. The rain had been steady and at times hard. Annabeth wanted to return home. She wanted to wake up in her own home with her own husband and go to her own bakery.

"We need to get home." Will smiled at the group gathered in the front room. He no more wanted to stay the night in a crowded house than Annabeth. He wanted to be home with her. After saying their good-byes and promising to come for Sunday dinner, the couple was allowed to go.

"I thought they would never let us leave." Annabeth moved closer to her husband. She wrapped her arm around his and laid her head on his shoulder.

"There was no way I was staying all night." Will nudged her a little. She giggled. Her face then turned sober.

"You know I want the bakery to be ours, don't you?"

"I'm not worried about it, Annabeth. I will help you in the bakery until we see what happens. Don't you worry about it either. You just concentrate on me, and we will be fine."

He had a mischievous smile on his face and bent to kiss her.

"I can't concentrate on anything else." Her lips met his.

A rut in the road broke both their concentration when it sent Annabeth flying across his lap. He caught her just before her head struck the side. Slowing the mare down to a stop, they waited for a few minutes for the rain to let up. Will didn't waste time on idle chitchat.

*****

Will found a note on the pillow beside him. His wife had left for the bakery. He lay there for a few moments. Counting his blessings, he didn't get any further than Annabeth. His life had changed. He couldn't put the feelings into words. He just knew he couldn't survive the rest of his life without her.

He rose quickly and headed to The Dowry. Annabeth was alone. She had begun to form the tarts she was making when she heard the back door open. She didn't need to turn around she knew it was Will. He stood behind her, his arms encircling her waist. "I am not fond of waking up alone," he whispered in her ear, his lips touching her neck. She leaned her head in the opposite direction, exposing more surface of her neck. The stubble on his chin tickled, and she squirmed.

"Well, what have we here?" The familiar voice of their coworker did little to detour Will's behavior. He kept his chin near Annabeth's neck and his arms around her waist. "Is this what goes on before I arrive each morning?" Vivian had a sassy look on her face. "You two better explain yourselves." Her hands were on her hips.

Will reached down and pulled up Annabeth's left hand. It wasn't hard to see the gold band.

"Why, you rascals! When did this happen?" She made her way over, giving Annabeth a big hug and Will a little shove.

"It happened while we were in Rapid City on Thursday." Annabeth was beaming.

Vivian looked from Annabeth to Will. It was hard to tell who had the bigger smile.

The couple didn't tell their customers anything. They figured word would get out sooner or later. Little did they know it was obvious something had changed between the two. People may have not suspected a wedding, but they certainly knew the two were smitten with each other.

Once the last customer had left, Annabeth and Vivian began planning for the Fourth of July celebration coming up on Monday. With tomorrow being the Lord's day, preparations needed to be started today. Will left them to help the townsfolk set up for the celebration. It was always a big happening in Sheridan.

*****

"Do I have to wear a tie?" Will asked his wife as he put on his suit coat.

"Help me with this." She turned her back to him so he could fasten the clasp of her necklace. He caught her staring at him in the mirror.

"I know what you are thinking, Annabeth, and you're right. You are a lucky girl." He broke out in a laugh.

"Just for that, you have to wear a tie." She turned and put the tie around his neck, tying it properly.

His eyes were intent on hers. "I do love you, Annabeth, and I know whose side fortune has landed on." He kissed her passionately.

"We're going to be late." She pushed away and then leaned back in for one more.

At the end of a resounding sermon, Pastor Grey had a few announcements. "I would like to remind all of you about the Fourth of July celebration tomorrow. Be sure and wish Quinn Sheridan a happy birthday tomorrow. He is our Fourth of July baby and will be six years old tomorrow."

The boy was sitting between his cousins Hunter and River, and they were pushing him from side to side. The three got to giggling before Hawk put a stop to it. "I also would like to congratulate Will Stanton on the cunning way he got our town baker Annabeth Lorton to marry him this past week."

The congregation turned to face the couple. There were smiles and a few surprised looks from the crowd. Two little faces like granite turned toward Will.

Lachlan Kennedy was asked to dismiss the service in prayer. From the moment he began, Will felt the heavy stares. He opened his eyes, something he would have been whipped for as a child, and peered to his right. Hunter and River Sheridan were boring holes through him. With a massive grin on his face, he winked at his nemeses. The boys' eyes narrowed, and Will bowed his head. It wasn't long until the boys' father flicked them both on the top of their heads. They resumed a posture of prayer.

*****

The bakery was closed to customers for the Fourth of July, but that didn't stop Annabeth from going in at the regular time. She had food to prepare for the celebration. The town had been kind to her, and she wanted to provide a wide array of treats. Will followed her in and stoked the stove.

"Where do we start?"

"Well, I think we should start a tradition. We should start with this." She put her arms around his waist and tipped her head a little to expose her neck. She felt him chuckle as his lips skimmed her skin.

"I like this tradition," he said in a low voice. He kissed her again.

The Fourth of July celebration was always a big affair. It started in the afternoon and went well into the evening, ending with a dance. This year part of the festival was a wedding reception for the Stantons. It was somewhat rushed, but so was their wedding. The couple didn't mind, and they were caught by surprise at the event.

They were swarmed with good wishes and kind words. When there was a lull in activity, Dan approached.

"Will, I have meant to ask you if you would like to take over and become sheriff. I have been thinking about retiring but just couldn't see giving the town over to just anybody. I think the town would accept you."

Will was caught off guard. He hadn't planned on getting back into that line of work. "Dan, you're not ready to retire any more than I am ready to be sheriff. I have a feeling this was an idea concocted by Aunt Trudy. Am I right?" Will leaned against the tree he and Annabeth were standing under.

Dan shrugged his shoulder. "I have mentioned it a time or two. She did seem to think it might keep you here." He had a slight smile on his face.

Will reached over and slipped his arm around his wife. "This is what is keeping me here. As long as she is here, I am here. Ask me again in a year."

"That's a deal." Dan turned and went to find his wife.

"What are your plans for the future, Mr. Stanton?" Annabeth was asking with a coy grin on her face.

Will grabbed her hand. "Tonight, I plan to dance with the most beautiful woman in Sheridan, and tomorrow I plan to wake up with the most beautiful woman in Sheridan. I reckon that would be about the best future a man could have." He went to step onto the dance floor, but the pair was stopped by the Sheridan duo.

"Hello," Annabeth spoke sweetly to her cousins. "Is there something we can do for you?"

The boys looked at Will. "Pa said we should come over and say something nice about you getting married." There was a pause, and the newlyweds waited. "We're glad you finally got it through your thick heads."

Will let out a hearty laugh; and picking up both boys, he swung them over his shoulder. "I am too," he said, leaning to kiss his bride.

Epilogue

One Year Later

*V*ivian Tyler hung the Open sign on the door of The Dowry. She smiled and waved to her husband as he placed the Open sign on the door of his mercantile. Will and Annabeth were no longer considered the town newlyweds. Vivian watched as Will headed her way with his son nestled in his arm. She held the door to let him in.

"Where is Annabeth?" Vivian asked as she smiled and cooed at Benjamin Thomas Stanton. The infant smiled and turned his face into his daddy's chest, his bright-blue eyes peeking out in a playful gesture. He was nine months old and very attached to his pa. The child's blond hair was going every which way. Vivian reached to smooth it down.

"She wasn't feeling well this morning. she was exhausted. That is why I am late. I thought Lydia might watch him for a little bit, just until the morning rush is over."

"I am sure she will. Who wouldn't want to spend time with such a handsome boy?" Vivian reached out, and Ben went to his aunt Vivian.

"I hope Annabeth isn't coming down with something."

"She is coming down with something all right. She won't admit it, but we both know what's ailing her. In nine months, she'll have to admit I was right." Will went into the back of the bakery, and Vivian followed.

"What makes you so sure she is expecting?"

"Three straight mornings of being sick. She is tired all the time, and last night I fell asleep on the couch holding Ben with her on one side and Thrive on the other. When I woke up, she was just sitting there crying. When I asked her what was wrong, she just said she didn't deserve me." He shook his head. "She's having a baby." There was a finality to his words.

Vivian laughed. "Maybe she should see the doctor."

"She will later this afternoon. Thad and Merry are having their annual family picnic. Hawk will pick up on it the minute he sees her."

*****

Thad made his way through town. Each year he and Merry set aside a day for the family to spend time together. Quinn squirmed beside him, talking nonstop to his uncle Franklin, who had little Nora on his lap. David and Gil were in the back. His first stop was at the bank to pick up baby Melissa who had just turned one.

Tommy and Josie had moved back after the death of Mr. Miller; he had suffered a massive coronary during his trial. Tommy had taken over the role of bank president of Sheridan. Jonah had taken to running the mill for his mother-in-law. He and Hannah were expecting their first child in a couple of months.

Thad barely got the wagon stopped in front of the doctor's office before River jumped in the back. Hunter appeared with Piper and helped her into River's waiting arms. Hawk brought Chase out and handed him to Gil. "Are you sure you and ma are up to this? I can send Avery with you." Hawk was eyeing his father.

"We will be fine until you all get there this afternoon. I am stopping to get Hannah. She and Molly have planned some games and such for the children."

Hawk gave a quick glare to his two oldest boys, and Thad knew his eldest son had directed his own boys to be responsible for their behavior and those of their siblings. The last stop was to pick up little Ben. Soon the wagon would be full of Thad and Merry's offspring. None of which were biologically theirs, but each grew out of a handful of purpose, a measure of trust, and a whole lot of love.

Books by Sarah Hale
Handful of Purpose Series

*****

Handful of Purpose
The Yoke
Hope Deferred
A Measure of Trust

About the Author

Sarah Hale was born and raised in rural Central Indiana. The defining moment in her life was when she answered the knock on her heart's door at age five. Since that time, she has dedicated her life to following the will of the Lord. The journey led her to the field of nursing in 1993. She currently is a staff development coordinator and nurse educator. In addition to writing, she enjoys cooking and traveling. She is an avid University of Kentucky basketball fan. She lives in the country near the small town of Mooreland, Indiana.

WWW.Sarahmhale.com
authorsarahmhale@gmail.com

9 781098 017422